DREAM

KEEPER

THE AMULET SERIES: BOOK ONE

By

Julie Pope Petrou

ISBN (E-Book): 978-1-966167-06-8

ISBN (Paperback): 978-1-966167-07-5

ISBN (Hardcover): 978-1-966167-08-2

JULIE POPE PETROU

ACKNOWLEDGMENT

The kickstart I needed to get the ball rolling on this book came to me in the form of my fellow "book clubbers", who have inspired me in ways I can't explain. I want to thank you all, Kathy, Marie, and Sonja for making me read outside my usual genre and giving me a taste of so many things I would have just looked past.

I need to specifically thank those people who volunteered time to help me hone my story. Cathie Bryant for her editing assistance, and Meredith McDonald for her professional advice and kind words. Pattie Wagner for your detailed peer review; one of the most fun things I've done outside of a vacation. Ruth Kleinjan, for the positive reinforcement and encouraging words.

To my BFF, Karen Anderson, who was and has always been my biggest cheerleader; not only on this project, but in my life. You are priceless.

Thank you to those people and experiences that inspired me throughout the years and have taken form one way or another in this creation. Trace and Deb, you're in here and have NEVER been forgotten. My family, who have given my life color, is always a constant source of fuel and adds pages to the next book on a daily basis.

The chapters in Dream Keeper where the police department is involved were descriptions I conjured after multiple conversations with my son, who answered my questions during random phone calls. The story is random and fictitious, but the fact that Human Trafficking is a problem in our world is not. I "googled" a few facts, so the sources are not confirmed.

Fact. Worldwide, there are an estimated 27.6 million people at any given time who are exploited and forced to perform either sex or labor under the precipice of slavery. They are of all ages, both sexes, all races, all ethnic backgrounds, and socio-economic statuses. No human on the earth is untouchable. The disappearance of men, women, and children often leaves no trace. I didn't want these facts to be cornerstones in this book; however, the information is eye-opening, and Andrea felt every bit of the terror a victim of such a crime would feel.

Regarding the Creek Tribe and the Native Americans that are such a large part of this book, it is all fictitious. In my research, I became interested in the time after the Revolutionary War and before the Indian Removal Act of 1830, knowing that many tribes were split in their loyalties and torn apart by war. My vision of what the world might have been like, I saw the Natives as a kind people, trying to hold together their traditions and livelihood in such a broken country. I pray that nothing here insults any culture — these are the stepping stones of our history.

JULIE POPE PETROU

CONTENTS

1. A World Upside-down

Andrea hears voices and muffled sounds, detecting the varied speech of three men talking in low voices. Someone was crying, but she couldn't see who it was through the dark sack placed over her head. Her heart was pounding, and she was trembling convulsively, terrified, so much she couldn't understand. She tried without success to wriggle loose from the bindings on her wrists, now angry and frustrated, unable to remove the head covering so she could see.

There were others with her; she could sense them. It was echoey, and she thought the others were all on the floor, just as she was. She grew more afraid now because she couldn't see anything. Tears welled up in her eyes, as fear pulsated through her, realizing the dream trip turned into a nightmare, changing her life forever.

Why me? She thought to herself. Then her friends came to mind, but she couldn't recall them coming to the lobby.

"Chelsea?" Andrea called out, scared that her friends were among the people in the van, just like she was. She heard a man's voice with a solid Spanish influence explode from across the vehicle.

"Shut up!"

She didn't care and dismissed the threat. "Brenna?" She said, followed by a short gasp, desperate to know if her friends were captives.

Someone slapped the side of her head with the back of their hand. Probably the same person who told her to shut up.

"Kiss my Ass!" She shouted in the direction of the voice.

She received another hand slap, bouncing her head off the van's wall, and everything went black.

She heard a voice – Another girl whispering, "Hey, are you ok?"

Andrea blinked hard and tried to focus, but everything was still blurry. She squinted hard beneath the black head covering, her ears ringing and a headache from hell reverberating from the hit. She opened her eyes again, and there was nothing to focus on, deciding she'd be better off with them closed.

She felt an elbow in her ribs when she heard, "Hey, are you ok?"

Andrea responded in a whisper, "Yeah." The girl's voice sounded so young. Andrea thought it best not to talk for fear of retribution, so she didn't openly talk to the girl, although she wanted to.

The van smelled like sweat and stale beer. She was sure the smell emanated from the three men she heard; they were the only ones talking. It was some kind of cargo van, she knew that, and as disgusting as ever. *Might as well be a sewer*, she thought. She tried to rationalize her predicament. She had gone to the lobby only to get a soda, and two men she nearly ran into grabbed her. One of the two stuffed a scarf in her mouth so she couldn't make any noise, drug her straight out the side door, and brutally shoving her into this van.

More lucid now, her mind rifled through scenarios of how the other girls might have been taken. The kidnappers shoved her roughly into the van and forced her to sit. She only had a split second to look around before everything went black, her vision blocked by the dark sack jerked over her head. All the captives had hoods on, just like hers, and figuring out who was there with her was impossible.

The van traveled for some time and finally stopped. She didn't know how long she had been unconscious, so judging how long or far they'd traveled was hopeless. The air smelled of fish, and she could hear the waves, which told her they were near the ocean. *Are they going to put me on a boat? A ship?* She thought as another flush of panic ran through her.

She would *not* let them take her away. Escaping now would be her only chance to free herself from these convicts. Andrea plotted the entire time she was waiting for the dickheads' next move. The van door opened, and she could hear them forcefully grabbing girls and pulling them out. The sounds of the other girls' struggles intensified, leaving Andrea feeling every bit of terror felt by the other girls.

A hand reached for Andrea, and they dragged her out of the van and onto her feet. Her heart was pounding out of her chest; she struggled willfully, then doubled over, faking illness.

She pleaded, "Please take off this mask; I have to throw up! Please!"

Gritting her teeth, she continued, "I'm sure you don't want vomit everywhere. Take off my mask!" She spoke urgently, making a scene until finally, someone jerked off the head covering. Andrea remained bent over, and from the corner of her eye, she could see the assholes holding guns and forcing the other unwilling passengers from the van toward the beach.

She took a minute to orient herself; then she consciously rose, quickly and solidly kicking the disgusting long-haired offender next to her in the balls as hard as she could. She caught a glimpse of the criminals when the slimeball she'd just kicked fell to the ground, swearing there was something familiar about one of them. *No, it couldn't be*, she thought.

Andrea gathered her strength and bolted, running away from the beach, hands still bound behind her back. Another guy with a wife-beater T-shirt gave chase and threw himself on her, forcing Andrea to crumble to the ground. She huffed loudly, and the smelly, disgusting man began to strangle her. She opened her eyes wide in sheer panic, gasping as she tried to scream, but this only made him tighten his grip. Feeling completely helpless now, lightheaded, the sand, the girls, and the kidnappers began to fade slowly to black. She tried to scream again, but it was too hard; nothing came out. Despite her determination to break free, she now felt her life slipping. She was no longer scared; she was tired. So tired.

2. Strange Girl in a Strange Place - 1798

Lazily, Andrea's eyes fluttered open, feeling the sun shining bright on her face. She was alone in the quiet. Her whole body ached. She gasped sharply, realizing her breathing was shallow; the air intake surprised even herself. Her eyebrow was sore, and reaching up to touch it, she felt the swollen bump oozing blood. *What the hell*, she thought.

She tried to recall what happened and why she was there. Andrea began shaking uncontrollably, not recognizing anything around her and sensing something was wrong. The flow of thoughts didn't come to her. The night – the day, it was all a blur.

As she lay on the ground, she slowly brought the things closest to her into focus. Tall, wispy grass surrounded her, rocking slowly, pushed by the breeze. She listened carefully as she heard the rush of waves. Still unmoving, her eyes reached in all directions.

Aching and scared, she blinked hard; glimpses of strangers and darkness came to her like flashes of light. Her heart sank, and she felt weak; she didn't know this place or how she got there. She scowled, wincing at the gnawing discomfort when she moved. Her heart began to thump wildly when she thought about her friends.

Andrea managed to pull herself up so she could look around. Having heard waves splash softly in the distance, she could now see what she thought she heard.

"Oh, it is the ocean," she said, whispering. She could see a wide beach, half shadowed by the tall trees above her. Palm trees.

But I. Where am I? Where is this place?

The details were murky; the lack of memory unsettled her. She momentarily sat, brushing the sand off her pants and face, knowing this much sand meant there was a struggle. There was a pain in her neck that was hard to describe.

Was I in a fight?

Rubbing her face, she recalled flinging her hands and pounding fists, kicking and running; a vast blank spot interrupted this reproduction. Fear and insecurity enveloped her like a wet blanket in the few short minutes she had been awake. She tried desperately to remember how she got there, mentally searching for an explanation.

It was morning, and she was not mortally wounded, she had been abandoned here in this strange place.

Andrea began searching for her cell phone in a half circle around her. Blinking, she remembered suddenly seeing it snapped in half as a dark-haired, grimacing man threw it out a window just before everything went black again. "That son-of-a-bitch," she said to herself, and there was no other memory of that man, or why he broke her phone.

Decisively, she rose and took a few steps from the beach. Moving slowly, she mumbled, "I just need to get to the road. It's right here. It should be ..." Andrea staggered slowly toward the imaginary road.

It should be here. It should be right here! She thought, panic beginning to rise.

There was no road. Where the girl thought she should find a road, she found merely a path. It was nothing more than a game trail and lay just beyond the grassy patch where she woke.

Follow the path, she thought to herself. *It must lead somewhere.*

Andrea tried to smooth out her disheveled hair; the curly brown locks jostled and disorderly. She couldn't help but think about what a sight she must be. As she walked, the soreness in her neck faded, but the bump on her brow was throbbing.

What I wouldn't give for a couple of aspirin right now, she thought to herself as she tugged on her pants to straighten them, then smoothed her shirt; it was a mess.

She wandered the path for quite a long time. The ocean was still in sight, but there was no road. Distracted, she watched her feet scuff through the sand, trying to invoke the details that brought her to this place. Still a bit loopy and in a strange place, she looked up, and standing in front of her were two native Americans, young and strong; she saw the muscling in their arms and chests. Andrea stopped, her eyes still trying to focus as her heart hammered.

What? Where am I? She thought in disbelief as panic took over. She frantically hoped it was only a dream, but the voices of the natives were resounding. She closed her eyes, wishing the vision would go away as she tried to reason with herself. *I must have been walloped; I'm not thinking clearly.* Looking for a reason, she thought her eyes were playing tricks.

One of the natives approached her, and Andrea's eyes widened. She stood rigid, terrified by the unknown intentions of these two men with her. He reached out, tugged at her hair, and spoke to the other young man.

His black hair was slicked back smoothly, and the darkest brown eyes she'd ever seen. She felt as though he could look right through her; the severity of his stare made her shudder, and tremors wracked her body.

He wore a vest decorated with many trinkets and colorful things. The girl could smell him as he stepped closer. He smelled of the forest - like an animal would smell. His confidence made her feel so small, like a creature caught in a trap. He began to walk in a circle around her, his soft leather shoes brushing intently through the sand. He pulled at her hair and laughed.

"Wotko-este Hokte'vcak'e!" The very forward native spoke to the other, who was only an arm's length away. The second young man was happy to egg-on the more aggressive cohort, his eyes trying to make sense of this strange woman in front of them who wore white pants. Although he trusted his companion, he kept his distance. He knew there was something very different about her.

"What do you want with me?" The tension in her voice intensified; her heart now pounding with fear.

She wrapped her arms tightly around herself, feeling so exposed. Standing still, she watched and waited, having no other choice. The muscles in her shoulders tightened painfully, as she wished she could hide. The two young men were speaking to each other in words she couldn't understand, and she realized there was no English spoken between them.

Glancing at the native's decorated vest, she abruptly thought about the turquoise bracelet strapped to her left wrist. She thought he might have a taste for such a thing. Hoping to bargain with him, she hastily took it off and held it up.

"Would you like this? I will give it to you if you let me go." The same native that pulled her hair grabbed at the bracelet; Andrea, scarcely able to breathe, pulled it away at the last second. The other native jumped slightly and, standing back a few feet, docked his arrow, the bowstring pulled tight. It was a split-second thought, but she realized that if he let go, she could be a murder victim.

Just then, as she faced an uncertain fate, something clicked that sent her into survival mode. She breathed in with a short, quick gulp; this time, when she looked at the aggressor, her eyes became laser-focused on the young man's face.

She set her jaw and stance, ready for battle, and said nearly shouting, "You leave me and take this. Leave me alone!"

He nodded his understanding, waving a hand at the other brave to lower the weapon. The young native took the bracelet and did as he promised; Andrea stood there, faint and panting, while watching them walk away, afraid to divert her eyes. She felt her cheeks flush red after the encounter, then sunk to her knees, overwhelmed with weakness. She was so scared.

When she put her head down, the amulet swung in front of her face; a glint of sunlight reflected brightly on it. She paused momentarily, feeling a pang of prophecy, then held on to the stone, examining it. The warmth of it was overwhelming, and she felt pulses within it.

She asked the stone, "What do you have to do with this - huh?" She'd said the words aloud, appreciating there was no one there to hear her.

Not having a choice, Andrea regained her strength, forced herself to stand, and began to walk; the throbbing of her heart began to calm. Her steps continued to a place still unknown to her. The encounter with the natives left her feeling numb; she kept asking herself, "Why me?" She felt so odd, and out of place. But here she was, and she could fall apart or gather her wits; this moment she was sure it was the hardest thing she'd ever done.

Simultaneously laughing and crying, she brought herself back to the moment; afraid and hopeless as she had no idea what to do next. Still unsure of her next move, she walked the unfamiliar path for a while, wondering about her friends.

I wish I knew what happened to them – or where they are. Why aren't they here?

She wracked her brain, trying to conjure a memory, anything that would help her get back to where she came from.

Passage of time was sluggish here, and she was unclear about how long she'd wandered. Her awareness snapped to attention when she suddenly caught a scent in the breeze: wood smoke. She glanced around and saw it lingering among the trees.

In seconds, she began to hope that she would meet up with some campers who might allow her to use their cell phone. She started in the direction of the smoke, watching it thicken as she got closer. Drawing nearer, she heard voices before she saw anyone, shocked at the sight as the camp came into view. She recognized tents, but they were not modern tents. She'd never seen a tent like that before. And horses, but no vehicles - not even motorcycles. She reasoned with herself, knowing there had to be a vehicle – she just couldn't see it.

Approaching slowly, she could make out several animal skins on a grass mat beside the tent. One of the men watched her as she got closer, stepping toward a bow propped up against a rock near the fire.

It took the man a minute to realize it was a woman. He stared at her, never having seen a woman in pants before. "Who are you, and what do you want?" Andrea pulled back a bit. Couldn't he see she was hurt?

"Hello," Andrea said weakly. "I –I seem to be lost." She looked at one man, then at the other, explaining.

"I hoped you'd let me borrow a cell phone or get a ride into town. Could you tell me where we are?"

The two men exchanged glances. The younger fellow seemed to be a teenager, maybe sixteen. He was tall but not much older than the young native she'd encountered only an hour ago. His blue eyes were bright and cheerful, exuding confidence and good humor. The other man, she guessed, was in his early thirties, had a beard and longer brown hair.

They both appeared shabby and unkempt. She wondered if these two would be more dangerous than the natives she just faced.

"What is a - phone?" said the older man hesitantly, obviously on his guard.

"A phone? You mean you don't know what a phone is?" Andrea could hear the shock in her voice.

"A telephone? Look, as I said, I'm lost, and I just had a terrifying experience with a couple of your local natives. I need to call my friends."

She insisted once more. "And where are we?"

The older man eyed her suspiciously as her agitation grew. *What in God's name was a woman doing alone in the wilderness? There had to be something wrong with her*, he thought, remaining cautious. The two men again looked at each other with blank expressions.

"We're a couple of days ride from Macintosh. Where are you lost from?" The older man answered, eyeing her suspiciously. Andrea wrinkled up her face.

"Macintosh, What? Where is Macintosh?" She now looked bewildered, her voice raising two octaves.

"Macintosh, Georgia, miss. Georgia territory" said the older man, whose voice now softened slightly, seeing she was getting upset.

He put his hand on his chest. "I'm Jacob Lofton, and this is my brother Johnny. Johnny Lofton. You must have got quite a bump on the head if you don't know where you are."

Andrea's frustration grew as she tried to remember. "Boy, you're telling me," She said, huffing loudly.

Knitting his eyebrows, Jacob said, "Well, yes, ma'am, I am telling you."

The older man shook his head, not understanding. "Why don't you sit down here and lemme' have a look."

Jacob touched his eyebrow to help her understand. Apprehensively, she stepped closer, and Jacob's eyes opened wide when he saw more clearly the red marks on her neck. He began to feel sympathetic toward this strange woman who dressed so curiously and appeared out of nowhere.

He looked at her and asked, "Did those Indians do this?"

She shook her head, reaching toward the purple-red marks on her neck. "No. Oh, I mean, I don't know how it happened. I came across the natives after. Are they dangerous?"

His tone seemed to change, sounding more surprised, understanding that she had suffered an attack. Raising one eyebrow, Jacob said, "Sometimes." Andrea heard doubt in his words.

"Would you happen to have something to drink? I'm dying of thirst," Andrea exclaimed.

The two men looked at each other again, bewildered by the language this girl used. This time Johnny jumped up, grabbing a bottle. He handed it to her tentatively, not trusting anything about this stranger.

Jacob took a piece of cloth and soaked it with some water. He got close to Andrea and began to dab at the cut on her brow. "How'd you get this?" he asked. Andrea's eyes sought the ground to avoid making eye contact with him, ashamed. She had some ideas but couldn't be sure.

"I don't know. I found myself down by the beach." She took a deep breath and shook her head, feeling tears stinging her eyes. "I don't know where I am, and I don't know where my friends are, and I don't know Macintosh." Andrea, suddenly overwhelmed by all the things she didn't know, began to sob quietly. Jacob and Johnny looked at each other, not knowing what to do for her.

Jacob softly said, "Aww, don't you worry, miss, we'll get you back to where you ought to be." He had heard a lot of different accents throughout his travels in the backcountry, but the accent of her voice was different; grateful, at least, that she spoke English.

He hesitated momentarily before asking, "Uh, where is that exactly?"

Andrea looked at him with tear-filled eyes. "I don't remember." Suddenly her sobs intensified.

Jacob shook his head slightly. He was focusing on gently cleaning her wound and asked another question, aiming to distract her.

"What's your name?"

Andrea shook her head slightly, forgetting she hadn't told them yet. "My name is Andrea. Andrea Bruer, but my friends call me Andy."

Johnny nodded. "Nice name."

She looked at Johnny, teasing him with the shadow of a smile. "Well, it is the only one I know," she replied, her voice lighter.

She wiped her eyes with her hand, and Johnny smiled. She felt utterly vulnerable and understood these two men could not help her. Her head ached and she was so hesitant;

her heart pounded randomly. It was not like her. She felt like such a stranger in this strange place. However, she was safe, for now, and they were kind, offering her what little comfort they had, so until she figured out how to solve her dilemma, she had no choice but to accept her current circumstances.

3. Georgia - 1798

Andrea sat by the fire while the men bustled around the camp. Johnny looked over his shoulder at her and asked, "Do you cook?" Andrea was not a well-versed cook but knew how to fry an egg.

"A bit," she replied.

Then he asked, "You ever made rabbit stew before?"

Andrea hesitated. "No, never, but it can't be too difficult. She stood up and looked around to see what supplies they had for cooking. She asked, "Do you have anything besides rabbit to put in the stew?"

Jacob gave her a blank look. "Like potatoes, you mean? No, not exactly. We have a couple of turnips and some collard greens."

"Well, I think that will work just fine," Andrea nodded.

Johnny had to check some traps, and Jacob tended to the recent rabbit harvest. "What do you do with all those ... bodies? You don't eat them all, do you?" Andrea asked curiously.

"I dry them; they keep better that way. You can bring it back by boiling it. Not as tasty but it's good in a pot of beans," Jacob smiled.

He kept his head down, intent on cleaning the meat from the hides, keeping one suspicious eye on the cook, still unsure what to make of the stranger. He took care of removing all the remnants of fur and hide from the meat. He weaved small branches around the edges of the carcass to stretch the meat, making it as thin as possible, then hang them by a rope strung between the trees. The meat dried quickly with the constant and gentle ocean breeze and the heat of the sun.

Andrea did what she could to put together a decent meal. She mindlessly stirred the pot, pouring in some clean water, and in a short time, the concoction began to boil. She needed some seasoning and the men gave her a little tin of salt. "Jacob, do you have any wine?"

He looked up, surprised at the request. "I might have a little," he replied and went to his saddlebag to fetch it. His saddle was in a pile on the ground, and he pulled out a bottle and said, "Here you go," he said, scratching his head. "Never heard of it going into the pot with rabbit though."

Andrea gave him a little nod and a determined, smirky smile. "Thanks," she said and walked back to the boiling stew. She poured a little of the wine into the pot and slowly stirred. The dinner began to smell very tasty. She chopped up a few leaves of collard greens and added them to the pot. "About an hour, and it should be ready," Andrea said to Jacob. He smiled at her.

After a few moments of silence, Jacob asked, "Why are you here? A young lady such as yourself. And dressed so strangely? It's dangerous out here alone."

He stopped, and his eye followed her as he watched every move. "Being so different, I mean." Jacob showed concern, second-guessing his decision to help this girl. She certainly wasn't like others he knew. *Why was she in pants?* He thought.

"Well, as I said before, I don't know exactly how I came to be here. I hope maybe with a little time, I will be able to remember ..." Her voice trailed off, frustrated that she was so clueless. Andrea shook her head, knowing it had to be a bad set of circumstances that ended her in this place.

Jacob and Andrea chatted calmly, making small talk the whole time he was cleaning the hides.

"What do you do with those?" Andrea pointed at the rabbit hides lined up on the mat. She hadn't ever seen freshly harvested hides before. Jacob raised his eyebrow to the question, as Andrea should have known better.

"This will probably end up stitched into a blanket for winter. Maybe I'll trade some of the hides for things we need more than fur. It's like money." He gave her a mischievous grin.

Andrea's eyes went to the ground as she made a subtle sound. "Hmmm." Quietly, Jacob rose and went to the tent. He brought out a blanket fashioned with other skins and handed it to Andrea. "Oh," she said, "This is beautiful and so soft." She suddenly understood the money reference, although she was more inclined to feel sorry for the little critters.

A short while later, Johnny came back with another handful of rabbits. Jacob had the other carcasses cleaned and hung for drying. Once the newest harvest was cleaned, those, too would to be strung and dried.

Johnny was happy about the stew Andrea had made. He walked over to the pot, then looked at Andrea and said, "Oh, ma'am that smells good. Thank you!" His response was enthusiastic.

Andrea smiled warmly and said, "You know, you can call me Andrea. I'm not all fancy about titles and such." Johnny boyishly smiled back. "Ok, then. Thank you, Andrea."

The rest of the day was spent puttering around camp, mixed with little bits and pieces of conversation. Andrea was as uneasy about her given her situation, just as Jacob was, knowing nothing, really, about what the hell she was doing there. *Either these guys are really out of touch with the rest of the world, or I'm so much more lost than I know.* She felt exhausted as she urgently rubbed her temples. She knew there was something very peculiar about how these men dressed; even their tools were antiques. She thought about how strange a question like, *What year is it?* Would be. Maybe less strange for her than them, but she wasn't sure, about opening that can of worms.

She was shaking out the blankets that lay in the tent when Johnny came up to her. "I plan to go down to the beach tomorrow to get us some clams; Jacob thought you should come along."

Andrea smiled. "I think I would love that." She silently hoped to find out more about her arrival on the beach.

"We'll leave real early in the morning. That's when you can find the clams." Andrea recalled walking along the beach at dawn with her brother many years ago. They watched people digging for clams, and it looked like fun.

As she watched the two men heartily eat the stew, Andrea went over the day's events in her mind, thinking about how very strange she felt and how these men appeared to her. She merely nibbled at the food as she thought, mindlessly grabbing at the amulet around her neck. She couldn't help but feel wonder and uncertainty when she touched it. Her world had been turned upside down, her friends were nowhere to be found, and she was stuck in this place.

A light breeze always accompanies the ocean, with the slow, easy sway of the trees. The sound of the rustling leaves was almost medicinal to her. Closing her eyes and taking a breath, she began to let a host of thoughts swirl in her mind. She wondered why this place, and if all of this was just a scheme, a trick. Then, with a scowl, she thought *it wouldn't be good to worry about something, you can't do anything about*. Her thoughts consumed her, and she jerked herself back to the present and to her meal.

As the sun sank low on the horizon, Jacob pulled out the bottle of wine that Andrea used in the stew and offered her some. She gladly took it. After he filled her cup along with his own, Andrea held hers up and said, "Cheers - to my rescuers." Jacob and Johnny joined in, tipping cups and feeling the warmth of friendship in the present company. The wine seemed more potent than just wine, but Andrea didn't care. Sitting around the fire was quite mesmerizing and very enjoyable.

After a couple of hours of stories and limericks, the threesome retired.

4. Adventure Bound – 2004

A yellow-orange hue reflected on the wall behind Andrea's pillow. The bright sunlight breached the edge of the windowsill and illuminated the wall in her room directly above her head. Letting out a grumble, she pulled the blanket up a bit more, protecting her eyes from the light. The bed was so cozy. Andrea had a mind to stay there all day. *Just a while longer*, she thought. She tried to drift off into blissful sleep again, pretending to be enjoying this in-between state, but it was too late. She was awake.

She carefully prepared her morning brew, anxiously waiting. The night before was a whirlwind of activity. A Friday at school, dinner with friends, a night on the town, and a 2 am pizza call. Ridiculous. And only a mere four hours ago. But the excitement was soon to begin for Andrea and her friends as they were about to embark on an once-in-a-lifetime trip to New Orleans and Mardi Gras!! The three brave friends had been looking forward to this for some time after deciding to hit Mardi Gras instead of spring break in Florida. *It will be a unique experience*, Andrea thought, recalling what Chelsea had said the previous night after a few drinks. She sounded like she was trying to convince herself it was the truth. Andrea wasn't sure, if Chelsea was keen on the trip, but she and Brenna were all in.

She picked up her cell phone and called her friend. She heard the phone click and a muffled "hello" came through. "Hey there, bright eyes!!" Andrea chirped almost too cheerful for such an early call.

"So, why the sleep interruption so early?" Chelsea said with a note of irritation.

"Don't you remember what today is?" Andrea paused for a reaction, although nothing came.

"It's Mardi Gras Day!" Then Chelsea hesitated and seemed to wake up a bit.

"Oh, crap, am I late?"

Andrea chuckled, knowing how Chelsea was in the morning. "No, not late, but I'm glad I called you, or you would be. The cab will be here in about an hour, so you'd better get a move on. "I thought it would be better to catch a ride rather than pay for parking. After all, it is going to be a whole week."

She was far too energetic in the mornings. Chelsea thought, yawning. Her jaw clicked in the background. "What time again?"

Andrea rolled her eyes, expecting Chelsea to see it through her phone, then she let out a giggle. "Can you make it in an hour?" Andrea said it slowly, like she was talking to someone with a hearing problem.

Chelsea responded with a bit more energy this time. "Perfect. See you then." On those words, Andrea clicked her phone off.

Chelsea was a striking, petite, blond-haired, blue-eyed beauty with a creative streak, a mile long. Her neatly highlighted almond-shaped eyes always had a sparkle to them, and no matter what Andrea came up with, she went along with it. Andrea had been her best buddy since grade school, and now, in college together at Northwestern University.

Chelsea was an Art major, and although they'd been besties forever, the two girls viewed the world very differently. Although Chelsea's world appeared perfect, it wasn't. Andrea could see right through her guise but always tried to offer her a shoulder to cry on and the support that only a good friend could give.

Andrea's next call was to Brenna. She dialed the number, and it rang and rang. Andrea clicked the phone off, checked the number, and then hit it again. This time, it rang twice, and she heard a "click." Just then, a text materialized on her phone. It said, *Outside, silly.* Andrea went to the front window of her tiny two-bedroom apartment, pushed aside the curtain and peeked through the shade.

There was Brenna, staring back at her from the sidewalk. Andrea giggled and ran to the door, pulling it open to Brenna's exclamation.

"Surprise!" Andrea's smile grew, and Brenna embraced her with a big hug, all the while saying, "I just couldn't wait any longer. Time to pa-ar-tay!"

Andrea glanced at her sideways and added, "I couldn't agree more. C'mon in and give me a chance to get my shit together."

While Andrea dressed and packed, Brenna chatted with her about the things she had read in the online travel chat she joined just a week ago.

"There is a lot to do in New Orleans, but it depends on what time of year you go, Mardi Gras is probably the biggest event short of the Super Bowl." She went on about the food scene, the little jazz clubs that dotted the boulevards, and didn't forget the art and cultural centers in the French Quarter. "Just talking about it, I feel as if I'm already there," Brenna said with enthusiasm in her voice. "I'm excited just to experience that old city. It is an old city; did you know that?"

Andrea smiled and nodded, rolling her eyes a bit. Brenna often was over-enthusiastic about things.

"I did know that - and I'm all about the experience, so bring it on!"

Brenna was a party girl, always looking for the next best adventure. The taller, brown-haired, brown-eyed young lady was an explorer at heart. She was almost lanky in her appearance with no natural curves. She wasn't one to get and keep a decent job, either. She came from a wealthy family and never really had to worry about working. She had all that she needed. Andrea thought briefly about her and Brenna's friendship, giving attention to how Brenna could merely suggest something, and she would go along, like putting a match to gasoline - crazy but a ton of fun.

They managed to make it to the airport on time, checked their baggage, and boarded the plane. Before they knew it, they were in New Orleans, off the plane, and on their way to the St George, giggling with nervous energy, was ready to hit the town.

5. Miss Josephine

New Orleans - 2004

The threesome stowed their luggage and freshened up before they set out to explore the city. Brenna had been scanning the travel chat for some time when she said, "So, on this website I've been checking out, and they recommend a string of 'Period' shops along Dauphine Street. It might be worth checking out." She had an animated way of talking that was perky and lighthearted. People couldn't help but like her. She continued, "And they're only a block off Bourbon Street."

Andrea added jokingly, "Well, that settles it. *That* was my next question."

Chelsea was, as always, adorable in her baby blue T-shirt and white capris. Her hair was so shiny and bouncy, and her eyes sparkled blue, hinting at mischievousness within them. Chelsea glanced over with her charming half-smile, and both Brenna and Andrea knew they were in trouble.

The girls went to the string of shops Brenna had read about. They found cool secondhand stuff in one little shop. Andrea might have bought something if the smell of the place didn't turn her stomach. Old, musty, and worn. She wasn't feeling it. A liquor store, a bookstore, and a hat store, of all things, were all on one block.

They made their way across the street, and Brenna said, "Now that is what I'm talkin' about - look at those cool things in the window. She said, pointing to the little pawnshop which displayed some old cameras and costume jewelry. Without thinking, Brenna just walked into the place. It felt eclectic and friendly. There was an older blonde buxom woman behind the counter who looked up when they walked in.

She spoke in a rather cheerful voice, "Hello, ladies, and welcome to Jack's Pawn. Y'all look around here. Let me know if I can help you." The woman said with the flip of her manicured fingers.

Andrea smiled, "Thank you, we will." Then, all three girls took off in different directions and explored the store.

Of course, Chelsea went straight for the paintings and drawings that lined the walls. She studied a piece, feeling its aura, investigating the method by which it was made. Brenna found some glass beads and record albums. She breezed through a few titles and picked up a string of mismatched beads. Andrea watched her smiling eyes examine the intricacies of each bead and could see she seemed to have a way of enjoying everything.

Andrea found herself envious. Brenna was a free spirit, letting the rough stuff roll off her like water off duck feathers. Andrea was more deeply affected by things. Everything. Andrea felt she was the "stick in the mud" out of the three of them.

Without speaking, she sauntered very slowly as if to savor the flavor of the things displayed all around her. She found a lapel pin that had to be fifty or sixty years old. It was dazzling, but she had no reason to wear it; she didn't have a lapel. She saw a knife that had an ivory handle. It was an intricately detailed carving of a mountain scene. It was very unusual, but that was nothing she would purchase for herself.

Casually browsing the various things in a glass case, she saw pieces of jewelry that would never be seen in another store. Andrea's eyes wandered around the case, imagining what each piece would look like on her or with one of her outfits. She caught sight of a stone necklace and immediately fell in love with it.

It was a deep blue color and had lines through it that shone like silvery ribbons with little smudges of black spattered about the unfinished rock. It was a rough texture in a setting that looked like antique brass or dingy silver. There was a twist of wire that held a tiny piece of carved bone or ivory. It was not distinct, but it was a simple little design and very pretty. The setting was suspended on leather lace that looked clean and new. Andrea looked up at the woman behind the counter. She said, "Can I see this necklace please?" The woman moseyed over to where she was standing and took a key out of her pocket to open the case. Andrea pointed out the necklace, and the sales lady brought it out for her, a smile forming in the corner of her lip-sticked mouth. "This is beautiful," Andrea remarked, amazed at the detail of the piece she held.

The sales lady gave her a little wink and said, "This is a special piece right here. It must have called out to you." Then she winked.

Andrea raised her eyebrow at the remark and then dismissed it. She asked her, "How much?"

The sales lady said, "How does fifty dollars sound to you?"

Without hesitation, Andrea said, "I'll take it."

Her budget had very little wiggle room for extravagant things, but there was nothing else she wanted to spend her money on. Both Brenna and Chelsea found something they wanted as well, and the three of them walked out of the little pawn shop with smiles on their faces, looking as though they'd won the lottery.

They continued their shopping adventure along the string of shops when Chelsea caught sight of a storefront she couldn't ignore, and her eyes brightened. "Oh - fortune tellers - I've always wanted to do that!" Without giving the others, a sign of any kind, she darted inside. Andrea and Brenna looked at each other, then reluctantly followed. It was pretty dark in contrast to the bright sun outside, but the little place was clean and well-kept.

When the ding of the bell at the door rang out, a voice from the back hollered, "I'll be right there." Brenna shrugged her shoulders and began to look around the room. The atmosphere was a bit mysterious, yet welcoming. Heavy, maroon-colored brocade curtains hid what looked to be a doorway. Andrea thought any fortune teller had a personal life, like anyone, but she imagined dark things, like summoning spirits going on behind that curtain. She shook her head in response to her own private, internal conversation, thinking *this is why I'm not sure a reading is the best idea*. It made her feel exposed. She found her mind racing through what-ifs and possibilities; she was incredibly nervous.

Brenna went over to a small desk adjacent to the entry door, noting a little amber-colored glass hand that held business cards. She picked one up. It read, "Josephine DeSpark – Fortunes - Love -Money -Future - Purpose." She thought to herself, "What else would anyone need to know?"

A moment later, a woman popped out from behind the curtain.

"Hello, ladies!" she said in a light, cheerful voice. "What can I do for you?" She was an African-American woman who had warm, welcoming eyes and a bright smile, making them feel right at home. She wore a bright yellow smock with embroidered trim and big red stone earrings.

A wide smile spread on Chelsea's face. "I would love to have you do a reading for me. Are you available?"

The woman gave Chelsea a quick nod and a wink. "Yes, ma'am, I am. You can call me Ms. Josephine."

Just then, Brenna said, "Me too."

Andrea hesitated a bit, unsure about wanting to know what her future held. She finally spoke up, "If you have time, make it three."

Ms. Josephine went over to a calendar tucked in the desk and examined it. She said, "I got about an hour." She winked at the girls; a playful smile shone on her face. "I think we can squeeze you in."

Then all three girls said in unison, "Excellent!"

Since it was Chelsea's idea, Brenna and Andrea insisted she go first. Josephine said to the other girls in a more serious voice, "You're welcome to be in here as long as you sit over there." She signaled to a few chairs lined up along the wall. "We don't want y'all to cause interference with her reading." Andrea and Brenna certainly had no objections and went to chairs along the wall, quietly taking their place. Josephine began.

"I will do the cross spread. Looking at you girls, I think I see deep thinkers looking to the future. Am I right?" The three girls nodded rather than spoke, not wanting to interrupt the process.

Then Josephine began. "The three cards in the middle represent the past, present, and future. Then, we read the one at the bottom, which will tell us a reason. The final one at the top will tell you the potential of what you learn from the rest of the spread. The possible direction you can take, if you will. Please, Chelsea, clear your mind and think hard about the question that has troubled you."

Chelsea closed her eyes and took a deep breath. She rallied her thoughts and gave the fortune teller a nod of acknowledgment. Josephine drew the cards. She methodically shuffled them, then laid them out one at a time. She spoke directly to Chelsea as she pulled out the first card. "This card clarifies your past," she said quietly. Then, as she organized the rest of the spread on the table, she began Chelsea's reading.

"This one," she said, her hand on the first card, "is the Star card and, reversed, it refers to your past. You have suffered discouragement and insecurity; most likely, had divorced parents or an interrupted home life." Miss Josephine explained a bit about her spread, then said, "Find a way to greet it and make peace with it. It made you a strong-willed individual."

Josephine then went for the middle card. "In the Present position, you have a Lovers card upright. This one shows a union. It could also mean a partnership. Part of this card in this position tells me you're ready to take the next step, whether in love or business. You're craving a relationship of some kind. It is also something you think of often. It is close to your heart."

Josephine's lips turned up in the corners, showing her satisfaction with this particular reading. She continued through the rest of Chelsea's reading, hitting upon things that, indeed, describe her life and what was in her heart.

"This spread shows us that you will have an exciting future, but because of your past, you will make good decisions, and they will lead you where you want to go. Bless you, child."

And with that, Josephine picked up the cards and reshuffled them. As she did so, Chelsea got up, and the expression on her face was one of relief. Andrea knew her well enough to know she had been worrying about something, be it life, love, or family, but she chose not to share it with Andrea. This reading made her feel better about it.

"So, pretty good, right?" Andrea said to her, looking into her light blue eyes. Andrea was looking at her as if her words needed reassurance.

"It says so much with just a few little cards," Chelsea remarked, happy and breathless, "I feel like a weight was lifted off my shoulders."

Brenna smiled at her friend and said, "I get it." In her next breath, she asked, "Andy, do you mind if I go next?"

Andrea had hoped to go last anyway. She couldn't even think through what questions she wanted answered.

"Of course! You should go next." With that, Brenna got up and plopped down in the chair across from Josephine.

The woman recited the exact words. "Please clear your mind, dear, then think hard on the question you would like answered." Brenna did as told, taking a deep breath and closing her eyes.

She paused briefly, then said, "Ok, let's do this!"

Josephine smiled wide, squelching a laugh. She began, "So, we'll do the same spread." She talked as she began to spread out the cards. "The first card represents your past. You have before you the Page of Swords. This card tells me you were a handful for your mother. That you were a curious child, probably the little girl who liked playing in an ant hill. Curious not only with the world around you but curious about the things you did not understand."

Brenna's eyes widened at the clarity of Josephine's words. "This beginning was a catapult to your life now. You see the world as a tool to make it what you want. That began to set the pace for you in your future."

The Fortune teller flipped through her cards, each describing things that Brenna could expect. "This card in the Future placement is a Page of Wands and is upright. It tells us you are going to have an adventure in the future. You desire freedom and crave excitement. You'll likely have it." Josephine looked her in the eye and smiled, then focused on the reading again. "It could also mean you will be taking a new path."

Brenna smiled, feeling the excitement rise in the pit of her stomach. The word adventure sparked her interest. The fortune teller gracefully turned cards, telling Brenna precisely what she wanted to hear. "And the final card in your reading today is Strength. Very fitting, don't you think?" Josephine continued her recitation of the cards displayed. "This is a beautiful thing that you see. That your heart sees." Josephine smiled softly. "Bless you, my child." Then, as if to close her thought and the reading, Josephine gathered the cards and shuffled them once more.

"I'm ready for the last reading," Josephine said, looking at Andrea. "Are you ready?"

Andrea hesitated momentarily, nodding slightly, "Sure, I'm ready." She'd never thought about looking into the future and wasn't sure she wanted to know. Getting through the day was taxing enough; seconds later, she felt silly. *It's just a reading. Only I can decide that.*

Just as though she was reading Andrea's mind, Josephine said, "Come along, Andrea dear, let's get started."

Andrea sat down across the table from Josephine, hearing her repeat what she told the other girls. "Then think clearly about a questions you want answered." Andrea closed her eyes and took a deep breath.

She sat quite still; then, she took another slow breath to calm her heart, which was, for some reason, beating quickly. In the split second between the exhale of her breath and opening her eyes, Andrea had a glimpse of a young girl. Red hair and dark eyes, and she fingered the stone amulet that hung around her neck. Her eyes widened suddenly, and just as quickly as the vision appeared, it left her. It took a minute to recover, unsettled by the girl in her dream she didn't know. At that moment, it did not have meaning to her or her reading.

Andrea struggled to bring her attention back to Josephine and her pending reading. She blinked and looked straight at the fortune teller, who smiled and began to flip the cards.

"Your first card is a Seven of Cups in the upright position. This card is a glance into your past and tells me you were a dreamer; you still are. You spent a good piece of your days dreaming about things that were out of your reach. You were looking for purpose because you did not feel direction or guidance. This emptiness continues. The search for a clear path continues." Andrea gave a little nod as if Josephine could see right through her.

"Your next card, in the present position, is the Two of Pentacles and is upright." Josephine looked very focused but struggled with finding the words. "You have inner turmoil." Andrea related the last description to the vision she saw, thinking maybe it was precisely the turmoil Josephine just spoke of. As the fortune teller talked, Andrea had a hard time focusing on her words. "It should inspire you to move on. Move forward with the path you've chosen and trust in it."

Josephine took a second and indulged herself with a drink of water, then began her recitation again. "Now, onto the Future card." Josephine flipped the cards skillfully, offering predictions for Andrea's future. She flipped the last card and hesitated; shock filled her expression. "This one represents the reason for your card set. It is the Six of Swords reversed. It tells us that you struggle to change your future outlook."

Josephine stopped and looked at Andrea with fear in her eyes. "I must stop here. Bless you, child." The fortune teller picked up the cards quickly and shuffled them, not saying anything else.

Andrea gulped and looked at Josephine in shock. "What does it say?" She was suddenly overwhelmed with despair – like she was left standing on the edge of a cliff.

"It is not clear what will happen, but I curse myself to tell it. You must have faith; now more than ever." Then she shook her head and walked away. Those final words ended her reading.

As Andrea rose, unsettled and dazed by her reading, she thought to herself, *I never should have done this*, leaving the table with a feeling of dread.

The girls paid their fees, and Josephine looked at Andrea, then down at her necklace that she hadn't seen before the reading.

"Wherever did you get that necklace?" Andrea heard Josephine's voice popping through her thoughts. "May I see?" Andrea took a step closer to the fortune teller.

"I've studied the powers of these rare stones. This style is likely tribal. This stone is Lapis Lazuli, one of the gemstones supposed to have mystical powers. It's probably why your reading suffered interruption. The legend says that the holder has the gift to travel through celestial time, a balance within the universe and allow you to move through the cosmos. It is extraordinary. You're lucky to have it."

Andrea began to fiddle with her new bobble. "I found it at a little pawn shop just down the way. I fell in love with it. I thought it was beautiful, too." Josephine gave a bob of her head in agreement.

As they bid farewell and walked out the door, Andrea was skeptical as she thought, *she just told us what we wanted to hear, or are these readings actual? Surely, there must be some truth to it.* She kept her thoughts to herself, fully knowing both Brenna and Chelsea found merit in Miss Josephine's words.

The girls continued along the sidewalk of the busy little shops. Andrea mentioned to Chelsea, "Visiting a Fortune teller was fun and something I would not have done without you guys." They wandered around the multitude of shops and finally, back to the hotel.

6. Uncertainty – 1798

Andrea began to stir among the furs and blankets, relishing in the warmth and softness of them. Her eyes fluttered, letting in little glints of sunlight and the reality of where she was flushed over her like a wave of cold water; fear engulfed her. Where am I? Instinctively, she grabbed at the amulet as it was the only thing that seemed to give her comfort, and just as if the stone answered her need; she was convinced to take a long, slow breath and close her eyes. Her heart and mind calmed, allowing her to focus on the present.

She heard voices. They were subtle and masculine. Andrea flung her eyes open abruptly and tried to orient herself. She saw woolen blankets and a pillow made of straw. Smelling the wood smoke and seeing the tent over her head, she realized she was in camp with Jacob and Johnny.

Andrea sat up suddenly, looking around the tent, feeling the sand and sweat on her skin. She began to run her fingers through her wild hair, trying to smooth it out. She had a string in her pocket, something she had randomly stuffed in there from the hotel. She pulled her fluffy, wavy hair back to tame it. She stood up and smoothed her clothing, then erupted from the tent.

"Ah, mornin'," Jacob said the moment he'd seen any activity from her direction. He couldn't get over how she just appeared, although he was slowly losing his reason to be suspicious.

Andrea kept her eyes down, saying, "Morning" to Jacob.

"Johnny's been waiting for ya'."

Johnny smiled and looked at her. "Get yourself some hot tea, and let's get going. Those clams are not gonna wait."

Andrea chugged down the warm liquid, very happy to have it. The tea was good, too.

"What tea is this?" she asked Jacob.

"It's Chamomile. It's wild here and easy to get and dry. We have a fair amount of it." Andrea was pleasantly surprised at this. It didn't taste anything like the chamomile tea she was used to.

"Well, I look forward to having more," nodding her appreciation.

Johnny threw a strap holding a bag over his shoulder. She noticed he had a flask with fresh water on a strap secured with his belt. He looked at Andrea and, with a motion of his hand, he gestured toward the ocean for her to proceed.

"After you," Johnny said, provoking a whisp of a smile to lighten her face.

Johnny strode up beside her, and they walked together. They were silent for a while, and Andrea thought about what she had dreamed. She remembered the parade in New Orleans. Reflexively, she grabbed the necklace as the memory of the pawn shop came to mind, and Chelsea was wearing blue. But what happened after that?

Johnny could see her struggling with her thoughts and started the conversation. "I don't know what happened to you, and I'm sorry you don't remember either. But I know that when these things happen, they'll all come around sooner or later. Just don't you worry! You can be our guest and stay with us until we figure this out." Andrea was not surprised at this outpouring of kindness. Johnny was that kind of guy. Then she thought her sudden appearance was probably on his mind as much as it was on hers.

"You have been truly kind, Johnny; thank you. Where I come from, people are not so kind." Andrea halted her words, thinking she'd said too much. She expected his next question.

"Well, where do you come from then?" Johnny asked as if reading from a script. Andrea thought quickly about where she could be from.

"Uh, New Orleans, I think. There are a lot of people from all over there. None are as friendly as you." She thought she'd covered herself pretty well.

Johnny shook his head. "Memory will come back to you."

He began to make small talk, bringing up Jacob and their hunting trips "We come out here a few times yearly to get rabbit and pheasant. We don't fetch clams all the time. They don't last long, but it's a good change. We live a few days' ride from here, but this place is wild with rabbits, and the furs are great for tradin' n' such." He paused his oration for a moment and looked up to the sky, squinting against the brightness of the day. "It's a nice change from deer and turkey sometimes," Johnny muttered in a faint voice. "Jacob knows some of the Indians around here, and he trades rabbit hides and copper cups – in exchange, we get baskets and deerskin. Jewelry sometimes, too."

Andrea's eyes widened in disbelief at hearing Johnny talk of the Indians, remembering the encounter she had when she took her first steps on the beach. It seemed so long ago, but it was only yesterday. Worse yet, the first people she saw were natives, and the encounter was not altogether pleasant. She had to give up her bracelet.

They had just reached the sandy beach when Johnny pulled a scoop-shaped tool out of his pocket. His eyes took on a mischievous glimmer, and he turned to her and said in a little more than a whisper, "They move fast. As soon as you see them, get under them, or they'll be gone." Andrea listened intently. "We need to look for little bubbles in the sand or tiny air pockets. Those are clams. You can get down and dig them if you want or show me where you see em' and I will use the big scoop." And with that, Johnny started his hunt. He kept his head down and moved slowly; Andrea followed closely behind. It was only a second before he found the first one. He reached down and scooped the sand, working quickly, then slowly shook the sand out of the spoon. There it was: a clam about the size of a quarter. He rinsed it in the ocean waves, then dropped it in the leather bag.

Andrea focused on a couple of bubbles, falling to her knees and grabbing as quickly as she could. The first one was a miss. She tried again and came up with nothing. She was not about to give up so quickly, and she kept trying, pulling one out on the third try. Her smile widened, showing Johnny a little whisper of joy; her playful eyes twinkled as if she were a child again.

"Wow, this is fun," she exclaimed. The two wandered all over the beach, looking for the tiny air pockets or bubbles and diving in to grab them. After about an hour, they had nearly filled the bag. Andrea began to tire of clamming and wandered along where the water washed up on the sand, kicking at clumps of sandy seaweed, letting the waves rush up against her legs.

She had taken off her shoes and rolled up her pant legs so they wouldn't get wet. Taking in the raw beauty of the ocean and the quiet droning of the waves, she looked out toward the horizon, her eyes scanning for anything, but she saw a lot of nothing. A glimmer of something reflecting a long way away caught her eye. "Johnny," she said with urgency in her voice. "What do you make of that?"

Johnny looked up from the hunt in the sand, squinting, then his expression darkened. "Oh, we'd better go. That could be pirates." Andrea shot him a look like he was kidding.

"Pirates?" she said urgently, needing confirmation.

"Yes, ma'am, there are marauders that sometimes make it here, and we don't want to be anywhere near them. Let's get going." In one motion, Johnny picked up the scoop, the weight of the bag full of clams over his shoulder and turned back toward camp.

Andrea grabbed her shoes, and once they were off the shore and away from view, she stopped, putting them on. She asked hesitantly, "Do you think they will find us?"

Johnny answered her in a low voice, "I don't know. Our camp is a distance away; we'll probably be fine." Andrea traveled along for a while, holding back her words. Johnny was quiet too. She could tell he wanted to distance himself from the so-called pirates.

After a short while, Andrea said, "I'm glad you brought me. I enjoyed myself." The statement lingered for a minute; Johnny understood what it was to find just a little happiness in the face of adversity.

He had confessed in their conversation that his parent had died, and that's why he lived with Jacob.

Andrea had to ask, "Can I ask what they died of?"

Johnny took a few seconds to answer. "It was smallpox. It's taken a lot of people. Everyone lost someone. It was bad around here for a while."

They walked, not speaking for a few minutes, then Andrea worked up the nerve to ask Johnny the question that had not left her mind in the two days she'd been there – wherever this place was.

"Johnny, do you know what the date is?" He looked at her, pity in his eyes.

"It is February. The 20th or so."

Andrea kept her eyes down when she added, "And the year?"

Johnny's step hesitated. She didn't think it would be too off-color to ask since she'd lost her memory. He let out a breath. "1798." Without making eye contact, she nodded slightly, shocked, realizing she knew it all along. Still moving through the bushy landscape, Andrea kept her eyes down, her thoughts backtracking and wondering where it all went wrong. What in God's name happened? How did I get to 1798? She thought. Her brain searching for rationality.

Johnny finished his thought. "I forget the day of the week when we are out hunting and such."

The two finally returned to camp and met Jacob's kind nod. He had a metal pot on the fire half filled with water.

"There you are," he said. "I got the water warmed up and ready for those clams."

Andrea perked up and said, "They'll need to be cleaned a bit before we cook them. Do you have any fresh water?"

Jacob walked over to a canvas bag and handed it to her. "I just went to the creek and got us some. Here you go." Andrea didn't know there was a creek. She hadn't seen one anywhere.

"Oh," she said with surprise. "Where is the creek?"

Jacob pointed in the direction of the horses. "Just yonder, down the bank."

She noted its general direction so she could wash herself later. She never thought she would crave something as simple as a bath until now, dreaming of the smell of the jasmine soap she bought at Pier 51. Gently roused from her daydream by the smell of wood smoke; she scowled about not having access to the bar of lavender-colored, delicious-smelling soap.

She took a cup full of water and the clams and went behind the tent where she was able to get the sand out of the clams. Once they were clean, she used large, flat leaves to carry the mollusks to the pot and threw them in. Then she asked Jacob for some salt. A bit of turnip was left, she cut it up and threw it in.

Everything cooked together for a while, and the "clam stew" was done. Jacob pulled out two carved wooden bowls from his saddlebag, and Andrea served. They ate their meal heartily, as it was the day's only meal.

Johnny told Jacob of the ship they had seen and could not describe it as it was too far away. After that, Jacob's eyes darkened with concern. "Well, it might be quiet now, but I think we might sleep in shifts tonight, just in case," Johnny nodded. The thought of being assaulted at the very least brought a shiver to Andrea's spine.

She went to the creek and gratefully cleaned herself. Her head was itchy, so she also washed it, at least as close as she could come without using any shampoo or soap for that matter. She pulled off her shirt and rinsed it as well. Wringing out excess water, she put it back on. At least for now, she could stand the smell of herself. She found some honeysuckle that was close to the creek and in full bloom. She took some of the blossoms and massaged them, then rubbed her hands on her neck and the soft part of her belly. If nothing else, this would make her smell slightly better.

After her "bath," Andrea felt much more presentable. Upon cleaning her hair, she combed through it, smoothing it with her fingers, then bound it up again with the string she had used before. The lump on her eyebrow was still very tender but was healing, as she could feel the scab. Not only would the injury take a while to heal, but there would also be an awesome scar from it.

She made it back to the little camp just as the sun began to set on yet another day, and found a place to observe the gorgeous sunset. She watched the sun slowly dipping behind the horizon, doing her best to recall the day and relishing the moments of peace it provided. Once she turned her attention back to the camp, she thought curiously about the earlier mention of Jacob's trips to trade with the Indians. Mulling over which tribes specifically were in this location, so she asked Jacob about it.

Jacob said, "They call themselves Creek. The place we visit is a smaller tribe that is part of the Muskogee Creek Tribes. It was one big tribe, and smaller groups broke away from it. They don't trust white people - and for good reason. I've been friends with them for a while, and I'm lucky they trust me enough to trade for things they need." Andrea watched him talk intently. He knew much about the tribe and seemed very comfortable speaking about them. "So, they're friendly to you? Are you someone they trust?" Andrea shrugged while was working it out in her mind.

Jacob responded to her question. "That is a fact. Many white folks have fooled them into a false friendship, only to double cross them. They've moved many times, and now they don't trust anyone." A person could tell Jacob took his friendship with the tribe seriously, even defending them. Few could do what Jacob did with the Indians, and many folks trusted him to do the talking.

As the evening was winding down, the new friend sat around the fire and told ghost stories for fun. Andrea was careful about how she phrased her story so as not to give up any truth and provide the men with something to question. She was surprised that people of the 18th century had ghost stories that were just as entertaining. After some wine and small talk, Andrea felt more relaxed, enjoying the atmosphere of the time and place where she radically appeared.

Jacob had a flute that he'd made, and he blew a tune on it as the coolness of the night began to pierce the little camp.

Andrea had gone into the tent and grabbed a blanket, flipping back the door flap as she reappeared. Curiously, she said, "Tell me about tomorrow," breaking the peacefulness of the night.

Jacob and Johnny were starting to get used to the funny way Andrea talked, and with a subtle shake of his head, hiding a smile, Jacob responded, "We'll be heading north in the morning so I can meet with my Indian friends.

Andrea thought momentarily and said, "Is it okay if I go along with you?"

Jacob wrinkled his forehead and said, "Of course, where else would you go?"

She was genuinely tentative about accepting their kindness. "I just thought that, well, I don't know how the natives would take to a white woman in their tribe."

Johnny came closer and put a hand on her shoulder, saying confidently, "Don't worry; you're no threat. They will see that. You're welcome to come with us." Although Andrea knew he was sincere; she was unsure showing up in the Indian camp was a good idea. After all, Jacob has a family, and she doesn't want him to risk anything, especially for her.

Jacob pulled a bottle out of his saddle bag of something she hadn't seen before. "Tonight might be the perfect time for this!" He smiled broadly, sporting a playful expression. Jacob pulled out the cork and took a swig out of the brown bottle. He clenched his eyes and wrinkled his forehead, then smiled through the pain of the intense sting of the drink.

He passed it on to Johnny, and the younger man also took a swig. "Whew, that is good!" Johnny's expression matched that of his older brothers.

Andrea realized it was probably very stiff booze, and although she was not much of a drinker; she was happy to take a shot out of the bottle. She tipped back her head and took a sip, trying to control the flow so she didn't take in too much at once. It tasted hot, like a whiskey.

She winced and let out a slight cough. "Oh dang!" passing the bottle around again, and Jacob put it away.

All three were sitting peacefully, watching the fire, getting lost in the licks of flames dancing about the rock ring that held it, hissing and popping as campfires do when the horses began to stir. One of them whinnied loudly. Jacob picked up his gun and headed over toward the tethered horses. He readied his rifle and cocked it, stepping very slowly toward the darkness that enveloped the horses, ready to confront the unknown disturbance.

Johnny grabbed his bow and arrow and followed his brother, signaling to Andrea with his open hand to stay back. She did as Johnny bade, staying close to the fire, as she had no weapon and did not want to confront anything or anybody in the darkness. The faces of the Indians she'd encountered came to mind, making her tremble, scared more now than before. What if they came back with more Indians? She sat with her knees up and her arms wrapped tightly around them, her head buried in her knees, holding on for dear life.

A hundred yards or so behind the horses was the creek, which looked to be where Jacob was going. A few moments later, Andrea heard a gunshot echoing among the trees. She closed her eyes, trying to shut out the noise from the blast. Jacob came back, his gun in his hand and a scowl on his face.

Johnny met him at the trail and asked breathlessly, "What was it?"

Jacob swung his rifle casually by his side. "It was a panther. She's on her way to the creek and startled the horses, that's all. I'll keep a watch for a while, but I spooked her; I don't think she'll be back."

The two returned to camp, and Johnny said, "I'll get a little shut-eye and come out to relieve you in a couple of hours." Jacob nodded, taking on the first 'guard duty shift.'

Andrea's heart was still pounding; having never encountered a wild animal before, except in a zoo. She was out in the wilderness, in the middle of nowhere, and having thought about it, this was probably a regular occurrence for people in 1798.

Still shaking she said, "Well, I'll try to get some sleep too – Goodnight," and she went directly to her tent.

Lying in the quiet for a while, listening closely for anything that did not sound like a camp sound, the recent events rolling through her mind. She listened to the soft rustle of the leaves in the trees above, watching the peak of the tent move so slightly in the breeze. She listened to the subtle noises and rhythms, eventually relaxing her; she felt her body grow heavy, pressing into the furs. After a short while, she drifted off to sleep.

*

Andrea tried to open her mouth to scream, but no sound came to her. She backed up as quickly as she could, not taking her eyes off the feline creature. A massive cat with big teeth was casually walking toward her, a low growl made the hair stand up on her neck. In a split second, something shot over her shoulder, narrowly missing the cat. The predator swiped its front paw along the ground, sending up a cloud of dust. In a blink, the cat was gone, disappearing into a mist. Just gone.

She shot up to a sitting position, eyes flying open, expecting a confrontation, but there was none. She looked around, seeing just a slit of moonlight through the tent. There was no noise, no threat, nothing. Then she grasped the idea it was a dream. It was so real, she thought to herself. I could have reached out to touch it. Relieved, she laid back down, taking slow breaths to help ease her back to sleep. It took a while, but she eventually closed her eyes, drifting off again.

7. Krew of Bacchus

New Orleans - 2004

Andrea pulled the hot pink, short-sleeved shirt over her head. It was one of her favorites, choosing comfort over style. It suited her. She began to run a brush through her mousey brown hair, which had a profound natural wave. Looking at herself in the mirror, she focused intensely on her dark brown eyes, reasoning that they were probably her favorite feature. She put down her hairbrush and grabbed her makeup bag, touching up her mascara and applying a little lip gloss. Andrea thought deeply about what Josephine had told her and wondered why here, on the trip of a lifetime, she was inventing something else to contemplate.

Brenna and Chelsea were chattering in the background as they, too, were getting ready for the night. All three girls were excited, sensing the stirring of the air around them. The city came to life, and soon, the parades would start. The crowd would get denser, and the drinks would flow. There was nothing Andrea wanted more than to be a part of the experience here. Her day was perfect, and she hoped to make some great memories as the future was a big gray cloud to her. Finding her path was important, but she felt lost most of the time. Being decisive about what direction to go in her life was so difficult. And why? Why did this always seem to be a hurdle for her? She loved adventure but needed to feel the arms of security. She felt the polarity of being between two different lives for too long.

She was taking far too long in the bathroom, slowly massaging an apple-scented lotion into her hands. Her mind drifted to a faraway place as she thought, wishing for something to change her outlook. Just as that thought came and went, she decided she wouldn't have to commit to any decision if she didn't speak it.

The three girls started down the street shoulder to shoulder and smiling from ear to ear. It was only a couple of blocks from the street where the action began. They found their way to a corner bar and ordered some "fru-fru" tropical drinks, then went out to the street and did some people-watching.

Brenna said, amused, "What else do you do in a crowd like this?" People-watching was one of her talents, and her game was great fun for everyone around her. She spoke to her friends in a muffled voice:

"See that guy over there in the green Bermuda shorts? He just told that lady in the big white hat that he

thought she had a great ass. She is thinking about whether or not she wants his attention. The kicker is that she thinks he has a great ass, too. See that right there? She just whispered in his ear, 'Hey baby, I wanna jump your bones.'"

Chelsea and Andrea began to laugh aloud, and the man in the green Bermuda shorts and the lady in the big white hat turned to look at the three girls. Andrea and Chelsea looked down as quickly as they could, holding back their raucous laughter; Brenna watched them, looking over Chelsea's head. The fact that they'd gotten the two strangers' attention made the story even funnier.

The girls drank and scrutinized the crowd. Everyone around them was cheerful and lighthearted. The weather was warm and sticky, nothing like the cool freshness of the air in the northwest. The moon was as bright as they'd ever seen, which made Andrea think it was the alcohol rather than an especially clear night. As she scanned through the people lined up for the parade, she witnessed a strikingly handsome fellow looking at her. She was sizing him up when his eyes caught her staring at him. Andrea quickly looked away, pretending to scour the faces in the crowd while smiling to herself. Chelsea caught sight of this exchange and began to coax Andrea to go over and talk to him.

"There is no damn way I'm going to do that!" Andrea said intensely. "I just don't work that way."

She grabbed Chelsea's arm and made her look in the other direction. And with that move, Chelsea's eyes found something, or someone, to look at.

Chelsea exclaimed, "Oh, my goodness, I'm in love."

Brenna heard their little private conversation, butting in. "Slow down, Tex, you need to cool down the horses." She always had a way of making a joke out of an emotional outburst. It was one of her talents. She was pretty content people-watching, partaking in a small serving or two of spirits as well.

Moments later, they heard a band only a few blocks away. They moved among the crowd to the corner of St. Charles Street for a better view of the oncoming parade. So many people were there, all kinds from all over the place. The lighthearted celebration was an escape from their worries and responsibilities; the three friends from Seattle felt it, too.

Brenna, being rather tall, was gazing down the street at the oncoming pageantry and Chelsea had been trying to find the lip gloss in the bottom of her clutch. Andrea's focused was down the street at the advancing spectacle when someone bumped into her. She didn't think much of it because the gathering crowd moved in all around her. Then it happened again.

Now feeling a little agitated, she turned to tell them to back up and saw it was the dark-haired handsome man she'd caught sight of before.

"Oh, sorry," she said, her heart sinking at the stupidity of her comment. The stranger searched for her eyes, and once they'd made contact. The dark-haired man began to smile. Andrea smiled back.

The young man said, "I hoped I would run into you. I'm Collin." There was a long pause. "You're in a great place to get the best view."

Andrea replied in a quiet voice, "Oh, great. I didn't know."

The relaxed way about him made her, even more, attracted to him if that was possible. "Are you from around here?" Andrea focused on his bright and engaging eyes.

"Uh, I'm Andrea, and I'm not from around here. Are you?" She began to relax a little as they conversed. His eyes drank up her free spirit. He stood for a moment as if he was contemplating what to say. The truth of it was he didn't want to say the wrong thing and make her walk away.

"N - No," he stated so hesitantly she might have thought him to be rather shy. However, he went out of his way to bump into her. "I'm from Colorado. Came here with a buddy." Andrea smiled. She admired his tall, solid build. He stood straight and proud. The kind of man her grandfather would like. Brenna and Chelsea had been distracted but looked over and saw Andrea's ongoing conversation with the handsome man.

They looked at each other, and Chelsea said, "That will be good for her; a man, I mean."

Brenna said calmly, "Hmmm. I thought it would be you to hook up with someone first."

Chelsea gave her a blank look, then said, "And what is that supposed to mean?"

Brenna cocked her head and responded, "You know. The thing that Miss Josephine said? That you'd have a union?"

Chelsea stared at her and remarked, "Right. You're right. It should be me. But I guess she never said when that would happen. She couldn't predict something like that." Getting louder as the entertainment got closer, the Krew of

Bacchus parade was underway. It was quite a show. The crowds lined the streets, seeing Winnie the Pooh, Ali Baba and his magic lamp, and King Kong, to name a few. The people on the floats were throwing beads as intoxicated revelers were spilling drinks. Andrea soon realized the crowd was as amusing as the parade. The whole time the delightful show continued, Collin and Andrea stood side by side. They talked back and forth about the meaning of some traditions around these spectacles, or at least the rumors. She was shocked to know some traditions went back hundreds of years.

Andrea noticed Chelsea was now standing next to the taller blonde guy she'd seen and commented about earlier. That was how she worked. And really, no one could resist her once they got to know her. Andrea watched her out of the corner of her eye and thought how the two looked together, like *a modern-day Barbie and Ken.*

Without warning, she began to giggle. Collin looked at her, first just glancing, then full-on looked at her. He smiled; his eyebrows raised high.

"Wanna let me in on the secret?" Andrea thought her actions were rude and smiled a pretty little smile before explaining.

"Oh, my friend Chelsea," Andrea said, rolling her eyes, "She's gone out and fallen in love again." He looked at her, not getting the inside joke intended for her closest buddies. He followed the direction of her stare, looking at the beautiful blonde "couple" but was barely swayed, if at all. Andrea's perspective had her right where she wanted to be. Next to Collin in the crowd full of strangers.

While her friend was getting to know the new acquaintance, Brenna met a couple of girls who were just in front of her and were talking. They were tourists and, like Brenna, began filling the other in on things to see and do in the Big Easy.

"Yeah, we went to a Tarot place this afternoon and had our fortunes told. It was really cool!" She spoke enthusiastically, making the girls want to visit Miss Josephine.

The two new friends, Brooke and Jen, got directions from her so they could give it a try. Brooke mentioned a museum of Mardi Gras history and highly recommended it.

"Sounds great," Brenna said, "We can see that tomorrow." They continued. The whole time Brenna was making new friends, Collin and Andrea were getting to know each other. They talked about work, and school, among other things.

Collin said, "I graduated from CSU last year with an engineering degree. I've been working with Union Pacific on their civil engineering crew. It's been okay; there are a lot of projects out there."

Andrea was quite impressed. "That sounds like an interesting job. I bet in the future you'll have plenty of opportunity to work on those more interesting projects."

Collin nodded and said, "How about you? What turns your crank?"

Andrea rolled her eyes to show that her life was much less interesting. "I'm a senior at Northwestern, where I am working on a degree in history specializing in Native American Studies." She brightened and added, "I am the lucky recipient of a Summer Scholarship to study the Salish and Kootenai Tribes in Montana. Should be exciting."

Collin shook his head and said, "Wow, the college I attended didn't have anything like that. It sounds intriguing. What exactly would a summer scholarship winner do? I mean, what could you do with it?" He stumbled over the words, trying to get his point across, but it just never came out right. Andrea smiled, understanding that her passion needed more explanation.

She held her head up and straightened her back before she spoke. "I'm very interested in a tribe's ability to hold on to and pass down their beliefs and traditions. This tribe routinely has celebrations like pow-wows for different occasions. I want to know what they're celebrating and how they pass down those traditions and their language. I wanna know if the kids go to 'Indian school' or if a medicine man teaches them about herbal medicines n' stuff. You know, live with them – get to know their lives."

Collin nodded in understanding. "I could see that about you. You want to know what makes things tick."

Andrea looked up and waved her friends over. Andrea said to Collin with a tinge of humor in her eye. "Wanna meet my friends?" Giving him no time to object, she perked up, leading the introduction. "This is Chelsea, and this is Brenna." Andrea smiled at her friends, giving an unintelligible wink.

Collin nodded politely and said, "Hello, ladies, it's nice to meet you."

The small group talked for a short while, and Andrea could feel her friends take an immediate liking to Collin. He was outgoing and polite. Charming. They addressed him as if he was just one of the gang.

Once the parade had passed and the crowds began to thin, Collin led them to a little bar down the block where they could get a table. Andrea was so close to him she could smell his subtle cologne, clean and masculine, happy to be so near. The others followed, weaving among the crowd.

They crossed the street and, on the corner, only a couple of blocks from where they watched the parade was a little bar named Shakey's. It looked cleaner than some of the other places on that block, but Andrea was sure it would look like all the rest once the celebration was over.

They pushed through a cluster of people and entered the old tavern. Andrea thought the decor looked more like an old-time saloon. It was rather dark inside, accentuated by the wood and walls having been painted black. The moldings were quite ornate, with a very high ceiling. There was laughter and smiling faces all around, enjoying the company and the cheerful atmosphere, enhancing the pleasantness of this place.

A speedy barmaid took their orders, and the small group began conversing. Collin could not take his eyes off Andrea. She hadn't stopped smiling ever since he'd bumped into her at the parade. She was pretty and feminine, without being too much so. Smooth; oh, she was smooth in the way she walked and talked. So easy to talk to and even easier to listen to.

Collin had reached over and grabbed her hand, then whispered to her, "I hope you don't mind." She was a little surprised but let him hold her hand while she continued chatting, a little wisp of a smile curled in the corner of her mouth.

The entertaining crowd continued drinking and pranking into the night. One of Collin's friends, Jake, had come over to the table and plopped down in a chair right between Chelsea and Brenna. He and Brenna began joking and provided the group with im-prov that would impress even professionals.

As the night went on and the scene turned raunchy, the girls decided it was time to go back to the hotel. Andrea smiled and looked at Collin with flirty eyes, blinking slowly, the long lashes brushing the high point on her cheeks.

Then she asked him, "Do you know a safe way back to the St. George Hotel? There are a lot of very drunk people out there, and I certainly don't want to get lost."

Collin raised an eyebrow, then responded. "Oh, you're staying at the St. George? It's a nice place and in a terrific location, close to downtown. How about Jake and I walk back with you?" Collin glanced back at Jake, who only showed him a sheepish grin. Andrea was quite happy to hear that. "Better to have a couple of guys hangin' around fending off the creeps," Collin said, an infectious smile slowly spreading.

Brenna and Chelsea enthusiastically said, "Yes, please." Andrea secretly thought, *"This is precisely what I hoped would happen."*

As they walked together back to the hotel, Collin and Andrea held hands and talked small talk. Andrea was thoroughly smitten. He was tall and strong, kind and funny, and had a commanding way about him that made people desire his company. It also seemed that Collin reciprocated. Whatever it was, Andrea didn't want it to stop.

They'd reached the hotel, and Andrea was sad their walk ended. She'd enjoyed his company and loved how interested he was in her. He couldn't stop touching her, even the tiniest bit, and she reacted like a cat to catnip.

Finally, as everyone began to scatter, Andrea said to Collin, "Well, I'd best be going, but what about tomorrow?

Would you like to show me around? Or do you have other plans?"

Collin's eyes sparkled as he responded, "I would love us to get together. When and where?"

Andrea gave him a little flirty smile. "How about you give me your phone number and I'll text you when we figure out our plan of attack." She rolled her eyes in the direction of the hotel's main door, through which Chelsea and Brenna had just disappeared. "I'll know better myself after we get our day started."

When Collin took out his phone, Andrea grabbed it and added herself to his contacts and then, she sent a message to herself to get his number. "There," she said. "Now you won't be likely to forget me."

Collin looked at her sheepishly and said, "I won't forget you."

He pulled her close and kissed her. It was longer than a first kiss should be, but told Andrea what she wanted to know. She kissed him back. There was something about the taste of him that felt right. And just as Andrea had that thought it, Collin said, "Mm mm. I like that."

He kissed her back once more, stirring Andrea's emotions. Her stomach fluttered like it was full of butterflies;

she hadn't experienced that since her first boyfriend in high school.

"Good night then." He smiled and looked back over his shoulder as he walked away. Andrea slowly went through the door and up the elevator to her room, sporting a goo-goo smile that wouldn't stop.

When she opened the door, Chelsea and Brenna "high-fived" each other, laughing. Brenna said, "Told ya'!" There were no words from Andrea, just a smile.

8. Henderson Point

East of New Orleans - 2004

The girls planned their day over a café' au lait and beignets. Brenna commented, pointing at the plate of pastry. "This is just what everyone said to do while we're in New Orleans."

Andrea responded with a tone of sarcasm, "Who is everyone? I don't know anyone who's been here."

Brenna quipped right back, "On that travel chat I subscribe to. It is a traditional treat in New Orleans." Chelsea and Andrea looked at each other, unable to argue.

Chelsea spoke up, curious about their plans for the day. "I just wanna see all we can see while we're here."

Brenna let out a giggle. "Sure, you do..."

Andrea rolled her eyes at her friends, adding, "I think that train tour starts in about an hour."

Brenna's eyes opened wide, glancing at her phone. "Yes, it does. We'd better get moving. We need to get to St. Charles Street to catch it."

Andrea gathered her purse and cell phone and said, "I'm ready." Brenna shrugged her shoulders and got up, too. They both had to wait for Chelsea, who ran back to the room; then, the threesome trekked to the train depot. After walking a few blocks, they were soon at the terminal looking over the schedule.

The sun was bright and clear, very different from the weather they'd have in Seattle in February. They stood among other tourists on the platform for nearly twenty minutes, finally hearing the train coming, ringing its bell, and tooting its horn. The train (trolley) was cute. Red and yellow with a brass bell by the driver's chair.

They paid their fare before waiting on the platform, seeking out a place to sit. The girls clamored into the trolley, getting the once-over from the driver. He was staring and smiling, trying to get the attention of any one of them but failed miserably. The girls noticed his attention and giggled about it. Chelsea declared, "Can't blame a guy for tryin'," which produced laughs all around. Andrea could not remember a time she had been so relaxed. She had dreamed of being in a different, more exotic place. New Orleans was different and strange but not exotic.

The trolley took them down to the French Market, only a couple blocks from Miss Josephine's. It was quaint and colorful. The girls decided to come back another time to shop.

A few minutes later, they saw the Aquarium, which the travel chat had yet to mention. The ride was nearly over when Andrea got a text from Collin. "I can't wait to see you," was all it said. While looking at her phone, her expression changed, catching her friend's attention.

Chelsea said, "What?" prying Andrea into telling her what the smiles were about, as if she didn't know.

"Aw, you know. Collin asked me last night if I would go with him to Henderson Point. He was asking what time would work." Andrea thought they would allow a few hours for the Museum and a short trip back to the hotel, then message Collin afterward.

New Orleans was an amazing, historic city brimming with unusual things. There is a certain charm about it, both mysterious and enchanting. She briefly wondered whether it had anything to do with budding romance.

Her hand went to her neck, loosening tension, thinking about Collin's eyes, and she paused for a moment, stroking her new amulet. She remembered what Miss Josephine said about the extraordinary stone. *Did it have powers?* She couldn't help but be skeptical about the mysterious amulet and thought almost the same about the tarot reading. The thought of it still made her wonder.

Collin came by right at 3 o'clock. Jake came along, too, admitting to messaging Chelsea and Brenna about hanging out. There was a Martini Bar just up the same street as the hotel, enticing the three friends to have a cool drink on a ridiculously beautiful day. It was a perfect opportunity for some downtime to relax, check messages, and get to know Jake.

Collin drove a Jeep. He opened the door for her, and she slid into the passenger seat. She thought it would be best to wear something light and fresh so she wouldn't get sweaty, so, she decided on cream-colored pants and a dark blue blouse. She didn't know what the Point would be like. As they hit the highway on-ramp, Collin told her the Point was the last place a sailor's family could wave to him as he went off to sea.

"It sounds sad, but they could come here and watch the ships pull into port, too." That thought made Andrea smile.

She had been hoping for this moment. A chance to be alone with Collin. Since their meeting, she had thought about it a lot. She was unexpectedly drawn to him, feeling a pull, like the ends of a magnet. Looking down, she saw his hand was on the shifter, and willfully, she reached over and put her hand on his. Collin was not expecting to feel her touch, and his head jerked to look, first at their hands, then at her as she smiled. He smiled back, feeling the natural connection. He pulled his hand from the shifter and laced his fingers through hers. Andrea wondered what would happen when it was time for her to go back to Seattle.

The jeep approached a stop sign, and Collin leaned over and kissed her. His lips were so warm and welcoming. She hoped his affections were not leading her, as she wanted to be in control of her emotions but his overwhelming charm made it extremely hard.

It took nearly an hour to get there, but when Collin pulled into the parking lot, Andrea knew this was a special place. Her eyes absorbed the view; the body of water with no end. She jumped out of the car abruptly and stood with her face in the wind. The ache deep in her heart just then had more to do with freedom than any other emotion she could think of. Standing there, still, the sea breeze wafting over her and ruffling her hair; she didn't want to be anyplace else.

Collin removed his shoes so they could walk on the beach. It caught Andrea's attention, bringing her suddenly back to the present. She took a minute to do the same. They went east, hand in hand, talking general small talk, wanting nothing more than time to share.

They made it down the beach to Harbour Park, almost two miles away. Collin laughed. "You'd never catch me going that far for fun, ever!" But he drew Andrea in for another kiss, never letting go of her hand, this time pushing his body up against hers. He smiled a dashing, heart-melting smile and said, "Now, this is fun!" The intensity of the embrace made her blush, but she didn't want him to stop, feeling entirely secure in his arms.

As he pulled away from the embrace, and looked her in the eye, she was warmed all over, melting in his arms. As he slowly stepped back, she watched him, getting the impression that he regretted it.

Still thinking about the kiss and his devastatingly beautiful eyes, they began to walk back toward the point, slowly savoring every minute as the sun drooped toward the horizon.

This afternoon was so perfect, Andrea thought, not wanting this time together to end. Collin's following comment surprised her as if he was reading her mind. "Today was great, and I'm not sure I want it to end. I want to get to know you better." Andrea gave the question serious attention and thought hard before answering. There was an awkward moment when Collin felt a twinge of doubt.

Andrea smiled sweetly, breaking eye contact with him. He knew there was a "but" somewhere.

"I love being with you, Collin. I will ride this ride for as long as I can. I want us to enjoy each other. No strings."

Collin decided not to make it more difficult. She was right, one day at a time. He smiled and put his arm over her shoulder, walking arm-in-arm for a while in silence. He wanted to be close to her, and she to him.

The light was fading by the time they'd returned to the car. They stood there, propped against the passenger door, snuggled close, and watched the sunset. The wind blew the warm, damp air around them, pushing them closer to each other. Their touching began to flow fluidly as water, picking up each other's rhythms. They kissed and talked and touched. It was the perfect end to the perfect day, and they reluctantly climbed back into the jeep and went back into town.

Chelsea, Brenna, and Jake were in the lobby waiting for them as they appeared. "Where have you been? The Krew of Orpheus parade starts in forty minutes!" Brenna was agitated. The three of them had gone to the Aquarium after Collin and Andrea left and spent the day behaving as tourists, but tonight was another parade, the "crescendo" of the Mardi Gras celebration. It was the event they'd looked forward to for the last couple of days.

Andrea said a little apprehensively, "I need to go freshen up. Can you give me ten?" Chelsea tapped on her watch. She got a sideways glance from Brenna and headed to the elevator. Andrea was floating on a cloud. She couldn't believe where her heart was right now and could not stop smiling. Was it too good to be true? She didn't want to think about it, but found it hard to trust that something this good could happen to her.

9. A Visit to the Tribe

Georgia - 1798

When Andrea awoke, she heard a bustling outside the tent. She stayed there on the blankets and stretched long and hard. Closing her eyes, she sighed. Suddenly, she felt her body was not under her control, her mind pulling away as though under a spell. Before she was fully awake, she had been overtaken once again with a vision of a man: a tall, bearded man with a stern face and dark eyes, not unlike the girl she'd seen in her previous dream. She then had a flash of a falcon, regal and commanding; her body tensed as a feeling of strength and determination filled her. She worked hard to open her eyes, and it was gone, whisked away by the wind. Her heart was pounding, and beads of sweat covered her forehead. She wondered why she would see strangers.

What does it mean? She thought to herself, blinking her way back to reality. Before she took her head off the straw pillow, Andrea reached for the amulet again, looking for the warmth and comfort it offered, curious about whether it had something to do with her visions and her current state.

Hesitating only a second longer, she sat up and straightened her wild hair, sighing out her frustration with its crazed tendencies, tying it back with the string. She thought about whether or not her expression would give away the unsettling dream she had and consciously did what she could to erase it, taking another breath before exiting the tent. When she threw back the flap, she saw that the two men had almost everything packed up. The men had left a few pieces of jerky for her and a still-warm cup of coffee.

Jacob greeted her cheerfully. "Good Mornin'. We're heading out soon and got things picked up and ready to go. I think it would be best if you rode along with Johnny. We put his bedroll on ol' Jack, so there should be plenty of room." In the two days she had been with the Loftons, neither had ever spoken of horses, so it was a guess which one was Jack. Once she was out of her own shelter, they had broken down the tent in just a few minutes.

She finished her 'breakfast,' rinsed out the cup, and stuffed it in the saddlebag. She did not want to be the one to hold them up. They mounted and got their trip underway.

Feeling the steady drum of the horses' hooves and seeing their tails sway gently back and forth, Andrea thought of the horse's names. "So, what do you call the other horses? Do they have names?"

Johnny jumped right in. "This one here is my horse; her name is Babe. She is strong and gentle. She can be fast as lightning if we need her to be. I've had her since she was a filly." As he spoke, Johnny stroked the long, muscled neck of the chestnut-colored horse, expressing his affection for her. "And that one is Skeeter. Jacob bought her a couple of years ago, and she's gone on these hunting trips a dozen times or more. She is a strong and steady horse and doesn't spook."

Jacob nodded in agreement. "They have served us well."

Andrea glanced back at the mule and back toward Johnny with a gesture of her head. "So that must be Jack," she said, smiling and looking at the brothers, waiting for some reaction and getting nothing more than a smirk and a nod.

Jacob exhibited a good-humored expression but kept looking forward. Andrea stared at the man, sitting straight in the saddle, obviously prideful; she couldn't help it. He was a reliable, respected man for his work and the kind of man he was. He was very gracious and would kill himself to do the right thing.

Andrea thought *this whole incident could have gone very differently*. Her mind picked through what happened all at once, and swallowing the lump in her throat, she suddenly felt blessed.

They traveled a few hours through the forest, hills, streams, and fields. This country impressed her with its unspoiled beauty. Andrea kept her eyes on the ever-changing horizon, in awe at its raw ruggedness. She gradually felt more connected to this place, craving the next beautiful view around the bend or hearing the birds calling each other. It was so serene.

There was little conversation between them, and tension seemed to build as the men focused on the meeting with the natives. Andrea felt their uneasiness as the day wore on. They paused at a stream so the horses could drink, and Jacob said, "We're almost there. I need you to trust me and do what I say - for the safety of all of us. These Indians can be unpredictable, and we don't want them to get their dander up."

Johnny looked over his shoulder, saying quietly, "Sometimes I just stay out of sight. We'll see how they are with Jacob before we move forward."

Andrea absorbed all the information and was frightened, but she trusted her companions that they were not in danger. They urged the horses on and, in a few minutes, reached a clearing where they saw the camp in the distance. Jacob merely raised his hand as signal for Johnny to stop, then went ahead toward the camp.

As Johnny and Andrea waited, watching Jacob's silhouette get smaller in the distance, she asked, "So what happens if they get upset that we're here?"

Johnny thought for a minute and said directly, "Jacob won't be gone too long. He'll come back, and we'll travel another hour away from this camp before we stop for the night. If they're in good spirits, they'll ask us to join them and offer up a place for us to stay for the night. They're good people, but they don't trust anyone."

Before long, Johnny saw Jacob waving at them with a gesture to "come." Johnny kicked Babe and tugged Jack's lead, Johnny and Andrea feeling the jerk of her sudden gait change, trotting toward Jacob. When they were within speaking distance, Jacob sounded relieved and said, "Today is a good day. They want what I have to offer and will share their evening meal with us."

Johnny and Andrea dismounted, and a young Creek boy who couldn't have been more than nine years old took the horses. Andrea's eyes suspiciously followed the boy, but this did not alarm either of the men as the tribe had a separate place for the horses. Andrea followed them to a clearing near their tents and teepees. Several men and women greeted them with nods and smiles.

The group before them stood tall and proud, proud to share their home with these strangers. Jacob spoke a little of their language and introduced Johnny as "Cuse (brother)" and Andrea as "Enhesse (friend)." Two younger Creek girls came up to her and touched her. It was very seldom, if ever, they had seen a white woman. The Creek women talked among themselves, and then one stopped in front of her, frowning, her expression flowing into one of astonishment.

Andrea shook her head and looked at Jacob, "I didn't do anything!"

The unusual scrutiny drew Jacob's attention and listened carefully to what the woman said. Jacob told her, "They're upset about the amulet you wear around your neck. Where did you get it?"

Andrea grabbed the stone and said, "I … traded for it in New Orleans." That was the truth; she traded money for it.

The Chief came over, observing the commotion, nodding and smiling for an uncomfortably long time.

Then, in his manly baritone voice, he said, "The one who wears the stone is blessed." He raised his hands in the air and spoke to all the tribal members that had gathered around. "We are fortunate the Great Mother has brought the stone to us. Por retv!"

Jacob turned to both Johnny and Andrea with a bewildered look and interpreted the Chief's words. "It's not bad, it means bewitched. They will honor it, and the person who wears it."

Andrea was quite surprised to hear that. She didn't think anything would make her significant to these people; she was afraid of the opposite, the onlookers who didn't give her a second glance before, now gave her their full attention. It was weird.

The Chief, Rakke' Taf (Big Feather), who was once skeptical of this new person, was now more cheerful and gracious. A short while later, the women who paid so much attention to Andrea led her and the Loftons to a gathering near the center of the camp. Several carcasses were roasting over a fire, in addition to a cornmeal-like bread. This band of Creek Indians was kind to the visitors; it seemed the stone was a "lucky charm" for sure. Jacob brought out whiskey he had planned to trade and shared it with their friends.

Among the onlookers, Andrea's eye caught sight of the young Indian whose confrontation with her on the beach still left lingering fear. She let out a gasp, unaware of what he was thinking. She kept her eyes down, fearful of making a scene, and stole glances at him occasionally, and when he saw her, he looked away, a bit more respectful than he was just a few days before. Her heart fluttered a bit, realizing he was now afraid he'd made an enemy of the "Blessed one".

The three travelers still drew a lot of sideways glances, but overall, they enjoyed a meal and sowed seeds of friendship that could be a significant advantage in the future.

Once night fell, the fire swelled as the tribe's atmosphere livened with gaiety. There was chanting and whiskey and a lot of smiles. Andrea and the two Loftons whispered amongst themselves, not wanting to cause an interruption.

"I never thought this amulet would be the center of attention." Andrea reached down and looked at the stone, admiring the mesmerizing sparkle of it in the firelight. Jacob uttered a small sigh and scratched his head, sounding tired.

"Neither did I, but the story that group was just saying," He nosed in the direction of a small group of men, "was about that very thing."

Andrea made a sound, "Humph." Her interest piqued; she now focused on Jacob. "And what did the story say?" She knew generally, how a story such as this came about, some truth and some fallacy.

"Well, go on," Andrea urged him. Jacob looked around to be sure other eyes were not watching too closely. "Pf'neta, a young hunter, was in the woods one day and found the amulet."

Jacob pointed to it briefly before he continued explaining. "He tied it on himself as a prize. A short while later, Pf'neta had fallen down a hill and right into the path of a bear. He lost his weapon in the fall and had no way to protect himself. He thought for sure he would get eaten by the bear, but as it approached him, it stopped. The bear lowered its head as if to bow to the hunter, then it walked away. The tribe swore it was the stone that protected him."

Johnny spoke first, his eyes brightening, "Wow, that would have been something to see."

Jacob nodded in agreement, trying to visualize what the hunter experienced. "Yes, it was, but now you can see why they think the stone has power. Why would a bear not eat a supper served to him?" Andrea nodded and gave a hesitant grin. Then she looked away and wondered *why a stone like this would end up in a pawn shop?*

As the evening went on, she reflected on the day, savoring her time in this place. Then, out of nowhere, she conjured thoughts about the demon-possessed men who assaulted her.

Maybe the fact that I got away from the captors was the stone's gift to me. She kept this thought to herself, but the mystery of this relic began to make her feel the amulet was more than just a necklace.

The following day, as the sun rose, the people of the tribe began to stir, as did the three visitors. Jacob successfully traded some furs for whiskey and some baskets for a couple of copper pots. Overall, the visit to the tribe was successful. When they went to the Chief to thank him, Jacob told Andrea to bow and lower her eyes, which is a sign of humility and respect. She did as she was told, and the Chief nodded to her and motioned for her to "rise."

She stood and faced him. He stated clearly in English, "We thank you for the blessings you shared with our tribe." Andrea nodded, dumbfounded. His voice was deep and proud, and an audience with him was highly valued. He continued, garnering her full attention. "The stone chose you. Be of good mind and heart." The Chief pointed to his head and to his heart when he said the words. As he did, Andrea felt a warming sensation where the amulet touched her chest. The Chief gave a quick nod as if to dismiss them and turned and walked away.

The three friends turned and went to their horses. Andrea was speechless, grasping the idea that she had connected to the - tribe on her own, making the amulet even more special. They mounted quickly, and as they rode away, Jacob said, "Now that was somethin," and shook his head. Andrea thought to herself. *Good trades, and we got out of camp in one piece, so I guess it was a good something.*

She grappled with the thought that her amulet made this visit so successful.

10. Becca

McIntosh - 1798

Johnny and Andrea trotted along with the pack horse in tow. Andrea raised her chin and spoke to him over his shoulder. She asked, "So, where are we going now?"

Johnny said proudly, "We're goin' home. He tilted his head to the left, making sure she heard him correctly. "If we ride hard today, we can make it." Andrea looked at him with understanding.

"And if we don't?" The question resounded in the tone of her voice.

"Well, then we'll stay somewhere, and the ride tomorrow won't last long." Both the men were cheerful, more so than at any other time. The three friends rode for quite a while without saying a word, and Andrea thought about how strange it was that she'd become accustomed to the quiet, given she'd come from such a busy, bustling place.

Out of nowhere, Jacob perked up and asked Andrea, "Are you remembering more yet?"

She confessed, "Why yes. I'm remembering my friends back in New Orleans. I remember a man assaulted me, but I can't for the life of me remember how I came to be here in Georgia. I truly am a long way from home."

Home, she thought. Andrea's mind wandered back to the beautiful bathtub in the hotel. It was big enough for two people and had a Jacuzzi button to make it all bubbly. The clean smells of linen, soft carpet on the floor, and a mattress. Oh, a mattress! She thought that she would never complain about the comfort of a mattress again.

After they'd ridden for a few hours, the group approached a stream where Jacob dismounted, allowing his horse to drink. Johnny signaled to Andrea to get down first, then he did the same for his horse. She walked downstream a few yards to relieve herself while the men undoubtedly did the same. She was pulling up her pants to button them when she heard a grunting sound coming from across the stream.

Andrea backed up almost to the horses and said in a very shaky voice, "Jacob, you'd better get your gun!"

Jacob saw the expression on her face, now white with disbelief and fear. He moved close to his horse and pulled his gun from its sheath on the saddlebag. Andrea's eyes remained locked onto the direction of the sound, and as she got closer to the horses and the Loftons, the thick shrubs near the bank of the stream parted, and a mountain lion emerged.

The creature slowly approached the three travelers, setting its gaze on Andrea. The Sound in the lion's throat made the hairs prickle on the back of her neck. Although being closer to the horses and the weapons gave her more confidence, there was little that could temper the urge to run.

The mountain lion pushed out a low growl, eyes on her, sounding a warning. Andrea had spent little time outdoors and did not know what to expect.

Would it attack her here with the men and the horses so close? Andrea backed into one of the horses, quickly realizing she'd seen this sight in a dream. Her fear began to build as she analyzed her thoughts, and she became scared of more than just the cat.

Jacob moved past her, putting himself between her and the lion. He was unsure what the cat might do but was ready no matter what. The lion swiped its foot across the ground in Jacob's direction, sending a puff of dust roiling into the air, a warning, trying to intimidate or distract him.

Jacob did not falter as he faced the cat. The creature began to make a loud "hissing" sound as he cautiously approached. Johnny grabbed a rather large rock and snuck up beside Jacob, holding the rock up just enough for him to see it.

He whispered, "Should I?" Jacob gave a subtle nod, not taking his gunsight off the cat.

Jacob gave an abrupt nod, and Johnny threw the rock straight at it, and the lion moved its head to miss the impact. Emitting a loud growl, the cat swiped its foot again, then wandered back to the shrubbery from whence it came.

Although the danger seemed to be over, They mounted their horses once more, never moving their eyes from the cat's location. They rode for half a mile before they relaxed back into the gentle rhythm. Johnny said, "Big cats will follow and wait for the 'weak' one to fall behind. They're not as strong as bears, but they are as patient as the day is long."

After they'd put some distance between themselves and the cat, the ride became more pleasant and relaxed. The day warmed quickly, accompanied by a light breeze, making it a breathtaking afternoon. The air was clean, a kind of freshness Andrea had never known. Not realizing it until now, the world in this century was unspoiled, unpolluted, and new.

Andrea thought, shaking her head with pity; *if they only knew what would become of it.* As they rode in the peace offered here, she thought about plastic grocery bags tumbling in the wind down the alley, near her apartment. She thought about the traffic at quitting time, the roar of engines, the smell of exhaust. Sadness swelled in her, wishing she could tell the future a thing or two.

The threesome had stopped only once more for a drink and to cool the horses. They located a little shade and some fresh cool water nearby and rested, fully knowing Jacob had his sights set on home. They mounted again, and after traveling an hour, Andrea realized Jacob, Skeeter, and other horses had a little pep in their step, and there was no slowing them down.

It was nearly sundown when they rounded a slight bend in the road and were in sight of a cabin, smoke rolling out of its chimney, and a lantern visible through the window. Johnny spoke over his shoulder, "We're home."

Andrea uttered under her breath, "Thank God." The last hour her ass hurt so badly, she thought she'd drawn blood.

The cabin looked comfortable and inviting, and the weary friends were only yards away when Jacob's wife came out the door. "You're home!" Andrea smiled at their affection, watching the little pieces of her pulled-back hair fall about her face. Although she didn't appreciate the uninvited guest, her greeting hosted a warm and welcoming smile.

After they kissed their hello, Jacob said to Andrea, "This is my wife, Rebecca. Becca, to those of us who love her." His smile was unstoppable as he gave her another peck on the cheek.

Andrea looked up, rather pleased to see a woman. "It's nice to meet you."

Becca was a bit confused because the two men went out hunting and brought back a woman. Jacob looked at her, humor spreading on his face. "I'll tell you; it is an interesting story."

Becca looked up at Andrea and smiled politely. "I bet you're ready for some supper."

Andrea nodded. She did not want to seem too eager, but she was famished. "Yes, ma'am. I could do with some food."

Johnny said, "I'll be takin' care of the horses. They've had a long day, too." He took the horses around the back of the house, with a paddock and a pasture.

Andrea didn't think it right that Johnny had all the responsibility and asked, "Can I help you, Johnny?"

He kindly shook his head. "You go on in and get some food. I'll be along real soon." Andrea nodded politely and followed Jacob and Becca into their cabin.

It was small, with a warm and friendly aura, and neat as a pin. It was just one room, making Andrea feel claustrophobic. She felt like she was imposing.

"I'm so sorry to show up and barge in like this. I just had nowhere else to go."

"Don't you worry yourself, Andrea. We don't have much, but we're happy to help a friend in need. Please make yourself comfortable." Becca's voice was most gracious, although she was a little shaken about this woman. *Why did Jacob bring her here?*

Jacob pulled out a chair and signaled to Andrea to sit. She obeyed, not wanting to be a bother, feeling a little out of place and more like a squatter than a friend. Becca served stew from a pot over the fire and some biscuits.

Andrea thought, *whatever was in this stew, it was delicious*. Andrea used her biscuit to sop up the little bit of gravy left at the bottom of the bowl. Just then, Johnny came through the door, and as quickly as she could, Andrea jumped up and moved to give her chair to Johnny. "He needs a meal and some rest. These boys work hard!" Andrea said with a smile, trying to appeal to Becca's sensibility.

Becca proudly placed a bowl of stew in front of Johnny as well. Small talk followed, and Jacob asked, "What did you do while I was gone?"

Becca asked, "How many hides did you get?" It wasn't long before Becca just had to ask, "And how did you come about?" She looked directly at Andrea. The girl was taken aback, her eyes finding the floor just then as she searched for an answer.

"Well, to be honest, I don't know. I woke up with no memory of how I ended up on the beach. I know I had taken a beating the night before and was in New Orleans. I even had to ask Johnny the date."

Becca looked down, trying to hide the pity she felt for her, but Andrea knew what she was thinking. With what little she knew about the encounter, there was nothing more she wanted to share with this family.

Blurry-eyed, Johnny looked around the table and said, "I think I need some sleep. Goodnight, everyone."

Jacob and Becca responded, "Goodnight, Johnny."

Andrea hesitated for a moment, and looking at Jacob, she asked, "Where is he going?"

Jacob answered, "He sleeps in the loft in the barn." Andrea blinked and looked somewhat surprised.

"Oh," she said, wondering why he went out to the barn, and she had the honor of sleeping in the house. Jacob went out for a moment and came in toting a straw mattress. In truth, it was just a burlap bag full of straw, but it would serve as a mattress well enough.

"If it's alright, we'll have you sleeping by the fire."

Andrea was flattered. "That is too kind. I'm sorry to put you through all this trouble." She was much more self-conscious now of feeling like a mooch, unlike the day she showed up on the beach.

Becca said, "It is no trouble at all. It will be nice to have another woman around here." Andrea reached out for Becca's hand, expressing how much she appreciated the hospitality.

"Becca, Jacob, I am so grateful for all you have done for me. I wish to repay you somehow. It's scary to think of what might have happened if I hadn't come across you and Johnny. Having a place and people to be with is so nice."

Becca pulled a blanket and a straw-filled pillow off a shelf and handed it to her.

"Thank you," was about all Andrea could muster. "Goodnight," she said.

Jacob and Becca replied in unison, "Goodnight, Andrea." With that, Andrea took off her shoes and laid down, feeling pleasantly relieved for not having to straddle a horse. As soon as she pulled the blanket over herself; she was fast asleep.

Morning came, and the sun shone bright and hot, even early in the morning. The day would be a warm one. A few clouds loomed in the distance, leaving the air sticky with moisture, however, the weather proved suitable for chores and duties around the little farm. It took very little time from when the sun first showed itself before the entire household came alive.

Andrea moved as quickly as she could, getting her bed and blanket out of the way. She immediately offered to help Becca in any way she could, hoping it might help her feel less of a leach. Becca put Andrea to work fetching water from the creek and retrieving eggs from the chicken coop.

Becca had given Andrea a basket to collect eggs. There were about a dozen chickens, and she found eight eggs, plenty for breakfast. She took them back to the house, as proud as she could be of her contribution. Becca boiled ground corn that had a texture like grits. She stirred in goat's milk and served with salt, eggs, and coffee. Andrea swore it was the best breakfast ever.

As the day wore on, she wandered the farmyard, around the barn, the house, and the pasture offering help where she could. She saw Jacob and Jack out with a plow in a field just beyond the pasture. The plot was not too big, a fair size for the mule to handle, and one could see it had been plowed before as the clumps of dirt and sod turned over quickly.

She watched, thinking the job was laborious for both man and mule, giving her new appreciation for everything at this little farm. Jacob told her that he and Becca had worked this land; it was nothing but a field of grass and trees. They did it all from scratch, having dug the foundation, cut the wood, and shaped it. They cut the grass that became the hay that was stored in the barn. They raised the chickens and fenced the pasture. They'd done it all and Andrea respected what an accomplishment it was.

This place was home for them, for all the sweat and sacrifice needed to make the land theirs. At that moment, Andrea felt selfish and spoiled, thinking about how much had been given to this land. She had it so easy in her time. So much was lost between this time and her own. She pondered what they might think of 2004. Would they be ashamed? She was.

She could have stood there all day watching the dust rising from the earth under the driving plow blade. She felt movement behind her and turned to see Johnny come up beside her and watch. He looked at her and smiled, then watched Jacob intently.

After a short while, he said, "Tomorrow, once Jacob is done with all the plowing, he will drop seed, and you and I will haul water to the whole field to help it sprout."

Andrea watched him as he spoke, his eyes on the field before him. "Sure. It might even be fun," she said lightheartedly. Johnny looked at Andrea with a smirk on his face.

"Well, alright then," his words filled with doubt. Johnny was a young man who appreciated gifts that were kindly given. Even the most minor things were essential. He knew what needed to be done and just did it. It was impressive how hard he worked. Chores on the farm were tedious, but Johnny knew the importance of each job and did all of them with the pride of a landowner.

Andrea followed him for a while as he fed pigs and cleaned the paddock where they kept the horses. He took the dung in a cart, hauling it to a pile near the pasture, and dumped it. He gestured toward the heap and said, "We'll add this to the field and help keep it green when it gets too hot."

Andrea remembered her uncle's place and how it would dry up in the summer heat, despite having irrigation. It was different here in this century. A lot depended on the rain; they would struggle all year if it didn't. The water would need to be hauled to the field as long as it held out. The thought of such a struggle was boggling.

Andrea went to the yard in front of the house, where Becca was washing clothes. Laundry was time-consuming and done daily, so Andrea pitched in. Becca was kind and was a straightforward person to talk to. Their conversation involved a few things Andrea could remember, including the kidnapping and assault.

She wasn't sure how to explain it to Becca but said, "I think they were going to sell me as a slave." Becca's face showed shock as a jolt of fear ran through her. She continued her work, quiet for a moment, processing.

The words gave her just enough information to keep her asking for more. "So, did they - uh, do anything else to you?"

Andrea shook her head and said, "No, but that is what I thought would happen."

She swallowed hard, recalling bits and pieces of that night, some of which she chose not to share.

Becca couldn't believe slavers would take a white woman but didn't discredit Andrea's story. Just as they were getting to the end of the pile of clothes, Becca remarked with a broad smile, "I bet you'd like to take a nice bath and put on some clean clothes."

Andrea was dirty and sweaty and had been wearing her clothes for days. She nodded and smiled, feeling every bit of grime on her skin and clothing. "Yes, that would be nice."

Becca stood back and sized her up. "I think I got something that would fit just right." She headed into the cabin; Andrea close on her heels. The space did not boast much room, but she had a place for everything if everything was in its place. She pulled another basket off a shelf filled with several simple house dresses, clean and folded neatly. Becca handed a couple of them to Andrea. She pulled a blue and white dress up to herself, and it looked as though it would fit. A pot of water on the fire, already warm, and Becca smiled, giving Andrea a wink.

"If you go fetch another bucketful, this should be enough to bathe in." Andrea quickly grabbed the bucket and headed out to the stream.

Undressing in front of someone was not a comfortable thought for Andrea, but Becca stood guard and watched the door while Andrea bathed. The water was neither hot nor cold, but it felt so nice! She began to relax as she washed away the days of filth. Taking a moment to draw in a slow breath; time nearly stopped for her.

Suddenly aware of just how long she'd been in the little tub, Andrea began to move more quickly and finish. She blotted the water off her now-cleaned body and slid into the simple linen dress Becca had loaned her. She scooped up her clothes, dropping them directly into the same water she just bathed in. Swishing them about, she wrung them out just as they had done earlier with the clothes on the line. She carried them to the front yard and hung her shirt and pants, with the others already drying. The silhouette of a smile crept onto her face, showing just how happy she was to be clean.

The shadows of the trees and the barn were stretching out long on the ground now as the day of work was ending. Becca had boiled a sizable chunk of salted pork with some potatoes and carrots that Johnny brought up from the root cellar. Becca stirred the stew in an iron pot over the fire. Andrea cleaned the table off (the dust from the plowing was all over everything) and set the plates out.

Jacob and Johnny came in after scrubbing themselves in the creek, and both donned clean shirts. Becca pulled a bottle of wine off the shelf and placed it in the middle of the table. After bowing for grace, the group sat down to share a meal. She naturally compared everything to the life she once knew, silently wondering if she'd been born in the wrong century. She enjoyed the peace immensely; no electronics or lights. Simple.

When night fell and all was quiet, the humble little group began to yawn and rub their eyes.

"It has been a long day," Jacob touted. "Why don't we all get some shuteye?"

Becca nodded and picked up the remaining dishes, putting them in the washtub. Andrea went out to the porch, picked up the straw "bed," and whacked it. The dust flew from it like it did from everything else. No items, either inside or outside, were immune to collecting it. Then she dragged it into the house and laid it in the same spot as the night before.

As each person said "Goodnight" and things began to settle down, Andrea yawned profoundly and stretched her tired limb. The world abruptly went black when she closed her eyes, another vision taking over.

It was her, and she was wandering in a forest, deep and dark. Two tall natives were staring at her, deerskin pants and hairless faces. They were gesturing to her to "go," but she couldn't go; the forest moved in, and the fear of being alone in this strange place overtook her.

She watched as one of the natives took the horse's lead, and she realized it was Jack. Her eyes flew open, and her heart pounded; the natives in her dream were so real and close to her. She looked around and heard nothing; the peace of the room was interrupted only by the subtle snaps from the dwindling fire in the hearth. She watched it for a while until she couldn't stop the weariness from taking control. She gradually fell deeply into sweet slumber.

11. Krew of Orpheus Parade

New Orleans - 2004

The group of strangers who had become friends flocked to the street corner they thought would offer the best view. Each had a drink in their hand, not unlike anyone else in the crowd. They were laughing and teasing each other as old friends would. Andrea and Collin held hands and flirted. This entanglement was not at all what Andrea had expected, but her heart was alive with the thought of having someone to share life with. Someone who might care what her day was like; just someone to care. It had been a long time since Andrea had someone in her life. She felt her body consumed by warm emotion; her eyes were the catalyst when she casually caught his gaze. Collin was always cheerful and attentive. Thinking of him now brought color to her cheeks.

When the parade was in full swing, the atmosphere was electric. It was the most celebrated parade and finale for Mardi Gras. They saw dragons and jesters, beads flying through the air above the crowd. There was such joy in the air that Jake's altercation went almost unnoticed.

The shouting began suddenly, which led to shoving. Finally, one of the obstinate adversaries threw a punch, landing hard on Jake's jaw. He was fast and able to dodge yet another swing while landing a short punch solidly with his left. The opponent hit the ground and was slow to get up. One of the man's buddies jumped in, pulling the punk away so the fisticuffs would stop. A friendly face among the delinquents approached Jake and put out his hand.

"I'm Adam," he said, "Sorry about that; he was pissed off and drunk, and you know how that can be."

Jake replied, "Yeah, I do." Then Adam and the others turned and were swallowed by the crowd. Jake turned back toward the rest of his friends and shook his head, rubbing the spot on his chin where the punch connected. "I'm glad I had three older brothers to teach me how to fight. Comes in handy." Brenna looked Jake over with concern until he said, "I'm fine," his voice writhing with agitation.

Andrea and Collin thought the climate was getting a little problematic and decided to head back to the hotel. Collin whispered to Andrea as they wandered away, "I want you. I want you so bad. Will you come to my hotel with me? I have my own room." Then pausing in the middle of the street, he pulled her close and kissed her slowly, passionately. Andrea felt a warm rush over her body, now roused with his touch. She responded, her eyes blinking, connecting with his, and said, "Yes."

They strolled, holding hands and whispering flirty things to each other. Collin's hotel was only a few blocks from St. George, but it was still just as close to all the action.

Collin held open the door when they reached The Rupert Inn, watching her intently. His emotions stirred at the thought of having her naked body next to his.

They made it to room number 109, and he opened the door, extending his arm to hold it as she entered, just as a gentleman would. Once the door had closed behind them, he pulled Andrea close and kissed her softly, his heart beating rapidly in anticipation. Andrea responded as her senses began to heighten, matching his. He kissed her neck, then pulled her collar back on her shirt to expose more of her chest. He didn't know what this did to her, as now she wanted to feel his body, eagerness blossoming as his touch electrified her skin.

She slid her hand up under his shirt and felt the firmness of his muscles flex with her touch. She could not stop the progression of the excitement stirring within her. They pulled the clothes off each other, not separating the touch of their skin by more than an inch. Andrea felt warm and filled with desire as they fell onto the bed, their naked bodies aroused by the closeness.

Collin kissed her and skillfully touched her in all the right places. Finally, when they couldn't wait a second longer, he thrust himself into her, and she let out a subtle moan of pleasure. The union made Andrea feel like Collin touched her soul, and although she had little carnal knowledge, she craved his touch and imagined this is what true love should be. They lay together on the bed, shoulder to shoulder, both with thin-lipped smiles, fulfilled.

"Wow, I never thought ..." Collin looked at her with his sparkling blue eyes, holding back his following words.

Andrea asked, "What?" She rolled toward him and pushed the entire length of herself up against him again.

He smiled, caressing her long, shapely hip, and kissed her softly.

"Nothing now. You just took my words away."

They lay together for nearly an hour, talking, touching, flirting, and absorbing all they could of each other before Andrea thought she'd been gone long enough.

"Will you walk me back to the hotel?"

Without much expression, he said, "Sure. Of course. This town is no place for a girl to be alone in the street, especially tonight."

Andrea dressed slowly, stepping into the bathroom to straighten her hair. They left the room and walked hand in hand back to the St. George, saying very little. Collin pulled her in close to him and kissed her very slowly and passionately once more. Andrea felt so weak and vulnerable in his arms.

"I'll see you tomorrow." Then he let her go and backed away, waiting for her to get inside the doors before turning and heading back to his hotel.

12. Jack

McIntosh - 1798

Andrea woke to a loud crack of thunder. Rain was pelted against the window, and its subtle sound was quite pleasant, but the thunder, my God, was loud. Andrea remembered her grandpa telling her that when the sound came quickly after the flash, the lightning was close. She lay still on her straw bed with the blanket pulled over her head trying to hide from the noise. There was a sudden bright flash outside, followed by a loud crack seconds later. A thump rattled the window from an impact.

Jacob jumped up, suddenly rattled by the chaos. He pulled on a pair of pants, and his boots and went out the door. He was only gone a few minutes and appeared in the doorway, dripping wet from the pounding rain.

Andrea heard him quietly say to Becca, "Looks like that big ol' tree was struck, and a branch fell across the fence. Jack got out." He took his boots off and climbed back into bed. "He won't go far. I'll go fetch him when the storm is over."

Andrea lay still as the storm passed, listening to the roll of thunder echoing through the canyons to the north, feeling the rumble of it under her. It was still raining hard, and the horizon was showing signs of the approaching dawn. Another hour later, the rain slowed, nearly stopping; the sun breached the horizon, and light began to filter into the room, signaling the start of another day.

The little cabin began to come to life now as Jacob got out of bed, put on his clothes and boots, and headed out the door. The women could hear him beckon to Johnny, recruiting him to help search for Jack. Becca and Andrea, being left to their agendas, decided to try and shove the big branch off the fence. The two women struggled; one pushed, and the other pulled. Finally, after wrestling with the darn thing for the better part of an hour, they flopped it on the ground. Becca laughed with relief, and both girls staggered from the effort, plopping down on the tree, and taking a minute to rest.

"There," Becca said with a note of satisfaction, "now Jacob can chop it up for firewood." Andrea was impressed by another chore that should be added to the list.

It struck them both simultaneously that the men had not come back yet from their search for the mule. Andrea wondered just how far that goofy animal had gone. The storm was vicious and loud, and maybe that had spooked Jack bad enough to make him run for cover.

It was another hour or so later when Jacob and Johnny returned empty-handed. They had been as far as the ridge with no luck. Jacob said, dismounting and clapping his hands together, "We can go out on the horses again later, but I want to eat first."

The four of them headed into the house to eat and construct a plan. Becca made porridge and hot tea. She pulled out a jar of honey to add to it, making it richer and more delicious. The tea was wonderful, and although the breakfast was simple, it was filling.

Jacob was out by the hitching post adjusting his saddle, scanning the pasture and hillside disconcertedly. He couldn't imagine why the damned animal didn't come home after the storm passed. He and Johnny decided to split up to cover more ground. Johnny rode to the end of the field that Jacob had just furrowed, turning Babe into the trees heading west, and Jacob swept south, crossing the creek and up the adjacent hill. The two men disappeared into the low brush under the cover of wet and drooping tree limbs, rapidly being swallowed by gray shadows lurking at the base of the timber.

Andrea and Becca watched as they disappeared, the farm overtaken by silence. The women were left to tend to the chores, including the ones that belonged to Jacob and Johnny. They took them on, one at a time, moving to another when they finished the first. Andrea would occasionally walk out to the end of the pasture, straining her eyes to see into the shadows and flora, looking for a sign of the mule, expecting Jack to pop out of the tree line any time. About midday, Andrea had traipsed out to the end of the field once again, coming back flustered.

"I can't stand just sitting here if I can help."

Becca warned her, "You don't want to go too far. That brush gets thick, and finding your way home won't be so easy." Andrea agreed, but the warning didn't deter her.

She found some yarn and cut off a few pieces, explaining to Becca, "I'll use this to mark the way, so I'll have a trail to follow home."

Becca nodded and smiled. "Now that's clever. Remember, not too far. Don't risk yourself."

Andrea looked back over her shoulder, winking to Becca as she headed in the same direction as Johnny - beyond the pasture and through the thick brush.

She thought about what she should be looking for: signs like tracks, broken branches, or dung. She was sure Jacob and Johnny were thinking the same thing. Andrea did not doubt their abilities but reasoned with herself that one more set of eyes couldn't hurt. She purposely broke branches and made deep footprints, thinking she could make her own trail to follow back to the house and Becca.

As she progressed deeper into the woods, her eyes strained to see through the tangled masses of shrubs and trees, which were beginning to look the same. She paused to tie a piece of the blue yarn to a branch at eye level so she would see it.

She finally made it to the top of the ridge and hoped she might have a view, but the woods were thick with trees and brush; finding anything beyond the next fir tree was impossible. She half expected to see the men or some sign of them while she was out, but that was not the case. She found herself alone and understood only a short while into her hike that returning to the little farm would be more of a challenge than she thought. She tied yarn pieces to branches on the way but realized later in her journey that her efforts were too little and too late. Facing the inevitable fact, she was lost.

Once Andrea reached the top of the ridge, she walked along it a fair distance to finally have a view. Able to see in all directions, she gasped at the sight. It was beautiful! There were rolling hills and green fields as far as the eye could see. It was such a raw beauty and different from the northwest. Everything seemed so new and clean.

After taking in the vistas, Andrea stopped to look around but didn't know what she was looking at, as everything was unfamiliar. She'd gotten turned around and was not sure which direction to go.

Finally, she called out, "Jacob! Can you hear me?" Then, "Johnny! God dammit, ANYBODY!!" Andrea bit her lip to help her hold back the tears; she was scared and frustrated.

Finding a stream, she followed it, not knowing if it would take her in the direction of the farm. She wandered around for what seemed like forever, frustrated, exhausted, and terrified.

She once remembered hearing that a person should stay put when lost. If others were looking for her, it would be easier to find a still target. She sat down near the stream and waited.

Andrea began to hum Yankee Doodle Dandy to herself and found little delicate yellow flowers stretching their little heads out of the moss growing near the water. Her thoughts wandered, taking her back to the day she woke up in the grass on the beach. Right now, this moment felt just like that. Her thoughts added to her frustration. Why can't I just pop back into the 21st century?

She sat in the peace of that place for quite a while and saw the shadows growing long into the afternoon. She heard a rustle across the stream and, of course, could not see through the brush. Unable to penetrate the shrubbery with her vision alone, not knowing what to expect, she got up slowly and trained her eyes directly to where the sound was coming from.

She recalled the mountain lion they had encountered only days ago, and fear welled up in her like a balloon filling with air. Andrea heard a snort. That does not sound like a mountain lion, she thought. Taking a second to find something she might use as a weapon, she found a rock about the size of a grapefruit and picked it up.

She heard another snort and thought it would be a bear she'd face. She swallowed the hard lump in her throat, afraid of having to fight for her life. She saw the brush move with force, and a nose erupted from behind it.

"Jack! You pain in the ass, mule! Where have you been?" she scolded but was thrilled to have a friend to keep her company, knowing night was upon them.

She had never been so glad to see a mule, but here he was. She petted and talked to him, knowing Jack felt as happy to see her as she was to see him. He rubbed his ears up against her, bobbing his head. "Now, I wonder if you can find the way home, huh, fella?" Andrea whispered to Jack. Some animals have the instinct to find their way home; however, if that were the case, Jack would have already been there.

Andrea was much more relaxed after finding him. She was anxiously hoping they could manage their way back, and she could boast about how much better she did at finding the mule than either of the "hunters."

She led the mule along the ridge and started down a slope that might take them closer to the farm, or so she thought. She was admittedly lost but figured she was safe going downhill. It was either to the left or the right. Andrea and the beast trekked for a while until she realized she should have seen the pieces of yarn, or her footprints, by now. They saw none of it, and it was growing darker by the minute.

Just about the time Andrea had given up and was looking for a place she could settle for the night, she saw movement again in the brush, some distance away. Deep in her heart, she hoped it was one of the men who she knew would be able to get them home.

Andrea cupped her hand around her mouth and shouted, "Jacob! Is that you?" She waited for a response and hollered again, "JACOB!" Still no response, but this time, a figure came out from the shadow of the bushes and moved toward her. A flood of relief swept over her as she now had her guide to lead her and the beast back home. It took a split second for her to realize it was NOT Jacob coming toward her.

A tall, lean native was moving forward. She grabbed Jack's halter and turned in the other direction, mumbling to herself, trying to calm the panic racing through her mind. As she shifted, another native stood behind them, stopping any progress.

"What do you want?" she said, desperately trying to steady the absolute terror she felt wrap around her like a wet cloak. Turning quickly to the Indian who had snuck up behind her and Jack, she said, "If I'm in the wrong place, I'm sorry, I'll go the other way. I just got lost, that's all."

The native approached her, grabbed at the mule's halter, and led Jack down the ridge. The tall native man in front of her was so close she could smell him: campfire smoke and animal hides mingled with the smell of the earth. His stride was confident and solid. This native was stone-faced, expressionless. He merely poked at Andrea, directing her to follow Jack and the other man.

Andrea didn't realize how close she was to a Native American encampment. She wondered if Jacob or Johnny knew about it, then revoked the thought because it didn't matter now. She was stuck. The feeling was almost more terrifying than being lost. As Andrea, Jack, and the two native men approached the multitude of teepees, dogs, children, and women, many stopped and glared at her. Andrea's thoughts were defiant. It's not my fault I'm here. They brought me.

The small Indian village was set up much like the one she and the Loftons had visited. They walked past several teepees and tents and came to the center, where there was a prominent "gathering place." Again, just as before, the Chief came to greet the party. Andrea looked at the man straight on, bravely. Her heart pounded so hard that it was unsettling, but she recalled a saying once told to her when she was young. If a person looks deep enough into another's eyes, you could see into their soul. The Chief looked at her just as deeply, making Andrea pull back as a shiver ran through her.

She observed the Chief and the other natives of this tribe who stood at attention in his presence. There was no anger or fear. She did not see a raging wild man like so many others described when they spoke of the local natives. "Savages" is something she'd heard many times referencing the native people. It was a term used loosely. No, that wasn't it at all. What Andrea saw was kindness, which was truly unexpected. He met her gaze, and his eyes fixed on her.

In distinct English, the Chief said, "Where did you come from?"

Andrea was shocked; it was the first time she'd heard a native speak more than staggered words. "I'm Andrea. I was looking for the mule and got lost, that's all. I don't want to be here."

The Chief was a tall, lean man. He wore a blue shirt and long braids with beaded leather wraps to hold the braids in place. He had several strands of beads and other things around his neck. He stood tall, straight, and proud; his features were aged and pronounced. He didn't seem old, but the years of weather and worry had aged him. She noticed some subtle tattoos over his eyebrows, and although his face was stern and severe, there was a softness; a gentleness about him. He held a confident presence, which explained why he was the most respected member of the tribe.

Her eyes slowly, methodically browsed around at the gathering crowd; one of the natives had what looked like a bone stuck through one of his ears. Another had his hair cut bald on the sides and a tuft on the top that stood straight up.

Andrea looked up at the Chief and, as calmly as she could muster, said, "What can I call you?"

The Chief looked ominously down at her and said in a baritone voice, "I am Menawah."

A younger man was by his side and maintained eye contact with the Chief. It must have been a sign of respect or obedience or something. Andrea put out her hand to Chief Menawah and spoke in a very official way.

"Nice to meet you."

The Chief was a little surprised that a woman would want to shake his hand, he took hers and shook it. Then he said in a low voice, "Friend." Andrea felt an "electric-like" pulse when she touched the Chief's hand, disappearing the second she let go. She looked at the Chief's face and expected a reaction, a smile, or at least pleasantness, but the Chief remained stoic and expressionless. Did he feel that jolt? She thought to herself. She found his absolute stillness and no physical or emotional reaction unnerving. Was the amulet trying to tell her something?

Andrea stood there, unsure of what to do after the introduction. The Chief turned, continuing with his other business.

The younger man who stood beside him said in noticeably clear English, "He doesn't shake people's hands."

Andrea cocked her head as if he had spoken in tongues. "Oh, you speak English well. Where did you learn?"

The younger native said, "We had an Englishman live with us after the big war. He did not want to return to his homeland, so he hid in our camp. We called him Eto Evkepter – a tree walker. He would watch everything from the trees above." The young man pointed up to the treetops. "He married one of our people and became one of us. Then, not long ago, he died of fever."

Andrea looked the young man in the eyes. "That is sad. I'm so sorry," she said to him, his eyes lowered with her comment.

Andrea wanted to keep the conversation going and was happy to have someone to talk to. "What is your name?"

The young man smiled and said, "You can call me Awahani."

Andrea also put her hand out to him and said, "Very nice to meet you." She was indeed satisfied.

In no time at all, she had begun to make friends. A few others in the tribe spoke broken bits of English at best. Andrea was lucky to have someone within the tribe with whom she could communicate.

She had asked Awahani about getting back to the little farm where she had a place and people who were her friends.

"You cannot leave. You must stay with the tribe until Menawah decides what to do."

Sadness welled up inside her as she pushed back the tears pooling in the corner of her eyes. She had had a harrowing experience and wanted nothing more than to be with the people she trusted. As the sun went down, fires began to burn around the camp. Andrea did not have a choice and resigned to stay put for now.

She ran through escape scenarios in her mind repeatedly, but she always arrived at the same conclusion. She didn't know how to get back to the farm. The thought came to her that even if she decided to escape, they would probably go after her, and if they caught her, the rest of her stay would not be so pleasant. She would need help to escape this tribe and her imprisonment.

She sat quietly, watching the tribe's people settle down for the evening. Food was eaten but Andrea couldn't identify what it was, however it was eaten with voracity by the tribal members.

She knew little about this tribe and these people, but they treated her very differently than the Creek tribe, she had met only the other day. After a short while, Awahani came to her and offered her a plate. It was fish and bread. Andrea was grateful to him, thanking him for not forgetting her.

"It is truly kind of you to watch after me. I didn't think I was going to eat tonight."

He kept his eyes on the food that he offered. "You'll not go hungry. We keep you here."

He offered her a sip of the water from the pouch hanging around his neck. She took a long drink, handed it back, and asked, "What are your people? What tribe is this?"

Awahani confidently raised his head and said, "We are Este Mvskokvlke - Creek."

Andrea gave a nod of understanding. "I've met other Creek people, but they are not like you. They did not speak any English and treated me like I was a princess. This tribe is different. I'm a prisoner."

Awahani looked down and shook his head slowly, thinking before he spoke. "A tribe follows the Chief, and our Chief does not trust the white people. Don't worry. If you are trustworthy, he will begin to trust you, too." Then he showed a snip of a smile.

Andrea's expression was one of doubt, but in her heart, she knew she had little choice except to believe him.

Curious again, she asked, "So, is this where you live?" Andrea looked around, her eyes catching everything in her vision when she asked the question. "How did you get here?" She knew Jacob was unaware that an Indian tribe was so close. She shook her head gently and thought he would never have left her or Becca alone if he did.

Awahani gave a small chuckle, shook his head, breaking eye contact with her, and said, "No, this is not our home; we are moving to a better one. There was a battle that killed many of our people. They do not want us there. Menawah leads us to a place where our tribe can have peace. This place is not our home." The young native looked around the clearing, then shook his head again in disgust, a bit melancholy. Andrea thought it must be tough to move a village, as she realized what was happening to them.

She soon began to view these transients differently. The reality was that they did not want her as a prisoner, but they did not want her to jeopardize their safety either. Her mind was busied with her thoughts again. Keeping me with them in their camp was the easiest and most efficient way to ensure I wouldn't give up their location. What they didn't know was that she couldn't do that. She was nothing more than a stranger in a strange land.

13. Outsider

Transient Tribe - 1798

Herusa was a young and curious Creek girl who followed Andrea around like her shadow. She spoke little English but wanted to learn more. Andrea went down to the creek to wash her face and hair, and Herusa did the same thing.

Andrea said, "Wash," then Herusa mimicked her.

"Waash."

Andrea ran her fingers through her hair and said, "Hair."

Then Herusa said, "Har."

In a short time, she could put the words together, and the two girls could carry on a conversation, kind of. They did a lot of laughing, too. Andrea did the same to understand some of the Creek words as well.

Once she had finished her washing routine, Andrea stood up and began to button her blouse. The stone she wore around her neck was exposed now, and Herusa saw the precious gem. She let out an "AH!" It was loud and abrupt enough that others in the tribe came over to investigate.

Herusa was pointing to the stone with a look of surprise and astonishment. Andrea looked at her, then down at the stone, touching it, holding it up, and asking, "Do you know about this amulet, too?" She was unaware that her hand was gripping the girl's forearm. "The other Creek tribe knew the power of this stone."

Awahani came up to her and looked closely at it. He said, "We know its power, but how do you have it? It should not belong to you. Did you steal it?"

Andrea looked at Awahani in shock, "No, I did not steal it. I traded for it, fair and square." Many other natives in the camp kept their distance, but others came close enough to get a glimpse. They were cautious because the chief was cautious.

Menawah came closer and pushed through the small group that had gathered to see what the fuss was. He reached out for it, then stopped, looking at her intently, and asked in a low husky voice, "Where did you find this?"

She looked at him, fearful, as if he would kill her if she gave the wrong answer. "I - I traded for it in New Orleans."

Knowing it wasn't the whole truth, she couldn't tell him she bought it from a pawn shop.

Menawah nodded, folding his fist and striking his chest softly. He said to her, "It chose you."

Andrea looked at him bewildered. Not moving her eyes from him, she asked, "Why me? What do you know about this?" She looked at him pleadingly, wishing for him to give her answers about what had happened to her.

Menawah looked down at the ground and then looked at the stone. He said softly, "The stone chose you; soon, you will understand." Still, being a mysterious and vague answer. Andrea thought for a moment.

"What, it chose me?" Menawah said something in Creek to Awahani to interpret.

The young man turned to her, letting out a long, slow breath, and said, "Open your heart to the stone and the lessons, it will teach." He then pounded a fist into his chest just as the chief did.

Andrea thought he was physically repeating what he just said, and she said again, "Why me?" Neither of the native men answered.

Andrea asked Awahani to explain. He spoke English clearly, and she needed help understanding. She talked with him as she would to Chelsea and Brenna, and she needed a friend.

"What did Menawah mean when he said it chose me?"

Awahani thought for a moment, then said slowly and clearly, "All things of the earth have a power we are not to understand. It's like water in a stream. It just flows without question and always seems to know where to go. It is not for you to understand. The stone chose you; it knows you need what it can teach you. Open your heart. Let your soul see the stone."

Awahani kept his eyes focused on Andrea, smiling slightly, while she processed the information. Then she asked him another question. "How do I do that?"

Awahani took little time to answer her most recent inquiry. "Do not resist. Trust. It will make you stronger." Awahani gestured with his hands as he spoke, making Andrea understand what he was telling her. She had no idea that her self-preservation was that obvious. She had sheltered her heart for a long time, and her natural reaction was to protect it.

Andrea said to Awahani, "Thank you. I understand, but it might be hard for me to trust as you say."

Her friend smiled. "Many things are not easy in this world. But it is important, and you will see more clearly after you succeed." They continued to walk for a while, as quiet again settled over the tribe. An air of suspicion and distrust still surrounded her among Menawah and his people.

Andrea thought hard about it, wondering how to change it. She'd only been in this century for a few days. What did she know? Then it occurred to her; she does know this century. She'd read about it in history books, and although this chief was wise, Andrea held the trump card.

Her heart now felt lighter, and she hummed a song while she and other Creek women prepared dinner. One woman, Okam'yeti, called Andrea a "Fuswa," which meant "bird." She smiled at the thought. Being called a bird made sense to her as the only other music she'd heard in camp was drumming.

Andrea continued her meal prep, now deeper in thought. She tried remembering what she learned about the early Creek tribes in American History. What she did recall was that as many times as the Indians trusted the white man, in return, they had been lied to and betrayed; eventually, the

English and early Americans pushed them off what little land they had left.

The upheaval of this tribe now seemed to be a direct result of it, as she saw History unfolding before her eyes. *They're simply seeking a new home.* She thought as she worked through some of the facts she'd recently learned.

Andrea's head shot up from her work, and an "Oh" escaped her mouth as she realized what was happening.

She asked Awahani about other tribes, curious if they were friendly, and he replied, "We have friends and enemies in all tribes. Some days, we share, and some days, we fight. Many Creek people don't understand honesty and loyalty because they only know betrayal." Andrea considered his words, thinking *if the white people were pushing them off their land, why don't the Creek band together and make themselves more substantial as a group? It's like they're destroying the hive to get to the bees - but why ruin the honey?*

In all her deliberation, she thought it possible that by cooperating, this native tribe could have a home for their families. As she touched the amulet, the stone warmed in her hand, and she knew it was divine intervention at work. She felt the amulet manipulating her thoughts and knew she would be able to help.

Finishing her chores, Andrea went to the teepee she shared with Herusa, flopping down on the grass mat with a thump. She was distracted, deep in thought. She needed to do what she could to help these people secure a home. The Indian Removal Act hadn't happened yet. They still have time. She was frustrated; how could she help them change their fate? Her thoughts were unsettling as she struggled to think of how she could influence them, and help them to help themselves.

Andrea laid her head down and closed her eyes, trying to sharpen her senses. She lay there, still, hearing the birds chirping and flitting about and the leaves flickering in the breeze. The smell of the outdoors cleared her mind like champagne cleanses a palette. She took a couple of long, deep breaths and stopped, holding the breath she just drew in. *Wait...* Andrea thought to herself. Out of the blue, she remembered something from the night of the attack. *That Adam*, she thought. He was one of the guys Collin was talking to the first night they'd bumped into each other.

What was he doing fighting with someone he already knew? Andrea gave up the thought of napping or even resting. She was restless now and wished she could talk to Collin about her recollection. "Maybe I'm not remembering very well." She tried to reason with herself, wanting to give him the benefit of the doubt. She pulled herself off her sleeping place and smoothed her skirt, then stamped out of the teepee.

14. The Search

New Orleans - 2004

Chelsea and Brenna waited a long time for Andrea to return, deciding to go to the lobby to see what was keeping her. She had only come down for a soda. Where could she be? Brenna thought to herself. They looked everywhere and asked everyone in the lobby, the halls, and the front desk, inquiring about their friend. The lobby was quiet, with only one desk attendant, and a maintenance man, along with a half-drunk customer in a lounge chair by the door. Brenna showed a picture of Andrea to each of them.

The answer was decidedly, "no."

The girls went out the door together; Chelsea yelled Andrea's name as they wandered down the block and back. There was no sign of her.

Chelsea panicked. "Oh my God, what do we do?" A tear rolled down Brenna's cheek as she stood there with a blank look, trembling, then shook her head.

"I don't know," Brenna responded glumly. The two girls wandered back up to their room and decided to call the police.

It took only a short time for the police to arrive and take down Andrea's information. Officer Raymond Blanchard was a tall, thin man with a trim and tight haircut. He spoke softly and caringly to the girls, he could see they were beyond worried about their friend.

The officer looked up and said, "I'm sorry, I can fill out a report, but often, those missing will show up out of the blue. Try to get some rest, and if she hasn't returned by morning, give us another call. Then we'll send out a bolo."

Brenna was furious, thinking about how unimportant she felt when this person was making them wait. The officer continued, hoping to offer relief, "You see, many times, there is a logical explanation for what might have happened."

Chelsea spoke, distressed, "But we tried her phone a dozen times, and she doesn't pick it up. The last couple of times I tried, it went straight to her voicemail. She NEVER ignores our calls."

The officer, showing concern, shook his head, "I'm sorry, girls." He handed Brenna a card with his name and phone number, and said, "I'll write up a report about your suspicions, and we can follow up in the morning," then he turned and walked away.

The girls were deflated, bereft of any semblance of hope. Neither could sleep, thinking about what Andrea might be going through.

The next morning, when Collin came to pick up Andrea for the day, he learned what had happened. Chelsea gave him a repeat of what the police said, and Collin's reaction was much the same.

"I tried to reach her last night and again in the morning, but she didn't answer. I thought she was probably charging it and didn't think anything else about it." Now, his face contorted, questions and doubt running through his mind.

Since it was morning and Andrea had not turned up, Brenna called the police again, this time, knowing they would launch a search.

The police arrived to gather the information for the report, and a different officer showed up. Officer Wink Adams was your average officer - all business. He looked like someone who would get things done.

After taking the girls' report, he went to the hotel manager and asked about security footage from the previous night with an approximate timeframe for when the disappearance occurred. Chelsea and Brenna provided some information but mostly asked a lot of questions. The officer suggested that someone remain at the hotel if she returned.

The officer on duty would come by on their regular rounds as well. The worst part was having to sit and wait. Collin had called Jake, who showed up only ten minutes or so after the officer left. Jake showed genuine concern, and when he arrived, both Collin and Jake began to plot and plan a search on their own. It was impossible for any of them to sit still and do nothing.

"We could go around town and look for her. Maybe she just went for a walk and got lost. It's a good place to start," Collin said in a faint voice to Jake. "Maybe someone like a gas station attendants might have seen something strange last night." Collin was logical about his thoughts, but felt it was responsible to do something and was not the kind to sit on his hands and wait for someone else to solve the disappearance.

Officer Adams had gone to the front desk, and after explaining why he needed to see any camera footage they had; the hotel quickly obliged. It was confirmed undoubtedly to be a kidnapping. Two men had masks over their heads, successfully disguising their appearance. The parking lot camera confirmed a black van pulling out of the lot just moments after Andrea's. The film confirmed what they all were thinking. Although the criminals were amateurs and obviously in it only for the money; they were quick and thorough. Following a trail would prove to be complicated.

This information made the girls feel even worse. Brenna had learned if they don't find her in the next twenty-four hours, the possibility of her still being alive drops dramatically. Why go through all the trouble to sneak in, grab her, and then take off in a van? Why her? Chelsea asked the question repeatedly in her mind.

Jake looked at his friend with concern. "I know we're going to find her, Collin. She'll be fine."

Collin bobbed his head slightly in agreement. "Well, I know that we won't leave any stone unturned."

Jake slid in behind the steering wheel, and they took off down the street. They could ask questions of gas station attendants and convenience stores. They could ask cabbies and bus drivers if they'd seen anything suspicious or had even seen the black van spotted on the hotel footage.

They drove through alleys and side streets, down highways, and investigated every dark crevasse they thought might make a good hiding place.

Hours had passed when Jake said, "We should go check on the girls. Maybe they've heard something. Besides, we need something to eat."

Collin agreed. The girls most likely had not eaten either. "I suppose you're right. Besides, we need new ideas about where those bastards might take her."

The boys stopped for a pizza and arrived back at the hotel. Brenna had sent a picture of Andrea to a local print shop and had flyers printed. She planned to go out and put the Posters all over town.

"That's a good idea," Collin said drily. He was a bit skeptical that it would do any good but knew the effort would make her feel better; sitting around waiting for word was hard. Brenna was proud of herself for thinking of the flyers.

They all went up to the room and shared the pizza. Neither Chelsea nor Brenna even tasted the food.

Chelsea perked up, breaking the silence. "I found this online missing person website. I submitted information about Andrea's description. Maybe that will help us." She saw nods all around.

"All it takes is one person to recognize her," Jake added, stuffing another bite of pizza in his mouth. He couldn't imagine what she must be going through.

They were almost finished with their lunch break when a knock came on the door. Brenna opened it, and there stood Officer Blanchard.

"Good afternoon," the officer said. "I thought I would check on you girls. No news yet?" Chelsea shook her head gently and smiled, more to be polite. She opened the door wider and said, "Come in and have some pizza."

Officer Blanchard held up his hand, his eyes turned to the ground, humbled. "Please, call me Ray."

Chelsea smiled back at him. "No luck yet," she replied.

Ray said a bit hesitantly, looking directly at Chelsea, "I thought you should know there were several girls reported missing last night. It could be some pranksters giving folks a scare, but Mardi Gras events seem to attract all kinds. It might comfort you to know she's probably not alone."

Chelsea and Brenna were anxious to hear that they'd found her or had word of her, but neither of them thought it wasn't good news; it was easier to hear Andrea was likely not the sole captive.

Collin stood near the window, gazing over the balcony's railing, staring at the city. All the while, the girls were talking to the officer, he was thinking about the previous day and the afternoon he and Andrea had at Henderson's Point. She had told him about the incident with her father when she caught him dealing drugs. Drugs, of all things, he thought. Andrea and her brother were at risk because of it. He did most of his dealing out of his garage, and Andrea's mother kept quiet. She stayed silent because her husband would beat her, and they seriously needed the money.

He remembered Andrea wiping away a tear as she told him the story. She harbored a lot of guilt because of it. Collin thought he should have told her she did the right thing. He should have told her it was best for the family, but he didn't. Now, he wished for the chance to do it differently, to do everything differently.

Jake noticed Collin appeared troubled and asked, "Are you doin' okay, man?"

Collin looked at his friend with a furrowed brow, his eyes glassy.

"Yeah." He paused for a second and asked, "Did you ever think of things to say to someone AFTER they were gone?"

Jake nodded, "Oh yeah. I think everyone does. Don't worry, we'll find her." Jake put his hand on Collin's shoulder and patted it. Although he was trying to be supportive, he had his doubts that this would turn out alright. Collin kept his eyes fixed on the trolley that just went across the intersection and thought he didn't deserve a friend like him.

Officer Blanchard asked the group, "Is there anything ya'all need?" That sentence came out with a considerable Southern accent.

Chelsea touched his arm and said, "Thank you for checking on us. Please keep us in the loop."

He smiled sweetly and nodded, then grabbed the door handle, twisting it. "We'll keep at it," he added as he went out the door.

Collin and Jake decided to go to the beach and see if there was any evidence that would give them a clue as to where the bastards might have taken Andrea. Sitting around seemed to make them more tense.

Driving the jeep down the road, Collin was distant and kept his eyes straight forward. Out of nowhere, Collin confided in Jake.

"I've never met anyone like her." Then, a moment of stillness languished in the air between them; Jake swallowed hard, not knowing what to say.

"Let's just find her and get this over with!"

Jake and Collin had been friends for half a dozen years. When Jake had a serious breakup with his longtime girlfriend, Collin was there for him. When Collin lost his mom to cancer, Jake was there for him. The two friends would work together to solve this puzzle because that's just what they did.

Collin drove along the highway that skirted the ocean, talking scenarios with his friend when Jake spoke. "Why kidnap her? She did not have a wealthy family; she wasn't a political figure, she's pretty but not a model."

Jake stopped with the shock of realization. "What about sex slaves? Could it be they took these girls to sell them into slavery?"

It was not an off-the-wall idea. It happened all over the country. Collin knew that if Jake had thought of it, then for sure, the police would have thought about it, too. Jake contemplated. He knew that if this were indeed plausible, then they would need some hard evidence to get the ball rolling. Where would they find the evidence?

15. Lucas

Transient camp - 1798

The afternoon had grown warmer with the long hours of exposure to the sun. Andrea was hot, and staying in the teepee was growing increasingly uncomfortable. Feeling restless, she sat up. She had been lying there, considering the memory bomb of Adam in her thoughts. Something caught her eye just beyond the open flap, seeming out of place. Curious, she rose and wandered out.

In front of her, she saw an African American man chopping wood. His chocolate-colored skin was almost as out of place as her white skin and fawn-colored hair. He was not overly tall and had large muscles in his arms and shoulders, probably because of the wood-cutting activity. Andrea hadn't seen an African American man in camp throughout the last couple of days. She approached him slowly, her gaze landing squarely on the figure before her, admiring him. He looked up at her and then quickly looked away, and he was just as surprised to see a white woman staring at him, living among the natives.

Andrea smiled and asked, "Do you speak English?"

The African American man nodded and said timidly, "Yes, ma'am."

Andrea smiled. "That is excellent." She unconsciously added the African American man to the list of English speakers in the camp. Without considering her next question, she said absently, "What are you doing here?"

The African American man kept his eyes down. The last white people he had known would have beaten him for even looking at a white woman, let alone speaking to one. He stared at the ground and replied, "I had no home to go. My massa was killed in da' war, and I walked and walked, and these Indian people found me. They brought me here. My home is here now." He had trouble looking her in the eye, tending to look at the ground instead.

Andrea had to contemplate the African American man's words. She thought to herself, *this man was a slave. Oh my God!* Not once in the time she had been in this era did she consider slavery. These tales, the kind ballads were of, she'd read about it in history books. She realized that the premise of slavery had forever affected the world, and shocking as it was, here was the proof of it, living history right before her.

From the time she had met the Loftons until this minute, Andrea had not seen a black person, likely because they had been in the wilderness. *Black people belonged to rich white people*. Andrea was uncomfortable about the thought. This African American man had truly kind eyes. He was quiet and soft-spoken, and a hard worker. *Why would a white person want to hurt or enslave someone like him?* She looked again at the man standing there next to the woodpile, holding his hatchet.

Andrea asked, "What is your name?"

The man, his eyes still diverted, said, "Lucas, ma'am."

Andrea approached him and put a hand on his shoulder. "Lucas, I want you to be my friend. Please don't call me ma'am. My name is Andrea."

Lucas smiled at her and gently nodded. "Friend ... Andrea."

Then Andrea returned the smile. She was happy to see a pleased expression on his face. *To think of all the suffering he'd endured.* The thought of this man, any man, answering to a whip gave her a chill. Maybe he's found peace amongst these people. She began to understand why he was there, why he wanted to stay, and why the tribe took him in.

Andrea went to the creek and splashed water on her face. Although she had escaped what might have been a life of slavery herself, it seemed the thoughts would keep chasing her. Without giving mind to what she was doing, Andrea's hand landed on the stone pendant draped around her neck, and without notice, she found herself pressed with another vision. It was her, standing in another Indian village with big fires. Lucas was there with her, but it was not this place. She strained, trying to make sense of it, and just as the vision had come upon her, it washed away, like a leaf on a river; it was gone.

Her mind came back to the present, and finding she had a death grip on the amulet, she let go, the warmth of it slowly dissipating. She shook her head, knowing that the magic stone had something to do with her being here in this camp.

After freshening up, she returned to the wood-chopping pile and found a place to sit and observe. *This day has been a challenge*, she thought.

Lucas continued his chore. The action and sounds were mesmerizing. Andrea watched Lucas' strong, steady movement with each strike of the hatchet. He was confident in his ability; each stroke was smooth and honest. His skin glistened in the sunlight, sweating due to his effort.

Her mind began to pick at some of the odd strings of her memories, and she found herself in a sort of droning trance; her mind faded to her mother's anger on the day she turned her father in and the police came to arrest him. Her brother teasing her at the dinner table. Chelsea's flirting. The abduction and her fight with the captors. These thoughts were darkening her mood, and feeling helpless to fight them, she considered the reasons. *Why am I focusing on something that has already happened? Something I can't fix, or change. Why?* She tried to suppress her frustration.

Lucas saw her face was all scrunched up as though she was suffering. "You alright?" She blinked and looked into the deep brown eyes of her new friend.

"Oh, yes, Lucas. I'm fine. Just deep in thought, I guess." He gave a slight nod and continued his work. Andrea was surprised he had noticed her expression.

Herusa recruited Andrea to help prepare the meal. When it came time to serve the food, Helsu Este', a Medicine Man, blessed it. The chief and his family were the first to eat. Then the warriors were next. People like Andrea and Lucas always got food, but only what was left. They were not held in high regard but were incredibly grateful to have food to eat. She watched Lucas close his eyes and clasp his hands together as he said a silent prayer before eating his food. Without interruption or ceremony, he opened his eyes and began to sup. Andrea had a life lesson here. She'd never given thanks for her food. She saw how easy it was for him to be grateful after all he'd been through and felt ashamed. Bowing her head and closing her eyes for just a second, she mirrored Lucas, saying a silent "thank you" for her food and comfort. She smiled, opened her eyes and began to eat her food.

The evening came and went. The tribe held a gathering that consisted of chanting and dancing, and again Andrea found herself mesmerized; caught up in the moment's experience. The rhythmic flow of the drumming, chanting, and dancing was beautiful. She felt weightless. Away from so many things that had burdened her heart and mind. She began to enjoy the peace here, this day with these people.

Andrea slept, eventually stirring near daybreak. She opened her eyes and saw a pinkish glow, realizing it was the tint of sunrise given to the clouds on the brink of dawn. She blinked again and unwillingly recalled the night of the abduction. No wonder these images kept haunting her. She remembered something else. This time, it was the voice. The voice of the girl who poked her with her elbow in the van, asking if she was okay. *The voice was that of a young girl she'd met in the crowd at the Krew of Bacchus parade at Mardi Gras. My God, that seemed so long ago.* The thought was no more than an echo; the sound of her voice was an echo. The girl with that voice was with Collin and Adam that night.

Andrea recalled he was very handsome and very blonde. He had his arm wrapped around the girl. She seemed so young and petite. Andrea did not know her name, nor had they been introduced. Her anger intensified as she remembered the girl with Adam. It gave her a chill. There she was, so far away, yet distraught, thinking about what might have happened to the other girls that night.

Andrea caught her breath. Who else did she know in that van? She gave up trying to sleep anymore and hiked down to the creek to splash her face with water. It was cold first thing in the morning, rather shocking. But she washed her face and dipped her hair in the cool stream. She stepped into the rushing water and washed her feet, hands, and every part of her exposed body. There was no soap here, and she remembered Becca overseeing her bath back at the farm. She craved that day.

As Andrea guided herself up the little path back to the camp, she saw people moving about, and felt the whirl of activity that signaled the start of a new day. Her eyes settled again on Lucas. He was a friendly face amongst many strangers. He gave her a polite nod, then headed to the area where the tribe kept the horses. *Jack*, she thought, suddenly remembering the rapid succession of events over the past couple of days. Jack was there, too. It occurred to her that she didn't even go to greet her long-eared friend the previous day, so with little hesitation, she followed Lucas.

Andrea caught sight of Jack munching on the fresh grass he could reach from his rope. She saw Lucas untie two ponies and lead them to the creek for water. Nearly a dozen horses were there with Jack, all needing water. Andrea grabbed Jack's halter and used his tether rope as a lead. She loosened the lead of another brown horse next to Jack, helping Lucas with his morning chores.

Following Lucas's path, Andrea found an open bank next to the stream. Lucas smiled at her when he saw the horses at the water's edge. He didn't have to, but his eyes said, "Thank you." She smiled back at him, then turned and stroked Jack's neck. When Jack and the other horse had finished, Andrea helped Lucas with the rest of them, two at a time. To the natives, it didn't matter who tended to the horses as long as someone did, and Andrea felt more productive helping.

Andrea returned to the teepee to shake out the sleeping mats and brush the dirt floor of the shelter. Herusa met her at the door, joining a different woman to weave baskets and make hairpieces. She signaled to Andrea to come along.

"I'll join you shortly if you don't mind. I want to go riding with Lucas." Herusa nodded graciously, happy to have her company when she could, as Andrea helped her practice her English.

Andrea joined Lucas, throwing herself onto Jack's back. It was no easy feat, and the clothing she wore was the house dress Becca had given her. Dresses were usually comfortable, but not "horse sensible." Whether it was practical or not, Andrea made it work. Lucas jumped on the back of another younger bay-colored mare. She was a spirited little minx, but Lucas handled her like a wrangler, and many natives appreciated his skills.

Lucas managed the unruly mare, and Andrea trotted along beside him. After a while "Nak vike" settled down and gave a rather pleasurable ride. Andrea asked Lucas about his life, and although he was uncomfortable at first talking about himself to a white woman, he opened up to her.

Andrea spoke gently but directly. "Tell me about your family."

Lucas shook his head and averted his eyes. "I was a child when my mum and pa' were put on a ship. They took me and my sistah because we were big enough to work."

Andrea paused a moment to process his words. "Where was your home?"

Then Lucas responded proudly, "We are from Ibibio. In Africa. They come many times to take our people. It was long ago." Lucas gave his head a shake as his voice trailed off.

Andrea paused momentarily, feeling she had struck a nerve, but Lucas turned to her, awaiting more questions. She asked about where he ended up when he came to America. "Here in Georgia, a place called Trinity Plantation. Massa Drew prays to the Holy Mother every day, he calls his place Trinity."

Andrea had another question ready to follow the previous one. "Did your family live all together?" She remembered hearing about the slavers and how they would separate the families to suit their needs, and a fortunate few would stay together.

"Mum and sistah and me, we stay together. Pa' go to another place." He waved his hand in the air, showing what he meant.

Andrea remarked, not looking him in the eye. "I'm sorry that happened to you." She tried to see the brighter side of his situation. "So, you got to be with your mother and your sister?"

Lucas allowed a whisper of a smile to appear on his face. "Yeah, das' right. Not long ago, my mum and sistah died of the disease. It was bad, and they die fast." Andrea imagined what it would be like to be a slave. To be forced to work and be forced to be separated from your family.

"Do you know about your Pa'? Do you know where they took him?" Lucas shook his head. "No, I don't know. I will look for him one day, though."

Andrea let the questions rest for a while but pondered the picture his words painted. The ride was nice for a while until the sun began to beat down on them, hot and sticky; it was hard to be away from the shade. It was only a few minutes later when they turned the horses around and headed back. Andrea might have tried to escape the camp while they were out of it, but had no idea how to get back to the Loftons, having no sense of which direction to go. It might just as well have been half a world away. *Would they even look for her?*

16. Seeing Deeply

Georgia - 1798

Andrea helped Lucas rub down and water the horses. When they finished, he gave her a slight nod of thanks, and Andrea headed back to her teepee. She was only a few steps away from her hut when an overwhelming feeling hit her; she saw flashes, bits and pieces of visions in her mind, that made her eyes hurt. It wasn't as though she felt like fainting, and she wasn't sick, but she felt suspended like she was floating in the air. For a moment, she thought maybe she'd had too much sun, but then the flashes became clearer.

She had stepped past the door flap of the teepee, flopping down on the mat, the only place she could call her own. She closed her eyes, suddenly grateful to lie down out of the sun. Abruptly, her vision came into focus. She saw Jacob and Johnny. They had worried looks on their faces, although their mission was a good one. It was all for her! She saw Johnny. He was in agony; he was injured and needed help. Frustration grew as she tried earnestly to speak to them, but no sound would come. It was as if she was in a dream, only she was wide awake, and it was so real!

Then she saw the two Indian chiefs, Rakke' Taf and Menawah. They were not enemies. They were shaking hands. She couldn't snap out of her vision and at the same time she wanted to see more. She saw a hospital room. It was her in the hospital room. She felt a deep sadness, then anger. Chelsea was crying. She saw ocean waves lapping against the side of a boat. It was a big boat. She heard angry voices but couldn't see the faces.

Then, as quickly as it came, the vision dissipated, and she was on her mat; silence took over the vision.

Andrea lay there breathing hard, her heart pounding like she had just run a marathon. It was as if she looked at things through someone else's eyes. She lay there, looking up, the sunlight casting subtle hues inside the teepee, then she slowly sat upright and tried to re-orient herself. When she was able to get her feet under her, Andrea walked down to the creek again and splashed water on her face. There was no real explanation for what she had just experienced, but she searched her mind to find logic in it.

She paused for a moment in the grass on the bank of the creek, trying to slow everything down. "Create calm," she thought, remembering a meditation she once saw in an online video. "To help clear your mind, use your breath to create calm." Andrea did just that. She closed her eyes and focused on what she could smell and feel. She breathed in the fresh breeze wafting through her hair and ruffling the collar of her dress.

She felt the sun's warmth and the coolness of the grass beneath her. She felt like she belonged here. Then it hit her. It was in the Tarot reading and the Queen of Swords. It described the clarity that Andrea would soon have. Is this clarity? She wondered, understanding that her tarot card reading could be right. In her reflections, she recalled the walk back to the hotel after reading and hearing about the "mystical" power of the stone amulet that she couldn't live without.

She thought about the few minutes she'd spent back at the hotel, searching the internet, finding the type of stone, a Lapis Lazuli, that had the power to assist in interpreting dreams and facing the truth. Looking down at the peculiar stone, she wondered why the amulet had been creating such a stir among the tribes. Is this whole thing, my assault and time travel, the stone's doing? She couldn't help but wonder if the stone brought her here for a purpose. Andrea had to find out why. Why her, and why here?

Andrea was searching her brain for a logical explanation for the mind-boggling experience she just had. Okay, so I saw the Loftons. Why were they a part of my vision? As she deduced, she attributed their appearance to the smells she had breathed in so deeply, perhaps something specifically, them. Or maybe the heat of the sun. It was hot the day she'd met them. Perhaps that was it. Then she thought better. No, that's not it. That didn't feel right. Her mind went to the Indian chiefs. She saw them together, but did they even know each other? So, was that vision a snapshot of what might come? The thoughts overwhelmed her because searching for the reason for this vision was like trying to find a raindrop in a barrel of water.

She had another idea that made more sense than any other disruptive thought. It's not for me to interpret. Maybe I'm just the conduit for the visions. Andrea almost felt relief for having that awareness. Once the vision was gone, her decision was clear that she didn't have to take action, she began to relax. Was she happy to have been given this power? Was it a blessing or a curse? She mauled around the idea until she felt comfortable with it. Maybe it was both, but she had determined she would not take it for granted.

Andrea got up and stood in the doorway of the teepee and just watched. Children playing, women preparing food, and crafting beadwork. She saw a young man walking by with a beautiful Appaloosa horse. Andrea thought, all these people are carrying on with their lives, even with no place to call home.

It was disturbing how relaxed they were. The roving tribe had to take it all in stride. They lived with faith that everything would be okay and their next home would be a wonderful place. The thought of these people struggling made Andrea uneasy. She wished she was not so selfish. So, entitled. In her world, in her place on this earth, she had been so self-involved. It was an ugly thought. Her perception of herself made her realize how lucky she was to have all she did.

Herusa came around the corner and looked at her, seeing the faraway look in her eyes. She moved in front of her to catch Andrea's gaze, then said, "You, okay?"

Andrea nodded and smiled at her. "Yes, I'm very okay. Thank you, Herusa." This answer made Herusa cock her head to one side as if she didn't hear correctly what Andrea said, or that she didn't understand.

Andrea knew better than to try to explain it but put her hand on Herusa's shoulder and said softly, looking her directly in the eye, "I'm fine."

Herusa nodded. "You come to weave with me?"

Andrea's smile lingered. "Yes, I would like that very much." Herusa grabbed her by the arm, and they went to the gathering place to weave.

17. Doing the Right Thing
McIntosh - 1798

It was late afternoon when Jacob arrived back at his house, and after looking for Jack the better part of the day with nothing to show for it. Becca met him at the paddock gate looking as lovely as ever in her pink and red floral dress. She had her hair pulled back so it wouldn't fall in her face while she was doing chores. Jacob imagined it down over her shoulders like she wore it when she was brushing it before bed. He loved it that way.

"Any luck?" She said, greeting him with a smile, gracefully moving close enough to plant a big kiss on his cheek.

"No," Jacob said with a frustrated huff. "Saw a lot of tracks, but not that stubborn mule."

Becca said to him worriedly, "Andrea headed out the same direction you and Johnny went about two hours ago and never came back. I bet she's lost." Then she shook her head, "I should have never let her go."

Jacob looked at her, shocked at her words. "She's out there?" He pointed in the direction of the thick brush beyond the pasture.

173

"Yes, she wanted to be helpful and was sure she could track him down. I know that forest is more of a challenge than she made it out to be."

Jacob was not sure how he should respond. He thought, *"You're a fool to let her go. She doesn't know anything about these woods!"* He used discretion before he opened his mouth to speak and hoped he would not air his opinion. "I know she doesn't like to take advantage of us. I know she just went out to help, but damn!"

Becca asked, "And where is Johnny? Did you see him out there anywhere?"

Jacob answered, "No, I haven't seen him since we separated, but I'm not worried about him; he's familiar with this land and can care for himself. It's a little different for him than for Andrea."

He paused and shook his head. "She's a fool."

Becca understood his angry response. "Well, I've seen enough to know she's not helpless. She'll be fine if she can avoid the occasional mountain lion or a run-in with a skunk. And besides, maybe she'll be the one to bring Jack home." Becca smiled and blinked hard, displaying her sense of humor.

Jacob took the saddle off Skeeter and led her to the trough for a drink. He turned the mare loose in the pasture, and she began to neigh. She was calling for Babe as the two mares were not separated often.

Becca grabbed Jacob by the arm, turned him around, and headed back to the house, trying to distract him. "I've got some supper ready; you must be starving." She said to him in a playful way, then thought to herself, *if a bit of food would do anything, it might sweeten his disposition.*

Becca no sooner placed her husband's meal on a plate before him than she heard Skeeter whinny again. The sound of clopping hooves followed. Jacob jumped up and headed out the door. It was Johnny whose expression radiated his happiness.

"Glad you made it. I bet you didn't expect that darn mule to have wandered so far." Jacob was relieved to see his brother. Although he could provide for himself, Jacob was much more relaxed once he knew his brother was safe.

"I don't suppose you saw Andrea anywhere, did you?" Jacob asked.

Johnny looked at him with a surprised expression. "What? She didn't hike out into those woods, did she?"

175

Jacob nodded, "She certainly did. And it will be nightfall soon. It would be a foolish undertaking for us to try to find her now. We'll have to try again in the morning and hope she's all right."

Jacob and Becca returned to the house while Johnny cared for Babe. The three ate their meal, and the penetrating silence was broken only by bits of small talk and a few deep sighs. Bone weary was the only way to describe how they felt. Becca, too, had spent the entire day worrying, which had also drained her energy. It was inevitable they would retire early, with the decision to begin their search anew the next day.

It was barely daybreak when Becca began to stir. The sun had just begun to lighten the sky, and she knew the men would want to start early. She wrapped some hard bread she had made the day before in a towel and threw in some jerky, easy things to carry. Jacob heard her milling about and pulled himself out of bed, ready to start the day. He stacked the items in his saddlebags, along with some water and ale. His tone changed, and Becca recognized when Jacob was all business.

"I hope we'll be back within the day, but we will most likely stay out until we find her, so, it may be more."

Becca nodded her understanding. "She didn't mean to get herself lost, and I'm sure once you find her, she will be a bit more wary about leaving the farm again."

Becca tried to sound reassuring. Milling over the truth, Jacob felt it was the Christian thing to do for the girl who had just dropped into their lives. Since they brought her with them to Macintosh, he felt a responsibility toward her.

A short time later, Jacob and Johnny were on their way. They headed in the same direction as the day before but did not split up this time. When they'd reached the end of the pasture, Jacob looked back and gave Becca a wave and a sweet smile.

The morning passed quickly, and the two Loftons dismounted to rest for a short time and to water the horses at a nearby stream. Johnny meandered about looking for tracks, some sign that would hint to them about where Jack or Andrea might be. If they got lucky, Andrea would have found Jack, and coming across them simultaneously would have shortened the search.

There were hoof prints, but they were not fresh. Jacob had looked around for signs of possible predators, suddenly aware that something could just as easily be hunting them.

Getting off his horse, he observed two sets of bare feet among the day-old hoof prints.

Immediately, he thought *of Indians* but did not say anything aloud. Jacob mounted Skeeter again, and Johnny followed. There was a subtle but consistent rise to the trail as they climbed to the top of the ridge. They hoped to have a vantage point from above that would allow them to narrow the search to a smaller region.

Once they were at the crest of the ridge, Jacob could see campfire smoke in the distance. It was still a long way off, and he doubted Andrea could make a fire without flint, making him suspicious. They also saw a woman's footprints, which wasn't fresh either. She hadn't been past this place for some time. He thought how unusual it was to see so very little evidence.

As the day wore on, the brothers were becoming increasingly anxious about Andrea's whereabouts. Jacob's thoughts were going to a dark place. *"Maybe we're too late. Maybe she's been attacked and injured. Worse yet, she's dead."*

Johnny was thinking very similarly but did not want to say anything for fear it would curse any possible good fortune.

Jacob and Johnny finally stopped for the night. They remained near the crest of the ridge, as it seemed to be a logical place to decide a direction they would take in the morning. Johnny gathered firewood and unsaddled the horses, and Jacob's frustration grew. *Why? Why did she take off in the first place? And why do I care so much?* Jacob's mind was racing, he felt as though he failed in his responsibility to take care of this girl, reasoning that it was his fault she was there at all; he didn't know or understand why it bothered him.

Johnny caught two fish out of the stream, and they cooked them over the fire. They consumed a good portion of the ale that Becca had packed for them. Just as twilight fell and they settled down for the night, Johnny said, "Do you hear that?" His frustration fogged Jacob's vision, and he wasn't paying any attention to sounds around them, a foolish mistake.

Jacob also heard the sound when he got up and moved away from the crackling and the hissing of the fire. It was drums and chanting. He looked at Johnny with surprise, and his heart sank.

"That's Indians." The sound was far in the distance, but it was there. As the words rolled off his tongue, the possibility that Andrea was with the Indians became more real.

Jacob and Johnny slept in shifts. They did not want to get ambushed in the middle of the night and had no idea which band of Indians might be out there.

After a long night of fitful sleep, daybreak came, and they talked about their next move. Jacob knew that a tribe usually had roving scouts who would look for game and watch for possible aggression.

"This wouldn't be a permanent camp, would it?" Jacob said, looking at Johnny with a question in his voice, searching his eyes for a reaction. "We can't just approach them; they might mistake it for an attack. We need to get close enough to see if Andrea is there." He stated hesitantly. The worry lines were growing along Jacob's forehead.

Then Johnny asked, "What do we do if we find she's there?"

Jacob shook his head in doubt. "Then I guess we'll barter for her freedom. I don't know what else to do. We can't just leave her."

Johnny responded, sounding concerned, "We might not survive this, Jacob." With his eyes, he searched the dirt-covered ground for an answer.

Jacob spoke softly, "Just pray, Johnny. I'm afraid you're right."

Johnny said, "We're doing the right thing. We won't be punished for it." Jacob nodded. He mentally prepared for the worst, not wanting to imagine what they would find.

The two Loftons decided to take the horses only a short distance for fear they would make too much noise and tip off any Indian scouts. Then, they would separate so that if one got caught, the other would be free to get help. They took only a few items with them, things they thought the Indians might barter for. They didn't have much, as they didn't expect the need to trade with anybody, let alone a tribe of Indians. The two men agreed Johnny would be the best choice for getting the closest to the encampment. He spotted a rise on the north side of the camp that looked like a good vantage point. From there, he should be able to see Jacob's approach and observe the tribe discreetly, possibly seeing Andrea. The two men hugged fiercely, fearing it might be the last they'd see each other, then headed off in different directions.

Johnny was young, but he was a proficient hunter and was skilled with a knife. He would be prepared and ready to confront any aggressor, just in case. He was stealthy, quiet and measured in his movements. He soon found himself perched near the top of an outcropping. He settled himself in a spot out of eyeshot of others but had a good view of the gathering place below. The lion's share of the activity within the tribe happened there.

As he'd settled, he felt a sharp poke with painful aftereffects. Agitated and surprised, he looked down, and realized he nearly sat on top of a snake. The snake had laid into his wrist, just above the wrist bone. Johnny bit his tongue, trying not to make a sound, but he was pale with the intensity of what had just happened. He was unsure what kind of snake it was, but if it was poisonous, he was in big trouble.

He knew if this were a poisonous snake, it would not take long for the venom to circulate, and he would be unable to do anything except die. He was able to reach his knife and sliced the bite open, taking care to miss anything vital. He began to squeeze as much blood out and as quickly as he could. He then sucked the wound to draw out more. He wrapped it up with his scarf as tight as possible and hoped for the best.

At the same time, Jacob's approach from below was more on the same plane as the encampment. He was as quiet and as heedful as he could be, expecting the worst but hoping for a non-confrontational meeting. He moved soundlessly through the trees, inching toward the camp, stealing glances of the hillside, searching for Johnny, but the brush and the forest trees were too thick. As he maneuvered himself from one tree to another, he breached the edge of a tree trunk and nearly ran directly into an Indian scout he didn't anticipate. The scout had a gun, and rather than shoot Jacob, he jerked his head, signaling Jacob to go ahead of him. With no words, the scout brought him to a clearing where another Indian met the two; this one smiled with the satisfaction of stalking and killing his prey.

What will they do with me? Jacob thought as a jolt of panic shot through him. It was evident to him that if they had intended to kill him, he would already be dead.

When Jacob and his captors made it to the camp, they walked him to the gathering place in the center of the tent village. As expected, the Chief came to see the visitor and approached him with a concerned look.

The Chief addressed Jacob, "Why are you here?" Jacob was pleased to be able to communicate with him.

"I'm here looking for a girl. She got lost searching for our mule."

Menawah nodded his head. "We have the girl. She cannot leave."

Jacob responded with questions. "Why? She is no danger to you." There was a sense of urgency in his voice, which the Chief recognized. Just then, Andrea and Herusa, out gathering herbs, came around a row of teepees and approached the gathering place. Andrea's eyes fell on Jacob.

"Jacob - Oh my God! You came for me!" She was overwhelmed at the sight of him. She wanted to hug him so badly but did not dare misstep in the presence of the Chief. She looked at Menawah, then at the ground as she spoke, giving reverence to him.

"This is my friend. He only came for me. He wants to know that I am well." At that moment, Andrea was overwhelmed by a sentiment she hadn't felt for a long time. Jacob was her "*family*". She hadn't had the support of family since the day she walked out, away from her own.

Menawah gave a short nod of acknowledgment and said, "I know who he is."

Andrea did not know how Menawah would know him but replied, still looking at the ground, "He means no harm."

She averted her eyes once more, suddenly bothered by her vision from the previous day.

She shot a panicked look toward Jacob and said, "Johnny is in trouble."

Jacob looked at her, quite surprised, and said, "What? How do you know that?"

Andrea shook her head slightly and said, "I don't know, but he needs help. Do you know where he is?"

*

Johnny was still watching from his rocky outcropping. He felt a bit faint and hot, realizing the snake must have been poisonous, he was now facing real danger. From his perch looking down on the gathering place; he could see Jacob and, like the sharp edge of a knife, fear shot through him. Then he thought, *what did we expect?* He was not comforted by trying to reason with himself.

As Johnny watched the conversation going on below him, he also saw Andrea and her reaction to seeing Jacob in camp. He was happy she looked well and was not hurt. With his focus on the activity in the encampment, he failed to see the Indian scout who had come up behind him. The scout made only the slightest noise, and Johnny whipped his head around, knife in hand. The Indian smirked and gave him a poke with the barrel of his rifle, tipping his head upwards to have Johnny stand. As he did, he felt dizzy and had to catch himself on one of the boulders he had been sitting next to. He held up his arm and showed the Indian his injury.

Then said "snakebite." The Indian gestured with his head in the direction he wanted Johnny to go, paying no heed to his injury.

It took about twenty minutes before Johnny and the Indian scout arrived at camp. By this time, Johnny was staggering and very lightheaded. When they finally made it to the gathering place, his approach caught Andrea's attention, and she ran to him.

"Johnny, what happened?"

Johnny said breathlessly, "Snakebite."

A moment later, he collapsed. Andrea was close enough she could slow his fall but was not able to prevent it.

She signaled to Herusa to come and help her. They found his wrist wrapped up in a kerchief. When Herusa unwrapped it, she could see he'd tried to cut the wound to bleed it but was not altogether successful. It was red and puffy, and the red marks began to show a trail up his arm. Herusa jumped up to get Helsu Este' to help. Andrea cradled Johnny's head in her hands while Jacob stood near the Chief, feeling helpless.

A few minutes later, the medicine man was by his side, chewing on some herbs. Herusa saw Andrea staring at the strange ritual and whispered, "Sneeka. It will help with the snakebite."

The medicine man chewed the cud to make it soft and release the medicine from it. He spit it into his hand, forming a wad that he pressed onto the injury. Johnny let out a growl at the intense, sharp pain from the action. The pain eased, and Helsu Este' softly chanted something.

He spoke to Herusa in Creek, which Herusa then translated, "It will take time, but soon we will know if the sneeka worked."

The thought that he could die was hard for Andrea to comprehend. Jacob swallowed hard. Reflecting on the events of that day, he blamed himself for Johnny's injury. He thought *I would still have come; we couldn't leave her.* He felt almost as strongly about protecting Andrea as he did about his brother or wife. The need to guard her and Johnny and Becca. They were his "tribe."

18. Good Medicine

Transient Camp - 1798

The Lofton boys, forced to stay at the camp just like Andrea, were considered more of a threat. The chief did not want them to run into any lingering troops or possibly any other aggressive Indian tribes, for fear it could prevent them from reaching a safe haven, wherever that might be.

Andrea asked the chief's permission to stay with the Loftons hoping to stay in the chief's good graces. He agreed she could help nurse Johnny and allowed Jacob to stay with them. Once they were led to a teepee and left alone without prying eyes, Andrea fell into Jacob's arms. "Oh, Jacob, I'm so sorry! It's my fault Johnny was injured. It's my fault! I'm sorry you had to come and get me. It was so stupid for me to think I could help."

Jacob's voice was comforting. "Now, don't you worry," he spoke softly. "Everything is gonna be just fine."

Still a little embarrassed about putting them in this position, Andrea felt relieved that he was with her.

It did not take long for Johnny's fever to spike incredibly high, and Andrea knew what could happen if they couldn't bring it down. She went to the creek to get a bucket of cool water, bathing as much of his body as possible and praying it would bring down his temperature. Jacob asked Andrea how they'd found her and if the tribe treated her well. Her answers surprised him.

"No," she said, blinking hard. "They've treated me very kindly. I must do chores and earn my place, but Herusa has taught me many things so I can be useful to them." Andrea looked directly into Jacob's eyes and said, "This tribe lost their home and many of their people. The chief decided it was time to move the tribe to a safer place, so - here they are." She gestured with her hand as if putting the whole camp on exhibit.

Jacob nodded. "I've heard of that happening more often since the war."

Andrea struggled to tell Jacob about her vision of Johnny and the chiefs. It was so abstract and unbelievable; she would never have guessed he would take it seriously. The fact was that her dreams and visions came true exactly as she'd seen them.

"I think it's this," And she held up the amulet that hung around her neck. She started dubiously. "I have seen things. What I think is a peek into the future." Jacob's face was wrinkled up with intense curiosity, trying to understand what she was saying. "I've seen Menawah and Rakke' Taf together. Do you know if they've ever met before?"

Jacob shook his head. "What? What do you mean you've seen them together?" She looked at him with pleading eyes, feeling naked by exposing her secret.

"A vision, I guess you could call it. A dream. Do you know if the two chiefs know each other? If they've ever been together?" Andrea insisted. Just by speaking the words, she felt lighter; the tension calmed considerably, and the tightness she held in her shoulders finally relaxed back to normal.

He looked at her, reflecting on the question seriously. "I truly don't know, but maybe we need to – get them together. They could double their size and the move might offer more protection to both tribes."

He didn't make eye contact with her, but she could tell he was working it out, comparing the good and bad. "So, you've seen this, you say?"

She nodded gently. "Yes, just like I saw Johnny hurt and needing help. Just like that."

Johnny woke, hearing his name, and writhed in discomfort. He saw that both Jacob and Andrea sat with him and said, "Good. You found her." Jacob and Andrea both could see he was delirious with fever, and she wrung out the cloth again with cool water and placed it on his forehead.

Andrea spoke softly, "It was smart of you to bleed the bite, Johnny. It probably saved your life."

He nodded. "Just did what my brother taught me," looking right at Jacob.

"Thank you for finding me, Johnny," Andrea said, gently kissing his cheek. Johnny smiled a weak smile; then his eyes closed again.

As Andrea bathed Johnny's head and torso with the cool water, Jacob and Andrea conversed about how she thought for sure Jack was a bear until he poked his nose through the bushes. They laughed, envisioning just how scared she probably was.

"The horses!" Jacob exclaimed. He told Andrea where they were, and she asked Awahani to send someone to get them.

When she returned to the brothers, she told them, "Horses are taken care of - Awahani sent two braves to get them. I'll show you where Babe and Skeeter will be kept. They will receive the best care." She smiled as she recalled Lucas' attention to all the horses in the tribe. Jacob nodded, feeling a bit ashamed. The farm, horses, the crops were his responsibility. He'd never surrendered his duties to anyone until now.

As time passed, the afternoon sun disappeared into the tree line; shadows of the fluttering leaf-filled branches stretched out along the ground. Andrea took the time to explain what she knew of this tribe.

She began, "This tribe of Creek people were attacked and forced from their homes. Menawah decided to move to safer ground, trying to preserve what tribe he had left."

Jacob nodded and said, "I have fought beside the natives and against them, and I know the difference between a wretch and a man. I know these people are not violent; they're villagers."

As Jacob sat quietly, he scratched his beard, hearing the abrasiveness of the spikey hairs against his rough hands. The creases in his forehead deepened in part from the internal conversation he was having with himself. Finally, he spoke.

"I think," he paused. "I think I might be able to help them." Andrea smiled, blinking long and slow.

"I knew you would think of something."

Helsu Este' returned to reapply the sneeka and check the wound. He pulled back the loose cloth that covered the wound and poked at the tissue around it. Johnny reacted to the poking and prodding as expected; it was puffy and red, tender to the touch. His reaction proved the nerves in his wrist were not severely damaged. The medicine man continued, giving the edge of the injured skin a squeeze, looking for any sign of infection. Luckily, there was none, but Johnny would have a long night.

Jacob and Andrea took turns watching over Johnny throughout the night. His fever ebbed and flowed but remained. When the morning came, Helsu Este visited again; this time, he brought another woman who chanted while he was doing his exam. Although the wound was still very puffy, there was no pus. There would be quite a scar, but it appeared Johnny would recover.

After the medicine man left, Andrea tried to get Johnny to sit up and eat. His facial color had improved, and although he only took a few bites, he did drink a fair amount of water. The hearts of the oddball family of friends were lighter and less burdened with worry after seeing Johnny's improvements. Andrea decided now would be an excellent time to show Jacob the encampment.

Awahani sat with Johnny while she and Jacob took a tour. It was a chance for him to see something besides the inside of a tent and to observe various activities that were part of the heartbeat of this tribe. The women did the weaving, mending, and bead sewing. The men worked at tanning hides, made shelters, and prepared the meat for cooking.

She showed him the nearby stream, and Jacob walked right into it, sticking his whole head in the water. It was cool and fresh and felt like a reward. He came up out of the water and giggled. He thought how silly he must look, but it felt good to knock off some dust.

He let the water trickle down, then returned his raggedy hat to his head, walking up the embankment with a smile.

Andrea watched him, shaking her head. "Refreshed?" She was sporting a wide grin.

"Yes, Ma'am. I am!" Then he joined Andrea again to finish the tour. There was little else to point out, except the teepee she stayed in with Herusa and where the tribe kept the horses.

Andrea saw Lucas giving a delicate wave as they approached the long tether line. "Lucas," she said like she was introducing her father to her prom date. "I would like you to meet Jacob. He and his brother Johnny are the closest thing I have to family here." Jacob looked at Andrea with surprise and thought, *I suppose you're right*. Lucas kept his eyes down, fearful of the formidable white man that Jacob was. Jacob had never met a African American man and had only seen one working in the fields, and he didn't understand Lucas' reaction. Jacob thought it only proper to put out a hand to him.

Lucas looked at it, unsure what to do, and Andrea's eyes sought his and said, "It is okay, Lucas." Then the African American man took off his hat and put out his hand, grasping Jacob's with a solid grip.

Jacob smiled and said, "Pleasure to meet you." Lucas gave a quick nod, replacing his hat, and went back to chores.

Andrea told Jacob, "Lucas didn't trust me initially, but we've become friends. I'm glad you've had a chance to meet." Jacob didn't doubt Andrea. He'd come to know that she was able to judge a good soul from a bad one. Lucas was a good soul.

She walked along the rope to Jack. Jacob caught sight of his old friend. "Well, you old devil." He gave Jack a scratch between the ears. "Looks like he's doin' well."

Jacob looked around for Skeeter and Babe, but he did not see them on the rope with the other horses. He found them on a separate tether nearby, separated because there were just too many horses on the same line. He walked around to the separate tether line, checking each horse to be sure they were safe and cared for. He found his saddle and saddlebags beyond Skeeter and Babe, under a tree. He gathered his and Johnny's things to bring back to their shelter.

Andrea let him know that Lucas tended to the horses. "He is the best; you can trust him."

Jacob could see her fondness for him on her face. He had no reason to doubt her words.

*

It was mealtime, and Herusa urged her and Jacob to eat. Jacob was humbled at the gesture and thought what a kind heart she had to give the strangers her place in the food line. She thought nothing of it.

Jacob put an extra piece of bread on his plate for Johnny. Awahani approached Jacob with a cup full of broth and said, "Here. For your brother."

Jacob took the cup with his head lowered. "Very kind of you. Thank you," he said, overwhelmed by the kindness of these people. Their generosity and warmth toward him were not expected.

Andrea, Jacob, and Herusa sat on the ground together as they ate. It was pleasant listening to the community of the native people.

"Peaceful, isn't it?" Andrea smiled, watching Jacob's face as his eyes scanned the tribe, seeing his pleasantly surprised look.

Andrea shared with him how Herusa had become her friend, and they taught each other their language. "She is my closest friend here." He was happy someone had taken on watching over her.

He had been waiting for a good time to bring it up, but he thought now, with Herusa's help, he could interpret his thoughts to the chief. He spoke slowly and quietly.

"I - uh, know another Creek tribe I trade with sometimes. I would like to speak with your chief about them. It could be a safe place for you to settle."

Herusa took in the information and smiled. "A new place? A home?"

Then Jacob smiled. "Possibly. Can you help us talk to the chief?" Andrea was clever but knew little about the politics of the tribe and had to rely on Herusa to get the information to Menawah. Once Herusa nodded her understanding, Andrea looked up at Jacob and said nervously,

"Now, we wait."

19. A New Home

Transient Camp - 1798

Andrea and Jacob had taken turns helping Johnny, who was now able to stand and walk. His strength depended on him eating and drinking enough to sustain himself. Except for Helsu Este', no one knew what to expect from a snake bite recovery. Now they did.

On a very cloudy, blustery day, Herusa came to them with news about her conversation with Menawah. She admitted that she asked yet another Indian hunter, Hesaket', to communicate with the Chief, as the Chief had great respect for him, and if he was to hear the words from a man, a hunter, she felt he would think about it more seriously.

It wasn't long before the young hunter returned to her and said, "Menawah wants to talk." To the misfit guests, this was good news. They had no real connection to this tribe, but all of them cared about the safety and welfare of these people.

Herusa led the Loftons and Andrea to the gathering place, where they waited anxiously for the meeting. A few moments later, Menawah greeted them, gesturing with his hand and encouraging them to sit.

He placed himself across from Jacob, looking directly into his eyes, and asked, "You say there is a place you *think* our tribe will be safe?"

The Chief emphasized the word "think." Jacob nodded, swallowing the lump in his throat before he spoke. "The Creek tribe I trade with have been settled at their location for many years. They are good people."

Menawah rubbed the palms of his hands together. Andrea watched his knuckles tighten and relax over and over as his hands release his pent-up tension. He was not one to make decisions lightly. Andrea wasn't sure if it was nerves or if the action might be the way the Chief processes things. Then he spoke slowly, his focus squarely on Jacob. It was as though he was measuring the truth of words before he began to ask questions.

"You know this tribe?" Jacob nodded confidently in response to Menawah's question and made it a point to keep eye contact with the Chief. "What is the name of this place?"

Andrea had heard Jacob mention the name only once before. "It is called Atiketiv, and their chief is Rakke' Taf." He and the Chief were so intensely speaking to each other that neither of them was aware of the others standing near them.

After hearing this, Menawah gave a short, quick bob to his head and said, "We go." The words led to a short discussion about a plan to visit, agreeing they would leave at sunrise the next day.

Jacob was happy to hear that Menawah would visit the other Creek tribe. The Chief ordered a couple of sentries to go with the party and act as guards and hunters, along with Jacob, to make the introduction. The travel to the other village would take days, bringing Jacob right by the farm and an opportunity to see Becca, who would surely be sick with worry.

As promised, the men headed out of the camp at daybreak. The Chief appointed Hesaket to take charge while he was away, so there would be a leader if something might happen to him either at 'Atiketiv' or on their travels. He understood the chief's hesitance, but Jacob assured him the passage was safe. Most of the trip would be his hunting and fishing territory.

Jacob knew these hills and trails very well and was undoubtedly the best man to lead this group through it. They traveled a while before anyone spoke, and Menawah was the first to break the silence.

"Why do you come to get the girl?"

Jacob smiled and answered with a shadow of doubt in his voice. "She was lost and frightened when she came to us. I felt the right thing to do was to go after her. She is a good girl and is worth protecting."

Menawah gave a quick nod, indicating he understood. "She has a good heart but an unclear mind. That is why the stone chose her." These words confused Jacob slightly, as he did not understand its ability as the Chief did.

"Oh ... the stone."

The Chief looked at him with solemn awareness and said, "We are blessed to have someone who bears the stone among us. I believe that is why you came to us. Now, you will help find safety for my tribe."

Jacob never considered this brush with fate as something the stone controlled.

They rode for most of the day and came down off the ridge in late afternoon and onto the flat. Jacob's farm was visible now, his eyes searching for Becca.

Jacob had told Menawah and his companions Poheko and Korru that this place was his home and a comfortable place to stop for the night.

Menawah graciously said, "I thank you for your generosity."

As they rode past the pasture and closer to the barn, Jacob saw Becca scattering feed to the chickens. She was taken aback, having seen movement out of the corner of her eye and looked up. The sight of the natives made her catch her breath momentarily, and then she realized Jacob was among them.

She dropped the feed and ran to him. "Jacob, I have been so worried. It was just a mule. Are you alright?" He dismounted, pulled her into his arms, and kissed her hard on the lips.

"Well, hello to you, too," he said to his bride. He looked confidently into her eyes, smiling, as she searched for an explanation. Jacob didn't see Menawah smile at his reunion with his wife.

"My precious," Jacob said, thrusting his muscular arm around Becca's waist, turning her naturally toward the Chief. "I would like you to meet Chief Menawah. He is the leader of the tribe holding Andrea. They provided shelter for Johnny and me as well." He blurted out the words before she had a chance to object.

Becca looked at him, her eyes smiling, then reached out to the Chief before her words did. "Hello, and welcome.

Thank you for bringing my husband back to me." Then she gave a polite curtsy to him and the others in the party.

Jacob showed the small group of Indians where they could put the horses and a place in the barn where they could sleep for the night. Jacob turned to Becca and asked if there was any food she could serve to the guests.

Becca said, "I'll think of something."

Jacob smiled, turning toward the house with his arm still around her. After gathering what soup and bread Becca had in the house, Jacob took it and some wine to their guests, confident they were comfortable and settled for the night. He was grateful to be home and just as thankful to see his wife. Her quiet, steady disposition had a way of calming his mind, which he needed desperately right now.

This time together gave him a chance to tell her of Andrea's capture and why the tribe insisted that she stay, then filled in small details of Johnny's snakebite and Andrea's vision, explaining that it probably saved Johnny's life.

Jacob told Becca with wonder in his voice, "There is something about that amulet she wears. It's like it speaks to her."

Becca looked at him, bewildered that he would believe such a thing. She was doubtful a stone could have magical powers, scoffing as Jacob tried to convince her. Jacob, however, had seen it work. Then she said with an exasperated sigh, "If that be true, you shouldn't have brought her with you. There is something extraordinary about her."

Jacob nodded slightly. "Indeed, there is, but it would be unchristian to not care for her. She had been attacked and was as scared as she could be. I couldn't just tell her to go away, no matter how strange she appeared. Besides, the Indians think she is blessed because she has the stone. That says something, doesn't it?"

Then, cupping Becca's chin with his long-fingered hand, Jacob tenderly kissed his wife. Fulfilled with his wife safe in his arms, Jacob and Becca fell asleep holding each other.

The dawn came with billowing black clouds and occasional bursts of rain. Becca was concerned for her husband. He'd slept hard. She knew nights out in the wilderness and the hard ground for a bed could not allow for a good night's sleep.

She rose, padding across the room with only a few glowing embers to light her way. She threw more wood on the fire, quickly bringing it to life. Becca put a kettle on to heat water for coffee, just like every other day. She thought again about the guests in the barn and added more water, figuring the men in the barn would like coffee, too.

She made biscuits and stewed quail for Jacob and the guests. Jacob went out to the barn and invited the Chief and his guards in for food and coffee before the group continued to Atiketiv. Menawah was gracious and appreciated the hospitality. He refused the coffee but partook in breaking bread with his friends.

Poheko and Korru were happy to eat and drink, and although they seemed awkward, the natives were comfortable at the little table in Jacob's house. Korru, who wore a brown shirt and pants made from deer hide, was moving his hands and scrunching his face. Jacob had not realized before that he was using his hands to sign for Poheko. The brave was deaf. Jacob smiled to himself and thought, *how ignorant of me*, ashamed he didn't know.

Jacob privately told Becca about the plan to get the two tribes together. "It is wonderful that you thought of it. Won't it be risky to put the Chiefs together, though? They could be enemies, too."

Jacob considered her words. "Yes, but the idea to get them together came from one of Andrea's visions. When it comes down to it, they are all Creek Indians. I hope the need to survive is more important than the need to fight."

*

Once sufficiently supplied, the Chief, his guards, and Jacob set out to Atiketiv, hopefully returning with good news. It was a difficult day's ride, and the plan was to allow Jacob to approach Atiketiv alone first. An introduction like this might have been impossible before the war, but so much had changed the tribes' culture that this idea was not so far-fetched. It was a matter of survival.

The wind blew, gusty and staggered, as though it was working to make way for the pelting rain that toyed with the small group. There were short breaks in the weather, and occasionally, the ride was pleasant, but minimal conversation took place. Jacob felt the tension build throughout the day, as though the group was teetering on the edge of a cliff.

Menawah was brave, and his guards were fierce hunters and warriors. He knew they were unsettled about the meeting of the tribes. Jacob felt the disquieted emotions of his friends and understood just how important this meeting would be.

They stopped to rest and give the horses water near a little creek. Just as Jacob and Menawah walked away from the creek; a wild commotion erupted by the horses. The animals were spooked, and their neighs were filled with fear. The men heard low growls and an eerie feeling swept over them, making their neck hairs prickle.

Korru grabbed his knife and ran to the stream, partially hidden by trees and shrubs. Jacob looked at the Chief, his eyes wide and wild, and turned, pulling his rifle from his saddle, running toward the disturbance.

When he pushed through the branches and bushes that blocked his view, Jacob saw Poheko with the lion on top of him, the Indian grunting as loudly as he could; his screams stifled. The lion had knocked him to the ground and had him pinned and helpless; blood everywhere. Korru had his knife drawn, and while the lion focused on his prey, Korru thrust it into the animal's neck right behind its ears, and almost immediately, the creature went as limp as a wet rag. Korru pushed the animal off his friend and helped him to his feet.

Poheko's blood-covered body was disturbing, coated with the sticky red substance. Jacob noticed Poheko had gotten in his licks as well. The ribs of the animal were exposed on one side due to Poheko's ability to drive his knife into the agile beast. He didn't hit anything vital but injured the creature enough to slow the lion down.

Korru paused by the Creekside and washed Poheko, enabling him to see his injuries better. He had puncture marks on his shoulder and upper arm and long claw marks down one side of his neck and onto his chest. It looked like he should quickly recover, but it would change the outcome if it were to fester.

Poheko's loose-fitting shirt reflected the crimson-colored bloodstain. The sight left even the hardiest of men trembling with regret.

Menawah brought over a bottle of whiskey, and Poheko took a long swig. Korru took the shirt off his friend and washed some of the blood off in the stream. He wrung it out and flipped it over a bush, then returned to the wounds. Jacob had a scarf in his saddlebag and handed it to Korru. The brave ensured the arm was as clean as possible, then tightly wound the scarf around Poheko's arm. The claw marks down his neck were deep, but the blood flow nearly stopped when Korru finished bandaging his arm.

Jacob stressed, "You are lucky the cat didn't go for your neck. You might not have made it."

Korru looked at the dead cat and, in one smooth motion, knelt beside it and began to skin it. He was skillful at removing the hide from the animal's body with his razor-sharp knife. After a few minutes, the hide was nearly clean of meat, and Korru rolled it up and tied it to his horse.

Menawah spoke only a few words to him and then turned to Poheko and asked the same. Poheko nodded, and the Chief turned to Jacob and proclaimed, "We should leave this place. The spirit of the cat remains."

He pointed to the carcass of the dead animal lying on the ground. Jacob had heard about the mystery surrounding a dead lion, something to do with the animal's soul, and all agreed to move on.

Not long after they'd moved away from the stream, Jacob told the Chief, "We should camp. It's still too far to make Atiketiv by nightfall. It will be a short ride tomorrow."

They rode on in the drizzle for more than an hour, well away from the place of the attack. Jacob saw a small clearing and a stream nearby, deciding it was as good a place as any to establish their campsite.

The disciplined Braves had a system that was quick and efficient in setting up camp, catching fish, building a fire, and retiring for the night. Jacob and the Chief watched the whole process flow as smoothly as water in a brook; Poheko was able to move without affecting his injury. He insisted on helping, and although slow and meticulous, the Braves got the job done. The group sat for a while and discussed how things used to be. Before the war, there was fear of only the British soldiers and not of other white people. Now, there were few men, even from the Americas that the natives would trust.

Menawah paused momentarily, held up the bottle to Jacob, and said, "You - I trust." Jacob smiled. He, too, trusted Menawah. No matter the place, many rituals honored Creek beliefs similarly.

Jacob rose from his place by the fire and held out the bottle of whiskey to Korru and Poheko. "Thank you," he said as he handed it to them. Korru accepted the bottle with a nod and took a swig. He offered it to Poheko, who did the same. When he returned to the fire, the Chief had retired to his bedroll to sleep.

Jacob was grateful not to have to lie in the rain. The shelter was crude but effective. He threw another log on the fire, then laid down to sleep.

20. Uncommon Handshake – 1798

Menawah was up with the sun as always, welcoming the daylight and a clear, spectacular sunrise, on his way to the creek to wash. Jacob sat up and stretched. A wide yawn graced his otherwise smushed face. He scratched at his beard, hesitating a moment to take in the brilliance of the day. He paused, contemplating how important this day was as a pang of uncertainty ran through him, feeling the strain. His eyes were focused on the horizon when Menawah came back, and Jacob's distracted stare continued.

Menawah spoke, interrupting his daydream. "Do not worry, friend. Our hearts are open, and Rakke'Taf will see us."

His words held a ring of prophecy as he spoke, soft and low. Jacob knew most natives took the time to see deeper into a man's soul than other human beings.

Whether it was a gift they possessed or just a deep-rooted understanding, the Indian culture could measure a man without words ever being spoken. Jacob acknowledged with half a smile and raised one eyebrow, but the reassurance didn't stop the chaos inside him. Menawah was a brilliant man, which made Jacob feel insecure; he was grateful to ride with him, hopeful they would soon be at ease.

Despite the attack of the previous day, Poheko moved slowly and carefully but seemed to be handling his injury as expected, bravely. Jacob looked at him and rubbed his arm, communicating without words, showing he was concerned about the puncture wound. Poheko picked up his elbow as if to show it to him. He walked over and slowly untied the scarf to get a look at it in the sunlight. It was red and swollen. The punctures concerned him because it could easily fester if deep, leading to a far worse outcome.

Jacob poked at it but didn't know what he expected from his actions. Poheko flinched under its pressure while Jacob nodded. He re-wrapped the arm, then gave a pat to Poheko's back. They parted, Jacob silently hoping someone could treat it when they got to Atiketiv.

Setting out, Jacob estimated they were only two or three miles away. As they drew closer to the encampment, Menawah looked to Jacob for guidance. He suggested Korru and Poheko stay behind until he and Menawah could initiate the greeting.

They both dismounted and walked into the camp, quickly being surrounded by various members of the tribe.

Some greeted Jacob with smiles, and others stared suspiciously at the pair, but neither Menawah nor Jacob felt threatened. Menawah spoke to a young man in Creek, who nodded and trotted toward Atiketiv's gathering place. Rakke'Taf came walking towards them only minutes later.

The chief kept his eyes on Menawah as he approached. Jacob looked toward him and smiled, giving a slight nod to satisfy the piercing glance that made him regard the chief respectfully.

He lowered his head and addressed the chief. "Please let me introduce Menawah, another Creek leader forced to leave his ancestral lands."

Menawah put out his hand, as it is a custom for the visitor to make the first acknowledgment. Rakke'Taf put out his hand to meet it, and although it was not common, the chiefs united with a hardy handshake.

The two made their way to the gathering place and sat. Rakke'Taf offered to share his smoke. They talked and smoked for quite some time. Jacob stood back and let it happen, but cautiously approached the two leaders, remembering Korru and Poheko.

"Sir, we have two men, hunters, waiting for us; one of them has suffered an injury," he said quietly. Rakke'Taf

213

gave a decisive nod, and Jacob moved to where he could see them and waved them in.

Jacob asked for the help of others in the encampment to assist Poheko and tend to his injury. One of the young Indian girls who recognized Jacob from a previous visit came and offered to clean and dress the wounds. Her name was Wenetef; she was kind and gentle; graciously tending to Poheko.

She led them to a tent-like shelter and helped Poheko down onto a grass mat, layered with burlap and animal skins. She went to work, fashioning a poultice of herbs and made sure she washed off all the dried blood around the punctures, then wrapped the injury up tight. She took a minute to clean the claw marks, knowing an animal's claws carried a lot of nastiness with them. Poheko was very grateful for the help and, using his hands tried to say, "Thank you."

Wenetef looked up at him, just glancing, but refused to let his eyes make contact with her own. Korru came closer. He spoke very softly to Wenetef so as not to startle her. Then she smiled briefly amid her concentration on her job. She kindly tended to the patient, smooth and calm, as if she were stirring a pot of stew. When the young girl finished her doctoring, she gave Poheko a short nod and left the shelter.

The two chiefs smoked, drank, and shared stories. Menawah told him of the fight with the white men who killed off most of his tribe, and the reason they were homeless and searching. The story was a sad one, as Menawah, as well as many others in the tribe, lost family members in the battle that crippled them. Rakke'Taf nodded in understanding but was apprehensive to just let them move in. Jacob had been standing nearby the whole time and knew the reason for the tension between them. The blending of tribes was a serious matter, but in this case, it was about surviving; survival for these Creek people.

Jacob came close to them, waiting to be acknowledged. Menawah looked at him and said to Rakke'Taf in the native Creek language, "Jacob would like to speak." They both paused for a moment, giving Jacob their full attention.

He started hesitantly. "Perhaps the arrangement would be more as neighbors, live side by side for protection."

Jacob used his hands to gesture what he meant. Both chiefs gave a short nod to Jacob's suggestion, then went back to their original conversation. The words were more than just conversational, and Jacob could not follow. Indians were not inclined to tip their hand, so even a concerted effort to interpret what they were saying was utterly impossible. It was private, and he couldn't read the faces of the men.

Much time had passed awaiting the outcome of the meeting and the everyday activities of the tribe continued around them. It was nearing mealtime, a time in the encampment when everyone gathered and fixed food, ate, drank, and generally enjoyed the company of others. The preparation and serving were not underway because the uprightness of the meeting took precedence over everything else, and the native community knew it. It would dishonor the chiefs to begin stirring around them with tedious activities.

Finally, Menawah stood up. He kept his eyes on Rakke'Taf, awaiting the final decision. Then Rakke'Taf rose, nodding to the other chief, signaling an agreement. He spoke clear and loud in Creek, his voice solemn and profound. Korru helped to interpret for Jacob. Rakke'Taf's booming voice was heard above all things.

"We will give our friends refuge from the white men who destroyed their home. We will share our safety and our food with them. They will commune with us as one tribe. Welcome to Atiketiv."

The Atiketiv people mumbled and cheered all around the center of the gathering place as the words were acknowledged and accepted by the tribes.

Jacob, overjoyed, could now negotiate his freedom and solidify his home's security as well. If he were looked upon favorably by this new alliance, he would have no reason to fear them. He also did the Christian thing by helping preserve the remnants of Menawah's tribe.

Once the meeting adjourned, the meal preparations commenced. The buzz of activity began, and smells of roasted venison and cornbread were wafting through the camp. Menawah, Jacob, and the braves joyously accepted the delicious meal, as they had not eaten all day. It seemed the atmosphere in the camp was much lighter and more cheerful than Jacob had ever remembered. He was especially pleased, feeling the weight lifted from his shoulders, hoping this union will succeed. A union that would grant the opportunity for the Muskogee Creek tribe to flourish for years to come. He was proud of the fact he contributed to its success.

When the meal was complete and the families were settling down for the night, Jacob asked Menawah about the decision to join the other tribe. Menawah was somber, reflecting on the significant change to come. He took his time answering the question, choosing his words.

"I wished the attack on my people never happened, but time only goes forward. My wish now is to preserve my people." He paused for a moment and drew in a long breath. "Rakke'Taf is a good leader with strong braves. Our tribe will only make them better and stronger." Menawah tightened his fists and shook them in the air, expressing the strength of his resolve as he spoke. "We agreed this was best for both tribes. Becoming one. Beginning a new, stronger Creek tribe."

Jacob nodded in understanding. Then he spoke softly but clearly, "I'm sorry for your loss. I wish you well."

Menawah showed a smile. Well, as much of a smile as he ever had. Then he said in a shallow tone, not meant to be heard by others, "This was a gift of the stone." Jacob's head snapped in the direction of the chief. He never thought of it that way but without Andrea and the stone she wore, he would never have met the tribe; he never would have suggested the joining of the two tribes, and this alliance might have never happened. So, the truth of it was all because of the stone amulet.

21. Fear – 1798

After the chief's small party and Jacob left for Atiketiv, things around the encampment went on as usual. The day was blustery and gray. A welcomed change, as it seems Georgia was quite warm and uncomfortable most of the time.

Andrea tended to Johnny, who appeared to be over the worst of his ordeal. He slept on and off, which was likely for the best. He needed to heal. Herusa was exceptionally helpful, making sure Andrea had what she needed to tend to him. He was hesitant to get up off the sleeping mat and furs, but Andrea successfully coaxed him. Once standing, gave her a cautious look. She could see that although she was pushing him, he was grateful to see something besides the inside of the tent, and he agreed it was nice to have the breeze in his face, even if it was warm and muggy.

The two friends walked around the camp briefly as Andrea shared bits and pieces she had learned about the Creek people's lives over the past few days.

They made their way over to the horses, and, as expected, Johnny had a few words for Jack. Also expected, Jack accepted them, rubbing his ears against his friend.

"You damn mule. I hope you're happy now," Johnny said to him, giving Jack a scratch under his chin, and the mule leaned into it.

Johnny looked up, blinking against the reflection of the voluminous black clouds and said, "I smell rain." Andrea had heard that expression before and never really gave merit to it until now. She held her head up and closed her eyes, realizing she could smell it too. Andrea could see Johnny was ready to go back and lie down. He was weak and needed time to regain his strength. They returned to the shelter; he ate a bit and then rested.

A bit later, on her way back to her own shelter, Andrea found Lucas dragging a big limb to the wood-chopping pile. Assisting the man, she grabbed one of the branches, smiled cheerfully, and said, "Hello, Lucas."

He gave her a quick nod and said, "Good day, Andrea." They walked together as the rain began pelting their faces, now being pushed by the wind. Lucas did not falter and merely continued with his chore.

"Did you see? My friends, Jacob and Johnny, came to rescue me," Andrea told him with a giggle.

Lucas looked at her and raised an eyebrow, unsure what she meant by her comment. His demeanor was passive and gentle. Even though he had seen so much misery in his life, his eyes twinkled as he seemed to be reacting to her happiness.

"You not gonna stay?" Andrea gave a little snicker and rolled her eyes.

"No, I'm not. I had been in the woods, and I think Menawah didn't know where I came from, so he just kept me here. He surely doesn't trust me."

Lucas gave a quick snort. "That is so. Chief, don't trust nobody."

Andrea understood Lucas' remark and acknowledged it. "I hope when Jacob returns, we can move the tribe, then Menawah will let me go home."

Lucas nodded his head. "I hope so. You are a good lady."

Andrea smiled at him. "You are too sweet, Lucas." He smiled a shy smile, then wiped the rain out of his eyes.

The weather was now pounding down on them, and Andrea had had enough. "I'm leaving you now, Lucas. I'll come visit with you once this storm has passed." She broke into a trot, holding her skirt out of the forming puddles, heading to her teepee.

Wavering, Lucas finally decided to give up his chores. Most of the time, the storms would pass in an hour or less, and he could return to it, picking up where he left off. Leaving things "undone" didn't feel right to him, but working in the poor weather was not very productive either.

He tried to dodge the pelting rain when he heard the roll of thunder and a loud clap. Instinctively, he ducked his head and stepped up double time to get to the tent. Seconds passed after the rumble of the thunder shook the ground when everyone on the west side of the camp heard the blood-curdling scream. The menacing storm prevented anyone except Lucas from running out into it. He was either very brave or very ignorant but couldn't let someone be hurt or stranded without doing the right thing.

He ran out into the pounding rain, and an ominous lightning bolt cracked, coincidentally in the direction of the scream, which was also over by where the horses were kept. The animals were very spooked. Wind, lightning, and rain surrounded them, and there was no escape.

Lucas had trouble seeing where he was going but found the rope they were tethered to and followed it. Once he reached it, he spoke softly to the horses, trying to calm them, the look of terror in their eyes. At the end of the rope, he found one of the horses on the ground, unmoving. The pink color of blood spreading in the fast-forming puddle below the horse's neck and shoulder caught his attention; he was unable to see the wound but could smell the sulfur stench of burnt hair and skin. The animal had fallen on the side of her body where the lightning struck.

He went over to the mare and lifted her head, looking for a response, finding blood oozing from her ears and nose. There was nothing. No life. No snort. No darting eyes. Nothing. The horse was dead. Sadly, he thought that her quick death was a blessing over how she might have suffered.

He disconnected the rope that held the mare and tugged as hard as he could to get it away from the others. Losing a horse was a tragedy, of course, but Lucas was still in search of the source of the terrified scream. If it was the horse that caused the reaction, the person should have been nearby. So, who screamed?

Lucas couldn't find the source. He was distraught over the loss of the mare, boggled over how the tribe could lose one of their horses to an accident like this. He checked the chocolate brown mare once more for evidence of life, then removed the halter. Once the weather cleared, he would get help with the carcass to move it away from the other horses and bury it. He could just as well leave it to the wild animals, but he didn't want other predators to think this was a hunting ground.

It took more than an hour before the weather broke and the wind died down enough that the members of the tribe would wander out of their huts and teepees. Andrea heard the scream as well and was curious where it came from. She headed out of the teepee in the direction of the disturbance, just like everyone else. Instead of finding a scared or injured person, she saw Lucas and a couple of others tying a rope around the dead mare.

The sight of the poor animal and the massive puddle of blood that had formed under her was a lot for a girl to see. The untamed nature of the unexpected death was terrifying, but she tried hard not to show a reaction to the sadness of it. Andrea stood there in the rain, which had slowed to a drizzle, watching Lucas, Awahani, and another young man drag the horse nearly thirty yards away. They dug a hole, the small shovels having a time in the solid rocky ground. Andrea knew Lucas was heartsick for the mare. He'd spent much time with all the horses, perhaps more time with the horses than with any of the people. Once, she had a chance and was able to have a moment with Lucas; she said she was sorry for him and for the mare. Then she patted him on the shoulder and headed back toward her teepee.

Andrea walked along the path that had now been trodden down by daily use, catching a sight out of the corner of her eye. A young native girl, who she guessed to be around sixteen, was on her knees just outside her teepee in the mud, soaked through by the rain. It was peculiar, for sure. Andrea thought, *what would make her behave like that? It was not sensible.* She took her next steps very slowly, keeping an eye on the girl. She looked as though she had been crying; her breathing was irregular, and her head hung low.

Andrea decided she couldn't just leave her there and went to see if there was anything she might do to help. As she walked closer, the girl got up on her feet and stood, looking terrified, mud dripping from her dress, still not making eye contact.

"Are you alright?" She was a very pretty Indian woman with big lashes and almond-shaped eyes, now rimmed with red from crying. Andrea knew the girl didn't know English but felt she would understand the sentiment just the same. "Can I help you? Let's get you out of the rain." With that, Andrea put her arm around the girl's waist, gently cupped her elbow in her hand, and tried to lead her back into her hut. The girl wouldn't go. She was adamant that she was not going into that hut.

Andrea also shook her head and remembered her stubbornness at that age. She led the girl to the teepee she shared with Herusa to get out of the rain, if nothing else. Herusa was in the hut when the girls showed up, and Andrea asked her to talk to the girl and find out what the problem was.

Herusa asked her question after question in Creek, all the while her expression changing from fear to shock, then sadness, then more questions. Andrea couldn't wait to hear the story. Herusa held up the girl's chin so she could look her in the eye, then hugged her tight.

Andrea felt she shouldn't be there but had rescued the girl. Herusa turned to Andrea and said, "Her name is Ehmeti. A man lie with her during the storm. She did not want this." Andrea's chin just about hit the floor of the hut.

"What?" she said, deeply curious about whom would do such a thing.

`Herusa continued, "It was a stranger who came to her. He took out his knife and frightened her. He lie with her." Her words sounded almost matter-of-fact, but both Andrea and Herusa could not be more surprised by the news.

"Oh my God," was about all Andrea could muster. "She was the one who screamed. She was asking for help, and nobody understood!"

Andrea asked Herusa, "What do we do now?"

Herusa answered slowly, letting out her stress with a big sigh. "I will talk with her mother. She will know what to do." In Andrea's mind, they must catch this guy.

"Should we go try to find him? What if he comes back?"

Herusa shook her head, still in shock. "We can't. Braves need to do it." Andrea was fine with that course of action, knowing some suffering was about to take place, and it won't be Ehmeti.

Herusa got a blanket for Ehmeti and sat her down. There was some Creek conversation going on, but Andrea knew it was just offering a distraction and some small talk to sway Ehmeti's thoughts. That was the best thing she could do under the circumstances.

A short time later, Herusa came back, leading Ehmeti's mother by the hand. There was a flurry of hugs and kisses, loud jabber back and forth, and eye-to-eye contact with Ehmeti. Her mother took her back to the hut where she came from, assuring Herusa the search party would find the random intruder who happened upon the transient Creek village.

Uneasiness shrouded the camp that day. For Andrea, she was fearful of a man who would do such a violent thing on a whim. She thought of just how appalling some people were in her time. Robbing stores, violence against families, drugs, and, of course, sex trafficking. *They're everywhere.* The thought made her a little sad. Andrea felt even more vulnerable since Jacob was gone, then just as quickly, she comforted herself with the fact that Johnny was there. Having him around made her feel more secure.

Andrea grabbed a blanket and wrapped it around herself. She walked again along a trodden path that circled other huts and closer to the gathering place. She went to check on Johnny, still convalescing, wishing for his company. She found him lying on his sleeping mat, throwing a cup in the air, and catching it with his hand.

"Hello there," he said, seeing her pop through the doorway. "That was some storm, wasn't it?" Andrea nodded. She mumbled under her breath a bit, although Johnny heard her words just fine.

"You have no idea."

Johnny stopped tossing his cup and looked at her. "Why, what happened?"

Andrea was bubbling over the facts of the story like hot water spewing out of a tea kettle. When she got to the part where she found Ehmeti squatting in the rain and the mud, a tear formed in the corner of her eye.

"It was such a horrible thing to happen to such a sweet young girl." Andrea's gave away her deep feelings of fear and sadness. Johnny sat, watching the tears rolling down her cheeks, not knowing what to do or say. Finally, he broke the silence.

"I'm sorry, Andrea. I'm sorry, there are awful people in the world." He remembered the day Andrea came to their camp with injuries from an attack. He thought her tears were left over from that time and maybe muddled together with tears for Ehmeti.

She wiped the moisture off her cheeks and breathed in deeply. "It's just ... so sad." Johnny grabbed one of her hands and made her look at him. He had such a kind demeanor. You could tell he and Jacob were related. They both were always ready to do the right thing and protect those they cared for. The thought made Andrea smile.

"You're so kind, Johnny. I'm thrilled to have you here – with me." She smiled at her friend with the slightest glimmer of a tear lingering in the corner of her eye. Sitting quietly with Johnny, she felt more connected to everything around her. Maybe it was that this place wasn't cluttered with cars and people and material things. No lights or noise to warp the mind, either. It was quiet and clean. Clear. She drew another breath and closed her eyes, calming the chaos fluttering around her.

Johnny was in the mood for conversation, and he kept Andrea talking for quite some time. He spoke of his childhood, pranks, and his parents; he asked Andrea about her upbringing. She thought about it, swirling ideas through her head, deciding it wise to be very vague. Her story differed vastly from Johnny's, but she felt it was realistic enough to make the conversation interesting.

Then Johnny asked her about her brother. "Is your brother in New Orleans?"

Andrea let a hint of a smile curl up the corners of her mouth. "He should be home. He's...." then she hesitated. "Well, he's your age. What would you be doing if you were back home?" She thought fondly of her younger brother, his sandy blonde curls wild on his head. Images of him romped freely in her mind. She had been self-involved as of late and hadn't given much thought to her brother. She'd decided right then when and if she ever got back in her century, she would make it a point to spend more time with him.

She was much more at ease after sharing some time and a few stories with Johnny. The conversation, if nothing else, was a grand distraction from the recent disasters that plagued this tribe.

Like a doctor, she paused and took a moment to look at Johnny's wound. It was gnarly looking, but the puffiness and redness had subsided, and he was regularly moving it, which should help speed up his recovery.

"You've been a good patient," Andrea said, giving him a wink.

Johnny let out a noise with effort, attempting to laugh. "I didn't have much choice."

Andrea's eyes were more alert now, and with questioning in her voice, she looked at Johnny and just smiled. "Don't you ever think that things like your snake bite happen for a reason?"

Johnny looked up and scowled at her. "What? Why on earth would the good Lord want me to get a snake bite?" Andrea spoke softly, trying to calm him and quiet her laughter at the same time.

"I mean how you got a chance to slow down and look hard at things. Maybe this was how God chose to slow you down. Up until the Indians caught you, you thought they were enemies. But they're not, are they?"

Johnny gave a quiet laugh and tipped his head with a nod, understanding precisely what Andrea meant.

"I can't say that I agree, but I understand what you mean. Maybe that is a fact."

Suddenly, Johnny suggested they walk. He needed to get out and was indeed enjoying his conversation with Andrea. They walked along the paths that trickled between the huts and teepees splashing in the mud and listening to the dripping of trees and tents as the last of the rain made its exit. They came to the trail at the perimeter of the camp and walked mindlessly, uninterrupted. Andrea chose not to talk, still uneasy about the random stranger who took advantage of the sweet girl. Stealing her virtue by committing rape, and because of it, the poor girl might never have a positive relationship with a man.

As much as she might want to say or do something that could help her out of the dark pit of fear and anger, Andrea was afraid she couldn't. She only hoped the men in the tribe would hunt him down and make him pay for what he did to her.

They ended up at the far corner of the encampment where the horses were kept. Andrea knew exactly where the dead mare had fallen; she could still see the dark puddle where her blood spilled all over the ground. Naturally, Johnny sought out Jack and Babe, taking a minute to look them over and scratch their ears. He had been their primary caretaker and was a bit like Lucas, in that respect. Andrea watched him, admiring that aspect of her friend.

They walked a bit longer in silence, and Johnny worked out an idea, thinking about what might have happened to the stranger.

"I've heard of a single Indian who did something wrong and was forced from their tribe. Then they're all alone in the world. Truly alone. Maybe this is what happens to someone who is so painfully lonely." Andrea nodded but had no words for a response.

Although it had stopped raining, mud was everywhere, and Andrea wanted to remove her wet shoes. She returned to Johnny's hut with him and brought him hot tea. The walk was a good diversion, and it seemed Johnny thought so, too.

She left him to rest, wishing to go to her teepee to dry out and warm up. She promised she would be back later.

She made it to the quiet of her shelter and sat in her sleeping place alone in the stillness. Thoughtlessly, she rubbed the amulet, hoping it would show her some insight, even though the stone was never inclined to give her answers. She let the stone interpret the aftermath of the day.

It was so peaceful in the quiet of her space, wrapped in a blanket. Her feet began to warm, and she continued to reminisce, enjoying the placidity. A peace she'd never experienced in her life. Her mind and body slowed, and she felt "entranced." That's when it happened.

Again, Andrea saw visions of things she couldn't explain. There was an Indian brave, for sure. Only he wore a brown shirt and had yellow streaks of face paint. There was pain in his eyes, so much so it saddened her. She would have never imagined such a thing until she heard Ehmeti's confession. The man she saw was covered in blood, and he was sad. Tears were streaming down his face. Then she saw Chelsea so happy she glowed. She saw Miss Josephine, who smiled at her and nodded as well, exposing the satisfaction of revealing another truth.

The stone let go of Andrea very gently, and there she was again, sitting alone in the quiet, picking up where she had left off, relishing the peace. As she began to regulate herself to her surroundings again, she could hear very acutely. She heard a bird in a tree a hundred yards away. She could hear women chattering in the gathering place, which was almost as far a distance. She felt the heartbeat of this tribe through the electrified air surrounding her. *What was the amulet telling her now?* She thought. She'd had such profound experiences since she had been brought to this tribe. In her heart, she knew it was the influence of the stone that rooted her so, binding her to these people. With all the chaos and unhappiness in the 21st century for her, it was a gift to have these luminous events envelop her like hugs from her friends.

She felt sheltered. Having a glimpse of what was in the future wasn't disturbing; it was empowering. Andrea became alerted to trapped emotions she'd been avoiding for years. A lot of things. She knew, in her heart, she had sidestepped the truth because it was uncomfortable. She also knew, sadly, she was comfortable ignoring it.

As she thought, her mind unloaded the trepidation and pent-up anger, suddenly feeling the need to fight back, to fight for her place. Determination swept through her like the wind blowing over the plains. Whether or not she could return to her time, she would fight against things that could bury her in fear or shame. Not anymore. Just face it and be done with it. Jumping into the past taught her to trust and not be afraid. Fear was a four-letter word.

22. Means to an End – 1798

Jacob proudly led the small party as they began their journey home, all the while planning the logistics of moving a village. The easiest route for a handful of men on horseback was by the Lofton farm and over the ridge, but that would not be feasible for the whole village.

Jacob knew it would be better to go around the ridge and cross the river. Although it would be nearly two days longer, it was the most intelligent choice for passage to their new home. He explained the suggested direction of travel to Menawah and why. The Chief accepted the suggestion, as it was a logical path, and although it was thought to be the safest route, none of them knew what lay ahead.

Jacob and Menawah were in the front of the group, backtracking the same way they'd come only two days before. The small party rode hard on the first day to get back to the farm for a hot meal and a warm, dry place to sleep.

Poheko seemed to be healing well. The care Wenetef had given him was precisely what he needed. The men avoided stopping at the place where they had encountered the lion on the previous trip, only stopping long enough to relieve themselves and water the horses. It was early evening when they made the last bend in the road and could see the house. Relief paired with delight swept over Jacob as a smile grew on his face. There was nothing better than this view, looking toward his little farm.

Just as the group of travelers approached the house, Jacob saw Becca's silhouette in the window; firelight behind her emphasizing her features. She saw indistinct movement a short distance from the window, and realizing it was Jacob and the Indian party, she went out to greet them. She showed them her beautiful smile, lighting up the evening shadows.

Becca approached Jacob, kissing him gently. She whispered, "How did it go?" Jacob smiled at her unchecked behavior, thinking she was brave for being so forward.

"Very well. It looks like we're moving a tribe."

Becca was proud of her husband, knowing he helped them find the middle ground. If this was not an agreeable resolution, there is no telling what might have happened. The tension might have been too great, and the consequences of a potential disagreement loomed large.

Jacob was confident that Johnny, Andrea, and he would be released once they were safe at Atiketiv. Becca was relieved. She had only met the natives briefly, and they didn't seem hostile. She hoped that they would appreciate Jacob's gesture and consider their family, friends to the tribe.

Jacob led their guests back to the paddock to feed and water all the horses. Becca readied a meal, enough to feed them all heartily. It was a feast fit for a king or maybe a chief. She served the guests and took what was left for Jacob and herself. The natives went to the barn loft, leaving Jacob and Becca alone again.

She cleaned the dishes and wiped down the little table, and the two sat quietly and listened to the night sounds of the Georgia twilight.

Becca said, "I've got news," to Jacob in a very matter-of-fact way. Jacob was wary of such a broad term. It usually meant something big, like someone had died or her mother was coming for a visit. This time, though, it was happy news.

"I'm pregnant," she said, looking into her husband's eyes for his reaction.

He smiled a broad smile and nodded. "You are? We are?"

Becca nodded, wanting more than "you are" for an answer. "Are you happy for it?" The question lingered in her eyes as she searched Jacobs for an answer.

He moved in closer and hugged her warmly. "Of course I am!" Then he pulled her to his chest, feeling her warmth and absorbing her sweet scent. There were moments of silence between them. Becca became unusually uncomfortable, afraid of what he might be thinking. Then Jacob pulled away just enough to look her in the eye.

He swept back a loose tendril of her hair, getting a look at her face, then raised his eyebrows and said softly, "We're gonna need a bigger house." They both chuckled.

Korru, Poheko, and Menawah were awake and ready and had geared up the horses as well. Becca made porridge and honey, a quick and easy meal for travelers. Jacob said his goodbye and told her if all went well, he would be home in about a week. Andrea and Johnny, too. He added it would hopefully be the last time he would have to leave her for a while. A plethora of work needed to be done, and he couldn't wait to start.

After taking the trails and paths from the farm to the camp and back again, it was now thoroughly marked. Jacob thought he could ask Menawah if he would let Johnny and Andrea go so they could be with Becca, and Jacob would accompany them to Atiketiv. He thought again, and decided that helping the tribe with the move would show his alliance in a kinder light.

By late afternoon, the small party returned to the transient tribe's camp. They were greeted by many, including Hesaket, who bowed respectfully to his Chief. Menawah nodded, acknowledging the Indian brave he'd put in charge. Jacob knew he would speak to him, and possibly others in private once they were settled.

Jacob saw Andrea smiling at his return. Johnny was by her side, and although he was pale and still recovering, he seemed well.

"Hello!" Andrea blurted excitedly, searching in his eyes for answers to the questions she had regarding the events of the past few days.

"I trust all went well?" Andrea looked at the travel party, trying to get a feel for the emotions, simultaneously asking the question. Jacob nodded before Johnny and Andrea could see the satisfaction on his face.

Johnny walked to his brother, grabbing his arm and holding him to look into his eyes.

"Very glad to see you, brother," wrapping Jacob in a hug. He'd missed him and was fearful, unsure of the outcome of his visit.

The gathering place came alive with activity. The fire was built with enthusiasm and seemed more significant than usual. There were healthy portions of venison, bowls of fresh berries, and corn biscuits. A drink of berry juice laced with whiskey was brought out and shared with the tribal members. It was a treat that was only shared on special occasions.

Members of the tribe were joyous about the return of their Chief. Anyone could see his people greatly loved him, and from Menawah's point of view, he loved them. He alone bore the responsibility of protecting them, and the move to Atiketiv would help him facilitate that.

Menawah was ready to speak to the members of his tribe. Hesaket' began to chirp a war cry, a way of getting the attention of the entire tribe and keeping the happiness of the occasion wedged firmly in their minds. Howls returned from others in cheerful response. The circle around the bonfire, the center of the gathering place, began to tighten, people drawing closer.

A hush fell over the crowd; anxious faces filled with anticipation waited for his words, knowing the Chief had something important to share.

Herusa came close to Andrea and Johnny, helping to interpret the Chief's words for her new friends.

Menawah began to speak. "Our village that was attacked and destroyed will now find peace and a home. Tomorrow, we will break camp and move to Atiketiv, a village of the Muskogee Creek whose leader, Rakke'Taf, has welcomed us. Together, we will make one Creek people. And together, we will protect our newly formed tribe." The Chief spoke loud and clear, exuding optimism. "We will respect all and will be given in return the same respect. Be happy and celebrate our new beginning. We thank the great Mother."

When he finished, he smiled and raised his arms in the air. Howls and cheers of happiness were heard all around. It indeed was a joyous occasion. The tribe no longer needed to roam or run. Herusa was happy. Andrea could hear the excitement in her voice and knew she was anxious to travel. This time will be the last, as she will now have a place on this earth to call home.

The celebration went on into the wee hours of the morning. It was a different tribe now than had existed before the Chief had returned. In the firelight, Andrea noticed faces she had never seen before, knowing they had been coaxed out of their teepees and huts by the bigness of the event and the joyous news gladly shared by the Chief.

Andrea thought about the bizarre morning of the day before and wondered who would inform the Chief of the situation and the hunt for the lone attacker? As Andrea sat with her friends, Herusa and Lucas, and her newly found family, Johnny, and Jacob, she took a minute to update Jacob on the weird series of events from the previous day.

"Which way did he go?" Jacob asked with a hint of panic in his voice.

Andrea responded, trying to calm his nerves, "Well, he was over by the horses and on the west side of the encampment. My guess is he was going south and maybe west." Jacob concluded that what she said was logical, but he remained suspicious. He knew Becca could handle a gun and was not afraid to use it, but hoped she wouldn't have to.

Jacob was bone tired, having ridden many miles in the last few days. Johnny followed his brother to their tent, looking forward to a good night's sleep. Andrea, Herusa, and Lucas also decided to turn in, having had their fill of the festivities, knowing the next day would be taxing.

Andrea woke in the wee hours before dawn to the howl of a dog or a coyote. She hadn't heard it before since she had been in this camp, but she knew the creatures were around.

She rose from her bed in the thin shift she wore, feeling a chill from the light breeze that fluttered the leaves and pushed the bristly tops of the grasses all around the teepee. She pushed back the flap at the door and looked outside, curious about the night. The clarity of the deep blue-black sky took her breath away. Through the course of the evening, the clouds had cleared, making way for a nearly full moon to show itself. It cast a soft, pure white glow over everything. She could also see the sunrise as it approached and knew the camp would be alive with activity before long, so she cherished this quiet moment.

As she had predicted, the flurry around her began soon after waking. The atmosphere was crackling with excitement despite the long trek before them. Without looking, Andrea knew packing, food prep, and overall coordination of all the people and all their things was under way. This whole transition was simply a means to an end. The end of absence and insecurity. Andrea was now excited for them and herself. Her connection with these people was deep; her heart connected in ways she didn't understand.

It took hours before the tribe was ready. Menawah had sent out scouts to find a safe, logical path. Many different hunters had been out beyond the creek, which was a natural boundary for their current location, but they'd never looked at it through the eyes of the chief, a leader who was responsible for moving the entire fellowship of people over a long distance with the mindset of protection and preservation. This migration was different for them than before. When they left their ancestral home, they fled, taking what they could, leaving danger and battle behind. This time was joyous, joining more Creek and reforming a tribe.

When the scouts had returned, they shared what they believed to be the best path. Hunters with weapons would be scattered throughout the mass migration to ensure protection and to help. Slowly, the encampment began to clear out. One by one, the families took their place in the departure until the last villager was gone from the grounds. Menawah stopped to give thanks and offer a blessing to the place that held his people safely and securely during this time of transition.

23. Migration – 1798

The group of Creek Indians and the subsequent misfits traversed the countryside gracefully and with little to no complaints. The afternoon was warm and clear, and a light breeze swept away any discomfort the pounding sun's rays might have brought.

For most of the afternoon, the group paralleled the creek, which converged gradually with others to form a river. It was big and moved smoothly and swiftly, little sparks of sunshine glimmered gold in the waves that would allow it. Many of the group were talking. It would be necessary to know at some point about the difficulty of crossing the river. Logistics didn't allow them to make it any other way. Choosing a good place to cross safely was a high priority to the chief and the members of the tribe.

The wagon train of misfits had made good progress on their journey, but none had any idea of how far they had gone or still must go. Jacob had estimated the entire migration would be about fifteen miles in total. By his calculation, they'd traveled only five before they made camp for the night. They chose a meadow near the river but would post guards because the scouts had observed game trails in more than one place. If there were deer and elk nearby, there would be bears and mountain lions as well.

They set up camp without the burden of raising the shelters to keep it simple enough for a quick start in the morning. Besides, with the guards posted all around the camp, there was little chance of any danger coming to the people of the tribe.

Andrea unrolled her sleeping mat right between Jacob and Johnny. "I think I will sleep better if I have my guards beside me." Jacob gave her a suspicious glance, thinking she was exaggerating.

"Is that so?" he said, raising one eyebrow. He enjoyed teasing the girl as she continued to straighten the bedding but was satisfied with the sleeping arrangements.

A simple meal of venison broth and flatbread was served. Enough to fill the stomachs of the hungry travelers, yet easy to haul and cook. The three misfits ate together and were happy to converse with others. The evening passed quickly, and as soon as the sun fell beyond the horizon, the encampment quieted, embracing sweet sleep.

It seemed the majority of the village slept soundly, rising with the first hues of the morning beginning to lighten the sky. It looked as though it would be another cloudless day, Andrea was glad not to experience the misery of bad weather during this migration. The tribe picked up and organized quickly and continued their way. Lucas rode along with Andrea and Johnny for a while, and he embraced the promise of a new home. Andrea asked him, making small talk, "Do you think you'll still work with the horses in your new home, Lucas?"

He answered with a broad smile. "I hope so. The horses are my friends – just like you."

His answer so touched Andrea and she blushed. She reached over and touched his arm.

"You're too sweet, Lucas." She knew Lucas did not allow himself to get close to anyone for fear of suffering another loss. She wanted him to know she cared and to have faith in his fellow tribe members. He needed them.

The migration went along uneventfully for the better part of the morning. Menawah had hoped they could travel the better part of ten miles this day. Reaching their destination was paramount. The scouts stayed about half a mile in front of the caravan and would backtrack to relay any crucial variations to their trek. Hesaket, one of the scouting team, came back and stopped the train's progress. He searched for Menawah, and finding him, they conferenced. Jacob, curious, investigated the concern.

He came back looking pale. "You know the stray Indian that paid the tribe a visit the other day?" Andrea nodded nervously, watching Jacob's expression change from one word to the next.

"Well, they found him up ahead hanging from a tree. Not sure if he did it to himself or if someone else did, but he'll no longer be a problem to this tribe or any other."

Andrea dismounted and walked hesitantly to where the Indian was hanging. He was now entrusted to the Braves, who would respectfully prepare his body. Andrea looked at him with a distasteful frown. Most women couldn't handle such a thing, but this didn't bother her. He was dirty and appeared to have been living like an animal for some time. He had filthy greased down hair; long strands of it clung to his neck. His face had gashes on his eyebrow and his lips, and he wore a brown shirt. She realized he was the man in her vision. It must have symbolized something unobvious to her, whether his fate had been left to someone else or by his own hand.

Menawah asked the scouts to cut him down. First, so all the members of the tribe would not be subject to the gruesomeness of hanging; and second, every soul should have a decent burial no matter what evils possess it. The unintended delay gave the tribe a few minutes to water the horses and take a break from the droning rhythm of travel.

The Indian scouts dug a shallow grave and laid the haco-hake' man in it. Awahani explained to Andrea this meant "crazy," and although it seemed disrespectful, it was a term that helped the tribe deal with this cruelty. Then Hesaket went to Ehmeti, and her family and told them the reason the whole caravan came to a stop. Ehmeti's mother expressed her gratitude that they tended to the body and got it out of the sight of her daughter. Ehmeti listened. She did not raise her head, did not look at Hesaket, and showed no reaction to the death of the stranger. It was her mother's wish that her daughter would return to everyday life and the whole thing would fall by the wayside. Forgetting was not as easy as it sounded.

Jacob joined Johnny and Andrea, who were somewhere amid the chaos. "You both faring well?" Jacob said, tipping his hat with his brows raised curiously.

Johnny's injury, though healing well, was throbbing. He and Andrea took a minute while the caravan was stopped to unbandage and redress it. Andrea caught sight of some mountain mint, and she crushed it in her hands to break loose the oils in the leaves. Then, she dampened it with some cool water and pressed it to his partially healed wound. Although it was primitive, it slowed the throbbing with its cooling sensation.

Johnny responded to Jacob with a tilt of his head, "Yes, we're fine. I've got a caregiver companion, and she's taking good care of me." He smiled wryly, then winked at Andrea and glanced back at Jacob.

Andrea said to him, slowly batting her eyes, "Thank you, Jacob. Yes, it's fine. I'll be glad when this whole trip is over. Long days in a saddle is hard, even for the best of us."

The migration began again and resumed the same rhythm as before. The carts and wagons jolted along a very rough trail, made smoother by the time the end of the train experienced it. The caravan stopped again when the path ended at the river. Rocky outcroppings hung over their heads on one side and the river on the other. It was time to plan the crossing. Jacob had been thinking about this event all morning, as it would be the most dangerous part of the exodus. He shared with the chief what he thought would be the best place and suggested a particular order for everyone to cross. Menawah would ask the strongest braves to escort the families as they crossed, breaking it down into smaller pieces. Jacob looked closely and crossed the current himself, searching for a smoother avenue for the carts and wagons.

Once a pathway was decided and strong braves were in place, the families went one by one into the water and across the currents that pulled at them. The process was slow, but gradually, a cluster of people, animals, and carts began to gather on the opposite shoreline.

Jacob had crossed back and forth over the river several times, helping where needed and assuring nothing was lost to the current. He had just crossed it again, riding up the riverbank, turning to view another wagon in the middle of the river. He caught sight of something that broke loose and was being carried away on the waves. It was a child! The young boy was seen with his hands waving and splashing, and when his head popped up, he was gasping.

Jacob and Skeeter took off running downstream along the shore to get ahead of the floating toddler. He found a clearing that offered a good view of the water, then jumped off his horse and ran right into the current, stopping in the path of the floating child. It was a small boy who could be no more than two years old. Jacob reached out and grabbed at his arm, missing it entirely but latched on to the leg of his little breeches and held on. He pulled the boy close as quickly as he could, walking carefully back to the riverbank.

The child was terrified, coughing and sputtering, but otherwise unharmed. Once he recovered his breath, he began to wail fiercely. Jacob trudged out of the water with the heavy, water-logged bundle in his arms. He kept the little boy close to him and then grabbed Skeeter's reins and found his way back to the caravan.

The boy's mother was racing in his direction, crying frantically, gasping, and whining as a caring mother should. It was a happy reunion. The mother held the child so tightly the poor boy couldn't breathe. She put her hand gently on the side of Jacob's face and said, "En'ke' Futciayet." Jacob didn't know what that meant but later discovered it was "God's hand." Of course, Jacob appreciated the gesture, but truth be told, he could not have just let the baby float away. It surprised him that others did not even attempt to rescue the child.

The river crossing continued slowly until the last few families had finally made it to the opposite side. Besides the baby and a copper cup, nothing else had been lost to the rivers current. As the last of the people, horses, and supplies made it to the eastern side of the river, the scouts again took the lead and found the smoothest route forward. The afternoon went by quickly, as the endeavor had taken some time, but once the scouts had found a clearing large enough to accommodate them, the decision was made that this would be where they would spend the night.

The land here was more familiar to Jacob, and he knew the rest of the trip would take only a few more hours to reach Atiketiv and the other Creek tribe. They were merely a stone's throw away from the trail Jacob, Johnny, and Andrea had taken after they'd left the campsite by the sea; the whole area was the hunting and fishing territory the Loftons frequented.

The first action would be to find food and settle for the night. The band of Indians was getting proficient at setting up just enough to get them through till morning, allowing for quick and easy readiness. Andrea preferred to keep her bedroll between the two brothers, and they were happy to accommodate. Jacob rolled his eyes; however, he did understand how sleeping between them would make her more comfortable.

The usual bustle that happens around families and their bedtime routines was familiar, even in a different century. *How things are so different, yet surprisingly the same*, Andrea thought to herself. She flopped down on her bedroll and surveyed the activity in camp. Soon her eyes were drawn to the horizon, and she scanned the landscape as far as she could from left to right, then from the muted pink and orange colors of the sunset to the dusty trail they'd just covered. The feeling of contentment was blurred with one of astonishment. Andrea felt so far away from the life she'd left and so present here, now. It made her wonder whether she was supposed to be here, living in this century. *Is this my destiny?*

She delighted in the vistas and reflected on the events of the last few days. Despite a smattering of some very disturbing exploits, her sense of well-being was completely intact. This time in the world was a dangerous one, full of surprises, but Andrea, in this moment, was as secure as a baby in its mother's arms.

Herusa came over and sat by Andrea in her sleeping place. She was quiet, touching Andrea's hand without saying a word. Andrea also remained silent. It was as if Herusa knew where her mind was and respected her space. She likewise wanted to experience her peace. They sat together and watched the sunset and its full range of colors blossoming in the sky.

Herusa waited a long while for Andrea to speak. Breaking the silence, she said, "It's beautiful, isn't it?"

Herusa smiled and nodded, "the paintbrush of God." Andrea smiled, feeling her friend's sentiment echoed her own.

"No one could ever duplicate it," Andrea whispered, closing her eyes, feeling the depth of the peace around her.

It was almost dark when Johnny strolled over and sat beside the girls. The boys had been drinking whiskey, and Andrea and Herusa could see in Johnny's eyes that he had also consumed his share. He had a goofy smile on his face and smelled of it.

"Having fun, are you?" Andrea asked him questioningly.

Johnny courteously answered, "Yes, ma'am. Keeping up relations an' all." Andrea rolled her eyes and laughed.

"We'll see how you feel in the morning. Those relations just might come back to bite you." Johnny gave Andrea a sideways glance, still sporting the same silly smile as before.

"Are you saying you think I'm drunk?"

This time, Andrea laughed harder. "Yes, that is what I'm saying." Herusa raised her eyebrows at the statement but got a laugh out of that as well.

Johnny laid back on his bedroll, and Herusa said goodnight to her friend. Slowly, softly, as the breeze brushed the tops of the trees, the tribe settled and drifted off to sleep. Andrea was slow to fall asleep. She closed her eyes, but she didn't feel sleepy. She picked through memories of New Orleans that she hadn't recalled until now. They just flooded over her. She thought about the Café au' lait. She remembered Shakey's bar and the black walls. She recalled the pawn shop where she got the amulet. She remembered holding hands with Collin and his passionate kisses.

Andrea thought about their visit to Miss Josephine's. She recited in her head the words, Miss Josephine told her. *Seven of Cups tells us that you lack direction.* Then she recalled another flip of the cards. *The Queen of Swords will give you the clarity you crave.* It was a curious thing just how *accurately* Andrea remembered her readings and how she'd bought the stone amulet just before she went there. Maybe the reading she received was because of the stone she possessed. Or not. Did the magical trip into the past happen because of the cards and the stone working together? And what did she mean, *the stone chose you?* What did the fortune-teller know that she didn't? Whatever powers brought her here, this event in this time was, without a doubt, the most crucial thing Andrea had ever been a part of.

She decided not to let those thoughts haunt her as she considered the whole adventure to be a blessing. She did so many things she would never have done. She saw and experienced sights, sounds, and feelings that never would have touched her life. Andrea had a new perspective, not just on her life directly but on everything. She gracefully opened her eyes, and a smile broke out. *What a great life*, she thought to herself, then closed her eyes once more and was finally overcome by sleep.

*

The weary travelers rose, filled with excitement and nerves, knowing the convergence of the two tribes would happen today.

Andrea sat up in her sleeping place, watching silently for a minute. Many tribes would have killed each other, but these two chiefs understood their future depended upon making peace. It was a rare thing. But here was history, right in front of her. She shook her bedroll, and saw Johnny and Jacob gathering people and property back to the caravan, ready to set this day into motion.

"Good morning," she said.

Jacob turned and looked at her while tying his bedroll to the saddle on Skeeter's back. She could see little beads of sweat on his forehead. The morning air wasn't hot yet, but she could feel the sticky humidity thickening by the minute.

"Well, good morning to you, too. Looks like we're all in a hurry this morning," Jacob said, handing her a piece of jerky and the leather pouch of water. She was hungry, but no more than she had been since her appearance on the beach. She had learned that the convenience of food was not the priority– there were much bigger things happening than the morning meal.

"Thank you, Jacob. Can I help?" He looked at Andrea as she chewed on a piece of jerky. He *really* looked at her. The ruffled hair on her head was spitting little curls out in a halo all around it. She had pulled it back, but much of the shorter hairs had let loose from the strap and fell nilly-willy around her shoulders. She was not tall but stood statuesque, like she could move this whole group of people by herself. Proud and strong, not unlike the band of Indians. Jacob was suddenly struck with the honor of knowing her.

Then he looked into her eyes and said in a muffled voice, "It might be good to walk round the wagons and families to be sure we don't leave nothin' behind. They probably won't want to return here once they get to Atiketiv."

Andrea beamed brightly and said, "Aye, aye, sir." Jacob shook his head and wrinkled his brow in response to her funny remark. He grunted at her directly as she turned on her heels and left to see what help she could be to others.

Small children were a big concern for everyone who had them. Keeping a child busy enough to avoid trouble was a full-time job. Andrea realized that the expectations of the children from the mothers and fathers were vastly different in this era. She saw 7-year-olds work like young men; certainly not what you would experience in the 21st century. They were physically capable enough to perform many tasks that would make a modern man shudder.

However, even though they were stronger and braver, and much more willing, the rhythmic sway of a wagon and dusty silence could make them lose their attention pretty quickly, leading to trouble. Nonetheless, Andrea offered help to whoever might need it. From fetching water to tying up a goat to holding a baby while their parents were busy with something else. Her pleasant face was a welcome one around the members of the tribe.

Soon, the caravan was underway. The mood was light and cheerful, as cheerful as a group of misplaced Indians could be. Andrea rode alongside Jacob for a while and pummeled him with questions as the boredom got to her.

"How long do you think it is from here to Atiketiv?"

Jacob humored her. "Oh, about half a day, I think."

Keeping the conversation going, she asked, "Do you think the chief will let me go? I hope they'll let me go." Jacob allowed a smile to grace his expression but did not want Andrea to see it.

Jacob humored her. "The chief likes you and he is a good man. I'm sure he'll do the right thing."

Andrea wasn't sure about what the tribe thought of her and worried she would be looked upon as a threat because Menawah made her stay. She tried to open her mouth to speak again, and Jacob raised his hand to make her hold her tongue for a second.

"Please, can we just relax and enjoy the ride?"

Andrea stopped short and bit her lip to help her avoid asking more questions. She replied, "Sure."

Feeling rejected and fidgety, she gradually moved her horse closer to Johnny, who always seemed to be happy to converse with her.

Johnny had watched the discussion between Jacob and Andrea and was snickering, knowing how Jacob was. He expected that reaction.

"Don't worry," Johnny said softly, seeing the frustration on her face. "He's just concerned. It's important to him that this goes well. It will all be different this evening."

Andrea was a stubborn girl, and although she was "pissy" about how Jacob was to her, she completely understood what it was like to perform under pressure and thought it best to leave him be.

Johnny and Andrea talked about this and that. "How does your wrist feel?" Andrea asked with genuine concern in her voice.

Johnny held it up and looked at it, twisting it left and right. "Much better now, thank you."

Andrea responded, "Excellent."

She talked to him about Lucas. She added, "He is forever grateful, you know."

Johnny nodded. "He is a man with a kind heart. That's why the chief lets him stay. He's a hard worker, too." Andrea agreed with him about that. She remembered watching him and thought there was no time during any day that she didn't see him doing something. She thought to herself, *I bet he's exhausted.*

The blue skies were clear and beautiful. The sun was bright, and the heat of the day began to bear down on the caravan. Andrea gave little thought to the weather up until now. It was humid most of the time, but the endless sunshine and warmth was something she was sure to crave forever.

Sitting upon Jack, she listened carefully to the sounds all around her. Of horse's hooves and how the giant animals would occasionally blow out their big nostrils. Mothers talking to their children, whom Andrea was sure were asking, "Are we there yet?" She smiled, relishing the thought that this life was pleasant and simple. The simplicity of just being in the world.

It was nearly noon when Jacob rode back to find Andrea and Johnny. "We're almost there." He moved his head, twisting it in the direction of the front of the procession. "Johnny, come and help me. We need to keep them all back until we get instructions from Atiketiv."

Johnny gave a sideways glance to Andrea, who nodded to him, letting him know she would be fine. She frowned a bit, knowing she was very capable.

Finally, after months of not having a place to hang their hats, these Creek people could accustom themselves to a permanent settlement to call home. Andrea looked hard at them. Hope showed on their faces, along with the pain of departure from the old and the trepidation of the unknown. The chaos will finally end, and before them, a new beginning. Andrea stayed about midway in the long train of people, horses, carts, and wagons, not wanting any part of the politics of setting up their camp.

She had dismounted and stood, admiring the treetops as they swayed in the afternoon breeze, listening carefully to the comforting sound of the rustling leaves. The light wind was welcome, and the shade was even more so. Young mothers walked with their children, allowing them to scurry about like children should. One could feel the cohesive group relax, like taking one great big sigh. Their journey was nearly over.

The handful of braves, Menawah and Jacob, had returned, having received clear directions from Rakke'Taf about where the new members of the tribe will make their homes. It was left to the individuals to decide where to place their shelters and tents, as they had done the same thing repeatedly over the last few months.

Together with others from Atiketiv, the families slowly dispersed to various locations over about four or five acres. This settlement was amongst the trees and near a creek that flowed south. It was perfect.

The medicine man, Helsu'Este, performed a blessing on the grounds, as well as the creek nearby, giving thanks and saying a prayer for the health and prosperity of the tribe. The caravan gradually broke up, and the members of the tribe found a place for their teepees. There was plenty of room to spread out, but they all chose to stay close to each other.

This group had been through so much and faced many a foe. Their security was in the hands of their neighbors, and together, they made a village. It was a rare treat to see this blending of tribes, a monumental task.

As the Creek people were getting settled, Wenetef approached Andrea and touched her arm. Andrea swung around, surprised. "Oh, Hello!" She greeted her friend with a smile and a hug. The two girls stood side by side and watched as a warm feeling rose in their hearts. *It was indeed a good feeling to know they would be safe*, Andrea thought to herself. She was quite sure Wenetef felt it, too.

24. Honor or Dishonor - 1798

Menawah and his people were still getting settled as the evening approached. Rakke'Taf had a couple of Indian braves show the Loftons where they could sleep, and Andrea was brought to a teepee of her own.

Since the first time they'd met, Rakke'Taf was always kind to Andrea. She knew it had more to do with his belief in the stone amulet than anything else, or maybe he thought she was special because she had it. Nothing more than a coincidence, but why not accept it? At least he didn't treat her poorly. She was grateful for that.

The whole time the new arrivals were getting settled, the natives of Atiketiv had been preparing a welcome dinner for their extended tribal family. They had fed her well, but that was not how natives ate. As they approached the spread of food, Andrea knew big meals were for special occasions; this was one of them.

It looked like rabbit or lamb cooking in large stew pots; there was also flatbread, venison, fresh bowls of berries, carrots, and other root vegetables. The meal appeared to be a weeks' worth of food prepared graciously for a celebration. Andrea's thoughts brought her back to her family's

Thanksgiving meal. She decided this was better than that. She had just enough time to look around at the spread of food and the people who prepared it before she caught sight of Jacob and Johnny.

Jacob looked tired but the good kind. He'd spent the afternoon helping carry tents, supplies, and belongings for people and made numerous trips. Johnny made eye contact with Andrea first. He smiled; his blonde hair shone bright in the oncoming sunset, emphasizing the brilliance of the colors it exhibited. She smiled a broad smile as she was always happy to see him and his delightful countenance. Jacob winked at her as they strode across the gathering place to address her.

"They went all out, didn't they," Andrea said to them. Jacob's face looked as though his mind was trying to wrap itself around her strange words. She realized then her statement was something that wouldn't have the same kind of meaning in this century.

Jacob savored the words, then muttered, "They surely did," swallowing hard.

The villagers of Atiketiv appeared to be dressed in their best. Hair was combed and braided or pulled back neatly. Their clothing was primarily made of hides, but some of the women wore cotton dresses with linen aprons, ready to welcome this gangly group. The sense of fellowship and belonging was evident.

Hesaket' walked up to Rakke'Taf and said something to him, then darted past the three of them in a hurry. Jacob didn't hear enough to be able to interpret it, but he thought Hesaket's duty was to summon the others to come and feast with them. A few moments later he discovered his guess was correct.

Menawah's people filtered into the gathering place, cautious and guarded, wary of how they would be accepted. Some sidelong glances were shared, and a few greeted the newcomers openly. It reminded Andrea of a church dinner, and she suddenly brought it to mind; in reality, it was these people's church. Then she smiled.

Rakke'Taf and Menewah stood together as Helsu'Este said something before the meal. It was maybe a welcome message or a blessing, but either way, people began to help themselves to food. The weary travelers were allowed to get their food first, a sign of solidarity and peace that made Andrea happy. The chiefs stood side by side and waited to fill their plates with food until the end, attempting to make the new tribal members feel welcome.

Once dinner was finished and new friendships and acquaintances were forged, the drums came out, and the combined groups started dancing. Some of the dancers wore bells and trinkets that would "clink" together as the dancing created music. It was a cheerful time, Andrea stood back and took it all in. She was witnessing an art that had been a part of the native culture for centuries. But she got to see it in person, the way the tribal celebrations used to happen. It was breathtaking. Andrea had to choke back tears; influenced by what she knew the future held for these people. She had to push it back in her mind, so she could enjoy the festivities, watching older men and young children, women and warriors, all joining in the dancing, drumming, and chanting. The heady celebration broadened smiles and lightened their hearts.

Andrea found Awahani in the crowd and gave him a pat on the shoulder. He smiled, obviously enjoying the celebration.

Andrea asked him, "What are they saying?" knowing there was symbolism and tradition in the dancing and chanting they do.

Awahani stood a bit taller just then and said, "They're wanting the great Mother to hear them. There are no words, just praying from the heart."

Awahani thumped his chest in obvious pride.

Andrea nodded her understanding. The tribe's connection to the earth was what bound them to their people. Simple and true.

The night went on, and of course, the celebration involved drinking. What type of celebration didn't? Andrea and Herusa were side by side watching the dancing when suddenly, she realized the commotion behind her. Andrea and Herusa turned just in time to see multiple braves dive into a brawl.

There was shouting and kicking, and an outnumbered tribal member in the middle of it. The Atiketiv people were outraged and tossing about, not giving heed to anything going on around them. Without notice, Andrea was swept off her feet, lying on her back in the dust, the brawl now, literally on top of her. Other bystanders were either kicked or knocked down, the brawlers entirely oblivious to the damage caused to the crowd.

Finally, after shouts and directions from the chief, the fight broke up, and everyone got a glimpse of who was in the middle of it. Hesaket. Andrea was shocked. He was Menawah's second in charge. What did he do to make them gang up on him that way?

Andrea took an inventory of her injuries, and despite a bloodied elbow and a scrape on the side of her head, she seemed generally unharmed. Andrea and Herusa stayed close by while the rather loud debate was taking place. Andrea would have been entirely excluded from the conversation had it not been for Herusa's translation. She was unable to translate all of it, as she was a relatively new English speaker but communicated with Andrea as best she could.

"Hesaket was showing a young girl, Onawa, too much attention, and Harjo, the brave who had been courting her was very angry." Herusa spoke quickly and quietly so others would not condemn her for the interruption. "This is not done in a tribe. Atiketiv is very angry."

Andrea got it. Hesaket was unaware she was spoken for and did what boys do; he flirted. But this was not the time nor the place for such a thing. It was poor judgment on his part.

Andrea looked at Herusa, a little distressed. "She knew Hesaket was a trusted confidante of Menawah's, but the decision of his punishment would be left to Rakke Taf' and it was unconditional. Rakke'taf was the one in charge, and it was an Atiketiv maiden who was amid his attentions. Rakke'taf stood stoic and would have none of it.

The chaos had turned to silence from all parties, and Rakke'taf spoke clearly and intentionally. He addressed all the people, but his eyes were focused on the newcomers.

"We come together in peace and joy; we all are Muscogee people. Respect our ways. Honor our women and our families. This man's actions were dishonorable. The brave, known as Hesaket will be banished from Atiketiv'. We must not see him; where he goes or choices he makes. Go now from Atiketiv - do not return."

Andrea's jaw dropped open, shocked by the abruptness of the chief. She was saddened for him. He was paying attention to the girl, not violating her. The situation was more than she could comprehend. *These people are so stuck in their traditions and customs, but he's human and not perfect.* He made a mistake! Andrea reasoned with herself, trying to tip the situation in Hesaket's favor, but it was too late. The next thought that came to her was that of the dead native man in the brown shirt. *He was probably alone in the world, too, and look what happened to him!*

This internal outburst she kept to herself for her own good. After hearing Rakke'taf's final decision, the celebration cooled off, and people began to separate and go to their teepees and huts. It was a long and wonderful afternoon that ended so violently, making Andrea feel uneasy. Such a broad swath of emotion in such a brief period. She walked with Herusa back to her teepee. They said goodnight, and now, in the darkness, Andrea stood at the door of her teepee, quite alone.

She had a cup with some water in her teepee that was brought to her just after they'd arrived, and Andrea used it to clean up. She took a corner of her skirt and wet it so she could wipe the dirt off her face. After using what little water there was in the cup, she decided to walk to the creekside to use fresh water.

"This darn thing will just get infected if there is any dirt left in there," she mumbled. Her dress was disgusting, and she wished she had clean clothes. Andrea stuck her whole head in the water of the creek. It was shockingly cold, but it felt good to immerse her head and to be able to run her fingers through her hair and freshen up as best she could. She spoke to herself, frustrated. "In a couple of days, hopefully, I'll be back at the farm and can get a proper bath." She craved the bath she took in the little tub provided by Becca, whom she missed just then.

Andrea was hunched over, wringing out her hair and extracting as much of the water as possible before she went back to her teepee. She stopped suddenly, listening intently to a rueful sound. Dismissing it, she began fussing with her

274

hair once more, then she heard it again. She listened closely and thought it sounded like crying. Soft and quiet but sobbing for sure.

Once she was able to throw her hair back where it belonged, she looked around, investigating. She understood that among the many strangers, a person could sneak off to have a good cry, but what if it was a child? She couldn't leave it be. She walked along the creek in the direction she thought the sobs were coming from. Then she caught sight of a young girl, just behind a rather large tree, sobbing. She felt for her.

Andrea spoke softly as she approached the girl so she wouldn't alarm her. "Are you alright?" The girl looked up at her, startled. She didn't see Andrea coming toward her.

Andrea put her hand up. "It's all right. I won't hurt you. I want to be sure, you're okay."

The girl was beautiful and had one rather large braid down her back, and big alligator tears streaming down her face.

She looked at Andrea, wiping away a tear with the back of her hand, still blubbering and said, "Okay." Andrea thought she was either responding to the question or mimicking her, not knowing how many English speakers there were in the tribe.

She extended her hands to the girl and said, "Can I help you?" The girl looked at her blankly, then shook her head as if she was shooing a fly. She recalled that morning when Ehmeti was all alone in the mud and crying. *God*, Andrea thought, *I hope it's not the same thing.*

Andrea decided to get Herusa and see if she might translate for her. The shelter Herusa was in was close by, and Andrea hoped she managed to find the right place in the dark.

She called her name from outside the teepee. "Herusa," she said in a loud whisper. Andrea waited a minute, then she saw motion in the teepee.

"I'm here," Herusa answered.

Andrea spoke again. "It's me." Herusa moved the skins that hung in her doorway. Andrea looked at her with pleading eyes, "Can you come? I need help understanding." She saw Andrea's concerned expression and followed her.

On their way to the Creekside, Andrea filled in Herusa on what she found near the creek, and hoped the girl was still there. She led Herusa over to the tree and found the girl there, still distressed and sobbing, alone in the dark. Herusa made her way over to the girl and squatted beside her. She said something to her in Creek, and the girl responded.

Herusa spent a few minutes talking with the girl as Andrea observed the conversation. Then Herusa signaled to her to come and sit with them. Herusa said something, then touched Andrea's arm.

The young girl nodded with acknowledgment, and Herusa said, "This is Onawa. She is sad because it was her fault Rakke'taf banned Hesaket." Andrea was relieved to hear this because, in her mind, she saw a similar situation to the attack on Ehmeti.

"So, what happened?" Andrea said to Herusa looking for the answer.

"Onawa was watching and smiling at him and should not have."

The beliefs and traditions that were the backbone of the Native American culture were primitive, but ones the tribe stood by unwaveringly.

Andrea shook her head, disapproving. "She has to tell the chief."

Herusa shook her head, then told her, "The chief is her uncle."

Andrea blinked in disbelief. "Oh," she said in a sympathetic voice, deciding there is more to it than just tribal politics. "It's personal. No wonder he blew a gasket." Andrea tried hard not to share her thoughts, though she was distressed at how rigid the people were of this time.

She patted the girl's shoulder and stood up. "Maybe I should talk to him."

Herusa shook her head, keeping her eyes on the ground. "Not good. It will not be good."

Andrea turned her eyes toward the creek, saying softly, "Well, we have nothing to lose, Hesaket is a good man."

She said, "Thank you" to her friend for stepping in and nodded to Onawa. She wanted to tell the girl everything would be okay, but shied away from making eye contact with the girl, as she felt it would give away her feelings of doubt.

Andrea knew talking to the chief was the right thing to do, but didn't know if he would see her. After all, she was only a woman, but she hoped he would see her as a guest. Taking in a deep breath and letting it out all at once made her suddenly feel exhausted.

Looking at Herusa, she said, "I've got to go lay down. Will you be, okay?" Herusa tipped her head in agreement, then Andrea looked Onawa in the eye and touched her shoulder and said, "It will all be fine." Then she turned to Herusa, with a nod, and departed for her teepee.

Shuffling back on the path, Andrea *thought, there is nothing we can do for her or for Hesaket. It's what the chief wants.* And with almost the same rationale, Andrea had thought about how Rakke'taf took a liking to her. *Perhaps I could be the one to change his mind.*

She approached her teepee, still stumbling over the feeling of helplessness. *Why am I fussing over this anyway? It's not my fight.* Andrea spent some time struggling with internal dialog, feeling overwhelmed, and wishing to do the right thing. She sat in the quiet and picked at her nails, frowning, then it went away as her mind flew blindly through thoughts of what could happen with Hesaket. It did not sit well with her. She fumbled with her nearly dry hair, laying on her bedroll, frustrated. She knew Hesaket well enough to know, however his intentions were perceived, he was not that kind of person. Without thinking, Andrea laid her hand on the amulet, her mind laboring through the recent events.

She drifted off to sleep, truly exhausted. The rigors of the last couple of days had been grueling, and she hadn't given it any thought until now. She slept without interruption and didn't wake until she heard stirring outside her teepee. She lay there on her back, staring up at the peak of the teepee, watching the gray-blue sky gradually lighten as the sun began to move higher in the sky. She recalled the conversation from the night before and wondered about Herusa and Onawa. The thoughts tumbled about in her mind, making her restless.

Andrea went to the teepee that was now Herusa's home to see what had taken place after she'd left the girls the night before. Herusa was gone. She stood at the door flap and looked out at the newly formed camp, in awe at the continuity of the two tribes, then refocused on trying to locate her friend.

She moved about the teepees and huts slowly, considering where she might be. After rounding a corner, distracted by two young boys fighting, she nearly bumped into Herusa.

Then she smiled, embarrassed. "Oh, there you are." Andrea sounded a little startled. "How was the rest of the night?" Herusa gave Andrea a slight nod and continued to her own teepee.

"She went home." Her answer was short and direct. Andrea turned to follow her friend hoping she would elaborate.

Andrea looked at Herusa, catching her gaze. She stopped wondering about Onawa for a moment, touching her friend's shoulder. "Thank you for being there to help her. I wish I could have done something more." Andrea wanted her friend to know she was happy to have her assistance.

Herusa said, "I help a friend."

As Herusa continued rummaging through her basket, Andrea said, "But ..." The native girl turned and looked at Andrea, tired of the conversation. "What will happen to Hesaket?"

She investigated Herusa's eyes with genuine concern and watched her blink hard. She tilted her head slightly, then said, "He may find another tribe. He may stay alone. Is up to Hesaket." Herusa's remark was very matter-of-fact. Andrea understood this was the way of the tribe, but her thoughts were still sprinkled with uneasiness. Herusa headed out her door and disappeared around another teepee and was gone.

By the time Andrea returned to her teepee, activity was happening all around the camp. She just stood and watched the village come to life. It was already a village and after the move, a much bigger one. Rakke'taf's house was on a mound just down the way from the gathering place and rested above all the others. It was the most permanent shelter there and the biggest. She wished there was something like it for Menawah but knew he very likely would now be taking orders from Rakke'taf to keep the peace. He may be assigned "second in charge," but that was up to the politics of the tribe. As she took in this communal atmosphere, she wondered if Hesaket's actions would have had any impact on how Atiketiv would accept Menawah. After all, it was one of the braves from his tribe who upset the balance.

Andrea sat in her sleeping place and ran her fingers through her hair. When it was smooth enough, she pulled it back into a ponytail and wrapped a leather thong around it. She took off her dress, which was an absolute mess, and shook it out. She held it up, targeting any blades of grass, dust, and dirt, swishing away the imperfections, trying to improve its look.

After satisfying herself with its appearance, she put it back on. The only looking glass was the water, so she went to the creek to find a place to see her reflection. Walking, she recalled how often she used to look into the mirror when she had one. It was strange to think of how unimportant her vanity was in this place and time. In retrospect, she had lived outdoors with the Indians most of the time since she woke, covered in sand on the beach. The night-and-day difference between her two lives made her crack a smile.

She found a place where the water ran smooth enough to see her reflection. It was as she expected. Thank God she'd dunked her head the day before and rinsed off a week's worth of filth, pondering how refreshing it was.

She pulled herself away from the water and decided to see if Rakke'taf would allow her a conference – to plead for her friend. She walked down along a line of teepees scattered with baskets and grinding stones, children, and dogs. There were small fires that burned most of the day and night that wisped smoke around her as she walked the path. It was all so simple and pure. It gave Andrea a completely different perspective on life, and she was happy to experience it, even though the nerves she felt were unsettling her stomach.

Asking for a meeting with Rakke'taf was a task of great importance, and she felt she had nothing to lose. The same young brave who had been tending the comings and goings the day before was standing there now. Andrea hoped to be able to communicate with him, as she retained only a little of the Creek language. She knew "chief" and "see." That might be all she needed.

Looking at the young man's face, she took a deep breath and tried to stand taller. Then she asked, "I would like to see the chief, please?" She spoke in English and didn't know if he understood. Without saying any words, the young man turned and went into the chief's dwelling. Andrea assumed he would ask, leaving her no choice but to wait. He gave no indication whether he would return, and she waited, unmoving, until she saw the slight frame of the young brave appear again in the doorway of the longhouse. He gave Andrea a nod and stepped to the side, signaling for her to go in. She looked at him again, wanting reassurance, his dark eyes focusing on her, this time more agitated; then he looked down at the ground at his feet, his hand still extended, inviting her in.

It was dark inside but warm, like her grandmother's house. It smelled of wood smoke and burnt herbs. Andrea saw the chief sitting on the ground in front of the fire in the far corner.

He was entirely still except for the slow, steady movement of his shoulders with the rhythm of each breath he took. She approached him, trying not to make any noise.

After she'd taken a few steps, Rakke'taf said over his shoulder, "Come. Sit," as he held his open hand out to the blanket on the floor next to him.

When she sat, his face came into view, his eyes closed. She didn't want to disturb him, deciding to wait for him to speak first.

"You wish to speak to me?" Rakke'taf said with the question in his voice.

"Yes." She cleared her throat and began to speak hesitantly, her voice quivering. "Please forgive my ignorance, but I believe the confrontation with Hesaket last night was not all his fault." She took a deep, shaky breath before continuing. "I've spoken with Onawa, and she does not feel he was forward with her at all. She was heartsick that you were so harsh on him. I know him. He is not that way." Andrea then paused for a response.

The chief gave a slight nod, waiting a moment before he spoke. "I understand discomfort with my decision, but it was not wrong." His speech was slow and steady, his tone and posture emanated respect. "Our Creek people are proud and have survived many years by following the rules of the tribe. It is not unusual that someone outside our tribe questions and tests our rules and beliefs. Questioning it does not make it change." The Chief's voice unfaltering as he continued. "You know better than most how confused the world is. Throw a rock in a pond to see the chaos." Andrea was nodding slightly the whole time he spoke. She knew of the tribe's rules and the penalties to pay when the rules weren't followed. But this was different.

Andrea spoke again. She felt the distress in her voice. "I understand the rules, but under these circumstances, could you forgive, just a little? He is new to your tribe. You are wise beyond all people and surely you could allow him to earn his way back into your tribe. I know what happens to people when they're forced to live alone. They go crazy."

Hearing those words, the chief paused momentarily before speaking again. "I will pray on your wish. The Great Mother spoke to me in my dreams about Hesaket." He closed his eyes again, and nodded ever so slightly. "Leave me." Rakke'taf sat quiet now, ending the conversation.

Andrea looked at the fire before her and paused just a moment to listen to the soft crackle of it. She nodded, lowering her eyes to the chief and left, her mood now flooded with disappointment.

She stepped out of the dwelling, and paused for a moment, letting her eyes adjust to the daylight, then looked at the tribal village to see it as Rakke'taf' saw it; it was a beautiful view. Then she slowly descended the stairs and headed back to her teepee, watching her feet take steps in the dusty ground. It was still unclear whether she made any progress on her mission. She spoke her piece and now would resolve to leave it be. *At least he received me*, Andrea thought. And he heard her. Ultimately, that's what she wanted.

25. Trading Day – 1798

As she approached her teepee, she saw Johnny peeking through the door flap. Andrea called out to him, and he turned in her direction.

"Good mornin', Andrea." He seemed exceptionally cheerful. "Jacob wanted me to look in on you. Would you like to come over and get some food? Jacob has enough for all of us."

Andrea looked at her friend and smiled. "Yes, thank you. Sounds great."

Johnny escorted her to his and Jacob's teepee, where he was dishing himself some porridge.

"Good mornin' to you, Andrea," Jacob said with a smile. Andrea was almost suspicious about the unusual cheeriness.

She finally asked, "What are you both so happy about?"

Jacob and Johnny looked at each other, then back at Andrea, and said simultaneously, "tradin' day."

A smile broke out on her face as Jacob continued. "Today we make money," Jacob said with a giddy grin.

Andrea had seen his bundle of supplies but didn't give it a second thought until now. She raised her eyebrows suddenly and said, "Oh, I see," she said, simply nodding in understanding. "So, what do you trade for?" she inquired.

Johnny perked up, happy to run her through the inventory. "Oh, lots of things. Beaded jewelry, moccasins, vests, bow and arrow. Lots of things."

"So, we will be staying one more night?" Andrea asked.

The two men looked at each other blankly, realizing just then the conversation about trading day between the two of them never included Andrea. Her eyes went from one to the other, waiting for some response.

"Jacob," Andrea said inquiringly. "Will they let us go?"

Jacob's expression changed when she asked the question. "I hope so, now that they're here and safe." Jacob turned his face away from Andrea so she couldn't see the fear in his eyes. It was something he hadn't considered, and he decided then he needed to meet with Rakke'taf.

Andrea took the bowls down to the creek to clean them, pausing for a minute to splash her face and thought about her meeting with Rakke'taf. She wasn't ready to tell her friends about it. Not yet.

When she got back to the boys' teepee, she handed Jacob the bowls for safekeeping, then said, "How can I help?"

Jacob's smile broke out on his face. "Yes, ma'am. Would you mind looking for a piece of jewelry for Becca? Something she would like. She deserves something special."

Andrea said, "Of course." She thought about what a sweet gesture it was for him to be thinking of his wife after all he - we had been through recently.

Jacob pushed the breakfast dishes into a very full saddlebag and closed it. He grabbed the bundle of blankets, furs, tin cups, and wool yarn he intended to trade, and out the door they went.

Jacob hadn't told Johnny or Andrea that Becca was expecting a baby. So much has happened in the last few days that the subject hadn't come up. He thought of it now, suddenly anxious and nervous about being a father. Jacob interrupted their tasks, thinking this would be a good time to tell them.

"I should tell you both that Becca is expecting a child."

Andrea gasped, "Aw..." covering her mouth with her hand, excitement in her eyes. Johnny's smile slowly grew, then began to beam on his face. He reached out and hugged his brother.

"I wish you both well, brother." Johnny was truly happy for Jacob and his wife. "Uncle Johnny," he said quietly, wondering what being an uncle would be like.

"So, there are many reasons to be happy today," Andrea declared. Although she was very happy for Jacob and Becca, she was still sad for Hesaket. And even though she didn't know Onawa very well, she felt terrible for her, too. The cheerfulness flowed around Jacob and Johnny, stopping short at Andrea. In her heart, she'd hoped Rakke'taf would give Hesaket another chance.

Jacob and Johnny moved toward the gathering place, carrying on very pleasantly. Johnny had opened the roll they had carried for days, and it spilled open with several items, some Andrea had seen and some she hadn't. All he had concealed was beautifully crafted and his pride was overflowing. He spread each item out so they could all be viewed. He held a couple of items in his hands that had remained hidden as well, including a white linen shirt and a short knife in a well-made leather sheath.

Tribal members immediately came around to see what they had to trade. They offered many items in trade, but very few involved coins. A maiden traded a beautiful, beaded bracelet for a cup and a couple of rabbit skins. Jacob was pleased with that trade. An older tribal member wanted blankets. He had a shilling and a pair of leather pants that were just about Johnny's size. Jacob allowed that trade as well. For well over an hour, they traded and haggled. By the time it was done, all the items they'd brought were replaced with other trinkets, coins, and clothing Jacob and Johnny could use.

They hauled their new items back to the teepee, and Johnny laid out his saddle blanket, rolling them up to protect them, just like he had before. Andrea watched Jacob's expression as he put the travel plan together in his head, mentally organizing the day so they could make it home by sunset. He was missing Becca; he visualized her hair pulled up off her shoulders and the little strands that fell out, brushing along her neckline. He missed the farm, and as time marched on, he was concerned that if they didn't get the planting done soon, there would be no harvest at all; the planting and cultivation must be finished.

Jacob still fussed with his saddlebags and did not look at her when he spoke. "I need to speak with Rakke'taf." Andrea didn't answer him but was thinking the same thing.

Once he was done arranging the last few items in his saddlebags, Andrea said, "I'll go with you." Jacob stopped, then looked at her, never having been side by side with a woman to talk to a chief or elder. He thought it wouldn't hurt their situation since Rakke'Taf had a soft spot in his heart for Andrea. He gave her a nod, unsure if it was a good or bad thing to show up with a woman next to him.

They left the confines of the teepee and walked down the path to the gathering place. Awahani was there helping to build a rack for drying meat. Andrea approached him and smiled.

"Hello, Awahani." He stood straight and gave her a subtle acknowledgment. She smiled, holding out her hand toward Jacob. "My friend Jacob would like to speak with Rakke'taf, would you come with us?"

Awahani smiled and put down his knife and leather strap. He said, "I will go," Then walked with them the rest of the way to the longhouse.

A young Indian stood by the steps. His duty was to announce visitors for the Chief, but he was not the same native who was there the previous day. Awahani approached him, asking for counsel with Rakke'taf for his friends. The young man went into the house and came back a moment later. "Chief will be out. You wait," and he pointed to the ground adjacent to the entryway steps.

The three of them waited out near the steps to the mound. It was apparent the house had been there for many years and possibly generations. Grass had grown up tall around it, and there was a bush that had grown over the back corner, nearly hiding the wall with its long spindly branches and full foliage. It was a place that was always revered. Standing there admiring it made Andrea feel as though she was addressing a king. In a way, she was.

Finally, the Chief came out, making eye contact with Jacob. He came down the few steps and stopped, making eye contact with Jacob. He waited for Jacob to speak.

"Hello," Jacob said with a courteous bow. "Thank you for speaking with us." There was an awkward pause as he waited for the Chief to speak, but Rakke'taf just stood there with his eyes locked onto Jacob's. "We wish to ask your permission to go home." Jacob paused again.

Then the Chief spoke. "What keeps you here?"

Jacob swallowed hard, hoping his request was taken the right way. He continued. "Our agreement with Menawah was to see his tribe to their new home. Now that they're here, we would like to go to our home."

The Chief looked over Jacob's head at the bustle of life in the newly expanded village, wondering what home would be better than this. "You are free to go. Menawah is now part of this tribe. Show him respect and ask for his blessing."

Jacob gave a slight bow toward the Chief, paying him due respect. He and Awahani were turning to go when Andrea's voice interrupted, and he stopped.

"I'm wondering about the matter we spoke of earlier. Have you made a decision?" Jacob's expression was minced with bewilderment. He didn't know about Andrea's earlier visit to Rakke'taf or even what it involved.

Rakke'taf spoke in a faint voice directed to Andrea. "I have prayed, and the Gods have answered. Hesaket must earn his way back to our tribe." The Chief drew in a breath and let it out slowly. "He must speak to me."

Andrea gave him a nod and a smile. "Thank you," she said and reactively took his hand and kissed it. She uttered "Thank you" again, then slowly turned left with her friends.

After walking a few yards, Jacob looked at her and asked, "What was that about?" Andrea was slightly embarrassed and understood his insistence, but this was her matter, not his.

"I talked last night with Onawa, the girl who was in the center of the calamity between Hesaket and Harjo. I asked him to show mercy on Hesaket. Onawa kept telling me it was her fault he was paying attention to her. I merely defended him because I knew him to be a good man. I know Rakke'taf likes me, and I thought I would have as good a chance as any to sway the Chief."

Jacob shook his head in disbelief. "I might have guessed if anyone could, it would be you." Then he let out a "humph," and they continued, Jacob now anticipating a sit down with Menawah.

Jacob, Andrea, and Awahani walked side by side to the place where Menawah now made his home. They found him sitting in front of a fire in the shade of a tree, braiding leather to make reins for a horse's headstall. Andrea thought it awkward, as his position was very different now; he seemed content to sit quietly and do his menial work.

Menawah greeted them as though they were old friends. "Why is it you come to me, my friends? Do you have something on your mind?" he asked, looking up from his task with a hint of a smile on his face. His features had changed and softened over the last couple of days, relieved that his tribe found safety, overwhelmed with the generosity of others.

Jacob smiled at his friend. He was happy that his relationship with Menawah was more relaxed than with Rakke'taf or any other leader in their position. "Thank you for allowing us a moment," Jacob said, bowing his head slightly, not taking his eyes off the Chief. "Since we have come to the new home, and the village is safe; we should like to go to our home now." Andrea thought his request was precise and to the point. Then Jacob added, "Rakke'taf told us it is your decision."

Menawah looked at the leather strips in hand and then looked up again. He took a moment to stand, then, gathering his thoughts, finally said, "Your home and your wife need you. Go." Gesturing gracefully, he threw his head back slightly, and just as if the words were water flowing in a slow, easy stream, his eyes lowered again, stopping once more to find Jacob's, and said, "This tribe and this chief are forever in your debt." He dropped one of the leather pieces and brought his fist to his chest. "Come visit." Menawah smiled.

Jacob smiled back and gave a nod. "I will, my friend. Be well." Jacob's cheeks flushed pink, and Andrea's eyes teared up. They were as grateful to Menawah as he was to them. Awahani said nothing but gave his Chief a nod. Then, turning to go, they slowly retreated to their shelters.

"Wow, the whole day was a success," Andrea spoke freely, feeling content. Jacob and Awahani remained quiet, absorbing the fellowship they felt from the words that were shared.

When Andrea got back to her teepee, she anxiously sought out Herusa so she could tell her friend what the Chief said about Hesaket. Walking among the new homes and shelters, Andrea weaved around many before coming to Herusa's teepee. She was sitting on a grass mat, weaving, as it was her favorite pastime. Andrea plopped down beside her to share the news of the day. Herusa didn't say anything to greet her; she just smiled.

"I had a visit this morning with Rakke'taf," Andrea began. "I asked him to reconsider his decision - to show mercy on Hesaket. I know him to be a good man and should not be cast out." Herusa paused her work for a minute to listen to Andrea. "Rakke' Taf agreed to give him a second chance, but Hesaket must go to the Chief personally."

A smile grew on Herusa's face as the reality of the words hit her. "I will find him and ask him to come," Herusa said determinedly.

Andrea nodded, then asked, "Please tell Onawa. I think she should know."

Herusa nodded her head enthusiastically. "It was courageous of you to speak with the Chief."

Andrea blushed slightly at the compliment and said, "It's what friends do." Andrea touched Herusa's hand, expressing her love for her friend.

Johnny had been strolling through the encampment, observing the community of these native people. As a young man, he had seen much and was very perceptive. He realized that although they'd lost so much, they retained equally as much. They had family and a new home. To find another home such as this and be accepted as part of an existing tribe was unusual. He smiled humbly to himself, knowing that he was a part of this, his and Jacob's actions helped it all come to pass.

Andrea caught sight of him; she saw his eyes watching a mother chase after her son. She quietly observed a couple of young boys swiping at a rock with sticks. Two men tanning hides as their women watch them. *A peaceful village*, she thought. Glancing back at Johnny, she saw his expression was ever-changing. His fair skin was pink from all the sun he'd seen; fine, scrubby whiskers were nearly translucent in the brightness of the day. He was a handsome young man and would be tall and strong when he was grown, but with what he had seen and done in his life, he would be wise, just like his brother.

Andrea thought, *if I ever get back, I'll expect something different from the world than I did before.* Although she was preoccupied, there was unmistakable contentment in her heart.

26. Home Sweet Home – 1798

The evening came quickly, and the group assembled again in the gathering place. The three misfits sat together on the ground in the shade of a tree and ate their dinner of rabbit stew. Andrea was unsure of what went into the stew, but there was a root vegetable-like potato and greens along with the meat. It was not delicious, but it was palatable and kindly given and accepted.

"We're heading home tomorrow?" Andrea asked. She knew Jacob was growing increasingly anxious to get home to his wife and farm and finish the planting.

"Yes, we'll leave tomorrow," he responded with a heavy sigh. "At sunrise. It will be a long day of travel, but we'll be home by sundown. If you want to say goodbye to anyone, do it this evening. We can't afford a delay in the morning."

Those words translated to a mission for Andrea to say goodbye to everyone. She found Awahani first. It was unusual at this time, with these people, to give hugs, but she gleefully wrapped her arms around Awahani. "You were my first friend in this tribe. I won't forget your kindness."

He smiled shyly. "We will see each other again."

Andrea nodded. "Yes, we will," she added, smiling at his timidness. He was reserved around women; at least he was with her.

"Until next time," Andrea said with a nod. She released her embrace and turned to leave. She felt a slight pang in the pit of her stomach as she did, realizing just how comfortable she'd been with the tribe; they'd welcomed her and treated her well despite her differences.

The next person Andrea wanted to see was Menawah. She proudly strode up to him, sitting outside his shelter. A smile broke out when she thought about Dorothy saying goodbye to the Tin Man and the cowardly lion in The Wizard of Oz.

"I came to say goodbye to you." Andrea then averted her eyes to the ground, respectful to the man whose tribe took her in. She squatted near him so she could see him, eye to eye.

"I'm so grateful to you for your help and hospitality. Thank you."

With that, Menawah stood up and reached for her hands, raising her to her feet and then looking at her straight on. "You came to us as a gift from the Great Mother. We were blessed to have you. I thank you, my friend." Then he placed one of his hands over his heart. "Safe journey."

Andrea gave him another quick nod and a smile, then slowly turned away, continuing her farewells.

She knew Lucas' tent was not far away. She found him in his shelter in the back behind the others among the trees. In Andrea's opinion, it was perfect for him. Lucas was whittling on what looked like a flute. Andrea sat on the ground next to him, sharing a smile and no words. She watched him for a minute, admiring how careful he was with every knife pull. She thought he would have been a craftsman if he had been from her time. So careful and methodical. He cared deeply about everything he did.

She interrupted the silence. "We're leaving tomorrow." Lucas stopped what he was doing, but kept his eyes on the wood, trying to find words.

Then he said softly, "You are a good person. You treat me like no other." Then he lifted his eyes to hers and smiled. "We see each other again." Andrea was tearing up. Lucas and she had bonded over their differences as much as their similarities.

"I will miss you, Lucas. You, too, are a special person." She put her arm on his shoulder and pulled him to her. Their heads touched, and their eyes found the ground under them, not wishing to look at each other just then. She got up slowly and said softly, "Goodbye, Lucas," and walked away. "See you next time," and threw her hand in the air, waving as she walked away.

Lastly, Andrea needed to talk to Herusa. If there were any person here who would have been her "bestie," it was Herusa. Andrea recalled when they met, Herusa could speak only a few English words, and Andrea was amazed at how quickly she learned. In no time, she spoke as well as Awahani. Secretly, Andrea thought, *I hope they practice their English together.*

She found her friend on the creek bank washing out a cup and bowl from dinner. She came up behind her; Herusa recognized the sound of her steps and knew what she was about to say. Neither was happy about it but knew this time would come. Andrea squatted down next to her and smiled at her friend. Herusa would not look at her for fear she would burst into tears.

Andrea spoke first. "You know, I won't be gone forever."

Herusa, still not making eye contact, said, "But you will be gone for a long time. You might not know me when you come again."

Andrea snickered at that. "I will never forget you." Then Herusa began to let go of her tears. Andrea wrapped her friend in a hug and just held her. She began to speak again, wanting Herusa to savor every word. "You are kind and smart, smarter than many I know. Let those things you love grow and become your harvest. Practice your English so we can speak again. I love you, Herusa."

Andrea loosened her hug so her friend could face her. Then she smiled broadly to lighten the mood. She did not want to leave Herusa in tears. "We are friends forever." Andrea had no more words.

Herusa said softly, "Forever." And with that, Andrea got up and walked away, afraid of looking back. She did not want to cry, and although she put on a brave face in the presence of her friends, tears streamed down her cheeks as she shuffled back to her teepee. These people touched her heart in a way that no others had ever done. She let those thoughts strum through her mind, continuing to be amazed.

Jacob saw her sauntering back toward her teepee. He walked over toward her and joined in with a slow-moving march. He could see she was crying but didn't have to ask her why. He draped his arm over her shoulder and walked with her in silence.

They reached her teepee, Jacob showing her a whisper of a smile. "Don't worry. You'll see them again soon enough."

Andrea looked at him and said, "It just doesn't feel that way."

Jacob looked at her and was trying to understand her reasoning. "I'll bring you with me when we take our next hunting trip. You'll see." Andrea gave him a nod, avoiding eye contact, and went into her teepee.

She lay down again in her sleeping place, and her mind began to roll through the day. She felt in her heart that this place was just a stop along the way, that she had other places to be in the world. She stopped weeping when she thought about how the stone necklace was deciding her future or how it could be. She admitted that she believed the stone brought her here and sent her to the Loftons, who had visited the tribe. Jack got lost, and she was driven to help find him, which brought her to the band of Indians in the first place. Because of the kind of man that Jacob was, he had to find her, which brought him to the tribe. They needed a place to call home, and Jacob held the solution that brought them here. Now. As she tried to make sense of the whole thing, she suddenly felt remorse. *Was this supposed to happen? Did I change history?* She wondered if it was possible, or maybe the amulet had it in the cards all along. She began to smile, in awe at how her life now was determined by the weird and wonderful amulet that hung around her neck. *My existence here helped people.*

Reflecting in this way lightened her heart. She decided she was never meant to stay but could rest easy now, knowing the reason she was there in the first place. She recalled Rakke'taf's words, somehow, he knew it all along.

*

The morning came quickly and started with a mist that lay close to the ground. When the heat of the day came it would be unbearably humid. She knew that much. Jacob was up, of course, and was having some coffee. He saw Andrea's head come out of her door flap, and he held up his cup to her. Andrea went over to him and took the cup, holding it out for some of the warm liquid. They looked at each other as they sipped the coffee, knowing the day would be a long one. Johnny was the last to come around. He was not his usual cheery self, as he was most mornings; he had been drinking with a couple of the natives which resulted in an awful headache.

Jacob looked at his younger brother, who had come out of the teepee, holding a hand in front of his eyes to block the daylight from hitting his face. He held out a cup to him, and Johnny took it, holding it out for coffee as well.

Jacob showed a sarcastic smile as he looked at Andrea, silently chiding his brother, who was sporting a hangover. She smiled and thought to herself how much he would appreciate the help of modern medicine right now. Her smile broadened as he squinted against the brightness of the morning coming through the mist.

In less than a quarter-hour, Jacob and Johnny were ready to go. They had the horses geared up and all their belongings wrapped neatly and loaded, fitting Jack so Andrea could ride him. They didn't have much for supplies, and the creature was more than capable of being Andrea's personal transporter.

The threesome mounted their horses and glancing over their shoulders one last time, began the trek out of the camp. Andrea was the only one struggling with leaving, as she knew Jacob and Johnny had done it dozens of times. Despite her unstable emotions, she looked forward to getting home to Becca and the farm.

They trotted along at an aggressive pace for quite some time before Andrea confessed how uncomfortable she was. Jack was sweet and obedient, but it was not a very smooth ride. Andrea tugged on her bedroll to use part of it as a cushion, but it didn't help.

She finally asked Jacob, "Can we slow down? This trot is killing me."

Jacob laughed aloud. "Why didn't you say something?" and pulled his horse's gait to a walk, and the others followed. "I'm sorry, Andrea, I guess I forgot Jack's gait wasn't like the other horses'," Jacob confessed. The walk was rough but not nearly as bad as the pounding pace she had experienced for the last hour.

At the more casual pace, the threesome noticed that the terrain smoothed out, giving way to open fields, allowing them to ride abreast and talk about odds and ends like horses and shooting a bow and arrow, and rabbit stew. Small talk among friends. The air was sticky and sweet with blossoms on various berry bushes and crabapple trees. Their path ended up parallel to a creek, filling the air with coolness, refreshing, and welcoming. The trees began to thicken as the scenery constantly changed. The horses rounded a slight bend in the path, and black Smoke could now be seen on the horizon. It was some distance away from them still, but Jacob was laser-focused on it, wondering what it might be.

"There is no reason to have a fire that big," Jacob growled as a scowl began to grow on his face. From the trail that ran from north to south, a person couldn't see houses or structures in the trees on the ridge above it. Jacob never knew this to be settled land. His thoughts went to the possibility of a wildfire, but he couldn't remember even a cloud in the sky on that day or the day before.

Andrea's first thought was Indians (not the friendly kind) possibly setting fire to a house or pile of hay. Or, it could have been an accident, and someone needed help.

"Should we go see what it is?" Andrea asked anxiously. Jacob looked at her, juggling the possibilities before he answered.

"Well, if someone needs help, we should try to help them. If it were attackers, they've probably gone by now." He paused again while his thoughts processed. "We'll go but be quiet," his eyes searching anxiously for theirs, wanting then to understand this could mean real danger. Johnny nodded, nervously pulling his knife sheath closer to his right hand.

As they got closer, smoke could be seen rising from an incline on the far side of the creek. The trees and shrubs were thick, and even though they went slowly and picked the path meticulously, being quiet proved to be complicated. They shuffled into a single file line. Jacob, Johnny, and then Andrea. She dismounted, preferring to walk with Jack in tow rather than ride him.

Jacob looked over his shoulder occasionally, making sure they were all together. He would never forgive himself if he lost either one of them. He breached a clearing from where the smoke seemed to originate. It was a house, or what was left of it. There was what appeared to be the outline of a body only steps away from a well. The house and the tiny smoke house adjacent to it was a total loss. Entering it was impossible, and they may never know the source of the fire; however, there was no evidence that Indians might have caused it. Had natives done this, tracks by both horses and human feet would be visible. There was nothing obvious anywhere near the house.

Andrea stood silent and watched as Jacob walked around the side of the smoldering building, making a wide path around the human remains. He looked suspiciously at the burnt pieces of the barrel staves, swiping its blackened edges and smelling it.

Looking up at Johnny, he said, "Bear grease."

If someone were lucky enough to kill a bear, they would extract as much fat as they could. The thick, greasy substance would be used to cook with and to light in lamps or torches and oil leather to keep it soft.

"It looks like this barrel of bear grease caught fire and went up like a powder keg." Jacob shared his suspicions.

The remnants found around the homestead were nothing out of the ordinary. A line of rope with laundry on it. Chopping block with an ax and wood that was likely cut recently. Andrea was looking out beyond the clearing for anybody or evidence of someone else besides the one who perished. She heard something faint in the brush nearby. The men were chatting about what events they "thought" led up to the explosion.

"Ssshhh," Andrea said abruptly.

Both the men stopped talking as they were told, straining to hear whatever it was she thought she heard. Andrea walked cautiously out beyond the brush and just out of eyesight for a moment. When she came back, she was carrying a dog.

"Look," she said with excitement. "A survivor." Johnny smiled. He loved dogs, pleased that there was a fighter who had escaped the flames.

The dog was a brown and white spotted hound and was so skinny Andrea was sure he hadn't had a good meal for some time. He was timid and looked like he wanted to run but had nowhere to go. Andrea put him down and softly spoke to him, gently stroking between his ears.

"Johnny, can we give him a piece of jerky or something to eat?" Johnny dug around in his saddlebags and pulled out a couple of pieces of dried meat. He knelt beside Andrea and the dog and fed him little bites. He was hungry. She grabbed the water pouch from her saddle horn and poured some out into her hand, which the hound lapped up eagerly. She continued to pet him and talk softly. Once the food and water were gone, he looked Andrea in the eye and wagged his tail. She'd made a new friend.

"He's a lucky dog," Jacob said, staring at the mongrel.

Andrea looked at him in a moment of realization and said, "That's what we'll call him, Lucky." Johnny smiled a broad smile, satisfied with her decision.

Jacob and Johnny found a blanket on the clothesline and wrapped the body that lay on the step, or what was left of it, so that they could bury the remains. Johnny rummaged around in the barn to find a shovel or some other tool to dig a grave. The dirt on the edge of the clearing away from the house was softer and easier to dig, so that would be this person's final resting place.

The men took turns moving the dirt and, in no time, had a shallow grave dug big enough to hold the body. Andrea found a couple of sticks about two feet long, and she tugged hard on a vine that had attached itself to a scraggly cherry tree, breaking it loose. She wound the vine around the sticks, forming a cross while Johnny and Jacob worked. They placed the body in the grave and filled it in. Andrea gathered some rocks that could hold up the cross, and when they'd finished, all three gathered around the grave while Jacob recited the Lord's Prayer.

It was sad to think this person died all alone, hidden by the foliage and trees with only a dog to bear witness. Jacob and Johnny were unable to tell if the corpse was a man a woman; it was so severely burned. All three referred to the person as "it," which was dreadful.

The body was buried, and the house was now a pile of smoke and ashes. The three travelers descended the incline once more and were on their way, one more added to their party. They paused at the foot of the hill near the creek long enough to water the horses so they could continue and hopefully still make it home by dark.

Lucky trekked down the hill with them and was happy to slosh through the water, lapping up some of the coolness as he did. When they mounted the horses to begin again, Andrea insisted the dog ride on the horse with her. He wasn't strong, and it would be a long day and a sizeable distance to trot along with the larger beasts.

Jacob looked at Andrea and said, "Here you go. He was your idea; now he's your responsibility." He lifted the dog up and patiently waited while Andrea got him settled into the saddle with her. She smiled, happy to take on that responsibility.

"It would be unchristian to leave the poor thing to the wolves." Jacob nodded. He agreed with her, of course, but he did not want to admit he wouldn't have left the dog either.

The rest of the afternoon went smoothly and passed quickly. There were times when the sun was beating down on them uncomfortably, and the air was hot and still. There were also times when they were by the stream or in the shade, and the cool influence was quite pleasant.

Late in the afternoon, there was a breeze that cooled the air around them considerably; the wind became stronger as the evening wore on, making them all anxious. Jacob and Johnny were in front of Andrea and Lucky, and Jacob pulled Skeeter to a stop when he heard a tree fall. They all listened to an eerie crack as the trunk gave way, followed by a thunderous sound, and the ground below them shook from the percussion.

A glance passed between the friends, and Jacob urged his horse on. "Keep your eyes open," he said, not wanting to stop their progress. Another couple of miles and they would be home.

The wind blew, and clouds began to gather, giving the sky an ominous appearance. The treetops swayed in the wind, and their black outlines against the deepening darkness gave Andrea a chill. It came on gradually, but she thought it was too early to be so dark. The collective group, even the horses, seemed on edge. Andrea kept her eyes on the sky and took a deep breath, letting it out slowly, wishing wholeheartedly for the adventure to be over.

Jacob and Johnny urged their horses to a trot so they could make it home before a storm hit. It proved difficult for Andrea to hold on to Lucky, so she let him down off Jack, and he happily, ambled along beside her.

Skeeter and Babe were hard to hold back now. They knew home was just around the corner. Jacob and Johnny joked with each other, laughing. Andrea knew their sudden happiness was relief from the obvious. They were almost home. Skeeter was the first to make the farm, with Babe in a close second. Andrea's smile grew as she rounded the final turn and the farm was in sight. She was just as happy to see the farm as the rest. Jumping off Jack's back, she walked the last few hundred yards with Lucky. Jacob stormed into the house, picking Becca up off the ground and gave her a playful hug. They kissed and laughed, genuinely happy to see each other. Becca was thrilled; her family was finally home. Andrea stood watching the display of deep affection; the warmth of the reunion was as good as she'd ever received from her own family, love filling her heart. The moisture built up in the corner of her eye as she couldn't help but feel this was home.

Becca paused, then hugged Andrea, holding her as if she hadn't seen her for a long time. Loosening her embrace, Becca looked at her sternly. "You gave us quite a fright." Then she touched Andrea's cheek, and looking into her eyes, her expression softened.

"I'm so sorry, Becca, sorry about all the trouble I caused," Andrea said remorsefully, unsure of how to make it up to her. "It was so stupid of me."

Becca smiled tenderly and said softly, "Yes, it was stupid, but you're all home safe now and that's all that matters."

Becca ruffled Johnny's hair as he walked into the house. She looked back at Andrea and said, "Let's go in and find us something to eat. I bet you're starving." Andrea smiled, grabbing the pot to fetch some water from the well.

Becca had some potatoes and green peas from the garden. The girls worked together to make a stew, quickly producing a meal. It smelled and looked delicious.

"This looks wonderful," Andrea said to her. She watched Becca move about the house as she carefully timed each step of the meal. She realized without difficulty that she was a steady, talented person.

"I wish I were like you," Andrea said decidedly.

Becca displayed a tiny grin on her face, not looking at Andrea. A slight "uh huh" was her only response.

Jacob, Johnny, Andrea, Becca, and Lucky sat around the table and talked for hours.

Becca brought out her "hidden" bottle of wine, so they drank a little. Lucky, the new addition, was the center of attention. He seemed content, although the strange events that brought him to this new place were tragic. Becca had taken a liking to him right away, although she did not take kindly to him being in the house, and without question, decided Lucky would sleep with Johnny in the barn.

The party broke up, and everyone went to their designated places to sleep. It had been a long day, and everyone, including Lucky, dropped their heads on pillows and went immediately to sleep.

27. On the Edge – 2004

The jeep stopped at nearly every gas station and convenience store along the highway coming into and leading out of the city. "It's like trying to find a needle in a haystack. That is a thing, you know," Jake said.

"Humph," was all Collin could muster. Collin showed pictures and Jake asked questions to anyone willing to listen. Unfortunately, no one person they talked to had any helpful information. Whoever these crooked bastards were, they did not leave much of a trail. At the same time, the boys pursued their search; the girls were back at the hotel waiting for word about their friend's disappearance.

Later that afternoon, there was a knock on the hotel room door. "Housekeeping," came a female voice from the other side. Brenna and Chelsea glanced at each other and looked around the room. They hadn't had the room "cleaned" for a couple of days. Both girls grabbed their cell phones and Chelsea opened the door to let the maid in.

"Thank you," Brenna said. "I think the room could use a good cleaning."

Phones and purses in hand, they headed to the lobby. As they came out of the elevator, Ray's lanky gait caught the girls' attention. Smiling cheerfully, they approached each other; Ray was exceedingly glad to see the young women.

"How's it goin', girls?" Chelsea's eyes brightened, seeing his face.

"As well as could be expected," she said, unknowingly letting her eyes search him; his eyes, broad shoulders, the day-old stubble on his chin. She felt selfish being happy to see him, as her whole reason for his being here was Andrea's disappearance. *He has such a warm smile*, she thought. Although he was a cop, he had a comforting way about him.

Ray asked, "So, still no word?"

The girls shook their heads. "We were kind of hoping you would have news for us." Brenna's sentence cut the facts to the bone.

"I sure wish I did," said Ray. "We have others who reported possible sightings of the black van, but we still need to follow up with them, so nothing to report yet." And with that comment, Ray looked down, breaking eye contact. He wished he could bring them more happy news. At the very least, a morsel of something that could give them hope.

Ray, Chelsea, and Brenna sat in the lobby for a while, making small talk. Ray was feeling a responsibility to these girls. He wanted them to know he cared and was there if they needed him. After a brief time, Ray got a text on his phone. He excused himself from the table and made a call.

After a quick conversation, he returned to the table looking anxious and said, "I'm sorry, ladies, I need to go. I'll check in on you a little later." The officer gave the nod and left, very official-like, leaving the girls feeling unsettled, and they decided to go back up to the room.

"At least he acts like he gives a crap," Brenna said in a muffled voice. Chelsea pushed the "arrow up" button on the elevator.

It was almost an hour later when Chelsea's phone rang. The room had been so quiet that the noise startled both the girls.

"Jesus," Brenna said, putting her hands to her chest, trying to calm her heart. Chelsea smiled teasingly, looked at the phone, and saw the caller, I.D., showing Ray's name.

She answered. "Hello there ... you miss me already?" There was a brief hesitation and Ray's voice could be heard rambling excitedly.

"We found her." Chelsea's eyes grew big as she drew a deep breath, unknowingly holding it.

"What? You did?"

Brenna jumped up, having a tiny glimmer of hope for the first time in a long time. Ray had to take a deep breath to slow down. He was as excited as they were as he continued.

"A couple was jogging down along the beach on Highway 10. They found her unresponsive in the tall grass with her hands bound behind her back and immediately called 9-1-1. She was brought to St. James Southern Hospital here in New Orleans."

The emotion was more than Chelsea could bear, and she started crying. "Ray," she said, her voice cracking, "Can you please come get us and take us to the hospital to see her?"

Ray responded gently, "Of course I will." When Chelsea hung up, she told Brenna what he'd said, and Brenna was nearly breathless, struggling to find words through the tears.

"I never thought we would see her again."

It was only a few minutes later, but it seemed like an eternity when Ray showed up in his squad car. He jumped out and met Chelsea and Brenna at the curb. They all three fell into an embrace.

Ray struggled to say, "Thank God."

Chelsea and Brenna were admittedly nervous when they arrived at the hospital, as neither of them knew what to expect. They peeked around the doorway of Andrea's room. Both were shocked to lay eyes on her finally. Andrea was not awake but besides a large bump on her head and some bruising around her neck, she looked fine. A nurse was in the room and Brenna was the first to ask questions.

"Do you know what happened to her?"

The nurse's name tag said "Maggie," and she responded using carefully chosen words.

"Well, she has an asphyxiation injury. It appears she was strangled but was lucky enough to survive it. The doctors will have to tell you more about that, but she hasn't woken up yet."

Chelsea wanted to know, speaking hesitantly. "When will she wake up?"

Maggie kindly smiled at Chelsea and said, "That's up to her."

The girls' minds were racing with questions. "Where did they find her?" Brenna blurted out.

"I'm sorry, miss, I don't know that. I can tell you her vitals are strong, and besides being a little beat up, she's fine. She'll wake up when she's ready." Maggie gave a quick shrug in the girls' direction, then left the room; a sudden emptiness surrounded them, as neither friend got the answer they wanted to hear.

Ray stood outside the hospital room door, trying to give the girls space. Chelsea motioned for him to come in, then asked, "When was she brought in?"

Ray responded, "I don't know exactly, but when the staff here sees there is an alleged assault or attempted murder, they call us, so my guess is she's been here a few hours."

*

Collin and Jake had been driving around for half the day. They went to a couple of parking lots along the beach where someone could have loaded the women into a waiting boat. They'd scoured miles of beach and the shoreline, looking for evidence.

Then Collin said, "Well, maybe they didn't take a boat. Maybe that's just something we came up with."

Jake nodded in agreement. "It's hard to know. And there are hundreds of miles of beach where someone could have pulled up a boat, but this highway would have been the most direct way out of town, going east or west."

Just then, Collin's cell phone buzzed. He saw it was Chelsea. "Hello?" Collin said. There was a pause while

Collin listened. "Okay, wow. Great. Thanks." Collin hung up; a baffled look replaced the expression on his face. "They found her."

Jake looked ecstatic. "Oh my God? Where is she?"

Collin answered very matter of fact, "She's at St. James."

Jake said with a lot more enthusiasm, "Let's go!" and the two climbed back into the jeep and headed west to the hospital.

Brenna was in the hallway when Collin and Jake exited the elevator. Brenna waved for them to accompany her, and then she stopped them at the door.

"She's not waking up. The nurse said her vitals were fine and she would probably wake up in her own time. I just thought you should know before you go in there. She can't talk."

They both nodded and peeked around the corner. Collin's heart sank when he saw the bruises on her brow and around her neck. He approached the bed. She looked so peaceful, although seeing her injuries gave them all the creeps. There was such a mystery around what she'd been through.

Collin said softly, "I'm so sorry you had to go through that, Angel." He wanted to touch her but was afraid. She seemed so fragile.

The party of friends was gathered around her bed, speaking very few words. Finally, one of the nurses came in to check her vitals. She was a younger woman with spikey blonde hair, reluctant to make eye contact. She took inventory of the cluster around the bed and said with a strong Southern accent, "You all have got to leave." With a wave of her hand, she said bluntly, "This is just too many people." They looked at each other, but no one moved. Brenna finally spoke up.

"One of us should stay with her in shifts, just in case she wakes up." The group nodded, and without hesitation, Brenna said, "I'll go first." Nobody argued, and the other three wandered slowly down the quiet hall of the hospital.

None of the friends were in the mood to talk, but Chelsea perked up, trying to lighten the somber atmosphere. "We need to be grateful she's okay." Then, putting on a braver face and taking a deep breath, she said, "Look, if Andy were in charge, she sure wouldn't want us all gloomy on her account. She'll wake up. She'll be fine," sounding like she was trying to convince herself more than the others.

Jake put his arm over her shoulder and said, "Yes, we have much to be grateful for. And yes, she will be fine. Let's find something to eat, perhaps ice cream." Then he fluttered his eyebrows like Groucho Marx, encouraging smiles.

Jake, Chelsea, and Collin left the confines of the hospital and headed to a coffee shop that was within walking distance. "Everything will seem better after a fine cup of tea," Chelsea said with a nod, half joking, half not. It was something her grandmother used to tell her when a serious issue was at hand. And somehow, it did make everything better.

28. Begins and Ends – 1798

It was a late start to the blustery, cloudy day, although warm despite the overcast skies. Andrea was up first this time and went outside to welcome the day. She stepped off the porch, stretched, and yawned, shaking off the stiffness of sleep. Walking around the side of the house, she blew a quick whistle to see if Lucky would respond. A moment later, he came, bouncing out of the barn and across the path to Andrea. It made her smile to see just how delighted the dog was. Lucky was quite skinny, but she knew he would fill out once he was settled in and getting regular meals.

Andrea found a stick and tossed it to see if Lucky would fetch it. He ambled off after the stick but was quickly distracted by some scent in the air and forgot his original mission. Andrea tried again but ended up with the same result. *That's okay*, she thought to herself. *Not every dog needs to be good at fetching*. She grabbed the stick and shook it at Lucky again before giving it one more toss, then stopped and looked around at the little farm. The emerald green blanket of grass was the backdrop for the outbuildings and farm animals. Despite the variety of critters all around her, the farm was so peaceful. The plantings that were already in the ground was popping out little green tufts. She hadn't asked what Jacob planted but was curious about the crop. She walked up to the perimeter to get a closer look with the intention of trying to identify what she could see of each plant. There was motion, just out of the scope of her focus, she jerked her head around, jumping with surprise, recognizing Jacob. He was awake and ready to get started on the rest of the sowing.

"Good morning," Andrea said with a cheerful smile, her heart still pounding.

"Good morning," Jacob said back to her. "Scrutinizing my work, are you?" Andrea nodded, then turned again to look over the field, trying to imagine what it would be like full of mature crops ready to harvest.

"I was trying to determine what plant this is." Jacob had pulled up right beside her, crossing his arms over his chest. She pointed to the new little plants, then looked at Jacob. He looked at her, bewildered that she didn't know.

"Well, these right here are barley." He pointed to the small plants laid out in a row in front of them. He continued. "It has a hearty yield and lots of uses. Next to it, I'll plant corn. It is also generous but fussier, although it is easy to preserve. The last few rows will be sweet potatoes. They keep for a long time and are right tasty. In the smaller section there," he pointed beyond the sweet potatoes, "by the barn will be tomatoes, onions, squash, and beans." Jacob pointed his finger at the more conservative patch that Becca typically tended to. "We can go into Macintosh and get anything else we need." Andrea, impressed by Jacob's vast knowledge of plants and yields, was beginning to understand farming a bit. They'd spent all they could afford on seed and prayed for a good harvest, hoping to produce enough food for themselves and enough to sell to get them through the winter.

"You're going to plant all of that today?"

He responded with a rather large exhale, "Yes, ma'am, I am."

She let her eyes graze over the land again and said, "I'll help you however I can. That's a big job." Jacob smiled and nodded his agreement.

"I appreciate that. It will need water once I get the seeds in the ground." Andrea turned to walk back to the house, speaking over her shoulder. "You can count on me."

When she appeared at the door of the house, Becca was up and had boiled some eggs for breakfast, along with biscuits that were baking. It all smelled wonderful.

"Good morning to you," Andrea said as she closed the door behind her.

"Good morning, happy wanderer. How did you sleep?" Becca said in an amused voice.

Andrea approached the table and put her arm around her friend's shoulder. She smiled graciously and said, "It was the best sleep I've had in a long time. Thank you." Becca lowered her head and gave a long, slow blink as she was tending to the food and the table managing a conservative smile.

Andrea asked, "Can I help you with anything?"

Becca looked at her, appreciating the gesture, and affirmed, "Would you mind fetching some water for the coffee?"

Andrea wrapped her hand around the handle of a water pail and went out the front door to the barrel just outside to fill it. She returned and prepared the coffee, helping Becca. The two women puttered around the hearth and table, and the meal was ready within a few quick minutes.

Becca stepped out onto the porch and poured out the boiling water, leaving nothing but the eggs in a round-bottomed pot. She looked over her shoulder as she did, smiling, and said, "It is nice to have another woman around. Makes the house seem right."

Andrea blushed a little. She was still embarrassed about taking off and getting lost, especially since Becca had warned her.

"It is so nice to be here," Andrea responded, giving Becca a shy smile. Becca went out to signal to Jacob that breakfast was ready. He hollered at Johnny, who still had not shown himself. When Johnny was finally roused, Lucky jumped up and began to run circles around him.

Johnny patted him and said, "You're lookin' lively today." He knew he wouldn't get a response, but the pup continued dancing around his feet.

The small group sat around the table and casually ate the meal that lay on the tab before them. Becca insisted that Lucky stay outside, which Andrea agreed with, but insisted she bring him an egg. "He's been starved, poor thing," Andrea said, seeking Becca's approval. Becca handed her an egg, and Andrea smiled and thanked her. Becca didn't feel it would be Christian to let the animal go hungry.

Andrea's heart was content. This gathering felt like a family. It had been so long since her family had gotten together for anything, and this shared meal was proof that perfect strangers can intertwine like family. They talked together and planned their day, which included fish for dinner and hauling water to the newly planted field.

The girls picked up after the meal and made the cabin tidy and comfortable. Andrea went with Johnny to catch some fish for dinner, and Jacob began to drop seeds, planting his field, picking up where he left off. Lucky went with Andrea and Johnny to the wide spot in the creek, where he was always able to catch fish. He hoped there would be a good harvest since he hadn't fished there in weeks.

The two friends used worms to bait their hooks and sat on opposite banks with their poles in the water. Johnny joked that girls don't know how to fish while desperately trying to keep Lucky out of the water. This favorite fishing spot was a prominent, broad, flat place in the creek that was perfect for the fish to gather. Half of it was shaded, which gave the creatures relief from the sun and a hiding place from predators.

Johnny was the first to pull a fish from the pond. He quickly gutted the fish, then stuck a rather long stick through its gill and placed it just downstream from where their lines were in the water. Andrea was more determined now to get her first fish. She very slowly moved her line closer to the shady spot, seeking an unsuspecting fish, and less than a minute later, one of the clueless fish took advantage of the free meal.

Andrea confessed she did not know how to gut it, and Johnny gave her a quick lesson. Then he placed the fish on the stick with the other, and the two began again. Andrea put hers right where she had just caught her fish, hoping there were more in the same place.

Andrea and Johnny fished for a few hours, bringing home plenty for dinner. She was in awe at the clearness of the sky and the depth of the greenness of the grass and leaves on the trees; she was so calm. It was almost unfamiliar to her. As they walked back to the cabin, Johnny told her about how Becca would prepare them.

"Fried in ground corn flour and crunchy on the outside," Andrea remembered when she was young; her grandmother would fix trout the same way.

"Do you eat fish a lot, then?" Andrea asked.

Johnny smiled and replied, "Don't know what a lot is, but once or twice a week for certain."

Andrea was reminiscent of home. "We weren't too close to a creek, so we had fish a lot less often. And my grandmother would fix it the same way, though; it was a real treat." The two talked like best friends, poking and joking, enjoying the task as much as possible.

Once back at the farm, Johnny went to see how Jacob was coming along with the planting. He was finished with the corn and had just gathered the seed potatoes for planting. Johnny grabbed half of them, and Andrea began to haul water for the corn that was already in the ground. She made many trips back and forth with buckets in each hand as full as she could get them, straining from the effort they took to lift. She finished adding water to the corn, pouring gently, right up to the last row of potatoes, still going into the ground.

It was afternoon, and the air was sticky with humidity. Andrea had waited as long as she could to bathe herself. She put the buckets down and gave a wave to Jacob, then went into the house and asked Becca for soap, deciding rather than having "assistance," she would bathe in the creek. She found her pants and shirt, the ones she'd worn on arrival, and then asked for a cloth she could use to dry off.

She anxiously went down to the wide place in the creek where they fished and stripped off her clothes, careful to stay out of sight. She laid her clean clothes over a bush so they wouldn't get dirty lying on the ground and sloshed into the water without hesitation and immersed herself. The dip was cool and refreshing; she floated about in the water, enjoying the peace and the rejuvenation it brought her. She took a minute to cover herself with the soap, scrubbing her scalp as best she could and dunked herself again to rinse the remainder of the soap off. She smiled privately about what they called "soap" and not at all what she was used to, but it cleaned her off and made her smell better, just the same. Her skin was spotless, and she felt more civilized than she had in days. She fluffed her hair with the cloth, blotting out as much of the moisture as she could, and pulled on her dark blue shirt and pale-colored pants, looking now as she did when she woke up on the beach.

As she buttoned her shirt, she felt a hot, stinging, burning sensation on her upper arm, then watched a bee fly out of her sleeve, only then realizing she had been stung. The damn thing was *on the bush, she thought*. Angry and frustrated, she made her way back to the cabin.

Becca had a comb, and Andrea used it to smooth out her hair, then pulled it back into the leather thong Herusa had given to her. Her upper arm began to swell, and she rubbed at it wishing for a bit of relief. She asked Becca to have a look, hoping she could remove the stinger. Becca, alarmed at the amount of swelling that had occurred, wrung out a damp rag and placed it on the bulk of the swelling, hoping the coolness might offer relief.

The boys had beaten off the dust from the field and stamped their way to the house, stopping long enough to wash their face and hands, now presentable enough for dinner. Their eyes lit up at the site of the delicious meal that filled the table. Once the collard greens were finished, and the table was spread. They all sat down again to enjoy the supper Becca had so carefully prepared.

Andrea poured the wine into the cups on the table. They ate peacefully, quietly sharing small talk of the day's events, and without warning, Andrea began to feel dizzy, unsure if it was exhaustion or the wine. She asked to be excused and went out and sat on her straw bed on the porch in the cool evening air. She laid herself down, hoping the dizziness would subside.

She blinked hard, glancing at her hand, curious about the swelling. She held it up and blinked again, thinking she was hallucinating. Her hand was translucent. At first, she saw her bones, and then they faded, and her hand and lower arm were invisible. Her heart began to beat faster, and she was nearly panting when she blinked again, and her hand was back, just like usual. She rubbed her eyes, which were

338

watering profusely. After staring at her hand for a short while, she dozed off.

It was dark, and Andrea awoke to Becca shaking her. "Andrea, are you alright?"

Andrea took a second to respond. "I, uh, I think so."

Andrea had trouble opening her eyes. Her cheeks were so puffy now that when she finally opened them, she could see only small slits of light.

Becca said, "Your face is," she hesitated, "puffy." Andrea didn't know she was allergic to bee venom until that moment and became scared. She knew a reaction could close off her airway, and there was nothing she could do about it at this time and place. She held tight to Becca's hand.

"Don't worry, Becca ... Don't worry." Andrea blinked hard, feeling her heart begin to pound as fear pulsed through her.

"Can I get some water?" she asked. Becca jumped up and brought her a cup of water, then helped her sit up to drink it. Andrea's throat was scratchy and sore, which made drinking very difficult.

Becca and Jacob worked together to pull the mattress into the house so Andrea could be by the fire. Becca looked at Jacob, and the concern on her face was genuine. She was not equipped to handle such a problem. She thought to boil some thistle. It might help to open her throat a bit. She finished steeping the thistle tea and brought it to her, helping once more to get her to drink it. The tea was bitter, and Andrea didn't like it, but the warmth was nice. She drank a small portion and chose to lie down again as the room spun around, making her nauseous and uncomfortable.

As she lay there, Becca was almost afraid to leave her, staring at her and watching her breathe. Andrea's body began to fade, becoming a vapor, then reappearing. Becca could not believe what she was seeing, thinking maybe she was starting to see things in her anxious state.

Andrea slowly faded out of consciousness, still breathing but more shallowly with every breath. Becca bathed her head and face as tears streamed down her cheeks. She witnessed Andrea's silhouette fade again but was still unsure what to make of it. She put another log on the fire smoothed Andrea's hair away from her face and neck, then prayed over her, not knowing what else she could do. Delirious, she finally went to bed, falling slowly to sleep, completely helpless to do more.

Morning came, and Becca's eyes fluttered open slowly, casually stretching before she threw back her blanket to get up. She suddenly recalled the night before and needed to check on Andrea.

She jumped out of bed wearing nothing but her shift and moved swiftly over to Andrea's sleeping place. Becca blinked, then blinked again. The bed was empty, and the blanket was smoothed over the straw bed as if she made it before she left. Her face twisted with wonder. *Where would she go? Or could she go?* When Becca went to sleep, she was fearful that Andrea wouldn't make it through the night; not once did she imagine her taking off in the darkness. She had disappeared.

Becca began to cry, frightened for her friend and the uncertainty of her condition, but somehow, she suspected Andrea's absence was due to some odd force of nature. She didn't leave on her own; couldn't. It wasn't possible. Jacob heard Becca's soft sobs and pulled himself up abruptly to see what she was crying about.

"Oh no ..." He quietly went to his wife, putting his arm around her while she cried. Jacob silently allowed a tear to fall; it disappeared into Becca's hair as he held her close to him. His mind began to rifle through all the events they'd been through. They never got the chance to help her get back to her own family.

"A sweet soul," he whispered in his wife's ear.

She turned and looked at him, determined to tell him what she witnessed the night before. "I saw her disappear, Jacob. She faded, then came back. Like a ghost."

"A what? When have you ever seen a ghost?"

"Jacob, I'm serious. I don't think her being here was real. I don't think she was real." She covered her mouth, masking her very rattled expression. He sat still, mulling over what she said. She did appear out of nowhere; she was accepted quickly by the tribes they'd encountered, and now, she just disappeared? It was strange, but he couldn't imagine they would ever know the truth of it.

Once Becca had regained her composure, Jacob went out to get Johnny and filled him in on what they'd discovered. Johnny and Lucky came to the house to investigate as well.

Lucky sniffed at her bed and would let out an occasional whimper. Johnny went out to the end of the field at the border of the property's northern edge and strained his eyes, searching for his friend. As he did, he was overwhelmed with a flood of memories of their time together and selfishly grieved for her. He grieved for himself, for the emptiness left in his heart. The place their friendship used to inhabit. He also felt that her departure was due to the wave of God's hand and nothing else.

Just to quell any doubts, Jacob thought it might be wise to ride out in different directions to search for her, in case she was walking somewhere, delirious. Macintosh was about an hour away, and Jacob rode in that direction while Johnny headed south of the house. At the very least, they could eliminate the possibility of her wandering off.

By early afternoon, the two men were back at the farm, singling out the odd chance that she'd wandered off. Her disappearance was indeed that. She just disappeared. It was not spoken about among them, but Johnny and Jacob suspected her appearance and her disappearance had been the work of the amulet. Not of evil; they'd seen it do good. It was that the amulet decided what happened to Andrea or whomever it chose. The wearer was merely a puppet.

"How could that be? She was fine, here, helping with the planting and fishing. Where could she have gone?"

As Jacob spoke, he shook his head, bewildered and frightened. The farm was tranquil that day and into the evening while the family dealt with trying to reconcile what they saw with what might have happened to her.

*

343

The next day, Johnny worked for hours making a grave marker for her. There was no grave to mark, but he kept her memory alive the only way he knew how. He constructed a cross with a flat front so he could carve her name into it. The marker read:

Andrea Bruer

D. 1798

Johnny proudly placed the marker near the boundary of the property where the thick brush began. He pounded it into the ground, making sure it was solid before he considered his job complete, struggling to believe that she was gone. He was keenly aware that she had only been with them a short time, but he missed her fiercely.

Jacob and Becca walked over as he concluded the final touches, and they all drank a toast to their friend. Shedding tears, but not able to speak.

29. Investigation – 2004

The decision to investigate a crime was based on the report and the evidence. The Commanding Officer of the New Orleans Police Department was Lieutenant Lloyd Watts, a 20-year veteran with the force, had seen many "strange occurrences" during Mardi Gras. Many times, there was no hard evidence to follow up on, so occasionally, crimes went unpunished.

The report of a possible sex trafficking kidnapping hit home with the Lieutenant. His daughter was victimized only a few years before, the emotional roller coaster of the aftermath would constantly plague her. The Lieutenant's resolve was solidified because of it. He was determined to find the weasels and bring them to justice, make an example of them and the attempted hideous crimes.

Officer Wink Adams and Officer Raymond Blanchard had been called into the Lieutenant's office to brief him on the numerous calls they'd received of missing young women over the past week.

"Is there a common location from where all five girls had been seen?" asked Lieutenant Watts.

Adams was the first to respond. "They were all reported missing in a twelve-block area, and all those locations were near parade routes."

Then Officer Blanchard added, "There are two of the kidnappings that had been caught on video, but the assailants were smart and kept their identity hidden from the cameras."

Lieutenant Watts sat back in his chair, drumming his fingers against the edge of his desk. His baby-blue eyes were unfocused, and he was deep in thought. A few moments passed, and the two officers remained silent. The quiet was interrupted by a gentle tap on the door.

"Come in," the Commander said, still gazing at nothing. The relatively small, neatly groomed, dark-haired young man popped his head in the door.

"I found something you might want to see."

The Lieutenant looked at him scrutinizingly and responded, "Let's have it, Scully." The young man entered the room and dropped a piece of paper on the desk in front of the Commander. He picked it up and read it. It was an APB about the black van that had been spotted in four of the five kidnappings. None of the cameras in any of the locations were able to get a clear picture of the plates, but regionally, this van had been mentioned in similar crimes from Mobile to Albuquerque.

The Lieutenant nodded, then passed the report to Officer Adams. "I'm pretty sure, given the wide footprint of these reports, the van is no longer in the area." The Lieutenant pondered for a moment. "I would like you both to work together on this. Walk the streets and ask a lot of questions. The bartenders are good. They've seen a lot. Sometimes, the bums have more info than they're willing to give up. Buy them a burger and a beer. It might be worth it." Officer Blanchard raised an eyebrow and broke in, sharing what he knew of the suspicious disappearances.

"I know more than one of the victims had friends who were with them around the time they were taken. Maybe they saw something that would help."

"Good thinking, Blanchard, do that. Report to me every morning. Record everything. Maybe we can build a plausible case when we put the pieces together."

Adams and Blanchard declared in unison, "Yes, sir."

They got up and left the office, determined to uncover unseen facts about the crime. Wink looked over his shoulder at Ray and shook his head.

"It's gonna be like finding a needle in a haystack."

Ray smiled back. "I think you're right. But we got this." He high-fived Wink, and the two officers pushed the huge glass double door open, spilling them onto the street.

They agreed the best place to start was where they'd found Andrea and to work backward. As they drove, Ray was making notes about what they knew.

"We know where Andrea was found. Maybe they boarded a boat near that location. So, we're looking for evidence of a boat large enough to carry quite a few people."

Wink nodded, "And we know Andrea was assaulted, so evidence of a struggle or maybe the direction of travel. We need evidence that they boarded a boat or got into a different vehicle."

Ray jotted down a: proof of boat, b: direction of travel on his pad. "We should talk to folks who travel to the beach daily. Maybe a fisherman or jogger; bums - bums know everything." Ray jotted "bums" and "joggers" on his pad too.

Wink opened the console in the car and pulled out a piece of chewing gum, stuffing it in his mouth. He smiled and said, "It helps me think."

Ray made a "humph" sound, and the conversation stopped. In silence, the two officers rode the rest of the way to where Andrea was found.

They exited the car and spread out, hoping to encompass a larger area. Since there were other footprints from the joggers who found her; they searched a wider area.

Wink found two sets of footprints with considerably longer strides, maybe Andrea's and someone who chased her. The other set was made with a substantially larger foot. As they expanded their search, Ray also found many footprints, all going in the same direction. Wink decided that those prints may have belonged to the others who were taken.

"Did she try to escape? Was that why she was assaulted?" Wink said questioningly. Looking along the numerous tracks, Ray found a hairband. It was black and simple but could have possibly belonged to one of the girls. Ray tagged it as evidence.

They'd scanned the whole area, turning nearly every stone. They noted a slight indentation that was possibly a drag mark from a boat. The tides have come in and out several times since, so it was hard to consider it as proof.

They had just about given up finding anything else that might be significant to the investigation when Wink kicked up something of interest in the sand. He reached down, finding the item that had been completely hidden before and pulled up a hotel keycard. The two officers looked at each other as though they had found a winning lottery ticket. The card had the logo of the "Rupert Inn," both recognized the name, recalling it was near the Saturday markets.

"Now, there is some possible evidence. We at least have a place to start," Wink said, his eyes wide with disbelief. The officers left the beach, went directly to the Rupert Inn, and asked to speak to the Manager.

Dave Gray came out of a room in the back and introduced himself to the officers. They told him of their suspicions and wanted to know which room the key belonged to. The Manager ran the card into the keying machine and brought up the information they were requesting.

"Looks like a couple of young men rented that room. It has been vacant since," the Manager paused while he searched the computer. "Yesterday." The man casually unloaded the information requested by the officers.

Wink said anxiously, "Do you mind if we access that room and look around?"

Dave gave Wink a curious look. "Don't you need a warrant or something? I don't want to set myself up for a lawsuit. Besides, that room has been cleaned. I doubt you'll find anything."

Ray looked down at his sand-covered feet and took a deep breath. He stepped closer to the counter where the Manager was standing. He cleared his throat. "We only need that warrant if you refuse to let us in that room. And if you refuse, we might have to implicate you as a suspect. Is it possible you know something, Mr. Gray? Ray's fixation on the eyes of the Manager intensified.

Then Wink interrupted, looking directly at Ray and avoiding the Manager's eyes, speaking clearly.

"Now, if Mr. Gray wants us to get a warrant, we can do that. I believe we have enough circumstantial evidence that we could easily get that warrant and possibly a subpoena for him and his establishment when this case goes to court. That's up to him." The Manager looked at Wink, then Ray, and back to Wink, sighing deeply.

Handing them back the key he said, "First floor, on the right. That key should still get you in."

They followed Mr. Gray's directions to room 109. Wink opened the door and found the room had been emptied of any personal items, and the maids had already cleaned.

They split the room and looked everywhere for prints, slips of paper, or anything that might give them a hint about the inhabitants. Ray found he was getting angrier during the search, frustrated by the lack of evidence. Unfortunately, there was not a speck anywhere they could use.

Just as they were about to walk out the door, Ray turned and looked once more, thinking they had to have missed something. It was just a gut feeling, but as he made a final scan of the details of the room, he caught a glimpse of something tiny and yellow. It seemed out of place, in a room that men had previously occupied.

He reached down, just under the edge of the dust ruffle around the bed, and found a little yellow daisy. It looked like a piece of a charm bracelet, a necklace, or something similar. Not knowing if this belonged to any of the missing girls, he stuffed the daisy in his pocket. It may help them confirm whether this key belonged to one of the kidnappers. The two officers returned to the squad car in relative silence.

They were returning to the precinct when Wink got a call from Scully. "Yeah, the Lieutenant wanted me to call and let you know we have a possible witness in the missing women's case."

Wink's eyes got as big as saucers. He looked at Ray and said, "You gotta hear this," and he placed his phone on speaker. "Go ahead, buddy." The other end of the phone was quiet.

"Scully?" Ray said.

"Yeah, I'm here. So, a man who was out at the beach that night said he saw three guys and four girls getting into a boat real close to the place the girl was found." Both the officers were nearly holding their breath. "He said he didn't think anything of it, Mardi Gras and all, but after he heard there was a woman almost killed right by where he walks every night, he thought he should at least report it."

Ray asked Scully, "Was the witness able to ID the boat?"

Scully responded, "I knew that would be your next question. He didn't remember a number or anything that stood out, but he said he could point it out if he saw it again. I will send a copy of the report to both your phones."

Winked thanked Scully and hung up, then looked at his partner and commented, "So, there is a trail to follow out there. Just needed a kick in the ass to get started." The corner of Ray's mouth curled with satisfaction.

They pulled into the parking lot at the precinct, and the two ambitious officers met with the Lieutenant to brief him on the evidence they'd found.

Lieutenant Watts said, "Good work today fellas. I think this proof is enough for us to be able to get our hands on the hotel's security footage. We'll do it the old-fashioned way so the manager at the Rupert Inn doesn't give us a hard time."

Wink said, "Thank you, sir." Ray echoed the same response, and they stood up, feeling satisfied with their progress and walked out.

The Lieutenant hollered behind them, "I want that full report first thing in the morning."

They both turned and said, "Yes, sir."

After the report was completed and Ray and Wink clocked out, Wink asked his partner, "Wanna go out for a beer?"

Ray looked down, avoiding contact with Wink's eyes. "Naw, I have a friend whose friend is in the hospital, and we've been hanging out a lot. I'm going to see her tonight. Thanks, though."

Wink nodded and headed out the door. "See you tomorrow!" Ray gestured with a hand, and the young officers parted ways.

He sat for a few more minutes on the bench in the locker room, wondering if it was wise to get wrapped up in a relationship with the friend of a victim. *What if the whole thing went sideways?*

Pushing the thought aside, he shot a text to Chelsea confirming her location, and as expected, she was still watching over Andrea. She and Brenna had been there continually since they'd found her. One or the other, often both girls were determined to be there when she woke up.

When Ray appeared at the door, Chelsea's expression went from melancholy to glowing, like someone flipped a switch. Out of all the things that happened to them in New Orleans, Ray was the best. His smile matched her expression, his eyes brightening when he saw her, softening her like butter on warm bread.

He signaled her to come out into the hall. She did, and once the door shut behind her, Ray scooped her into his arms and kissed her very playfully at first, but then the spark turned into a flame.

Once the kiss had ended, Chelsea said, "Now that was a nice surprise," and a mischievous smile crept onto her face.

Ray held her, not wanting to let go. "I've been thinking about you all day." Holding her close made him feel secure and satisfied like it was meant to be. He pulled away slowly and looked into her, eyes bright and happy.

He did not want this moment to end, but Chelsea broke the silence, first with an "Mmm," then a question; "So, did you come to see how Andy was, or did you come to see me?"

Ray let out a chuckle. "Well, if you must know, a little of both." He winked at her teasingly. "How is our friend today?"

Chelsea's eyes focused on him: his voice, his breathtaking eyes, and his tall, slim, muscular shape. She hung on to his every word. It was the first time they'd done more than let their hands touch, and she couldn't help but think it was worth the wait.

She sighed softly, "She hasn't woken up, if that is what you're asking. Her vitals are strong and stable. The doc said it could be any minute."

Ray gave a tip of his head in acknowledgment and said, "Well, that's good then. Any minute is good." He paused momentarily, looking through the little window in the door.

Then, redirecting his eyes back to Chelsea, he said, "I got some news." Chelsea was not in the same mindset as Ray, but his words brought her back to refocus on him.

She smiled and said, "Oh, good news?"

Ray grinned, letting his beautiful white teeth show. "Well, I think so. Wink and I were investigating these kidnappings all day and found something." Ray crossed his arms, a furrow now gracing his brow. "A key card to a hotel. It was in the sand near where they found Andrea."

The thoughts that popped into Chelsea's head overwhelmed her, and she was suddenly full of questions. "So, did you get prints? Did you see any video?"

Ray dropped his arms to the railing in the hall he was leaning on and answered sheepishly. "Well - no. We did get access to the room occupied by two men. They were probably under aliases paying cash, but we're checking that part out. The room had already been cleaned, and the men had taken all their belongings, but it's at least a start. And now, we have enough to get an order for the hotel security footage, which will probably tell us a lot more. The Manager there was kind of a jerk, so the department will just cut through the bull crap and get an official search warrant."

Chelsea grabbed his hand and said, "That's wonderful news! Something is better than nothing. And this is something!" she said excitedly. This time, Chelsea moved in for another kiss. It was warm and sweet, and the private time they shared in the hall was all that was needed to fan the flame of romance.

Taking their time lingering outside Andrea's room, they overheard a conversation going on in the next room. Listening but trying not to be obvious about it, Ray heard something that caught his attention. A young woman's voice said, "I think I was roofied. I was fine and dancing one minute, the next I woke up in a hotel room half naked. I knew I'd been raped, cause my underwear had been ripped off." He understood her hesitation. "He just left me there."

Then Ray heard another voice, "Where did they leave you?"

The young woman's voice was heard again. "At the Rupert Inn. I didn't remember going in, but I sure remember coming out."

Ray's heart skipped a beat. He told Chelsea, "The key we found was for the same hotel that girl was in. I need to talk to her."

Chelsea's eyes opened wide with surprise. "Did you say the Rupert Inn? That's where Collin took Andrea that night after the parade, and they, uh ..." Her voice stopped abruptly.

"Hold on," Ray said to her, quietly walking over to the next room.

He knocked softly, and a muffled "Come in" was heard.

Ray entered the room and said, "I'm sorry to interrupt."

He pulled his badge out of his pocket and said, "I'm Officer Raymond Blanchard with the New Orleans PD. I overheard you talking about an incident at the Rupert Inn. I've been investigating crimes that happened just the other night, and I found evidence that might lead us to believe the intentions were more than rape."

The girl was taller and relatively thin. Her dark hair drooped across her forehead slightly disheveled, as would be expected from someone who was in the hospital.

"If now is not a good time, I can come back, but I have a couple of questions if you're up to it."

The other voice he had heard in the room was of an older woman, maybe the girl's mother. Her gray eyes gazed at Ray and then looked back at the girl in the bed, inquiring.

"Sure. I'm up to it."

Ray asked her name. She replied as if she were in an interview. "I'm Brooke Simms."

Chelsea, still in the hall, remembered the name. *Was she one of the girls Brenna had been talking to the night of the Bacchus parade?*

Brooke continued. "I met this guy, Adam, who came on strong, but we got along really well. He was charming."

Brooke hesitated, looking down at her hands, wringing in her lap. "And a sly son-of–a-bitch. He had me eating out of the palm of his hand." Her expression changed, and Ray wasn't sure if she would cry or scream.

He was summing up her words in his mind. He wondered what could make a man abduct and rape a girl. She was so pretty and delicate. He must be an animal. Then Ray said to her softly, "Go on." Gently urging her to continue.

Brooke started talking again. "We were at a club having a perfect time dancing an' all. Then, before I knew it, the room began to spin, and it just went dark. When I woke up, I was in this hotel room with my clothes ripped off me."

She took a deep breath, letting it out unsteadily. "I don't even know if it was just Adam or if there were others. Adam was with a couple of other guys most of the time." Brooke's eyes teared up, and she bit her quivering lip.

Ray shook his head, disgusted with what he heard. "Has the hospital done an exam?" He asked softly.

"I believe so," Brooke said. Ray had another thought.

"Did you remember seeing the hotel room number by chance when you left?"

Brooke gave a slight nod. "Yeah, it was 109," Brooke answered straightforwardly, sounding very sure of her answer.

He pulled the yellow daisy charm out of his pocket. "I got one more question. Does this look familiar to you?"

Brooke started to cry, "That's Jen's. We can't find Jen." Brooke's tears turned into sobs.

Ray said in a low, comforting voice, "I'm so sorry to upset you. All this information is very helpful. I can't tell you how much I appreciate your time. Have you spoken to anyone else with the police department yet?"

Brooke nodded. "Yeah, someone came and took a statement. That's all." Ray nodded slightly, sensing her fragility, knowing what she'd been through.

"Thank you." He found a notepad on the table beside the bed and wrote down his name and phone number.

"Please call if you think of anything else. Again, thank you for your time." And with the tip of his head, he left the room as quietly as he'd entered.

Ray was back in the hall, where Chelsea was waiting for him. She had a concerned expression, anxious for him to share what he found out. Ray asked, "Does the name Brooke Simms ring a bell?"

Chelsea answered, "Yes — yes, it does. She was one of the girls that Brenna was talking to at the first parade."

Ray remarked warily, "I think the location where you went to view the parade was prime for stalkers looking for girls like you and Andrea." He thought for a minute as Chelsea could see the unsure grimace on his face change. "How about the name Jen?"

Chelsea's beautiful blue eyes met his. "Yes, she was with Brooke that night, too."

Ray's head hung just slightly. "She's missing."

Chelsea's heart stopped the moment she thought *it could have been Andrea*. Ray grabbed her hand, slowly lacing his fingers together with hers, and they pushed through the door to Andrea's room.

Ray and Chelsea sat in Andrea's room, trying to reconcile the latest information they'd received with what they already knew. It was easy to let a story develop; thoughts and suspicions begin to lead the narrative. Ray was very thorough in juxtaposing the facts, and with every detail they learned, the picture of Andrea's abduction and assault became clearer.

Ray made a call to Wink to let him know what he'd discovered through Brooke's interview and the questions he asked her about Jen's disappearance.

Chelsea was deep in thought. Once Brooke had mentioned Jen was missing, she feared deeply for her. If Brooke was roofied, it could be expected that Jen was, too, especially if they were in the same hotel room with the same group of guys. She wondered why the kidnappers took Andrea and Jen and not Brooke.

We may not know until Andrea wakes up, if ever. Chelsea's thoughts took her to a very dark place, but she reminded herself Andrea was safe; she had been found.

30. Closing the Circle - 2004

Andrea's eyes fluttered open at the streams of sunlight bursting through the gap in the curtains of her hospital room. She blinked repeatedly, trying to bring things into focus, coming to the realization that she didn't recognize anything. Where am I? She closed her eyes and saw a flash of a man running after her; the sensation of being breathless overwhelmed her, and she gasped. The feeling was so real, yet she was in this room and not going anywhere. When she opened her eyes again, her heart was racing. No man was chasing her, and she could breathe.

She looked at the door and saw a fluorescent light through the tiny window. She slowly rolled her head, looking the other way. Sitting in a rocking chair between herself and the window, Chelsea was sound asleep. She had her navy-blue jacket lying over her, and what looked like a towel under her head. Andrea tried to smile but had trouble getting all her parts to wake up.

Then she spoke. "Chelsea," she said. Her voice was raspy and weak. She cleared her throat and tried again.

Chelsea opened her eyes after hearing her name. Her first thought was to look at Andrea. To her surprise, she was awake and looking back at her. Chelsea choked up and couldn't say anything but went to the bedside and hugged her friend.

"I knew you'd be okay. I just knew it." Andrea tried to nod her head but was barely able to move it.

"Where am I?" she asked Chelsea, who looked at her, relieved, reaching up to stroke her hair.

She said, taking a breath, "Well, you've been asleep for almost a week, and we are at St. James Hospital in New Orleans."

Chelsea immediately began to make phone calls, the first one to Brenna. Andrea could hear Brenna laughing and crying on the phone, as there was no other noise in the room that would distract her from perceiving it.

Andrea said, "Tell her to come." Her voice was not very strong, but Brenna heard it.

Her response through the phone was, "I'm coming!" A moment later, Chelsea hung up, assuming Brenna was on her way.

The next call Chelsea made was to Ray. Andrea could hear a man's voice on the other end of the phone but didn't recognize it. Chelsea filled in the details, and he told her he would be down with Wink as soon as they could get there.

When Chelsea hung up this time, Andrea said, "Who was that?"

Chelsea blushed a little, but a smile grew on her face. "That was Ray. He is the officer who has been investigating what happened to you."

Still groggy, Andrea said, "What happened to me?"

Chelsea's eyes looked to the floor, having a tough time recalling the events of the last week. "You don't remember?" Just as Chelsea was about to speak, Nurse Maggie came through the door, her face lighting up when she saw Andrea's eyes for the first time.

"See, I knew she'd come around when she was ready." Maggie updated the dry erase board with details of the day, then slapped her hands together like she was clearing away chalk dust. "How are you doing, young lady?" Andrea blinked hard but didn't say anything to the nurse. Maggie went to the bedside and took Andrea's vitals. "Everything seems perfect," she remarked.

366

The nurse asked Andrea to follow her finger with her eyes. Andrea did as she asked but was a little slow to respond. "That's a good reaction, given you've been out of touch for almost a week."

She jotted something down on her clipboard, then looked up at the both of them, smiling warmly. "I'll get a report to the doctor. You should hear back soon." Maggie winked and left the room almost as quickly as she had shuffled in.

After Maggie left and the girls had a little privacy, Andrea looked at Chelsea and asked bluntly, "What happened to me?"

Chelsea took a deep breath before spilling the answer to that question. "Well, you were abducted, shoved into a van, driven about an hour out of town, and nearly loaded onto a boat. Best we can guess, you tried to run, and someone tried to strangle you, unsuccessfully, of course. The latest hypothesis is they left you for dead because later the next day, a couple found you and called 9-1-1. And here you are. You've been unresponsive up till this morning."

As Chelsea talked, Andrea began to relive the events of that night. She had gone down to the lobby and never made it back to the hotel room. Again, her heart began to beat rapidly and trepidation grew. Chelsea could see how agitated she'd become and put her hand on her friend's arm.

"I'm sorry, Andy. I didn't mean to scare you. You asked."

Andrea nodded. "Yeah, I know." Andrea took a slow, deep breath and asked, "Can you help me sit up?" Chelsea fiddled with the buttons on the bed, and it slowly rose to a sitting position.

Chelsea offered her friend a cup of water, and Andrea slowly sipped. She had been hooked up to an I.V.; the tube tugged at her hand when she moved it. Andrea glanced down at her hand.

"I bet it was a long week for you." Andrea now felt regret about what her friends had gone through, imagining what it would have been like to be one of them.

She felt as if she'd gone on a long trip. The events of last week came back to her in little bits and pieces. She wasn't ready yet to share all she'd done while absent. But soon. Then she remembered some of what she had left behind that night.

"Did anybody get in touch with Collin?" Andrea realized his name hadn't come up yet. Chelsea slowly moved her head from side to side, not wanting to share what she knew.

"He was here the first day they brought you in and came by on the second day, but we haven't seen him since then. I've tried calling his cell phone multiple times, but he won't pick up. I've left half a dozen messages, too. It's like he just disappeared."

Andrea said, "I'd call him if I could, but one of the shitheads busted my phone and threw it out the window." That part she remembered clearly. "Did he say anything? Was he worried?"

Chelsea answered her as best she could, "Yeah. He and Jake searched all over until you had been found. Then it's like he stopped by to be sure you were good and left. I wonder if something happened to him."

Andrea was ready to speak, and Maggie entered the room again. This time she had a tray of food in her hand.

"I'm going to take that I.V. out of your hand now, and you can try to eat something. I brought you yogurt and fruit, Frosted Flakes and some milk, a couple of pieces of toast, and a blueberry muffin. I figured you should like at least one of those things." Then she blinked her big brown eyes at Andrea and smiled.

Maggie moved over to the side of the bed where the tube was connected. She turned off the drip and pulled out the I.V., then stuck a bandage on the spot where she pulled it out.

"There you go, good as new," Maggie chirped. "You eat up now." Andrea smiled back at her as she bustled out the door.

Andrea was hungry; truthfully, she tried a little bit of everything. It beats venison; she thought to herself. Chelsea was busy texting someone while Andrea ate.

Then Andrea's eyes perked up, and she asked, "Could I have you run and get me some coffee? It sounds perfect right now."

Chelsea smiled and jumped up, thinking she would love some, too. "Sure. Be right back." Andrea was visualizing as she ate her food and recalled the taste and smell of the rabbit roasting on a spit over the fire. She remembered the rabbit stew she fixed with the turnips and wine. She remembered the porridge that Becca had fixed. She tasted it. All of it.

Does that mean I was there? How did I get there, and how did I get back? Her mind was now murky with her thoughts.

The concentration was interrupted by the door swinging wide and Brenna bursting through it. She ran across the room and wrapped her friend in a bear hug. Andrea almost laughed but was still weak enough that it came out sounding nothing like a laugh.

Brenna was full of questions. "How does your neck feel? Let me see your hands, you look good. I'm so glad to see your face again." She was so excited to see her friend that none of her thoughts went together. Finally, she calmed down long enough for Andrea to get a word in.

"I missed you, too."

Brenna laughed, loosening up, genuinely glad to hear Andrea's voice. Chelsea came back into the room with Ray by her side. Andrea looked at him and blinked. The tall blonde lanky man smiled at her. Giving him the once-over, she could see a badge clipped onto his belt loop, as he was otherwise dressed casually, like everyone else.

"Look who I found," her eyes looking up at him adoringly, then back to the others in the room.

Brenna casually said, "Hey, Ray." As expected, Andrea looked at him blankly. Chelsea said proudly,

"Andy, this is Ray. He has been looking into the back story of what happened to you. Sounds like there were other girls kidnapped, too."

Then Andrea said softly, "Yeah, I know."

Ray looked at Chelsea with questioning eyes. Then he looked back at Andrea and said, "When you're ready, I need to ask you some questions." Andrea took a sip of coffee. It was warm and delicious. She never would have thought how much she missed something so simple as a regular ol' cup of coffee. She paused for a minute to savor its taste, in love with its warmth.

"I would love to help out any way I can."

Ray pulled out a notepad that was tucked in his back pocket. He picked up a chair next to the window and sat in it right next to her bed. It was then that Wink Adams came into the hospital room. He was strikingly confident and had a bright look of intelligence about him. Ray smiled, looking at Wink, then back to Andrea's curious eyes.

"This is my partner, Wink Adams. I wanted him here in case he came up with any questions or thoughts about the investigation that I might forget." He opened his notepad and said, "You can start where you want, or I will start with questions. We have a few."

Andrea said, "I'll start."

Ray nodded and gave a friendly smile, "Okay, perfect."

She thought back to the beginning. "Well, I went down to the lobby to get a soda. It had to be close to midnight. When I got off the elevator, I walked around a corner, and a couple of guys grabbed me. They had hoods over their heads and wrapped a scarf around my face so I couldn't scream. Then they hurried me out the door and into a van. I could tell it was a dark -colored van, but I wasn't outside long enough to tell the model."

Ray was scribbling, trying to catch up as Andrea spoke. He interrupted. "We got security camera shots of the van as it was leaving the parking lot of your hotel." Andrea nodded gently, fear suddenly jolting within her. She paused for a moment and swallowed the lump in her throat. Ray waited patiently until she regained her courage and started again.

"As soon as they got me in the van ..."

Wink interrupted. "Who are they?" Andrea blinked, stopping her data dump to process his question.

"I really don't know. There were three men in the van, and two of them had a Spanish accent. The one that chased me was Spanish, for sure."

Wink nodded, glancing at Ray to be sure he was writing down the identifying specifics. "Thanks. Continue," he said softly.

"I never got a good look at the ones in the van; I just heard them talking and knew there were three of them. They put hoods over our heads. I was able to see four or five others girls in there with me but couldn't see their faces. One of the guys took my cell phone and broke it, then just tossed it out a window like it was nothing." She paused for an instant and closed her eyes, head down, doing her best to recall all the details of that night. "I mouthed off to one of them, and he smacked me. He hit me twice, and the second time knocked me out. I don't know how long I was out, but I woke up when the girl beside me asked if I was alright. She kept bumping into me until I answered. When I thought about it, I recognized that voice, too."

Andrea's lower lip quivered before she spoke again. "She was with Adam the evening before. And I remembered that Adam and Collin spoke to each other like friends. Why would he get involved in a fight with a friend?" Andrea's eyes were full of questions when she raised her eyes to look at Brenna, hoping for an answer.

Ray tried to keep up but did not want to interrupt Andrea or have her slow down. He was glad she paused for a minute to catch her breath and take another sip of coffee. She started again. "The van traveled for a while longer after I woke up, and when it stopped, they started to unload all the girls. I could smell the ocean, and I figured they were going to try to load us in a boat to go - who knows where. So, when they pulled me out of the van, I pretended to be sick and told them I was going to throw up and take off the hood. I was pushy and loud, so finally, someone ripped off my hood. Then I kicked the one nearest to me in the balls and took off running as fast as I could. I ran away from the beach, but he came after me. I would have gotten away, too, if I had my arms free, but they were tied behind my back."

Wink looked at Ray with raised eyebrows, thinking about how unpleasant it would have been to be the assailant. Ray nodded his head and went back to his notes. Chelsea and Brenna looked on in horror. It was a graphic description; more importantly, Andrea lived it. Neither of the girls knew what to expect, but they wouldn't have imagined this in a nightmare. The details repulsed them.

Andrea continued, "Then the stinkin' bastard got his arm around my neck, and he squeezed. Hard. I couldn't do much because my hands were tied. I swear, as I was running away from those slimy assholes, I recognized a couple of them from the parade that night. I wanted to ask Chelsea and Brenna about that."

She took another breath, her mind working quickly after a week of rest "Then everything just faded, and I went unconscious, and that is all I remember about it until just now."

Ray finished writing and looked up at Andrea. "You are so lucky." He shook his head from side to side in disbelief. "You not only survived the kidnapping, but you also beat certain death."

Andrea automatically credited the amulet for her stroke of good luck, but that was not something she could share. Not just yet.

He wrinkled his brow in thought. "Did the gang say anything about where they were going or the boat's name?" Andrea took another sip of coffee, which was almost cold now.

"I heard the water splashing up against the boat, but aside from seeing a white bow up on the sand, I didn't see much that would be helpful." She stopped for a split second, staring off into the abyss. "I do remember some numbers on the boat's bow. N7. There were more, but that's what I remember."

Then Ray asked, "Do you recall any names they might have called each other?" Andrea closed her eyes and thought. "Goober. That was a name - or a nickname I heard. Besides dork or dumb ass, there wasn't much talk." Ray expected as much.

Taking a deep breath and slowly letting it out, Ray said calmly, "I'll fill you in on our theory." He looked at Wink, getting his go-ahead to bring her up to speed. "We think the group of girls who were picked up were being bought by another party, possibly the cartel. We know the guys who did the dirty work were just in it for the money, and there is big money in trafficking, so it must be a big player. If we knew who, then we might know where, or at least where to start."

Ray shifted in the rigid wood chair. "We know that Jen, the girl Brenna had met, was taken, too. We still have no sign of her."

Andrea's face had a look of shock. "Oh my God," she uttered under her breath. "So, in that place on the street where we watched the parade, that's where we all were. Really close together. Is that why they picked us?"

Ray nodded. "That is our take on it." He was confident in their hypothesis. "All of you girls who were there near each other were marked. It made it easy for them."

Then Ray asked her questioningly, "Can you tell me more about Collin? Do you remember him communicating with anyone on the street that night? Possibly any of those you ran away from that night on the beach?"

Andrea was focused on the bed sheet that covered her. "I had just met him. He was nice, but I can only remember one he spoke to. I remember Adam. The others in the van were Spanish. I think they spoke Spanish. And to be fair, I was running away from a greasy, long-haired dickhead at the time, so I didn't see the faces of the others."

Ray began writing again. "Do you know Collin's last name?"

Andrea gave a quick nod. "Yeah, he said Brown. Collin Brown. He also said he had just graduated from Colorado State in Engineering."

Ray was writing quickly. "You don't suspect him, do you?" Andrea snapped.

He did not look at her but said, "Well, we suspect his associates."

Wink said, now changing the subject. "That is some valuable information."

Ray looked at her with a serious face again. "Tell us about the hotel room."

Andrea gave him a bewildered look, "Our hotel room?"

Ray smiled and said, "No, the one that Collin took you to."

Andrea looked surprised and said, "Oh," her face flushed pink. "Well, Collin and I had a great day together, and he didn't want to wrap it up. He told me he had a room, and it was private. Someplace we could be alone." Andrea stopped abruptly, not wanting to share all the details. Then, thinking again, she decided it was all part of the investigation, so she continued. "It was really nice. Romantic. We were only there about an hour; then he escorted me back to my hotel."

Ray said directly, "So you willingly had sex with him?" Andrea nodded.

"But it wasn't violent at all."

Then Wink said, "Just so we get the story straight, it was consensual?" Wink diverted his eyes as he thought, curious about why her abduction was different. "Other girls were drugged and raped, but that wasn't the case with you." Andrea looked at him with a scowl on her face.

"Yes, consensual," she answered curtly.

Wink and Ray looked at each other, and Wink said, "We think they used that room to stage the girls they wanted to take. Your friends Jen and Brooke were both raped. We also found evidence that put Jen in that room, and Brooke gave us more details. Do you remember the room number?"

Andrea nodded. "It was room number 109."

Ray picked up the pen and wrote in the book, asking, "Can you think of anybody else that you might have seen talking to Adam or Collin? Man or woman." Andrea was raking through other faces she had seen and if they acted like they knew Collin.

Suddenly, Andrea's eyes grew big with surprise, and she gasped. "I do remember," she exclaimed. "I remember walking to his hotel room; we passed a guy on the street who high -fived him and laughed, then looked at me. That 'guy' was one of the guys in the van. I remember that laugh. Oh my God!"

Wink said, "Eyewitness."

The two officers exchanged glances. Ray asked Andrea, "Would you be able to testify to that in a court of law?"

Andrea held her breath. "Yes, I would. Absolutely. For myself and the other girls in that van."

Wink gestured toward the tablet-sized computer under his elbow and said, "Do you think you might be able to identify any of them if I show you the pictures?"

Andrea took the device and swiped through the hundreds of pages of mugshots with Wink and Ray by her side.

"How do you get all these criminals' pictures? I had no idea."

Wink responded, "Well, there are many of these who have been on the wanted list for decades. I tried to filter out some that would not be suspected of this type of crime, but if they've had any association with a criminal who has been involved in a similar crime or involves people that are known associates, they'll show up."

The three viewed the shots together, and Andrea paused at one of the pictures. "This is the one Colin and I passed on the street," she spoke very pragmatically but swallowed hard when she spoke. Her finger lingered on the face of the man in the mugshot as Ray printed the name and number of the suspect down on his notepad. Andrea continued. After ten more pages, she saw another familiar face. "This is Adam." Ray followed the same routine and noted her identification of yet another suspect. Andrea turned to the very next page, and her expression changed completely. She went from relatively cheerful to pissed off and hurt. "This is the asshole who strangled me." Without a word, Ray noted the third man on his pad.

Wink picked up on the swell of emotion that washed over her and suggested, "How about we take a break?" He gently removed the tablet from Andrea's grip. She let go and skillfully averted her eyes down toward the sheets that covered her. It was gut-wrenching to see these guys, remembering the violence and flat-out heartless attitude toward the girls. They were property. Stolen property. Nothing more.

The part that got to her was just how much she cared for Collin and how scared she was for him. She was sure that if the people involved were his friends, then he was coerced. That's all there was to it.

"So, I voluntarily had sex with Collin, and you say Jen and Brooke were raped. Why did they take Jen and not Brooke? And why me? How did I become a target?"

Ray took in a breath, letting it out with a sigh. "We think it might be because of Brooke's association with Jen. They just took one, not both. There was less chance they'd make trouble. It was merely the luck of the draw."

Andrea thought about how very easily it could have been Chelsea or Brenna. She took a swig from a tall plastic tumbler full of water, trying to disguise the emotion that thought brought. The process was not easy, but she knew how helpful it would be if she identified those involved.

She looked at Wink and said, "Okay, let's get this thing over with," then reached over and took the tablet out of his hand, picking up where she left off.

She repeated the same process as before and was able to identify the kidnapper who broke her cell phone, having seen his profile before they jerked the sack over her head. Andrea's mind wrestled with the thought that Collin knew these assholes. He really couldn't be involved, right?

Chelsea saw the distress that Andrea was feeling and walked over, putting her arm around her friend. "This is not on you, Andrea. These people are snakes, and that's how they do it. You were a victim and happened to be in the wrong place at the wrong time. We are so glad you're here with us. You were so lucky." She tightened the hug with her friend.

Andrea was suddenly in a faraway place, remembered the scraggly spotted dog at Chelsea's mention of the word. Her heart sank briefly with a pinch of sadness at the realization that she was virtually unharmed and in a very different place. "Luck was on my side." Andrea grabbed at the charmed necklace she'd worn since the second she bought it, and an overwhelming swell of panic ran through her. The amulet wasn't there. She looked at her friends, agitation showing on her face.

"Where's my amulet?"

Brenna looked at her, alarmed by the reaction. "Well, they put all your belongings in this bag. Maybe it's there." Brenna got up and went to the wardrobe by the sink and brought out the bag of Andrea's things. She frantically rummaged through the bag, focusing solely on finding the stone.

"Ah, there," Andrea said, breathing a sigh of relief. The stone had settled at the bottom of the bag. She pulled it out and, as quickly as she could, put it around her neck again, reverently comforted by it.

Brenna and Chelsea were both taken by surprise at the reaction. What was up with this rock? Brenna thought. She's been without it for almost a week. Andrea inhaled long and slow, settling her anxiety.

"A good luck charm," she said and smiled while looking down, fondling the unique stone.

Wink and Ray gathered their notes and tablet and stood to leave. With a warm smile, Wink said, "We'll turn in what we know. This is great information, Andrea. We might be back with some other questions as they come up, but for now, we'll leave you girls alone."

They both pulled themselves away from the gathering around Andy's bed. Chelsea got up to show them out of the room, Ray putting his arm around her waist. The door opened, and the two officers left, but not before Chelsea could steal a kiss from Ray. Andrea looked at Brenna with surprise. Brenna smiled and nodded, not saying a word.

31. Pure Magic – 2004

Finally, the three fearless friends were alone. Chelsea and Brenna sat close to Andrea, touching her, wanting to know she was undoubtedly okay. Chelsea choked up and said, "It was so awful not knowing where you were. You just disappeared."

Andrea grabbed her hand. "I'm here now, aren't I?" Chelsea and Brenna smiled. And there was the reality of it all.

"Better to go forward than backward, I always say." Brenna joked, trying to sound more upbeat. It was terrifying to think of how things might have ended up.

Andrea asked Chelsea point blank, "So, what was that about?"

Chelsea looked at her, not quite sure what she was referring to.

Then it hit her, "Oh, do you mean Ray? We're an item now." A glimmer of satisfaction showed in her expression.

Andrea smiled, "I knew you wouldn't get out of New Orleans without some kind of hookup."

Chelsea looked at her, half mocking, half proud. "What do you mean?"

"You know what I mean." Andrea rolled her eyes dramatically, making the other girls chuckle.

"So, tell me about him," Andrea said. She was gaining her strength by the second now, after food, drink, and conversation.

"As you can probably guess, we have been spending more time together. Ray and Wink were doing their investigation, and we often hung out at the hotel. We get along great. What do you think of him?"

Andrea raised an eyebrow, and a smile curled up on one side of her mouth. "He gets my vote if he's good to you – it doesn't matter what I think."

Chelsea nodded. "He is very kind and caring, I know that. He checked in on us every day till they found you and have checked on you every day since they brought you in."

Andrea smiled very tenderly at her friend. "That's all I need to know," Andrea said, genuinely happy for Chelsea.

There was a moment of silence between the friends, and Andrea felt it might be the time to talk to them about the "web" woven by the stone's magic.

She took a second to clear her throat, then began hesitantly. "I need to tell you guys something, but I need you to have an open mind." Andrea's tone was serious, and the other girls were both concerned, focusing their attention on their friend.

"Sure," Brenna said. Chelsea nodded, almost afraid of what she was about to hear.

"After the near-death experience on the beach, I went somewhere." The other girls were listening, but neither would make eye contact with Andrea. "You guys might have seen me lying in this bed, taking a nice long nap, but I was not here. I went somewhere. I woke up on a beach in the sand in Georgia in 1798. I had strangulation marks on my neck and a bloody knot on my head from the tangle with the kidnapper."

Brenna remembered the knot on her head that was so badly bruised when she first came to the hospital, and the purplish-red strangulation marks on her neck, barely visible now. She pulled out her phone and showed Andrea a picture of what she looked like the day they found her. Andrea looked at herself in shock. Her eyes teared up, and her chin quivered as she held back the flood of emotion the picture brought her; it made the whole nightmare very real once again.

She paused for a moment, regaining her composure, then continued. "I was in a strange place at a strange time. I stumbled across these two brothers who were camping in the woods, and they took care of me. Jacob was a trader and had dealings with a local Indian tribe and on our way back to his farm, we stopped at Atiketiv, an Indian encampment. They saw this stone and told me about its power." Andrea held up the amulet, feeling it warm in her hand. "I didn't believe it, of course, but the whole tribe treated me special, like a queen, the whole time I was there."

Andrea held the stone tight with her hand and said with passion, "This stone helped me to see visions of the future. It kept me safe, and it brought people together. It solidified my belief in Native American traditions. I was already a fan, you know that, but it taught me to stay the course, no matter what." Then, she emphasized the last part of the confession, "This stone is special."

Chelsea's chin just about hit the floor. She was thinking, *she is so intense about this. She truly believes it happened.* Chelsea was cautious about her reaction to this strange but exact information. She didn't want to stir up something to upset Andrea, but she knew it was only a dream. Then, another notion came to her. Andrea had not seen herself when she was first wounded. Her strangulation marks are nearly gone, and her bump is a bruise and a scab now. How did she know about the marks? About how she looked?

Although investing herself in Andrea's words was a leap of faith, this almost made Chelsea a believer. It was an odd feeling not trusting a story that your best friend spoke so passionately about. Chelsea wanted to place her confidence in her friend.

Brenna's reaction was vastly different. She wanted to know more about this mystery trip into the past, holding back her skepticism.

"So, what was it like? Did people dress funny? Did they stink? They didn't have deodorant then." The questions came in rocket-fire succession. Andrea chuckled a little at her curiousness.

"Okay, let me see if I can answer them all. Yes, they did dress funny, but it was what they did in those days with the fabrics they had. Georgia, back nearly 210 years ago, was beautiful and fresh. The air was clean, and the ocean and beach were clear and flawless. And, yes, they all stink because there is no deodorant, but I spent a lot of time in the outdoors and that fresh air made it more tolerable. Besides, I stunk, too." She stifled a snicker.

Both girls were awed at how she recalled the "dream." To Andrea, it all happened yesterday. There was no delineation between the two separate lives she'd lived. She breathed in deeply and closed her eyes. When she opened them, she began to speak once more. "This was a lesson for me. Things that I needed to learn and people who needed me to be the vessel of their good fortune. I learned selflessness and sacrifice. I learned about honor and friendship. Whether or not you believe me doesn't matter. I know it sounds crazy, but it was real. Real to me, and real to the Loftons, and real to Menawah and Rakke'taf. I was real to them."

Her insistence took Chelsea and Brenna by surprise. They didn't know what to expect after she woke up from her weeklong sleep. She'd been out of it long enough that they needed to bring her up to speed. Thus far, this reality of the 21st century must have been scary and disappointing. She had been through the most terrible thing and lived to tell about it. It was a miracle, to be sure.

Brenna put her arm around her friend. "You know we love you, Andy. We know you've been through a lot, and we'll see you through this. Don't worry about us. And for the record, we're keeping an eye on you!" Andrea felt the comment was to pacify her, but she didn't care; she knew Brenna's words came straight from the heart.

Keeping her eyes down, she thought, *how will I pick up where I left off anyway?* Neither Brenna nor Chelsea would believe this fantasy she lived was real or could, at the very least, understand what she went through. But it was real. The recollection of details was so clear.

Brenna would grasp just about anything someone told her, but this was a bit much. She decided that even her besties didn't believe her or understand, and if she kept it up, a psychiatrist would be the next call.

After a very intense morning of faces, food, and water being consistently shoved into her face, a pummeling of questions, and poking of needles, Andrea had enough. She was happy her friends were glad to see her back amongst the living, but she wanted to be alone.

She said as gently as she could, "You know what, guys, I'm still really exhausted right now. Would you all mind if I just slept for a while and had some peace and quiet?"

Chelsea and Brenna looked at each other and were a little embarrassed. Brenna said, "Oh, gosh. So sorry, Andy. I was just so glad you were awake. I never thought about how you might be feeling."

Then Chelsea said, "Of course. We'll go and get some food and do something. Then we can come back this afternoon. Do you want us to bring you anything?"

Andrea smiled. "Yeah, bring me a soda pop when you come back."

Brenna stooped to kiss her friend on the forehead. "We'll see you a little later."

Chelsea went over to the window and closed the blind, making the room's lighting a bit more subtle. Then she turned and winked at Andrea.

"Get some rest. We'll be back." Andrea gave a little wave and a smile to her departing friends and lowered her bed.

Andrea didn't need to sleep. She needed quiet and stillness. She lay there on the bed and held tight to the amulet around her neck, realizing the strength of the magical stone changed her. What she felt in her heart was remarkably different. She felt so much more connected to her emotions but had less control over them. She felt so much more deeply and had less need for material things.

As she lay there in the dim quiet, she breathed deeply. Her breath calmed her and slowed the rush of thoughts that had bombarded her in the relative peace of her room. The power of the amulet took her over again. There was a brightness to her vision now. She saw falcons, or what she thought were falcons, darting around, playing a bird's version of "chicken." It made her heart feel so weightless, and she wanted to raise her arms and fly with them. The young girl she'd seen her vision before was happy and held her arms out to soar with the birds. Her spirit was luminous.

Andrea felt this new enlightenment and was driving her to do good. Her vision faded, and again, her heart was pounding, but this time, it was exhilaration and not fear. She knew now it was her job to do things in this world and, this time, to make it a better place. She was a person who always had to have a plan, but now, she saw that everything would be okay, even if she didn't *plan*. She may be unclear about many things, but her determination was laser-focused. "I will help the tribes. The Native people of this country." Her summer scholarship with the Salish was the start of something great.

Happier now, she smiled, remembering Rakke'taf's smile. The one he only let a few people see. He was wise, so much more so than was evident to others. He felt the rhythms of the earth in his soul, but sadly, he couldn't stop the shit storm that was coming. Andrea wondered if her presence there gave him insight into what the tribes faced in the future. Despite their discomfort, the Native people were getting on with their lives, but she remembered the look in their eyes. They knew this upheaval of their existence was just the beginning.

Andrea's mind returned to the present time and her hospital room. She was shaking, and feeling every bit of the sadness the indigenous felt. It touched her core; in her heart, she knew she would never be the same. As the vision dissipated, her heart calmed now as she looked around the room. Her thoughts now shifted, and she couldn't help but wonder, "When will they let me out of here?"

32. The Plan – 2004

Ray and Wink went back to Headquarters to lace together the bits and pieces of information they had and presented it to the CO. Ray went through his notepad to find a beginning and an ending and all the chronological events in between. In some of his notes, he would recite, and Wink would type, but there was a lot of "yeah, put that in there" kind of remarks. In their follow-up at the marine fuel station, it was common practice for the attendant to record all the boat numbers and gallons pumped to help them maintain their inventory. They were able to confirm a boat style from the man on the beach the night of the kidnappings.

Wink pulled together different pictures of boats for the beach walker, who was then able to identify the model. Once they had that information, the two officers went through the journal of boat numbers and copied down any of them with N7, narrowing it down according to the identity confirmed by the man on the beach.

Ray paused to ensure Wink was getting everything he said in the report. Wink looked up at him, waiting for more narration. Then Ray said, "The attendant's list only had two boats in which the number N7 appeared. One of them was light green and dark green. The other was all white."

Wink finished typing that sentence and paused for a second. "I don't suppose you know whose name the white boat is registered under, do you?"

Ray had a suspiciously devious smile and answered, "Yes, sir, I do. Dave Gray."

Wink began to grin. "You think they'd be better at covering their tracks."

Then Ray pointed out, "When we paid a visit to the hotel, he didn't seem like a very bright sort of guy. I think he would be the type to jump at an opportunity to make a buck, no matter the situation it would put him in. Now he's an accessory to kidnapping and sex trafficking. Oh, and add attempted murder." Wink nodded, knowing they now had one in the tank.

The officers still had to finish questioning the hotel manager, but they both agreed he likely was an active participant in supplying the room where the kidnappers staged their somewhat romantic endeavors.

Wink remembered there was little to no camera footage from the St. George that night, but they successfully got the subpoena to gain access to the tapes. Once the recordings had been thoroughly scoured, two of the five missing girls had been recorded entering the building with one other guy who they hadn't seen yet.

Wink mumbled to himself, "It pays to be persistent."

Ray and Wink began to brainstorm. Ray shared his thoughts with his partner, "Think about this. What if we can get the attendants of the filling stations to plant a tracker on the boat? We'd have to rally all the attendants within a 50-mile radius and supply them with the trackers, but it should be easy for them to stick it on or in the boat. Then we could get the 'little boat' to lead us to the 'big fish.'"

Wink blinked hard, not speaking for a minute, then his eyes widened. "Or, we could plant officers at the filling stations. It would be hard to know if we could trust all the station attendants. Besides, there are only four or five stations in that 50-mile stretch."

Ray nodded in agreement. "We need to write up a request for that, and soon. If we wait too long, the trail will get cold. It's already been a week."

The two wrapped up the first part of the investigation but decided to leave Dave Gray alone until they were successful in catching the criminals in his boat. Otherwise, it would be hard to prove their connection.

Wink and Ray went to Lieutenant Watts with the data they had pooled together and presented their idea of catching the kidnappers in action. "We know they will try it again, and we know the general area where they frequent. It would just be a matter of time before they try their hand at another 'snatch and grab.' We want to be ready," Wink said, hopeful the Lieutenant would see it their way.

Lieutenant Watts was quick to reply. "You mean to tell me you want us to take five, maybe more officers off the street to post at all the Marine fueling stations around the gulf on a chance that the kidnappers would strike again? That is not a very smart application of resources if you ask me." He paused and strummed his fingers on the edge of the desk, his eyes not focused on anything. Then he suggested, "Why don't you two grab one more officer and split up? Try to find that boat. It must be out there if it needs fuel frequently; it can't go far."

Ray and Wink looked at each other, neither one ever thinking about the inefficiency of their plan. Wink smiled and gave a nod. "There are thousands of boats out there in the bogs and swamps, but they all must be put in and taken out of the water somewhere. Since we know where they fueled up recently, it's pretty safe to assume we can start from that point and go backward."

The Lieutenant nodded. "If you split up, three people can cover a lot of territory in a day. I'm willing to invest those resources in the search for now." Ray was ready to get started when the Lieutenant suggested, "Take Lambert. He'll be good at that sort of thing, and all three of you report back to me daily."

Wink replied, "We will chief. Thanks." Then, the two men left the office in search of Alex Lambert.

Ray popped his head into the dispatcher's office and asked them to track down Lambert's cruiser. Once he had been located, Wink took a minute to fill him in on their investigation, and that Lieutenant Watts asked for him specifically. Twenty minutes later, the three officers met up in the precinct's parking lot with a map and a plan. Wink was very thorough in disclosing information to Lambert about their investigation and the next steps that might catch the kidnappers in the act.

"Ray, you cover this area, from Weston's landing to Henderson Point. Lambert, you start at Henderson's Point and go east; I'll take from Weston's landing and go west." Wink took his phone and forwarded pictures of the boat model they were looking for to Ray and Lambert. "The boat registration numbers end with N7. If you see anything, let us know." The three men took off in three directions to search for the captor's boat.

The search was arduous. The day was hot and humid, which was quite common for New Orleans, but hours in and out of the car, looking in driveways and causeways on the off chance they'd pulled the boat out of the water was almost painful. Since they didn't get started until afternoon, the search continued until nightfall. Ray, as did Wink, had decided he'd only gotten about halfway through his section. When Lambert finally called in, he was sure there was still a lot of territory to cover.

Lambert was a small man, quick, strong, and intelligent. His reddish-brown hair reflected the sunlight, giving the illusion, somehow, that he was taller than he was. He had been credited with being thorough, and in hindsight, there was a lot more real estate to cover in his section, but the other two officers had his back and would pitch in when their sections were sufficiently raked for sought-after evidence.

They met back at the precinct parking lot, where they had started. "So, ready for another go tomorrow?" Wink was tired and hot but confident that if the boat was anywhere near this city, they would find it.

"Of course," Ray answered, thinking it was a dumb question, then realized it was directed toward Alex.

"Sure," Alex said with a brief exclamation, and although he was hot and tired like the others; he was ready to go when they gave the word. "What time?"

Wink was happy to have the help. "How about seven?" Lambert gave a quick nod of his head and walked toward his car.

Wink and Ray talked for a couple of minutes about what they saw and other suspicious findings to investigate at another time. "I feel it's close, Wink. We're going to find 'em'." Ray sounded optimistic about their accomplishments, and they were not giving up hope. "At the very least, we found where the boat wasn't."

Wink smiled at that. "Yes, at the very least, we know that."

Wink and Ray were not friends at all before this hunt for the kidnappers threw them together, but found they were like-minded about a lot of things and began to rely on each other, almost without question. There was no doubt, they felt very much the same when it came to devoting time to this project. It is a miserable place to be when an officer is sent to a home or, in this case, a hotel, unable to offer a lifesaver of hope. Wink stretched his arms up, looking for relief from the tension in his back.

He said, "It's been a long day, I'm heading home. See you tomorrow."

Ray nodded and said, "You bet. G'night."

Ray went into the changing room and undressed for a shower. He shot a quick text to Chelsea to find out where she was so he could go straight to her when he was cleaned up. She responded almost immediately.

"I'm at the hospital, but I'm good to go somewhere. Brenna will stay."

He worked at getting the day's sweat and stench off his body. Ray thought to himself, *it feels good to have someone to care about*. His mind was busy thinking about how Chelsea muddled his mind as he fluffed his hair with a towel and smoothed it out, smiling in the mirror at himself.

When Ray arrived at the hospital, Chelsea greeted him at the main door. She was looking forward to having a little quiet time with him. He walked up to her with a smile, like usual, and gave her a lovely kiss. Instinctively, her eyes closed as she drank in the scent of him. He pulled away slowly as if he didn't want the kiss to stop.

"So, where are we headed?" Chelsea said, open to just about anywhere with Ray.

"No place special. Just somewhere I can have a little time alone with you."

His eyes met hers, twinkling with the sheer contentment that reflected her happiness. Ray escorted her to his silver SUV and opened the door like a gentleman would. Once he got in, he found a station on the radio that pleased them both, and off they went. He headed down the highway, thinking a beach stroll would be nice; perfect, actually. He pulled off the highway and into a lot near the beach. Chelsea read the sign. "PEARL BEACH" She'd never heard of it but trusted Ray to pick an excellent place for them to be together.

He pulled into a parking space and stopped. They got out and went hand in hand down a short path to the beach. As they walked and talked and listened to the sounds nearby, their minds and bodies were so in tune with each other, the ocean waves drumming their low, rushing sound that could lull a person to sleep. Suddenly, the rest of the world slipped away, and they were just with each other; nothing else crept in.

Chelsea was anxious to know more about him. Although they had spent time together recently, neither one knew much about the other. They began playing a game to learn little morsels about one another and have a little fun.

"Two truths and a lie," Chelsea said with a fun-loving twinkle in her eye that gave way to mischievousness. "You tell me three things, two true and one a lie. Then I guess which is which."

Ray laughed aloud, thinking there were a lot of things he wouldn't want her to know for fear it would make her turn and run, but he played along. Then he said, almost daring her, "You go first."

The two 'would-be' lovers played the game and had a wonderful time "guessing" facts and lies about each other. They walked and kissed and counted the stars in the sky. Ray said, "I think we've walked a couple of miles by now, we should head back." So, they turned and backtracked the way they'd come. Chelsea thought it must be nearly midnight, thinking she should get back as well, not wanting to leave Brenna high and dry. They both needed some sleep. Chelsea has been feeling every bit of stress from the last week.

As they strolled back toward Ray's car, he noticed activity just beyond them on the beach. Ray stopped; he grabbed Chelsea's arm and forced her to stop. They listened closely, hearing shouting and cursing from the men who were now only fifty or sixty yards away. Ray put his arm around Chelsea's shoulder and led her away from the beach. The berm was laced with long grass and thick bushes where Chelsea would be hidden from the harsh eyes of the other men there creating the stir. Ray looked at her, his eyes serious in a way she'd never seen before.

"Sit here and be quiet. If that group doesn't know you're here, you'll be safe." He gave her a quick peck and walked along the make-believe line between the grass and the beach. He turned and looked at her, whispering, "Record this." In one motion, Ray pulled out his phone and began recording the activity as well.

He moved methodically toward the scuttle on the beach, being as inconspicuous as possible. A moment later, a boat ran ashore. Ray missed it completely, as he was so laser-focused on the apparent barbaric activity before him. Two men, similar to the description that Andrea had given, were manhandling two girls, or what appeared to be girls, hidden by hoods, toward the boat. Ray was visibly holding his breath. He couldn't believe he'd stumbled upon the exact situation they had worked out from Andrea's witness statement.

He slumped down, staying low so his movement wouldn't catch their attention. He listened carefully and recorded the activity. He was as still as he could be and zoomed in with his camera on the faces of the men and the numbers on the boat. It was tough to see, but he thought the lab could get a good image. Ray was cursing under his breath, knowing he couldn't get a tracker on the boat. He thought they might know where they were taking the girls if they could watch the boat's direction.

Chelsea was slumped in the grass, straining to see. While Ray was inching closer, Chelsea called Wink.

Speaking in barely a whisper, she said, "We're down on Pearl Beach, and we are watching the same guys wrangling a couple of girls onto a boat. Ray thinks it's the same thing that happened to Andy. He doesn't want to get too close and jeopardize the girls. Is there any way you can get an eye in the sky, or the Marina Police, or something out there to find out where they're taking their victims?" Wink was amazed at what he just heard.

Before Chelsea had a chance to forward him a picture she had taken with her phone, the loud crack of a gunshot rang out. Chelsea dropped her head down into the grass; she saw Ray dive into the grass as well, attempting to take cover. Someone caught sight of him inching his way down the beach and decided to try to slow him down. Ray had gotten a second to look at the person holding the gun, creeping close enough that he could make out some features of the culprit. Under his breath, he said, "That guy fits Collin's description."

The bits and pieces of their investigation kept leading them to Collin being a suspect, but it was more about his association with them, not that he was in on it. This hard evidence would prove otherwise.

Chelsea was as low as she could be amongst the scraggly shoots of grass but kept recording the unfolding events. After the gunshot and the recovery from the shock of it, she focused the camera on the pistol toter in the boat and realized she knew the shooter. She had difficulty holding the camera steady, shocked at the sight. "Collin," she said to herself in a whisper. It was no wonder he'd disappeared after they found Andrea.

The whole time the shocking events were happening, Wink was on the phone and heard everything.

"Chelsea … Chelsea." It took a moment for her to realize her phone was talking to her. "You, okay?

She gathered her wits about her and said in a muffled voice, "Yeah, fine. Ray's okay too, I think."

Wink sounded relieved. "I'm calling the Lieutenant."

Chelsea covered her mouth, afraid that her voice would carry. "Can we get a boat in the water? Isn't there someone we could get out here?"

Wink hung up the phone abruptly, and Chelsea half expected him to show up personally. She hoped the Lieutenant would get a helicopter in the air to the location shared with him third hand. As for now, Ray and Chelsea could only watch as the girls were loaded into the boat, their heads hooded. The criminals knew there were alleged witnesses in the vicinity and moved swiftly. Chelsea, still squatting low in the grass, faced the fact that it was a replica of what Andrea described, and a shiver ran up her spine.

Once they were all loaded, one of the kidnappers shoved off on their way to an unknown location. As soon as the little boat was out of range, Ray came back to Chelsea, crouching in the shrubbery and raised his phone to call the Lieutenant to report what he'd seen.

Chelsea grabbed his arm, interrupting. "While you were getting shot at, I called Wink, who contacted the Lieutenant, who I hope will send a helicopter. With luck, it will be here any minute."

Ray looked at her, surprised by her quick thinking, and smiled broadly. "Well, you little angel you." He wrapped her in his arms and kissed her. He was so happy that moment, happy with his connection to Chelsea, happy about finding the pot of gold at the end of the rainbow.

"We might not get them all, but we'll get some of them. With a bit of luck, we can find the missing girls and return them to their families."

Ray and Chelsea had just turned to make their way back to the car when they heard the helicopter's choof-choof sound in the distance. They stopped on the beach and watched the bust unfold before them. They could see a spotlight searching for the little white boat. From what he could see, they were too far west of where he believed the kidnappers to be.

Ray called dispatch and asked them to relay his cell to the chopper. Once he got through, he was able to direct them to the target. From their beach vantage point, Ray and Chelsea could see the spotlight stop as the officers in the helicopter homed in on the little white boat, registration numbers, LG-2021 N7. They could see from their perch on the distant shoreline that the Marine Police were almost upon them, red lights flashing.

He and Chelsea smiled at each other. "Wow, that is really satisfying," Chelsea said to Ray, who was sporting a toothy grin.

"It is, isn't it?" Then Ray bent his head to steal another kiss, feeling very satisfied with their accomplishment.

Chelsea huffed a breathy laugh and said, "So, if anyone asks me what we did on our first date; can I tell them we busted kidnappers?"

Ray openly laughed this time and remarked, "Doesn't everyone?" They held hands on the beach, under the stars, and returned to Ray's SUV.

33. Quagmire - 2004

Brenna was showing signs of boredom. She had been filing her nails for some time when Andrea expressed, "You know you don't have to babysit me. I'm fine." Brenna put down the file and looked at her friend.

"I'm bored for you. You must be ready to get out of here by now."

Andrea nodded. "Why are they keeping me?"

Brenna shrugged, looking at Andy with a surprised look on her face, then said sarcastically, "It might have something to do with your week-long nap. It's not normal, which makes you a bit of a Phenom. Just eat and drink and talk; they'll have no more reason to keep you."

She winked at Andrea, and then her expression became concerned. "You know, this was the trip of a lifetime. I'm sorry you didn't have much time to enjoy it." Sitting on her bed, Andrea wrapped her arms around her drawn-up knees, and her eyes were dreamy.

"Don't worry, Bren. I had a wonderful time. It was like seeing the sunset for the first time. You don't know what is missing in your life until you experience it, then you're never quite the same."

Brenna rolled her eyes. "What a messed-up thing to say," she thought to herself. Then Andrea looked at her with saddened eyes. "You and Chelsea are the ones whose trip was all messed up because of me. You've spent your week here in a fucking hospital."

Andrea gave a pitiful shake of her head. "You guys are the ones who gave up your vacation for me. I'm so sorry."

"Oh, Andy, don't you worry any. We had plenty of fun. We met cool people, ate great food, and saw some interesting things. There is nothing to be sorry about." Brenna's soft smile was very comforting. After all, Andrea didn't choose to be kidnapped. It just happened. At the same time, Andrea believed it was fate - written in the cards played for her and why the amulet picked her.

An affectionate smile grew on her face, and with a heavy sigh, she confessed, "I believe all things happen for a reason."

A moment later, Andrea's brow scrunched, labored in thought that came to her just then. "What about Jake? Weren't the two of you getting all sweetsy-sweetsy with each other? Whatever happened to that?"

Brenna rolled her eyes at her friend's description of her and Jake's relationship. She cocked her head, and her expression changed slightly. "I don't know, but he just disappeared. He stopped answering his phone when Collin did."

Andrea shook her head from side to side, showing her displeasure. "There is something just not right about that. I wonder if they're ok."

Brenna reacted. "He's kindhearted and it's easy enough for someone to want to take advantage of that. You might be right. Or maybe they just went back to Colorado."

Then, it was Brenna's turn to get all dreamy-eyed. Her friend could tell she was drenched in memories. Andrea reached out and touched her friend's hand, saying softly, and "Don't worry about it, Bren. Together or not, maybe it just wasn't meant to be."

Brenna pulled up her lips into a subtle smile. "Maybe you're right, Andy. For whatever reason, he didn't follow through, and you know how I hate a guy who doesn't follow through."

Andrea was out of bed and pacing around the room. Her legs were stable and strong, and her mind was clear. "I'm ready to go home." Without warning, Andrea thought about the hotel room and the plane fare. "Oh, we should have left - yesterday, right?" Andrea couldn't recall the date.

Brenna said hesitantly, "Yeah, I think so." They both looked up and at the dry erase board by the door, where the nurse had written February 27, 2004. Andrea was right. Their return flight was for the 26th.

"Has anyone called and changed our flight plans?"

Brenna smiled at her friend's concern, giving a nod, then said in a consoling tone, "Chelsea called the airline and told them you were in the hospital. We'll be charged a fee, but they let us change our flight. The hotel feels somewhat responsible for what happened, and gave us a couple of nights for free."

Andrea gave a nod. "This kidnapping crap has caused a bit of a quagmire, hasn't it?"

Brenna did an "uh-hum" under her breath. "Why yes, it has." Then the girls laughed, lightening the mood considerably.

"So, Chelsea and Ray are out on a date?" Andrea mainly asked to see what Brenna's reaction would be, but she was curious as well.

"Yeah, that's what she said. They've been glomming onto each other lately but haven't had any time alone. I thought it would be perfect for her, uh - them, to have some private time. Ray is a great guy. He cares a lot about people, and you and I both know Chelsea needs that."

Andrea nodded in complete agreement. "I think she needs that connection, and Ray is perfect for her." Brenna wrapped up her feelings about Chelsea's relationship in a nice, neat package.

"I think it's high time Chelsea finds happiness. But long-distance relationships are hard. Not sure how she's going to work that one out," Andrea commented. Her words were only an opinion, but down deep, she hoped that her best friend would find a man to treat her right.

"Bren, if you want to go back to the hotel, go for it. Don't stay here because of me."

Brenna was quick to answer. "Chelsea and Ray will be back, and Ray will give us a ride back to the hotel. I trust they won't be too long." She suggested, "How about we play some rummy?" and reached into the nightstand's top drawer for the deck of cards. Brenna smiled. Andrea knew she loved to play; she also knew she loved to win.

The game went from one game to two, then three. It was much later when Chelsea and Ray returned, wide-eyed and exhilarated. Both Brenna and Andrea were surprised at the exuberant expressions.

"What have you been up to?" Brenna asked with a thin-lipped grin on her face.

"You'll never guess in a million years." Chelsea paused for a moment, then slipped her arm around Ray's waist. Ray began to explain like it was his queue, drawing in a deep breath.

"We were walking down on Pearl Beach and on our way back to the car when we saw men on the beach; one of them matched the description you gave us, Andrea. They were herding a couple of girls out to a boat. Something we thought you would have experienced."

Andrea's eyes got as big as saucers. Her response was one word, and she whispered, not realizing she was now holding her breath. "Yes."

Ray gave a tip to his head in acknowledgment and continued. "So, we hid in the brush and grass nearby and filmed. Chelsea was smart enough to call Wink, who called the Lieutenant, and when they heard the gunshots, the Lieutenant hopped to and was able to get a chopper out. They spotlighted the little white boat on its way out to a ship that was anchored about a mile out in the bay. Caught the whole friggin' bunch."

"Gunshots?" Andrea said in a breathless heave. She suddenly felt numb. Her face was blank and her limbs motionless.

Brenna's jaw dropped. She said, "What, are you kidding?"

Chelsea smiled and looked very satisfied with herself. "It was just dumb luck we were there - at the right place, at the right time."

Andrea turned to her friend and said, "This is more like a terrifying predetermined series of events, not the right place." She hesitated. "It's perfect." She reached out, wrapping her arms around her friend, and tears began to fall. Andrea was overwhelmed with gratefulness and relief.

Holding the embrace, she said again, "I can't believe they shot at you."

Chelsea and Ray took turns reciting the play-by-play of the event as it unfolded before them. Down deep, Andrea wished she could have been there to identify them and feel the satisfaction that this whole thing would end right here in New Orleans. Just like that. Chelsea put her hands on Andrea's shoulders and forced her to sit on the bed. "Andy," she said with a serious face. "I gotta tell you ..." She looked down momentarily, gaining courage. "It was Collin who shot at us. He was the one holding the gun." Andrea's face went red. She was embarrassed and angry at the same time.

"I'm sorry," Chelsea said, eyes staring at the specks of sand still on her feet. Andrea was dispassionate in her response.

"I should have known. I - I should have known," trembling now and gently shaking her head from side to side.

Brenna stepped over to her with a quick retort. "But how could you? Remember, he fooled all of us."

Andrea, still numb from Chelsea and Ray's news, thought to herself, *it's too good to be true, but still, I should have known.*

Ray explained that the Marine Police were the ones to bring them in for booking, and there are still a lot of questions that need to be answered. Then he asked, "Could you come to the station and pick the ones you know out of a lineup? It would be particularly important for us to have a positive ID from you."

Without words, Andrea nodded in agreement. Her mind went to what it would be like to see them again. Brenna was curious about the girls and was inquiring about finding any of the others who were missing.

Ray responded with a shake of his head. "I don't know what they've found. I'm sure I'll hear all about it in the morning."

Andrea began to shake, becoming weak in the knees. She never expected this kind of reaction to the news delivered by Ray and Chelsea. *What will they find out? Who will they find? Will they discover the other girls are still alive?*

Andrea's thoughts began to haunt her. She soon realized the remorse she felt wasn't for herself, it was for the others in the van. The ones who were victims. She went over to the chair by her bedside, unable to focus on anything. She just sat, staring off into the distance.

Seeing her friend's distress, Chelsea squatted down beside her. "This is the beginning of the end for those guys, Andy. Maybe we can end it all together."

Andrea tilted her head toward her friend. "I know, I hope so."

The conversation continued, but Andrea could not focus on it. Her thoughts went to Collin and their time together. He was a fun and exciting person. He could have been an excellent catch for anyone, but he was the one holding the gun. He was shooting a gun.

Worse yet, he was shooting at her friends. She couldn't help but see the darkness of this day amid the utter relief radiating through her. There was a good outcome for her, but she was one of many, possibly hundreds, who thought Collin was a 'good guy' or one of the others of his gang was a 'good guy.' And here they were, literally the scum of the earth, and she had gotten mixed up with them.

Chelsea and Brenna were chattering like squirrels, and Andrea was ready for a little time alone. Looking up at her friends with a forced smile on her face, she feigned tiredness, putting forth a fake yawn and stretching long and slow.

"I think I need to rest now. It has been a day."

The other girls looked at each other again, concerned for their friend. "I bet it has, Andy. I'm so sorry." Chelsea grabbed Andrea's hand.

Then Andrea looked at her friend, a faint smile still on her face. "No. It's all good. I'm just so tired right now - Like I ran a marathon."

"I get it. You really have." She reached over and squeezed her friend instinctively. "Get some rest. We'll be here in the morning." Ray, Chelsea, and Brenna then left the room and turned off the light, leaving only a warm glow from the vanity light in the bathroom that shone along the tile floor.

Andrea lay there in the dark as her mind searched to make sense of the news she was just given. *It's a miracle*, she thought, then grabbed the beloved magic stone that hung on her neck. *An absolute miracle.*

34. Friendship and Adventure - 2004

Andrea drifted in and out of sleep all night long. She blamed her restlessness on the emotional roller coaster that began with the initial assault, minced with the relief of never having to find out what those convicts had in mind. The peace of the night while she was alone was blissful. Andrea loved her friends, but since her return from the 18th century, she required more isolation. The chatter, beeps, and alarms were so loud. So many beautiful things are missed when you can't hear past the noise.

When she could clear her mind between the constant but subtle noises, she recalled Miss Josephine's words and reflected on all that had happened last week. *I see things more clearly.* It saddened her to think of how easily a sane, average person (at least, that is what she thought of herself) could get tangled up with such shady people. She, indeed, was a victim, as were the others in the van. She also understood now the far-reaching grasp of these criminals and to the extent they would go to find their victims. It was pathetic.

Then Andrea nodded to herself and thought about everything that had happened the whole week, questioning her decision-making ability. Had the decisions she acted on been necessary and meaningful? She decided it was foolish to go after Jack, but it did lead her to Menawah's tribe, and the whole debacle that followed prompted the Creek Indians to what could be called a happy ending, including getting Jacob's family back home safely. Jacob's family was her extended family in a strange home away from home. She missed them so, just now. The lines between the past she visited and now, today, were incredibly blurry.

The culmination of the tarot reading and the magic twist from the Lapis Lazuli amulet she wore was complete, and she felt accomplished. It suddenly came to her; *its power is wisdom and understanding*, but it is much more than that. It allowed her to be something she wasn't and never thought she could be. Her mind, now scattered, drifted back to her tarot reading, and thinking there was so much truth about what the cards told her. Andrea thought, smiling to herself; thinking it ironic, how the amulet and the reading worked together. The thought of its magic made her tingle. She allowed herself a moment of happiness, experiencing the thoughts now so vivid and real.

She had been given a rare gift to share with the world; she was sure of that. After a long while and a plethora of emotions, sleep overtook her, and she rested so soundly that no dreams came.

*

The daylight peeked around the entire length of the curtain, the sun bright and clear. It wasn't the sun that woke her; Maggie had managed to rouse her out of her slumber.

"Good Mornin'!" Maggie was always so cheerful in the morning.

"Good morning," Andrea replied in a sleepy voice.

"The doc is going to give you a final once over, but he will probably let you go home today if everything checks out." After hearing that, Andrea quickly pulled herself up to full alertness. Maggie said in almost a whisper, "Don't let him know I told you that." She winked at Andrea.

"Wow, that would be great!" she responded, wiping the blur out of her eyes. She needed to call Chelsea and have her bring a fresh change of clothes, as the only clothing she had with her she'd worn for a whole week. She blinked hard trying to wrap her head around what was real and what was a dream. The week's events were prominent in Andrea's mind, and she smiled at herself. *I could use some clean clothes, though.*

Maggie finished fussing. She updated the dry-erase board with the new day's information and headed out of the room.

Andrea glanced at the clock on the wall. It was 7:00. The perfect time for her to call morning, but a little early for Chelsea.

Not long after Maggie left the room, a server came in from the kitchen, bringing Andrea some breakfast. She hadn't given it much thought, but she was famished. The breakfast smelled delicious. Eggs, ham, toast, apple juice, and coffee.

Andrea licked the plate clean and removed the paper cover from her cup of coffee. She breathed in the delicious smell and took a sip. It was delightful. She'd missed coffee almost as much as she missed her friends.

By the time she was done eating, it was nearly 8:00. Time to call Chelsea. As expected, she woke her up, but it didn't deter her from completing the request. Without coming right out and telling her, she hinted that she might be released soon and needed fresh clothes. Chelsea agreed, happy her friend could finally be set free.

Dr. Jared Armesto was the attending physician who was the next person to enter the room. He politely nodded but appeared to be a bit shy. Andrea thought he was a handsome man, younger than an attending should be, but he professionally tended to her. The doctor did a quick overall exam and, when finished, made some notes.

Andrea commented, "So, what is your prognosis?"

Dr. Armesto pulled up the corners of his mouth with a faint smile. "Well, I really can't find anything wrong with you that would stop me from letting you get on with your life. Would you like to go home?"

Andrea was almost giddy inside. She tried very hard to contain it, but her excitement was brimming. "Yes, I think I've had enough of this hospital, no insult intended."

He laughed casually. "None taken." The doctor responded quickly, and Andrea thought he'd probably heard it before. He told her he would get her release paperwork done, and she should be free to go. Then, as quickly as he'd come, he was gone, the heavy wooden door shutting softly behind him.

Andrea was relieved and maybe a little scared. She hadn't been just a regular girl on the street for a while. At least it seemed so. She hoped she wouldn't have P.T.S.D. because of the kidnapping, but she thought it best to expect to feel a bit out of sorts for a while. She was up and pacing around the room now. It seemed best for thinking. "*The Indians abducted me, too. I was kept as a prisoner in that world as well. Why did it seem so different?*" She knew in her heart, the natives of the tribe never intended to hurt her; in contrast, she was quite sure of the trafficker's intent. *What would have happened if I didn't fight back?* She caught herself getting agitated, repeatedly putting herself in the shoes of the girls in the van who didn't escape.

Brenna was the first one in the door, interrupting Andrea's thoughts. Pushing herself into the room, not even saying 'hello,' she looked at her with a strained smile and asked, "So, are they gonna let you out?"

Andrea looked at her friend and returned a cheerful expression. "Yep, they just need to wrap up the paperwork, and I will be free to go."

Chelsea then came through the door, toting café 'au 'lait. "Oh, my God, you were reading my mind!" Andrea reached for the cup, removed the lid, and held it to her nose. "I've died and gone to heaven," she said, inhaling as the final word trickled off her tongue.

Chelsea laughed and said, "Thought you'd want to celebrate; hold the vodka of course." Andrea nodded and sipped simultaneously. It really was heavenly.

With clean clothes in hand, Andrea went into her bathroom and showered. She pulled out her clean clothes and stuffed her other clothing into the same bag. As she pulled out the shirt and pants she'd worn in her dream, or, other world experience, she caught the scent of Becca's washing soap tinged with wood smoke. She paused and put her blue shirt to her nose. It was! It smelled of the clothing that hung on the clothesline in the front of the cabin. She paused for a minute and took in the scent, then decided she would bag it and never wash that shirt again, so she could breathe in that wonderful, vivid memory.

"Now, this is something that was sorely missed in 1798," Andrea thought as she stepped into the warm, wet sprinkles of the shower and washed. She shook her head at the thought. "What a bunch of spoiled babies." She washed herself thoroughly, then toweled off and slipped on her fresh clothing.

Andrea flipped her hair with a towel and squeezed it until it was nearly dry. She massaged it, and the curls just popped. "The humidity will fuzz it up, so I might as well just go with it." She looked at her friends, who knew she would always fuss over her hair. Fuzz was never a good thing.

Walking past a mirror, Andrea noticed how baggy her clothing was. She hadn't given much thought to it before now. The reality was that she hadn't eaten much for a solid week before yesterday. *Thank God I wasn't skinny before*, she thought to herself.

The three girls sat and talked and drank coffee for another hour. Finally, Maggie came in with her release paperwork in hand. She showed Andrea where to sign and handed her some instructions, which Andrea thrust into her pocket not even glancing at them.

"You are free to go now." Maggie sighed. "We're gonna miss you around here. It's not every day you meet someone who experienced certain death and lived to talk about it." Then she winked. The other girls saw the humor in what Maggie said, but Andrea didn't. It was a little too soon, striking too close to home.

Andrea said her goodbyes, and with the help of her friends, they gathered the few things she had, and out the door they went, like three peas in a pod.

The girls found a bench at a bus stop and sat. Andrea was getting her bearings, and Chelsea was on the phone with the airline, trying to arrange flights. Andrea and Brenna could hear the voice on the other end running through the schedule and availabilities. Chelsea told her friends,

"Tomorrow afternoon would be the soonest." Both Andrea and Brenna nodded.

They didn't know what to expect. None of them were able to guess when the hospital would release Andrea. So, now that she was free, what would they do all day? With several things in mind that she never got to do, she turned to Brenna, now dubbed the activities star, and asked, "So, what haven't we seen yet?"

Brenna showed a half-cocked smile and pulled out her phone. She scrolled through some things and said, "You know what? We haven't been to the Mardi Gras Museum yet. Wanna do that?"

Andrea shrugged, then looked at Chelsea. "Sure," The two girls recited in unison. Brenna got the directions, and Chelsea looked at the bus schedule.

"Looks like we need to take that bus over there," she said, pointing across the street and just down the block. The three friends walked the half block to the other stop, arriving just as the bus pulled in. They traveled like tourists do, fingering at points of interest and looking up locations of other interesting sites. There were few others on the bus they chose, far fewer than the week of Mardi Gras.

The bus pulled into the stop that seemed nearest to their destination, and the girls departed. Brenna led the three enterprising friends down the sidewalk, looking at the street signs as they went along. The downtown area was quaint and dirty but eclectic and interesting. Chelsea told Andrea about Ray, and Brenna would sprinkle in the little things that Chelsea skipped over, making her the center of attention.

"So, what will you do about him when we board that plane tomorrow?" Andrea asked point blank. Chelsea scrunched up her eyebrows, as thinking such a thing was painful.

"We talked about it a little. Not sure. He wants to be with me, and I want to be with him, but he has his career and all.

Andrea nodded her understanding. "It's hard to be away from people you love." The very next thought that crossed her mind was her little brother. She thought of his smile and his wild head of hair. Those thoughts warmed her heart. Her brother was always funny and fun. She remembered her promise to herself about spending more time with him.

"So, are you considering moving to New Orleans to be with him?" It was a blunt statement, but Andrea wasn't beating around the bush. Not anymore. In the last week, she'd learned that nothing was guaranteed. Live in the moment.

Chelsea paused a moment and finished her sentence. "The thought crossed my mind," she said plainly. Just hearing herself say it made her feel like a traitor.

Andrea stopped and looked at her friend. "You gotta do what's good for you, Chels. Don't worry about us or other things you need to do. Brenna and I will be fine, and the other things can wait."

Chelsea nodded, nearly expressionless. It was clear to her besties that this was indeed a trying decision.

Brenna was in front of the other two and had kept walking, not realizing Chelsea and Andrea had stopped. She turned and doubled back to them, catching sight of something just over their heads and behind them. "Look," Brenna said, her eyes wide with awe. Andrea and Chelsea turned in time to see a funnel cloud coming out of the gray sky above. It was over the water in the gulf, creating a waterspout, something none of them had ever seen.

They stood quietly and watched the phenomenon. It didn't take long for it to fade and the clouds to break enough for the sun to peek through, revealing a rainbow. "Would you have ever guessed?" Brenna said with perfect timing. Brenna and Chelsea held up their phones to capture the odd timing of the force of nature. The aftermath left them feeling calm, blessed by the chance to see something so incredibly rare.

Out of nowhere, Andrea changed the subject. She said, "I need to replace my phone. Those kidnapping bastards busted it, and I could have used it just now." She was a little jealous about her friends being able to take pictures or share them.

Chelsea said, "I bet we can find you a new one." The words got Brenna started, scrolling on her phone again, searching for a store close by.

"Looks like there is a place about a block up from Miss Josephine's. It's not far from here. Wanna walk?" Andrea and Chelsea looked at Brenna as if she had asked a silly question. They both put their arm around Brenna, and the three of them marched down the walk toward Miss Josephine's. It was only a few blocks away, and they stood at the door in minutes. Andrea pushed through it and was helped almost immediately. She got set up with a new phone, and retrieved all the voice messages and texts from the previous week.

The other girls shared with Andrea several pictures they'd taken, which cheered her up considerably. She scanned through her texts and eliminated the voicemails that weren't important. One of the voice messages was from Collin. In listening to his message, Andrea was suddenly flushed with emotion. The more she thought about it, the angrier she was at her inability to call "bullshit" on Collin. She listened:

"Hey, Andy, it's me. By the time you get this, I will be long gone, and you'll know it was me who marked you for the taking. For what it's worth, I did like you. It was hard telling them all where they could find you, knowing it would let the cat out of the bag. I wanted to say I'm sorry."

Andrea heard the click that ended the call. She was breathless. They were standing just outside the store, and Chelsea and Brenna could see Andrea had gotten news and didn't quite know how to react to it. Her body language gave away the feelings she didn't show on her face. The other girls stood there and waited for Andrea to spill the news. She was non-animated but quietly said, "It was Collin."

She half expected him to reach out; at least, she thought he owed her an explanation but never got one. She said, "He just said he was sorry." Brenna, who always had something to say, was speechless. Chelsea had covered her mouth with her hand to hide her look of surprise but knew words were not necessary.

Without a word, Andrea began to walk down the sidewalk away from the store. She didn't know where to go but didn't want to stay there. The scenery needed to change. The other girls walked right beside her, one on each side. No one spoke, waiting for Andrea to open up about what she was feeling. Finally realizing her mood was a severe buzz kill, she thought it was time to talk.

"I'm not mad at Collin. He was getting paid to do a job. I'm mad at myself for falling for a guy who had no respect for me. No appreciation for my feelings. I was stupid."

Brenna put her hand on Andrea's shoulder. "Well, you're not the only girl who ever fell for a schmuck. Don't worry, we got cha'." Andrea smiled, knowing that Brenna was her own personal cheerleader.

Chelsea grabbed her hand. "He's gone. Good riddance to bad rubbish."

Andrea laughed and said, "My Uncle used to say that." She took a deep breath and let Brenna guide them to the museum.

When Ray called Chelsea, the three friends were paying their entrance fees for the Museum. "Whatcha doin'?" Ray said with a cheerful tone.

"We just walked into the Mardi Gras Museum. What are you doing?" Chelsea said, sounding more flirty than usual.

"I was hoping I could get Andrea to come in and identify the kidnappers. We have them in holding right now."

Chelsea relayed the question to Andrea, who nodded her consent. The girls were able to get their money back from the entrance fees they had just paid and grab an Uber to the station.

Ray met them and got Chelsea and Brenna situated, then led Andrea back through a maze of hallways, finally entering a room where they could see the assailants – through a two-way mirror.

Andrea was unexpectedly emotional about seeing the accused, trembling slightly, and sweat built up on her brow. She had fought hard against them the night she escaped and didn't expect that, seeing them would affect her, but it certainly did.

Andrea positively identified three of the five in the lineup as part of the crew that participated in her kidnapping.

The officer in the room with the accused separated the ones she'd pointed out and sent them out of the room and into the hands of Wink Adams, who was just outside the door. A different officer took the others, and the room was empty.

Andrea thought, "*Is that it?*" Before she could answer, a different officer escorted Collin and Adam into the same room.

The sight of him swept Andrea's breath away. There were so many thoughts of the time she'd spent with Collin, utterly oblivious to the ruse she was a part of. Her emotions became hostile, and through gritted teeth, she said, "That one is Collin, and that one is Adam," pointing to each as she said it. Saying the words aloud lightened the burden she had carried with her since the night on the beach. Although it was difficult, Andrea had done her duty and assisted the N.O.P.D. in getting hideous criminals off the street.

When Ray took her arm to lead her back into the lobby where her friends waited, Andrea was shaking. As they walked down the hallway, she drew in a long, slow breath, relieved. Aside from appearing in court, the hard part was over, or so she thought.

She heard his voice, pleading with the officer escorting him to loosen his cuffs. There was no disguising it. They were taking Collin and Adam to a different block of holding cells on the other side of the lobby, which meant they would be face-to-face. In a split-second, Collin looked up, right when Andrea's attention was drawn to him. Chelsea and Brenna both gasped, concerned about their friend, who was struggling with anxiety about her capture and near-death experience.

Andrea took a step toward Collin. Brenna rapidly reached out for her arm, but Andrea shook herself free. She abruptly said, "STOP!" and the officer holding Colin turned to look at her. She walked up to him, unable to dampen her anger, moving her body and her face so he would have to look her in the eye. She couldn't stop the flow of words.

"I hate you to the core, but I should thank you. What you did to me – what you do to all of these girls taught me so much more about life and dickheads like you. I know you were in it for the money and didn't really give one shit about me. But here are a couple of facts you will have to live with. You will not be rich, you will not be happy, and you will not be free. Not for a long time, if ever. I hope the years you spend in prison are worth it; it's right where you belong."

When she was finished, she took a deep breath and walked away in disgust. Collin's eyes followed her for a moment, then fell to the floor. He knew her words were valid, but wished he could have come up with something to say back to her. Nothing he could say would make her think about him in a positive light ever again.

*

The rest of the afternoon was easy by comparison. The girls shopped, ate, laughed, and photographed through as much of New Orleans as they could. In the evening light, they ended up on the balcony in the hotel with drinks in their hands, watching the sunset. Andrea held up her glass and made a toast with a smile. "Through thick and thin, we made it. Here's to friendship and adventure." She held her glass up in between her besties, and they clinked to the truth of the words.

35. Let go – 2004

After a drink-laden night and lacking sleep, the morning was a whirlwind of activity. Packing up all their things after nine days of occupation required some attention to detail. Chelsea was the first to claim she'd gotten it all and told the other girls in an anxious voice, "I'll meet you in the lobby." Andrea guessed Ray was down there, ready to give them a ride to the airport.

Brenna gave the place one more look, satisfied there was nothing left in the room that didn't belong there "Are you coming?" Brenna asked Andrea, heading toward the door with her suitcase in tow.

Andrea nodded and said, "I'll be right there." Brenna went out the door and headed to the elevator, leaving Andrea alone in the room.

She stood there in the stillness, relishing just a moment of peace before saying goodbye to this city. It tested her to be sure, but she knew what she would take away from this place was so much more than just trinkets and photos.

She pushed her hair back over her shoulder, away from her face, and stooped to pick up the handle of her purse. A shadow of a smile grew on her face, reflecting on the crazy week and a half she had there. She left the room and let the door close softly behind her.

Andrea realized her hunch was correct when she reached the lobby; Ray was there. He greeted them with a smile and a "good morning," but the four friends knew it was going to be a tearful farewell. Andrea was aware of Ray and Chelsea's affection for each other but didn't know, or even try to understand all they'd been through while she was "out of it," lying in that hospital bed.

Ray had seen Chelsea's tears and apprehension many times over the last few days, and accepted them, along with the beautiful person she was. Andrea wondered if Ray's driving force to find her had to do with Chelsea or the mission to see that the criminals face justice. *I don't care, I'm here*. Andrea shook her head at the thought of what a gift her "happy ending" was.

Ray scooted the threesome into the car with their luggage, and they were off to the airport. The terminal was bustling with all kinds of people. Most of the faces were disinterested in the goings-on around them, but for the three brave friends, it meant leaving gleeful and painful memories behind. It only took a few minutes to check their bags and make their way through security. Ray escorted them, wanting to be with Chelsea until the very last second before she boarded the plane. They sat quietly together and talked privately, holding hands and were as close to each other as they could get, in the middle of an airport, surrounded by strangers.

Andrea watched closely, trying to see what they were saying to each other. She finally gave up, knowing Chelsea would share soon enough. Her heart ached for her friend, though. It was so far away, and Ray was a fantastic guy. Perfect for Chelsea. She was a bit jealous of the private world they shared. Although Andrea had many alluring partners in her past, she'd never had that kind of connection to someone. Given her most recent experience, it may be a while before she lets go of her inhibitions enough to involve herself in a relationship. When the call to board the flight came over the speakers, they all got up, including Ray. He hugged Chelsea deeply as if trying to absorb her; his expression saddened. They kissed goodbye, but Chelsea couldn't hold back her tears.

Ray said to her softly, his face close to hers, "It won't be long, I promise." Brenna gave him a quick hug and thanked him, almost unmoved by the emotions shared between the two love birds.

Andrea stood before him with a tear in her eye as well. "I can't thank you enough for not giving up on me or the other girls."

Ray nodded and smiled, taking hold of her hands. "We will need you to testify when the kidnappers go to trial."

Andrea signaled her understanding. "I look forward to it." She hugged Ray as well and turned to get in line.

She was behind the others in the row of people boarding the plane, when she looked back at where she had been sitting, she saw her sweater lying on the ground. "Oh, crap," she said, flustered. Dropping her carry-on where she stood, she hurried over to the chair, bent there to pick it up, and the amulet strap tugged on her neck. In that second, she heard the speaker make one more last call to board their plane. She quickly grabbed her sweater and ran back to the line and to her carry-on. Andrea was the last one to walk down the corridor to the door of the plane.

Brenna and Chelsea were already seated, Chelsea's eyes rimmed in pink, still recovering from her emotional departure. Andrea stowed her carry-on and moved across the front of her cohorts to the window, happy that neither of the other two girls was interested in the view.

Just as the plane moved into position on the runway, Andrea thought silently about the time she'd had here. She was unconscious most of the time, but in reality, it was a hectic week. All the good she'd experienced made her want to pay it forward one day. Then she smiled a faint little smile. As she watched the plane move away from the terminal, she felt a tightness in her chest, sad to leave this place, her mind fluttered softly about with thoughts of home.

The plane began to accelerate, thrusting them back into their seats. Andrea reached for the amulet around her neck, looking for a little emotional support, and found it wasn't there. She let out a gasp. "My necklace! Brenna and Chelsea looked at her, then at the empty place where the necklace should be.

"Aww ..." Brenna expressed. "That was so cool."

Andrea felt an emptiness she had never expected, like she'd lost a friend. As the plane circled on a northwestern heading, Andrea had a full view of the vastness of the Gulf of Mexico. She saw a few smaller boats, along with one rather large ship dotting the surface, shrinking away as they gained altitude. Although she was angry that she had lost the necklace, she felt her connection to it fade.

Then she thought, maybe someone else who needs it will find it. She smiled to herself again, remembering how she just knew after seeing it for the first time that she couldn't live without it. Now, she was ready to let go. In retrospect, it wasn't about Andrea letting go of the amulet; it was that the amulet had let go of her.

36. Out of Nowhere – 2004

"Bobby, will you please leave those things alone?" The four-year-old was darting around the black rows of seats at the South terminal, making a game of it. Atina Brighton was a young mother who just about had enough. New Orleans was the last stop along the way to Denver and home. She had decided she would never travel with a toddler again, as it was way too hard to wrangle all that energy. There were so many people coming and going about the airport terminal, she was afraid he would disturb them, but she had been chasing him for most of an hour and needed a minute to sit. She flopped down in a chair and watched Bobby run around, never taking her eyes off him.

The voice over the loudspeaker finally announced their flight, and Atina got Bobby's attention so they could board the plane on the final stretch home. The agent examined the boarding passes, and once aboard, she found the assigned seats and got settled, having Bobby sit near the window, hoping it would keep him busy and less curious.

The plane taxied down the tarmac and stopped before turning onto the runway to begin takeoff. Bobby was quiet, which usually meant something suspicious was happening.

"What ya' doin' baby?" Atina asked him, more patiently than before.

Bobby looked up and said, "I have a surprise for you, mama." He held out a strikingly beautiful blue stone necklace.

Atina's heart sank. "Did you steal that? Where did you find it?"

His expression was deflated as he expected his mother to love his gift. "I found it. It wanted me to give it to you."

She shook her head, thinking he was telling a story. "I think it's beautiful, honey, but when you find something, you need to turn it into lost and found. Someone probably lost it."

"Okay, mama." and he dropped the conversation there.

Atina held the necklace. It was old; she could tell that for sure. It didn't have a chain; it was a leather strap that looked like it had been replaced recently. The thin metal wire that held a small piece of ivory, intricate and beautiful. And was the white piece ivory? Maybe bone? As she admired it, the warmth grew in her hand. She was flushed with a feeling of empowerment and determination. It was the strangest sensation she ever experienced. Atina was Native American and believed in the powers of the earth and all things, heartbeat or not, had a spirit. This product of the earth was showing off its power by speaking to her, and unlike other gifts, she heard - and felt it.

This amulet touched her unexpectedly, and she realized what Bobby said was true. It spoke to him, and it grasped her soul. Her thoughts led her to the stone's previous owner and how on God's green earth had it been left here for her son to find.

She craved knowing more about it and knew that in the coming weeks, she would find out. A moment later, she sat back and closed her eyes, and for the first time in a long time, she was completely calm.

Epilogue: Savannah – 2010

Brenna turned around to her friends, smiling, and couldn't help but tell them, "I have been so excited for this day. I can't believe it has been so long since we've had a girls' trip." Andrea smiled cheerfully, "It's long past due!"

Chelsea put her arms up to stretch, which only emphasized the roundness of her belly to her friends. "Yep, it won't be long before I can't do this, so we'd better enjoy ourselves!" She swiped her arm across the little bulge, admiring the life growing inside her.

"So, Andrea, how have things been at Northwestern? Do you like your new job?"

Hearing Chelsea's question, her eyes shined with enthusiasm, her internal joy showing on every inch of her face. "It has been wonderful. The new program is getting a lot of attention now, thanks to our research and generous donations. My team will be spending time across the nation learning about the Native cultures of thirty tribes or more. It will be a challenge, but well worth the work."

Since their last girls' trip and Andrea's summer with the Salish, she had a newfound passion for helping these native populations keep their heritage alive within their tribes, and

450

securing ways to share their cultures with the world. She absolutely lit up when she talked about it.

The girls climbed out of the rental car and scuffed through the sand, anxious to get a peek at the spans of the Atlantic Ocean. Andrea drew a deep breath, turning her face to the sun. Seattle had been drizzly and miserable lately, and the sunshine was warm and welcoming. They continued on a path that appeared to lead down to a little cove. It was hidden with tall scraggly bushes that had been beaten by the wind regularly, but when they'd pushed past the overgrowth, there was a beautiful white sand beach, palm trees on one side, and a rocky outcropping jetting out into the bay on the other. Brenna and Chelsea did the usual "oohhs and ahhs," but the experience for Andrea was quite different. It was unmistakably Deja-vu. With no warning, the memories of her trip into the past came flooding back. She instinctively took off her shoes and went directly to the water's edge, looking into the sand for bubbles and tiny breathing holes, trying to spot clams. Before she knew it, she was on her knees with her hands thrust into the wet sand. A second later, she came up with a small, dollar-sized clam in her hand, holding it up like a prize.

Brenna and Chelsea stared at her like she was sporting two heads. "Where ... um, did you learn to do that?" Chelsea said with an undeniable look of bewilderment on her face.

The three of them hadn't spoken about Andrea's visit to the 18th century for quite some time, but she couldn't attribute her knowledge of her actions to anything else. She smiled and said, "Johnny."

Chelsea came back with a quick retort. "Who's Johnny? Some new beau you haven't told us about?"

Andrea looked at them, drinking in the shock of their expressions. She quickly tried to cover her tracks. "Oh, no. Never mind. He's just a friend, that's all. You guys should try this. It's fun!"

Brenna approached her, looking in the sand just as Andrea was, then said, "Okay, show me how."

Andrea gave her a few simple instructions, and her friend dove in, dashing about the sand, finding the happy little shells, desperate to stay out of the hands of the girls, who now were giggling and covered with sand.

Chelsea watched them scamper around the beach, preferring to walk along the water's edge, letting the refreshing waves splash against her legs. "This place is beautiful," she said with a dreamy look in her eyes. "It's like time stands still right here."

Andrea shot her a look. "What did you say?"

Chelsea heard the change in her voice. "Doesn't it feel like this spot, right here, has been here for thousands of years? It's breathtaking." Andrea felt the rush of warmth drench her soul. She closed her eyes and breathed in deeply, smelling all the things she smelled that day she woke up on the beach. Taking a minute to let the memories flow through her, she smiled to herself and thanked God for allowing her the reflections that had eluded her these past years.

Andrea sat up and watched Brenna dash about the beach, acting like a schoolgirl, then looked at Chelsea and asked, "Would you mind if we did a little exploring today? I have something I'd like to check out."

Chelsea looked at her with that twinkle in her eye and said, "Sure, I'm game for anything."

Finally getting Brenna's attention long enough to get her off the beach, they climbed into the car again and headed north, along the ocean for a while. Then it fell away, and they were in the roaming hills just inland from the beach. Andrea, staring out the window of the passenger seat, was trying to manage her pulse, her heartbeat quickening as she recalled so many of the locations she'd passed in the previous century. On the left, she saw the river, the transient tribe was forced to cross, and a while later, on the right, the lower edge of the settlement of Atiketiv' Indian village.

They drove along for another half hour when Andrea sat up abruptly and said, "Here. Slow down."

Brenna looked at her and asked, "Are you going to be sick?"

Andrea shook her head very slowly. "No, this is it. Please pull over here and stop."

Brenna was a little agitated at her friend's insistence but stopped anyway. Andrea got out, crossed the road, and walked up to a mound of rubble. It looked like the remnants of an old cabin. Andrea was shaking now but intensely looking all around, remembering where everything was: the barn, the pasture, the chicken coop. She breathed heavily, as her eyes couldn't cover the landscape fast enough.

The other girls got out of the car and followed behind her slowly, passing suspicious glances at each other, wondering what was up with Andrea and how she knew this place. She seemed to be looking for something, but what? They both wondered, but neither were inclined to speak.

Andrea strolled out to the end of the field, studying the place she'd crossed into the thick brush and disappeared; merely the beginning of the journey the amulet had in store for her. She remembered what it used to look like; the huge plot now covered with weeds and scraggly bushes. Something caught her eye that she didn't remember before; now, she focused on the item that seemed out of place. Approaching it, pushing the knee-high weeds out of the way, she saw a dilapidated makeshift cross with A. BRUER – D – 1798 etched on the cross bar. She fell to her knees in a rush of emotion, openly crying at the sight, laughing through the tears.

Brenna and Chelsea rushed to her now, wondering what happened, as they couldn't see her face. They came up beside her, one on each side, both kneeling to get to her level, catching sight of the source of Andrea's reaction. Brenna gasped, covering her mouth at the sight.

Chelsea swallowed hard, choking back tears that were now ebbing in the corner of her eyes; both girls were reeling from Andrea's reaction.

Brenna slid her arm around her friend. Chelsea began to tremble at seeing the name on the cross. Still unsure of what this cross meant, Brenna asked, "What is this? Who is this?"

Andrea nodded very slightly. "It's me." The reality of Andrea's words made her gasp.

"Who would have thought ..." the remaining words disappearing into thin air. Andrea felt what Johnny, Jacob, and Becca felt when she disappeared.

Chelsea and Brenna both rose to their feet, taking a step back. "What?"

Brenna whispered, unable to wrap her head around the reality of the dream that Andrea lived during her ordeal in New Orleans.

"We thought you were just hallucinating. No way this could be real." Chelsea blinked hard, then swallowed the lump that formed in her throat.

"I didn't know how I left, but I know I went from one time to another. I know it." Andrea was almost detached from the words.

They stayed there and stared for a long time at the grave marker, none of them able to speak. No one moved until Andrea got up, wiping a tear from her eye.

Chelsea said softly, "How?"

Andrea was clear-minded when she said, "I believe, it was the amulet. It was magical; bewitched. I told you the tribes in this region revered it. That is the only way I could have done this," Andrea held her hand out to the broken down ancient cross.

Neither Brenna nor Chelsea could believe what they saw, but it was indeed a deep emotional response, a reaction from Andrea that still left them numb. The other girls followed Andrea's lead as they walked back to the car; Brenna and Chelsea taking in more than they did when they began their walk through the property.

"I bet this was something to see," Brenna remarked, admiring the view.

"It was." Andrea breathed in deep once more, taking in all she could. She closed her eyes, then thought to herself, *I wonder if this property is for sale?*

Author Biography

Julie Petrou is an experienced writer with a rich professional background, blending diverse skills and perspectives. She advocates for Native American communities' drawing from years of close connections with local tribal members. Through extensive research on events between 1783 and the Indian Removal Act of 1830, Julie brings to light the voices of those often overlooked in history.

Dream Keeper, her debut novel and the first installment in The Amulet Series marks the beginning of extraordinary journeys' with the magic stone.

www.ingramcontent.com/pod-product-compliance
Lightning Source LLC
Chambersburg PA
CBHW031141050726
47495CB00018B/288